Nae-Née

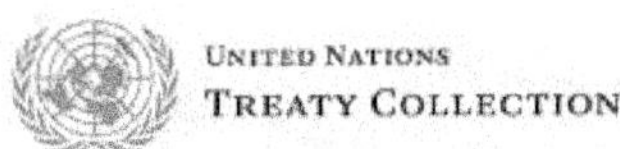

The United Nations Convention on Planetary Human Population Reduction by Birth Control

Full text of the Convention in English

INTRODUCTION

On 21 December 2012, the Convention on Planetary Human Population Reduction by Birth Control was adopted by the United Nations General Assembly. It entered into force as an international treaty on 22 December 2012 after the twentieth country had ratified it.

The Convention was the culmination of nearly 10 years of work by the United Nations Commission on the Status of Human Overpopulation, a body established in 2001 to monitor the situation of human health and quality of life. The Commission's work has focused attention on the results of human overpopulation on overall quality of life, highlighting the need for restraints on population growth.

The full text of the Convention is set out herein:

CONVENTION ON PLANETARY HUMAN POPULATION REDUCTION BY BIRTH CONTROL

The States' Parties to the present Convention,

PREAMBLE

Noting that the Charter of the United Nations reaffirms faith in fundamental human rights, in the dignity and worth of the human person and in the equal rights of men and women,

Noting that the Universal Declaration of Planetary Human Population Reduction by Birth Control affirms the principle of the inadmissibility of discrimination and proclaims that all human beings are born free and equal in dignity and rights and that everyone is entitled to all the rights and freedoms set forth therein, without distinction of any kind, including distinction based on sex,

Noting that the States Parties to the International Covenants on Human Rights have the obligation to ensure the equal rights of men and women and future generations to enjoy all economic, social, cultural, civil and political rights...

Nae-Née – Birth Control: Infallible, With Nanites and Convenience for All
By Stephanie C. Fox, J.D.

Nae-Née confronts the major taboo of our time: the conflict between human overpopulation and the human desire to pass on one's DNA – and to thus rest assured that the next generation will care for the previous one and continue all that matters to it.

Our planet is being stressed past capacity due to biodiversity loss, rising sea levels, floods, droughts, overdependence on fossil fuels, and climate change. The human species is in dire trouble due to overpopulation.

But nanite technology has brought about Nae-Née, a safe, reliable, user-friendly form of birth control. Nae-Née is a microscopic robotic device.

All that the inventors – a husband-and-wife team of inventors named Hamish and Avril – wanted was a convenient device that would prevent pregnancy every time without constantly pumping a woman's body full of artificial hormones. So they created one, and assumed that once it was marketed, their customers would be happy and that would be the end of the story. Its name literally translates as "not born" and was chosen by Avril to reflect her husband's Scottish background and her own French ancestry.

But that wasn't the end of it.

The world's leaders have drafted a treaty at the United Nations, and every nation has signed it. All women must have a government-registered Nae-Née device. Every birth must be licensed, and not everyone who wants a license will get one.

Nae-Née
– Birth Control: Infallible, With Nanites and Convenience for All

Stephanie C. Fox, J.D.

QueenBeeBooks

Bloomfield, Connecticut, U.S.A.

Library of Congress Cataloging-in-Publication Data
Name: Fox, Stephanie C., author.
Title: Nae-Née – Birth Control: Infallible, With Nanites and Convenience for All. / Stephanie C. Fox.
Description: Connecticut: QueenBeeBooks, [2011].
Identifiers: ISBN: 978-0-9996395-1-1 (paperback)
Subjects: FICTION / Science Fiction / Hard Science Fiction. NATURE / Environmental Conservation & Protection. POLITICAL SCIENCE / Public Policy / Environmental Policy.

www.queenbeeeedit.com

Cover design by Stephanie C. Fox
Cover Illustration by Katelyn Marie Gagnon
Printed in the United States of America

This is story is a work of fiction.

Any similarity to persons living or dead
is purely coincidental.

The names, characters, and incidents
have all been created to build an engaging plot.

The places are real restaurants, shops,
and museums in Manhattan.

Also by Stephanie C. Fox

Vaccine: The Cull
Nae-Née Wasn't Enough

New World Order Underwater
The Nae-Née Inventors Strike Back

What the Small Gray Visitor Said

Intrigue On a Longship Cruise

Scheherazade Cat:
The Story of a War Hero

An American Woman in Kuwait

The Book of Thieves

The Bear Guarding the Beehive

The Slamming Door:
Bone Cancer, Asperger's, and Loss

Elephant's Kitchen
– An Aspergirl's Study in Difference

Almost a Meal – A True Tale of Horror

Hawai'i – Stolen Paradise:
A Travelogue

Hawai'i – Stolen Paradise:
A Brief History

The Visitor Experience at the Mark Twain House

This story is dedicated
to the next generation of human beings.

I wish that the previous generations
had thought ahead more on their behalf.

"A human being has a natural desire to have
more of a good thing than he needs."

Mark Twain, *Following the Equator*

Table of Contents

Chapter 1

Home, Without a Home

There were just too many of us now; too many people preparing for the best of everything, competing for too few slots. We couldn't all be successes, but we didn't accept that. Hamish and I had to be able to make something of ourselves, and contribute something important to the world. I couldn't let myself believe otherwise, despite the foreboding I often felt.

Our generation's futures – along with our own – seemed to be over before the fact.

My husband and I lived in idyllic suburbia with my parents and a cat, in West Hartford, Connecticut, in a beautiful chateau of a mansion. It was both lovely and oppressive.

Who wanted to live with their parents after getting married?! No one in Western cultures, that's who. Nothing like the sound of a parent's footsteps moving about the structure to quash any amorous inclinations…it made me wonder how couples in multi-generation homes did it.

The house was halfway up Stoner Drive, situated among a collection of similarly styled homes. Many had been built during the mid-twentieth century, at the peak of American prosperity. They were almost uniformly gorgeous, with beautifully manicured lawns and attractive landscaping to match. Our home was no different.

I liked everything about the place, except for the fact that it was long past the time when I should have been able to have my own home with Hamish, my husband. We had been married for several years, and our wedding had easily lived up to my mental image of a fairy tale – the image that I had been building on since childhood, one which my parents had made a reality, on the summer solstice of 2002. I had done my best to hold up my end of the deal by finding my soul mate, so that the fairy tale would extend beyond the wedding to the marriage.

At least, that had been the idea. We didn't want kids. We wanted a home of our own in our own country. I also wanted the satisfaction of seeing my husband become a financial as well as a professional success, to share our own pet cat, and the chance to travel to places of our choice rather than where work took us. I still believed that I had chosen well, despite Hamish's constant requests for reassurance from me. He was living with the crushing expectation that he produce a continuous income from his efforts, and one sufficient in earning power to house us in comfort, convenience and togetherness.

Instead, here we were with my parents. I, Avril Antoinette Châtelet, D.Sci., J.D., published author of various books, medical historian and violinist, was now 40 years old and Hamish James MacDonall, M.D., Ph.D., doctor and engineer, was 50. It was frustrating.

We had met at Harvard, in a library, when I had needed some medical history data for a law paper. But we were working in our fields: I wrote books on all sorts of topics, and he worked with nanite technology, albeit in my parents' basement when he wasn't off teaching somewhere.

We had left many times to do fascinating things, both professionally and through our travels, but we had no steady income. Our curriculum vitas read like those of famous intellectuals in human history. But we were economically nonviable and back in my old room, with a portion of my parents' finished basement allocated to Hamish's engineering tinkerings. Tinkering pretty much summed it up; he knew his stuff, his work contributed appreciably to the scientific journal articles that he routinely co-authored, but none of it brought in a cent.

It was mostly funded by the small income generated by my own writing – a travelogue, a women's medical history (herstory, really), and a children's book – all published within the past few years. I co-authored scientific articles along with Hamish, but as I mentioned, none of it paid. Science articles aren't written for the money; they are written to get the word out on one's work. Once a scientist has a sufficient number of articles out in circulation, grant applications are more likely to be funded, thus bringing in a temporary income. The books that I had written were something to be proud of, but they didn't make enough money to support an apartment.

Hamish and I had that pleasure once, and only once. After 10 months in a beautiful faculty apartment in rural Connecticut, the grant was up, our lease was up, and we were forced to put the contents of our household into yet another storage unit. I had cried about it, despite knowing what was coming. We never really enjoyed our time in that apartment thanks to the knowledge that it was only temporary. That had been almost 4 years ago. And thus far, we had only succeeded in acquiring the contents of a home – not the home itself. It wasn't good for our self-esteem.

At least my old room was still mine, with a queen-sized canopy bed made of carved, varnished cherry wood. My mother was a whiz at trolling estate and antique sales, and this bed was one of the many results. It was a heavy Victorian style one with curlicues and a pattern of roses and lilies on the headboard. White gauzy fabric was draped over the canopy, along with a pale pink rose-patterned fabric with matching curtains and pink wall-to-wall carpeting. I swore I would never allow my mother to change it. She loved to redo the décor of the house, while I loved to find the perfect thing and just take good care of it. The décor of my old room was perfect as it was, and I was lucky that my parents would have me back in it any time.

Only my books were missing.

My parents had boxed them all up after Hamish and I were married, when we had headed to Washington, D.C. for 6 months. I didn't mind; I knew that they would treat my things carefully, not damaging any of them. When I thought of all the trees killed to produce books, and when I looked at how beautiful they were – whether they were coffee-table books full of glossy, colored photos, children's books full of prints of watercolor paintings, or just novels – I wanted to keep them forever. I was careful not to even crack the spines on the paperback ones.

At least I had the cat to keep me company. He was a beautiful, short-haired, silky gray boy, a Chartreux cat bred by my maternal grandparents in Provence, France. His name was Spock, for the *Star Trek* character, and he was 12 years old; I always got to name our cats.

Earning an income seemed like climbing Mount Everest as I hoarded news articles in my computer. The economy was a mess all over the planet, jobs were vanishing rather than being created, and the planet itself was heating up and losing more and more beautiful, useful species of plants and animals that we humans needed in order to survive.

I had quite a stash of data saved to my hard drive, plus a couple of memory sticks, an external hard drive, and a laptop computer. Hamish had an identical array – all assembled and maintained by me. I was taking no chances; since I couldn't afford as yet to pay for a remote storage service such as Acronis or Carbonite, I did what Mark Twain suggested: I put all of my eggs in one basket and watched that basket. This meant having everything under one roof.

My computer – a desktop – was in my room, on an antique (what else?) table in my old room. The stash was as virtual and as neat and organized as could be. Folders with subfolders and more subfolders, all named with precision and accuracy, were carefully stored and duplicated in the desktop, laptop, flash drives and external hard drive. It felt like my whole life was in there, and in a way it was: digital photos, scans of my published and unpublished pastel drawings, and all of my writings – fiction, legal, historical – plus Hamish's writings.

At least a lot of it had been published for the world to see and read, and stored at the U.S. Copyright office. That was what I wanted to leave behind when I died (presumably of old age). That was the legacy I valued: not kids, but publications, and preferably those in book form.

I had asked my parents when I got engaged to Hamish – and told them that we didn't want kids – if they were upset about their only child not wanting kids. My father had said "No – that just means that I won't have to baby-sit." My mother had said "No – I just want you to be happy. No one should have kids unless they really want to." I had felt relieved.

Hamish spent the bulk of his time in the basement, working on his nanites, which are microscopic robots, so I pretty much had the place to myself for reading and writing. Despite the removal of my books, I had continued to amass more. There were piles here and there on tables and chairs, plus some boxes of CDs and DVDs that my mother would gripe about from time to time. I told her not to touch them; I wanted to be able to get at them sometimes.

But Hamish was wearing thin on my parents. His role, as they saw it, was to provide a home for us, not keep us living an itinerant, stressful existence. I felt trapped between wanting him and only him as my husband and secretly agreeing with my parents, wishing he could actually provide that home. The past 2 years had just been more of the same stress. My parents didn't mind keeping me with them, but their patience with Hamish was running out.

He worked incessantly in his basement lab, but none of his inventions or formulations had yet been picked up by any major corporation. They all wanted the same thing: hand over full legal control of whatever he created, but keep paying all related expenses until we were bankrupt. No deal. I already knew what it was like to have something with potential, I told one of those vultures; I had no intention of learning first-hand what it was like to have signed away all future chance of having a continuous income from it.

If Hamish were to surrender and get a job, he could kiss that chance good-bye. The mere thought of doing so terrified and depressed us. My parents didn't get any of this, but they thought my career was okay as it was. I got the Kuwait book published. I was just going with the advice of Mark Twain, writing what I knew. The proceeds paid the bills, kept the computers running, kept Hamish supplied with nanite tools, and allowed us to eat out together occasionally. It also maintained our car, a gift from my father, but with little left over.

Unfortunately, my father didn't like the fact that Hamish was a big eater, despite being tall and thin. He once bitterly complained to Hamish that it cost $4,000 extra dollars when he stayed with us for a few months. I didn't know whether that was a guesstimate or a perfectly accurate accounting, and I was afraid to check. Hamish started making a lot of trips on buses to food pantries after that, and finding work that kept him away for months on end. I hated it.

My father was a hugely successful international patents attorney whose clients included the company that had developed RU486. My mother was a former hospital nurse; she had worked mostly when I attended the Ethel Walker School, coordinating her schedule with mine. I was in school plays, taking violin lessons, and in the French club. That last activity was all too easy for a girl whose grandparents were all from France, but I loved it. I even spent part of every summer in Provence, visiting my maternal grandparents, helping them with their Chartreuse cats. It was fun spending time with Nana, who had lived into her eighties.

When I met Hamish, I was impressed by his ability to adjust to anything; I couldn't.

Hamish could just toss his stuff in a corner and get to work, but I would have to organize my surroundings to perfection in order to settle in and start to feel at ease. Even then, I might have to sit in my dorm room at college or in my grandparents' apartment in Paris, surrounded by my books, for a few days to feel calm. I stayed in their beautiful Haussmann-era apartment on the Left Bank while I worked on my doctorate at the Sorbonne.

Those were fun times; I would wander the streets of Paris at all hours (well…not the middle of the night!) as what Grandpère called a flâneur – literally, someone who walks around, exploring and observing. It took care of the anxiety, and was fun. Grandmère used to worry about me, warning me not to stay out too late, not to fall in with strangers or be too trusting, and not to go in any lonely alleys. But I heeded all warnings and nothing happened to me.

I hated myself for having such trouble with anxiety, but I had learned to live with it and to work with it. My solution was to just do everything that I either needed to do or really wanted to do, regardless of that fact that a case of crippling anxiety was often coming. I wasn't going to let it stop me from writing, studying, publishing, or traveling.

It was either that or swallow fattening pills that dulled my thought processes to the point of not being able to write anything worth reading. Why bother? I had been there and done that. I would be unhealthy, unattractive, and nonproductive, not to mention no longer very interesting to be with. No…back to being my original, authentic, high-strung, but attractive and talented self. I was forty years old now; I would just have to live with the anxiety.

Hamish was beautiful to look at, despite his age. Being fifty years old made no difference; he was tall and thin, with thick, short dark hair that was just starting to go gray. I thought he resembled a depressed Craig Ferguson. I wished I could help, but aside from editing his letters and articles and talking to him, I was at a loss. As it was, although I didn't hear anyone asking about my employment status, I knew that my own record wasn't spectacular. The pay from my books came in fits and starts, tapering off to royalties after a short burst at the start. I had to be careful with it.

There was a television and DVD player in our room, which was great if we felt the need to hide while trying to forget about our predicament. But Hamish was an early bird, and I a night owl. He spent his time tinkering in the basement, trying to invent the perfect nanite device or e-mailing people, frantically trying to market whatever was ready. I was in there more than he was.

When I thought it over, I knew that I hadn't had any really terrible problems.

My nice husband wasn't interested in anyone but me, and was impressed with my intellect, work, hobbies, cooking and baking. We even collaborated on some work. He thinks I am beautiful, and we both like and dislike the same things.

By now you know what there is to know about me. I don't care whether you approve of me or not, or whether or not you agree with me about everything or most things. Obviously, if weren't curious to read this, you wouldn't be doing it.

It was now June of 2010, a couple of days before the graduation party for my cousin Jacques, who had just finished high school. I had promised to provide a dish for the party, so I went to the Whole Foods store in West Hartford.

As I drove, I thought about the pollution that the blue, 1996 C-Class Mercedes was spewing into the atmosphere, contributing to the carbon monoxide levels and heating up the planet. I felt bad, but it must be okay to go out to buy food, I reasoned. That was one reason why I didn't use the car much. The other reason was my writing career; I wrote at home.

The Mercedes had been a law school graduation gift from my father. It was safe, like a tank, reliable, and would last a long time. I liked it a lot. But it burned fossil fuels, so I wondered whether I ought to get a Prius if I could ever afford one, but I didn't trust their computer controls. I don't approve of allowing computers to run things, thanks to the moral of the *Terminator* movies: if humans create something that can think independently, it will just push us out of its way and threaten us. Plus, the Prius was a light-weight car – not so safe, Dad had taught me.

Driving along, I mused about alternative fuels.

Electric batteries: not that great, because the same fossil fuels were burned to energize the batteries, with a significantly smaller return on the investment. The car would go too slowly and run out of energy a lot sooner than a tank of gas would. Realistically, people who were used to driving at sixty to eighty miles per hour wouldn't willingly give that up. No, the replacement would have to be something that didn't force people to slow down.

Biofuel: again, not so great, because producing it took away land that could be growing food for the Earth's exponentially increasing human population. Also, it hadn't yet proven that it could overcome the same difficulties that electricity as car fuel presented.

Wind energy: a great fuel alternative, just not for cars. The white turbines were attractive enough to look at – not eyesores – and when placed near other ambient noise, seemed quiet.

Nuclear energy was no good; why trade one dangerous fuel for another?

So what was the solution? Driving less was one, but most people had to get to offices or other jobs, which meant using their cars. We couldn't all avoid that by working at home.

Too bad nuclear fusion hadn't yet been perfected. That would burn cleanly, but it was still in the works at CERN in Switzerland. As soon as it was ready, I was sure that the German engineers of Mercedes would get going on the idea of a fusion-powered car. Meanwhile, CERN had to plod along slowly, because they used electricity for their underground experiments. That meant taking winters off, because they couldn't deprive the Alpine residents of heat.

So it was the fossil fuel-powered Mercedes for now.

I pulled into the parking lot at Whole Foods and found a space, took my plastic bags with handles that the store sold, and headed inside. In Manhattan, if you forgot to use those bags, they would charge you 99 cents per paper bag, plus it might break as you walked back to your apartment. Why didn't they do that in the suburbs, I wondered?

The place was stocked full of wonderful fresh fruits and vegetables. As I began shopping in what was a monument to the top of the food chain on a planet that was currently operating at 20 percent above its capacity to feed everyone on it, I filled my cart with red raspberries, and then pushed off in search of several wheels of brie cheese and puff pastry from the freezers. This store was a place to buy stuff that couldn't be found easily at another, less expensive store. Since I was shopping for a special occasion, I might as well enjoy Whole Foods, I had told myself.

Free samples of fresh and packaged products were being offered every which way I turned. I tried some of everything, had a cup of Mocha Java coffee with almond milk at the coffee counter, and found some blueberry beer. It was fun in here for a gourmet cook and baker.

That is, until I started tripping over all the little kids; school was out and camp hadn't yet started. Damn. The little brats raced around, crashing into me and other strangers as they played, heedless of the fact that we didn't want to deal with out-of-control games and potential crying fits. Mothers smiled stupidly as they reined them in, stopping them from running on ahead. I didn't smile back. I thought of the strain on the public school system, wondering about the quality of the town's high schools by the time they were old enough to attend.

What was wrong with these people, wanting so many kids without a thought as to their slim and slimming future chances at an education and access to all these wonderful foods? The planet couldn't produce enough to satisfy such demands, so it simply wouldn't. Not that anyone would listen to me, so I just kept my thoughts to myself. I had Jacques' party to prepare for.

Jacques had been very busy at school, with a huge role in his senior play, a spot on the varsity lacrosse team, and singing. As a result, he was headed to a good college and his parents were satisfied. He was their youngest child; his older brothers were in college. Edgar – who hated his name and insisted upon being called Ed – was set to graduate from Penn State next spring. Fabian would start his sophomore year at Union College in the fall.

They were lucky, and I was glad. I followed the news and noticed that more and more teens were finding that schools did not have room for them, regardless of their qualifications. When I had applied, the standard practice was to apply to one's dream school, plus a safety school – usually the state university – and some in-between schools.

Not anymore…now state schools were glutted with applications, and could take their pick. Overpopulation had to be behind this; there was no way that a failure to get accepted someplace decent was always the kids' fault when you saw high GPAs and lots of extracurricular activities. Then what happened after college? No jobs.

Everyone wanted to be an educated, middle-class professional now. That left too few Americans to take other jobs which were still crucial to maintaining a functioning economy. Who would do the manufacturing that remained in the U.S. (not exported to China/India/ Philippines? Who would do the farming? Some Americans still wanted to do that, but often only after getting a Bachelor's degree in agricultural studies. Everything seemed to be running on intellectual achievements; without them, you just weren't in the club.

I drove home and got to work on the Brie en Croute with raspberry project. It took the whole afternoon, with a break for dinner, and into the evening, so I watched *Bones* as I worked. She drove a blue Prius to a crime scene. Interesting, but I still didn't want one.

On Saturday, the four of us headed out together for the party. Jacques was looking forward to college in the fall, even though the school, Wesleyan University in Middletown, Connecticut, wasn't his first choice. Northwestern University had turned him down. To his great disappointment and the undisguised satisfaction of my uncle, he would be going to college close to home. Uncle Charlie expected Jacques to join his real estate business after college.

But Grandmère, who lived with them, said it was a party school. When did the students study? I didn't see what all of the fuss was about. Wesleyan was a perfectly respectable school. At least it wasn't what Hamish called an academic mill, like our state university, which kept raising its tuition to devote more of its budget to sports. I wished Grandmère wouldn't compare everyone to her oldest son, my father, who studied at the Sorbonne and Cornell Law School.

Aunt Zoe and Uncle Charlie had moved into a McMansion off of Beacon Hill in West Hartford. The house was a huge cookie-cutter affair with small trees, little privacy – except for the fence around the huge rectangular swimming pool that they had added – and as yet minimal landscaping. Uncle Charlie was a real estate developer, and he had been involved in projects all over the state and some in Massachusetts. Aunt Zoe did the payroll at his office one day a week.

The guest list included the family, business contacts of Uncle Charlie's, friends of Aunt Zoe's, and Jacques high school friends. Grandmère was inside, I knew, and not interested in swimming, bright sunlight, or noise. I didn't blame her. She had moved in with them after Grandpère had died, 6 years earlier, and sold her Haussmann apartment to my father. Time to be near her other children, she said, after being near Tante Adrienne and Oncle Pierre for so long.

"Camille! Henri! Good – you can help me set up." Aunt Zoe came rushing to greet us as at the front door. "Camille, Avril – I need help setting up trays of hors d'oeuvres. Henri, Hamish – Charlie needs help setting up chairs and tables out back. Oh, Avril – you made the little Brie en Croute things! Thank you so much!" Aunt Zoe, whom Uncle Charlie had met after moving to Connecticut, was always effusive. She grabbed one of the containers from my mother.

"They are Brie et Framboise en Croute," I said. Aunt Zoe paused, lifted the lid to admire them, and rushed toward the kitchen with the box. We followed her with the other ones.

Hamish glanced back at me, gave me a slight smile, and headed out back with my father to help with the chairs. Uncle Charlie had a huge pile, and I could hear him thanking them for arriving early. He was rushing about, setting up 20 round tables with 8 chairs at each.

There was Grandmère, sitting with her customary glass of cranberry-raspberry juice, on a deep, comfortable chair in the living room, where she could watch the party until the sun went down. After that, she would go outside and eat with us. Her own Chartreux cat, a female named Simone (after Simone de Beauvoir), sat on the arm of her chair, purring.

I went over to kiss her, complemented her on her outfit, went through the usual reassurances when she said she didn't look good anymore, and headed back to the kitchen. She did look nice; she just hated what the aging process had done to her appearance. She had been gorgeous when she was young, with thick, dark hair, eyes the same sapphire blue color as mine but deeper-set and smaller, and a nice figure. Her thick, snowy white hair was coiffed elegantly. She even had a nice shape, despite being 90 years old and the mother of 3 children – my aunt, her middle child, still lived in Paris and worked as a curator at the Musée d'Orsay.

After saying hello, I went back over to the kitchen to put the Brie en Croute on plates. Grandmère watched quietly from her seat; the kitchen was a nice, well-lit, open area with an island facing the living room. I was glad to have something to do for a while. Unfortunately, I was finished in 20 minutes, thanks to my mother's help. Back to Grandmère on the cushy sofa.

After she had quizzed me about my writing, violin-playing (Had I brought it? No. Why not? This party isn't about me, and there are little kids running around who might try to touch it.), Hamish's work (No sales yet? Why doesn't he just quit and get a job? Job – where? There are no jobs, and he doesn't have a driver's license.), kids (When are you going to have kids? Never. What?!), she had exhausted her repertoire of inquisition.

I tried to distract her with some questions about herself. How was she? Fine, except for a few minor heart palpitations. Red wine helps with that, she added. What had she been doing lately? Just a few drawings. Grandmère had taught me how to do beautiful pastel drawings, and she was very pleased that I had published a book about Nana's Chartreux cats using our shared talent and skill, as was I. (Could I see her latest work? Sure, later on.)

But then she went back to the subject of kids. "Why don't you try baby-sitting? You might find that you want kids if you do that."

"No way. I hate being around kids – the younger they are, the worse it is. I've told you this before; all while I was a kid, I was eager to get older so that I wouldn't have to spend time around kids any more. Hamish doesn't want kids either; we want a cat. I won't baby-sit."

"But who will take care of you when you are old?"

"I don't know. But I don't believe that one's kids would automatically do that. If we had kids, I could still just as easily get stuffed into some horrid nursing home with awful smells and group activities and bad food so that they wouldn't have to bother with me."

"Not if you raise them right."

"Really Grandmère – did someone drug your drink? I don't know why you would believe in such fantasies. Even the most properly raised kids will find a way out of doing something if they don't want to do it. You were lucky you could move in with Aunt Zoe and Uncle Charlie."

"It's Charles," she said irritably, making a Francophone "sh" sound for the first 2 letters.

"How many times do I have to tell you that I agree with you about that, Grandmère?! You're preaching to the choir." I said testily. "The problem is that it is Uncle Charlie's name, and we can't enforce our wishes onto it or him. I think I'll go see what else is going on now."

She looked glumly at me, and said to go talk to Mindy. Mindy was Zoe's younger sister. I didn't want to spend time with her. Mindy was 15 years younger than Aunt Zoe, the same age as me, and always pregnant. I found her sitting near the pool, looking bored and vacuous as she watched her 6-year-old and 4-year old girls running around the pool, jumping in and out, and yelling "Look at me!" every few minutes. In her lap was her 11-month-old baby boy.

I decided to get it over with and went outside to say Hi to her.

"Avril!" Mindy waved to me as I approached. "How are you?"

"Fine. How are you?"

"Tired. Would you mind watching the kids for me and holding Sam?"

"Yes, I would mind. Do NOT hand him to me. I'll disappear if you try."

She looked offended at me. I didn't care. I pointed out that her phrasing of that question was an open invitation to an honest response. Any other response – including, but not limited to a polite one – would entrap me into child-care. "Why did you ask me – chance or deliberation?"

"Chance – and you have never sat for them."

"So the answer is both. Well, choose someone else. I don't want my own kids, and I don't want to watch any – not for a nanosecond. Some interaction with them will just go wrong if I do, and you'll hold it against me. I'm not setting myself up for that."

Great attempt at entrapment, Grandmère, I thought to myself. But that would have required acquiescence on my part. As I mused about that, Mindy spoke to me again.

"Avril, you really need to learn some social skills – and maybe blink some more."

I looked at her, cold and amused. "There are some social skills that I just don't want, such as those that lead to child care. I'm deliberately breaking the rules. It's premeditated. As for the excessive blinking that most people do, that is like fingernails on a chalkboard to me, combined with inanity, and an irrelevant criticism. My husband doesn't blink much either, and I love that."

She looked annoyed, but couldn't resist asking me, "What's a nanosecond?"

She had always treated me like a child, even though we were both in our teens when we met. I was so glad that she had gone to Conard High and not the Ethel Walker School; she would certainly have been a bully to me. But she was without her old clique of friends here, so she wasn't at her worst. The weird thing was her curiosity; always because of some remark of mine.

"A nanosecond is a billionth of a second," I told her.

With that, I rushed over to my father and Hamish. "Can I help with this? It looks like you have a ways to go, and I need to get away from child-care requests."

Dad looked at me, grinned, and handed me a folded chair. He didn't like Mindy or little kids much either; I had gotten interesting when I was old enough to study, which was – fortunately for us both – when I was 6 years old. Before that, I was a quiet, staring kid. After that, I would suddenly fire a long string of questions at him, interrupting his thoughts.

Hamish grinned too, and said, "I heard what you said. Good for you." Lucky Hamish; guys didn't get so much pressure to deal with kids. I was glad to be female; I just didn't like the pressure. Resistance was not futile, and could be entertaining; it certainly had shock value.

All too soon the chairs were set up. Not to worry; Aunt Zoe came out with balloon-patterned tablecloths, plastic cutlery, and paper plates and cups. Back to work! She dashed off to let the caterer in. My mother appeared with the Brie, and I told her that Mindy was looking for a respite from her kids, so if she knew of some willing person other than me, to let her know.

Mindy looked at me sideways, but kept her mouth shut. My mother looked at me, but didn't say anything. She knew that every time I had ever dealt with little kids or been a substitute teacher or sitter, I got a galloping migraine and was clueless as to how to handle the noise and exuberance. I needed quiet and independence. It was like oxygen to me.

My mother went over to Mindy and sat down. "Would you like me to hold Sam so you can go use the bathroom?" She always asked exactly what people wanted to hear, but then my mother was a nurse and a mother…and conventional.

"Oh! Thank you so much!" Mindy handed the baby over instantly and got up. I didn't feel the slightest guilt; I had informed someone else that she wanted help as soon as I saw a likely candidate. Before heading inside, Mindy paused. "Camille, did you hear our news?"

"No. What news?"

"I'm pregnant again!" She beamed at my mother.

"That's wonderful!" My mother smiled sweetly at her.

I didn't agree, but I said "Congratulations" as Mindy passed me. I didn't deliver that line with any enthusiasm, however, so she just said thanks, having taken it down a notch. People with kids were never my friends. Sooner or later my anxiety would resurface, and they wouldn't want me around their kids. That was why I didn't bond with people who had kids.

The caterer arrived and brought out dish after dish of food, forming a buffet on a long side table. This coincided with the arrival of Jacques and 10 of his friends. I got a plate of guacamole and chips, found a seat, and silently watched as he and 6 other boys and 4 girls in swimming trunks and bikinis swarmed around a table, chatting happily, ignoring the adults around them. Aunt Zoe had to come over and order Jacques to go and greet the adults.

Strange…I never had to be told to meet and greet everyone when my parents threw me a party. I did it each time I graduated from a degree program, and when Hamish and I got married. The nonconformity that I exhibited was always something other…like keeping my own last name after marriage, and not preferring to be with a large crowd of people my own age. I'm better one-on-one, and I love being with older people. They always have great stories to share.

Observing people of all sorts is endlessly fascinating, and I spent the evening doing that.

When Jacques came back to sit with his friends, they all chatted happily about the colleges and universities that had accepted them. One kid was very quiet, but when asked, he said he was going to study pre-med. I couldn't hear where he said he was going, and the girl next to him was so animated about Brown University, that I just listened to her talk for a while.

As the evening wore on, I moved around a couple of time to chat with different people. The conversation revolved around college, jobs, and where to buy or build a house, and all I could think was, Easter Island, here we come. I had human overpopulation on my mind constantly. We would use up all natural resources, kill each other over what little of value that remained, and that would it. The Earth would be just fine without us, and eventually recover.

Another topic that kept cropping up was *Star Trek*. They thought their kids were going to have an optimistic future like the one in *Star Trek*?! Not at the rate we were going; with the collision course that humans had put the environment on, we were more likely to suffer the resource scarcity of *Mad Max* and the misery that went with it, and soon. Too many people were being born, let alone in existence already. That people would continue to have lots of kids, regardless of their future, bothered me whenever I thought about it, which was a lot.

The mere thought that many teenagers who had worked and studied so hard to qualify for admission to competitive colleges and universities would not be admitted to those schools was enough to put me into a black mood. No new places were being created while the pool of applicants continued to expand exponentially as people continued to reproduce with seeming abandon, oblivious to these grim realities. And none of this was what the parents wanted to hear.

If a kid couldn't get admitted to a competitive college or university, it was assumed that she or he had to have slacked off. But I knew that this just wasn't so. Kids who attended private school kids had an edge as did the ones at public schools in wealthy towns – with a high tax base – might as well be attending private schools. Those schools would not have cut the arts.

But even the kids from the finest private schools were likely to soon find some of their numbers not being accepted to competitive schools: kids who played the French horn, the bassoon, or the violin…kids who had roles in a school play every year…kids who served as class president…kids who wrote for their school newspaper. It was going to get worse.

I wondered how bad it would get before the parents understood what was happening. Could those parents ever accept that what they had was gone, and that their kids would miss out on it? Aunt Zoe and Uncle Charlie sat fielding questions from about their sons, happy and unaware. These details were important, but they didn't see that change was coming.

If Jacques stayed out of trouble and found academic subjects that interested him, he would do well. At least he wouldn't have loans from college. I was horrified whenever I considered the costs of a 4-year degree. When I graduated, it had cost something like $80,000 to $100,000 for the whole experience. Now it was double that…

Until it was time to go home, I worried that my mother would find fault with me somehow, criticizing my behavior at the party, and pointing out some sign of social ineptitude. I still wanted my mother, despite the conflicts that still occasionally cropped up between us.

It was just that I felt such safety and calmness when she was near, and could focus easily. My best work seemed to have always been done knowing that I could bounce ideas off her. My father and Hamish praised my creativity, but I wanted my mother for that sense of calmness.

I wanted it so much that I never ceased to be startled and angered when she criticized my social skills. All of them had been learned by rote due to her coaching. I had long ago accepted that I would never be able to pick up on subtle cues from what, to me, were illegible expressions in other people's eyes. Unspoken signals were just an indecipherable code to me. The only solution that had ever worked for me was not to care.

Hamish was okay on his own, even if he talked a bit too loudly sometimes. (He had some hearing damage in his left ear from the Kuwait War, but I would just remind him not to yell.) Hamish had fun regaling people with tales of grenade fishing, descriptions of how haggis is made, explanations of how nanites interacted with human tissue, and on and on.

When at last it was time to go home, my mother simply congratulated me on having had the sense to just tell her that Mindy wanted help with her kids and walk off. I was surprised. "But you said you thought it was wonderful that she's having another kid. Do you really think so?"

"No, I don't. But it was what she wanted to hear."

"Why say what people want to hear if you don't agree?"

"I don't know; it's just easier. But you don't have to do that."

"I won't – I won't lie. I won't say what I really think if they don't ask, and if I know that they won't want to hear it, but I won't say anything that isn't true just to please people."

"Mindy said that she likes kids when they're babies best," my mother confided.

"She loses interest in them as they get older?! That's when they get interesting!" I was outraged. Dad and Hamish laughed and said that they agreed with me.

Later, my mother told me that she didn't see any real problems with me, or any point in arguing over every social encounter. She just wanted to enjoy being with me, she said.

Hamish was relieved when I told him so as we went to sleep. He worried about how I was getting along with my parents as he still hadn't made a continuous income for us. Why couldn't we manage that together?!

My husband was a nice person to be with – my best friend and soul mate.

Chapter 2

My Awesome Idea

A week went by.

I spent it as usual, frustrated and scared about the future – our own future in particular – our chances for making it through life let alone making a living, plus the litany of problems that I couldn't stop noticing as I read about the world.

I also spent it trying not to obsess about this too much…by playing my violin on my usual ruthless schedule, which certainly helped, every day at 3 p.m. for an hour. I liked the music by John Williams best – I loved movie soundtracks and scores – and Danny Elfman, Howard Shore, Leonard Rosenman, Rachel Portman, Alexandre Desplat, Hans Zimmer…and so on.

My father and grandparents didn't approve. Why didn't I like the classics best? What about Claude Debussy? Mozart? Well…for a Tanglewood concert, sure, those were my favorites, but I just loved to imagine that I was at the movies, with my mood rising and falling in a manic dash through the plots of my favorite stories.

When I wasn't playing the violin or helping with the cooking, I would read, hoping for more inspiration to write. I was currently in a state of writer's block, wishing for a new project. To pass the time, I read a book on the history of Paris – the seamy, seedy side of the city – and a Pulitzer Prize-winner, *Hot, Flat, and Crowded*. Hamish said that it did nothing for my mood, but I couldn't stop reading it and then thinking about the reasons why the world and opportunities for enjoying it seemed to be narrowly exponentially…and seemingly in direct proportion to the exponentially expanding human population.

Late at night I would watch David Letterman and Craig Ferguson on television, and then Hamish would say that I was watching his substitute, allowing myself to be entertained by his stand-in while he slept or toiled in his workshop. I didn't deny it.

It was a bit weird; the Scottish comic was from the same city as Hamish – Glasgow – and although they had never met, I did feel as though I was watching a stand-in for my often mentally as well as physically absent husband. The sad part was that when Hamish was away, which was often and for long stretches of time (a few months at a time in Hungary, Austria or Kuwait), I used Ferguson's show as a substitute to keep me company. It had gutter humor – but it resembled Hamish's style, and I missed him, so I watched it just before going to sleep.

Despite the comic's self-deprecating habit of saying that his audience must not have cable or high-definition television, I did, and yet I chose to watch him. I would remind Hamish of this silly irony whenever he suggested that his work wasn't sufficiently spectacular or otherwise up to par, when in fact the problem was a lack of hype, through no fault of his own. The comparison would perk Hamish up; he knew his work was excellent, even if it wasn't making tons of money. It was good, honest, peer-reviewed science that suffered from a lack of appreciation – financial appreciation. At least it was published in high-impact factor journals.

Part of our problem was that we were both Aspies – adults with Asperger's Syndrome, which is high-functioning autism. At least we each had great educations. We were lucky that way. Granted, one makes one's own luck by applying to graduate school and studying to completion of a degree, but there are so many Aspies who either don't have that opportunity or who just have such a tough time with change that they can't make it through any program. I was just very determined; I would endure the crippling anxiety brought on by change, suffering through it for a few days after arriving in another geographic location, then settle in and work.

Hamish seemed to have less trouble with a change of venue than I did. He also hoped to get us settled someplace that we would both enjoy living in, but as yet we had only gone through various false starts.

Shortly after we were married, Hamish had applied for several grants at Georgetown University while we stayed with a professor he knew, a bachelor with a townhouse in Foggy Bottom. But the grants weren't funded and we had been forced to return. At least I had made the most of my time there, visiting all of the Smithsonian Museum branches on the National Mall, plus the monuments to Lincoln, Jefferson, and the sprawling, 4-part, outdoor one to FDR and Eleanor. Once, I even dragged Hamish out to see the cherry blossoms from Japan when they bloomed around the Jefferson Memorial.

My husband and I had traveled because of our work, teaching and writing. Work had taken us to Austria (all too briefly!), Hungary, and Kuwait. Ironically, I had had a better time of it in Kuwait than in Hungary. This still amazed me, because I had not loved being in Kuwait either, and because I had always wanted to visit and explore Austria, but the actual day-to-day experience of being in those places had led to this odd conclusion. Hungary was not any place that I had wanted to spend time in, and the experience of it cemented that feeling.

Austria had been a short stopover for a couple of scientific conferences on the way to a semester in Hungary. I loved the opportunity to see Mozart's hometown of Salzburg, and Hamish and I had managed to see it for a few days together while attending a conference there. I also loved to wander around Vienna. It was a beautiful city, and we even got tickets to a performance of *Die Zauberflöte*.

Then it was off to Hungary. But we were doing little other than guest lecture while writing more journal articles (for months), and eating some really awful food. Hamish got along well with people, except for a brief hospital stay after he had stepped on a sharp object at a faculty picnic in the countryside. That was when he finally understood what I had been trying to tell him for the first half of our stay: Hungarian people are very nice, but they only understand their own view of the world. They really aren't interested in anything different. So if you got depressed – and Hamish got very depressed when he couldn't call me or e-mail me whenever he liked, or just keep working – they just didn't understand.

We had no laptops then, and Hamish keeps calm by working nonstop. I have to drag him to restaurants, bookstores, movies and museums, but he does go when I insist. Then he says that he can't relax and enjoy himself until he makes money.

When his week on IV antibiotics was up, the doctors let him out of the hospital –
and the university footed the bill.

Hamish does well in rough environments with lousy food. It's a byproduct of
his background: he was in the British army as a chemical weapons officer during
the Kuwait War, plus he is Scottish, so he was raised on lousy food with few fresh
fruits and vegetables. He ate dehydrated, vile MREs (Meals Ready to Eat) in the
army. He claimed to be able to eat almost anything, and he likes to try exotic foods
from other cultures, just for the adventure of it.

Not me. I got very sick in Hungary. I hate cabbage, turnips, beef, pork, organs
(such as liver), pickled foods…in short, just about anything that was standard fare
there. I had warned my husband about this before going. But he just didn't
understand that I won't eat if I am repulsed by the food or its smell, even if I am
hungry. He had to see that to believe it. I did cook on the tiny stove in our
apartment, but it was difficult to find ingredients that I wanted to use. Sometimes
I dared to eat fresh fruits and vegetables, but always with the same result:
galloping diarrhea. I lost a lot of weight. That was two years after we were
married.

When we came home, my mother had a fit as soon as she saw me, and my
father gave Hamish a terrible look. Hamish had been worried too, but he couldn't
force-feed me. A trip to the doctor confirmed it: she said that I was malnourished
and would have to eat more and a lot of the things that I actually loved to eat:
fresh fruits, vegetables, fish, and even some French fries and dessert. A month
later I looked and felt okay. I would remind Hamish of this whenever he talked
about getting us another teaching assignment in a foreign country.

My mother had responded to my weight loss with what she thought was the
perfect solution: she had taken me to a psychiatrist who put me on antidepressants
and anti-anxiety pills. My weight, never a problem before, suddenly ballooned by
40 pounds. I was constantly hungry. I was still eating healthy foods, but too much
of them.

I was really upset. My clothes didn't fit, and I stopped writing and playing
the violin. I wheezed when I walked up stairs. My heart raced and I wondered if I
would get diabetes from the excess weight. My thought processes had dulled and
slowed. I was entirely too complacent about everything, and Hamish said he no
longer recognized the person he had married. That was it; I stopped the pills. And
the result was impressive: in just 3 months, I was back down to my normal size
and shape. I looked and felt great.

One person later asked me, "Wouldn't you rather be fat and happy than
anxious and pretty?" "No way!" was my vehement reply. Never again. Not be
pretty anymore? Not be able to write or make intelligent conversation?! Forget it
– life wasn't worth living on those terms.

Better to feel things intensely and be creative and able to write. After much
explanation and arguing with my mother, she had to accept that. So here we were
again, with me writing and playing violin and watching Spock stare at me all day
– or fall asleep, purring – while Hamish tinkered away in the basement.

All of the reading I did just added to our glum outlook about chances for
earning money; more and more indications that Americans must seek jobs in

foreign countries rather than in our own cropped up. And I didn't want to leave my own country; I don't care how that sounds. Travel is one thing, but I get so anxious with a change in my environment. I applied for jobs, but when it said "Are you willing to relocate?" I always checked "No."

Living in Kuwait for several months only served to confirm this. But it was an adventure, and I am not sorry I went. We went because Hamish was working with a colleague that he had collaborated with after the war there, a physician and pharmacologist at Kuwait University. They were studying the effects of chemicals released into the environment, to help their patients.

I went along mostly as Hamish's companion, though I did deliver a couple of lectures at Kuwait University. That was interesting enough in itself; I spent half the time studying the students and half focusing on delivering the lectures properly. Just observing them made had me determined to learn all about their culture and religion. While I was at it, I figured that I might as well write a book about it all. Armed with a laptop and a digital camera, I wrote a detailed journal of my experiences in Kuwait.

The only publication I had found before going there was a chapter in a *Lonely Planet* guide to the Middle East. At least it had told me enough so that I could give my informed consent to accompanying Hamish: No veil, scarf, or robe was required.

I was pleased that I could dress as usual, with my hair fully visible, wear makeup, and my usual long pants, short-sleeved shirts, and sandals that showed raspberry pink nail polish on my toes. I had long, wavy, black hair, sapphire blue eyes with long lashes, clear skin, nice features, and didn't need much makeup. I could also possess and control of my own passport. So I had agreed to the adventure.

What I didn't like about Kuwait was the religiousness; I don't like religiousness, regardless of which religion it is that crops up. I also did not like the persistent pressure to conform to the group. Being female and different just made it more noticeable. I met Kuwaiti women whose husbands made everyday decisions for them, Kuwaiti men who didn't want their own daughters (it was like they wanted to send them back to the store and exchange them for sons), and everywhere I went, people asked us when we would have kids. We didn't want to!

Having kids just to take care of you when you are old is selfish. Having them to perpetuate your DNA is selfish, too. And unless I could afford to give a child everything that I had: private school, music lessons, travel, college and graduate school – plus have a great interest in spending lots of time with them – that kid should not be brought into existence. It's just not fair or right; either the best can be afforded with the child wanted, or forget the whole thing. The world is overpopulated anyway. Hamish was in complete agreement, as were my parents.

Those were the aggravations of living in Kuwait…plus I got hissed at by some men (In the West, they hoot; in the Middle East, they hiss). It would happen whenever Hamish and I went out to buy groceries, which was after dark when it was cool enough to walk about outside.

Other than that, I did enjoy the cuisine of Kuwait, with its fresh fish, fresh fruit (the most delectable, sweet, red, flawlessly ripe strawberries grew at the Wafra Farms Oasis!), and saffron rice. A Kuwaiti woman I made friends with showed me the cakes that she made: each one was a plain pound cake, infused with saffron, cardamom, and vanilla, the world's three most expensive spices, in that order. Kuwait tea was super-brewed, awful stuff, and they all wanted to load it with sugar, but Hamish I found the most wonderful coffee at the local grocery stores: it was a Turkish blend of finely-ground, cardamom-infused heaven. We loved that.

I dragged him to every museum I could, forcing him to abandon his scientific work for a day here and there, thus compiling enough notes to proceed with my book. He didn't mind, and the book was worth the effort. I figured that if a good one for foreigners didn't already exist, I could write one, and I did! When we came back from Kuwait, at least this time I looked healthy enough. I had the beginnings of a book and a huge collection of photos.

When I wasn't writing books, I was researching women's medical and herbal history: corsets, midwives, so-called witches who were really herbalists and cat lovers, women who became physicians like Elizabeth Blackwell, Margaret Sanger with her birth control advocacy campaign, and so on and on. I would write and publish articles on legal herstory and medical herstory. I loved it; it was something that didn't pay, unlike the book-writing, but it enabled me to draw upon my French language background and the rest of my education.

Because I already knew French, I took Latin in high school. (I hated the idea of studying Spanish.) Knowing Latin had made it easy to follow the subject matter at the Sorbonne when I was working on my D.Sci. in the history of medicine. I had done my thesis on RU486, of all things, and a large portion of my dissertation had been about the history of gynecological treatments all over the world.

In my college days, I had worked a couple of retail jobs – everyone should try that at least once, so that they won't be spoiled and will learn to appreciate what people-pleasing is like. The jobs were nothing special: just selling books at a small, independent shop, and counter help at a take-out joint. Never again…the owner liked to publicly humiliate the staff.

The best "retail" job I ever had was as a historic interpreter at the Mark Twain and Harriet Beecher Stowe House Museums. That job got me over my fear of public speaking. I loved being a guide. I read everything and anything by and about the authors, and then delivered a self-crafted and humorous lecture throughout each house. And…I got to tell people not to touch anything. It was the coolest job, and I did it for years – the last 2 summers during college, and then again off and on whenever I was home visiting from graduate school in Paris.

My only problems had involved working with children, which was mostly when school groups came on tours at the museums. I just don't relate to them well. Toddlers and babies screech, and little kids make personal remarks. It all reminded me of actually being a kid, when I found groups stressful, exhausting, and irritating. Playground shrieks just tired and depressed me. I wanted to get home to my quiet room, and just read.

Having kids my age to visit had tended to be a failure, too. "Let them play with your dolls," my mother would say. Why, I wondered… can't one just make up stories in one's mind? Once that's done, the story is over and there's no point in moving the dolls around, combing their hair, and thus destroying them. I was hopeless socially, and I still am. I kept in touch with the friends I had by phone and e-mail. These friendships dated from college, graduate school (not law school!) and the job at the museum.

Then I went on to law school at Harvard, and met Hamish; he was at Harvard Medical School. The Latin was useful again, and I did an independent study about outer space law – plus more medical history and health law. I loved it, and fell in love with the crazy Scotsman who liked to hone his skills with nanite technology while searching for medical applications for it. He had one year down and 3 to go, with his Ph.D. from M.I.T. already completed.

And why did I go to law school? Well…it was fascinating, but the other reason was that my father wanted it. It was with great relief that I heard my international law professor inform him of what I had understood about myself from day one as a One-L: that I did not have the aptitude for the practice of law. We were at a gathering of professors, attorneys and law students at the Café Fleuri in Boston after attending a symposium on patent law at a nearby hotel.

What a relief that was. I looked up and said "I know – but I'm not quitting. I'm finishing whatever I start, including this degree." The professor looked at me with respect in his expression – smiled, even – and said that he wasn't suggesting that. He told my father that there were plenty of other uses for a law degree.

My father didn't bring it up again, but my mother later told me that he was deeply disappointed to hear that. Apparently, it had long been his secret hope – no, his unspoken assumption – that my D.Sci., which I had finished when I was 26 years old, would go very nicely with a J.D. as I followed in his professional footsteps.

But he got over it and said he was proud of me anyway. I was certified in his mind as some sort of intellectual heavyweight, and obviously talented in several respectable ways. Plus, I had met a very promising bioengineer while attending Harvard Law School. Little did he suspect that Hamish's education would fail to produce instant riches. What degree did that without inside connections?! Hamish was stoically doing his best to create the perfect lucrative technology that would improve human health, and thus far he had invented some valuable things. Alas, none of them were showstoppers.

I had my parents to pay my tuition; Hamish had stipends. I suppose I might have done it with scholarships, but I agreed with my parents: it wasn't right to take one away from an equally qualified candidate who lacked financially willing and able parents to foot the bills just to prove that I could get one. So I let them pay, studied hard, and finished on time.

Hamish was similar to me in terms of intellectual achievements and curiosity yet different in terms of his ability to rough it and live on the edge. He came from a rough area of Glasgow, and had left to attend Edinburgh University. I had left a sheltered home environment – with my usual sense of anxiety upon leaving home each time a break between terms ended – to attend the rural but beautiful William Smith College.

Hamish had left home without intending to move back, and known little comfort or security since then, but lots of adventure. I admired him; I couldn't spend long periods of time on my own without a loss of productivity and constant anxiety. Any time that I had done so had begun with several days of adjustment, eating fruits and cereals and little else, seeing a gray haze in front of me rather than people and places, and just waiting for the cloud to pass. It literally looked like a cloud, even though I now understood that it was a physical view of my anxiety.

It was nice to have all that behind me and just enjoy watching show's like Ferguson's.

Spock would watch with me, staring with complete calmness at the graphic of the cat at the end of the show, regardless of what became of it: crushing, detonation, decapitation, whatever. Ferguson never failed to mention that if the cat got virtually clobbered, it was just a photo so that people wouldn't write or call in, upset that he had murdered a cat. Spock just stared coldly during that explanation, looking like his intelligence has just been insulted.

I went walking sometimes in the sunshine, noticing that now that school was out, the swimming pools owned by wealthy grandparents were being frequented by their descendants. I liked the green grass, iris bulbs in bloom, lilacs, rose bushes, and bees buzzing around the flowers. The enjoyment didn't seem to last long enough. The exercise, fresh air and perfume of the blossoms gave me a brief high, and then I would start brooding again: Letterman was always commenting that in 50 years, half of the species on this planet would have disappeared.

At least someone like Letterman was bringing it to the attention of the general public; his was the kind of show that was enjoyed by followers of popular culture. I liked it for a chance to observe human interchanges and humor – watching Charlie Rose and public television wouldn't do nearly as much for me in the way of illustrating how most people thought. Intellectual discussions were good, but…I wanted to see regular people, and watch them. Letterman had a studio audience, and he trained the cameras on them routinely. Rose didn't do any of that.

Here we Americans were, smugly commenting upon the fact that soon China and India would swell the Earth's ozone layer with more carbon dioxide in order to have the same standard of comfortable living that the Western world had been enjoying for most of the 20th century. Never mind that we had done it first and now they wanted their fair share of enjoyment – they ought to be stopped, the Green Reformers seemed to be saying without actually saying it, because the Earth couldn't provide it without coughing and chugging the whole engine of comfort to a sudden and unpleasant halt!

Well…with sustainable and renewable energy that would be sure to infuriate the petro-dictators in the Arabian Peninsula things might be okay, but I wouldn't hold my breath that the developed and nearly developed parts of the planet would actually scale back in time.

I remembered a trip to New York City with Hamish the year before, when we each lectured at Columbia University at a symposium on women's health. The lectures went well, and then I dragged Hamish off for some fun: there was an art tour at a series of studios in SoHo. We had walked all over the area, visiting several different temporary exhibits.

One of them stood out in my mind: it was all sculpture and installation art, and each exhibit appeared to have been created with the assistance of the NOAA (National Oceanic and Atmospheric Administration). It also reminded me of my law thesis, which had been on international environmental law – I wrote about outer space law. The NOAA uses sonic impulses to determine ocean depths projected from satellites in orbit.

The back wall was a mural. Around several small islands with greenery and small mountains were scattered across that back wall were swirls of white, then light blue, then a deeper blue, and finally an ocean blue. It looked sort of like Fiji or French Polynesia, but it wasn't a real geographic area. The purpose was to illustrate a point. We were told to get closer and see what was on the islands: broken bits of ships that had been wrecked and abandoned.

It was then that the guide, a former professor who had given up a tenured university position because he could make enough money to live on giving art gallery tours, told us that it was about the wastefulness of humans toward the planet: trash left behind after we have been anyplace, including by cruise ships. I told him that cruise ships have dumped so much garbage at sea for so long that there is now a floating island of trash in the northern Pacific Ocean the size of Texas – plus 4 more elsewhere around the planet. He was so fascinated that he told the group about that. I helped him with the details (he kept looking at me for prompts).

In the next room, we saw another exhibit under glass with lots of greenery. It was an oil refinery that had been reclaimed by nature after the last drop of petroleum had been extracted and then abandoned – more about our wasteful culture. The idea was that after everyone who is now alive is dead, the last drop will be pumped. I think this will happen sooner.

Another model was mounted on the back wall, and it was all dark and light grays. It was Antarctica with no ice – and NOAA definitely seemed to have helped the artist with the shape. The continent had decompressed, relaxing upwards without the weight of ice and snow. There was just one inaccuracy – the sea level was the same, and that was a logistical impossibility. But I could see that the artist needed to keep a recognizable shape in order to illustrate the point about global warming, resource guzzling, and failure to recycle.

Finally, a display case by the doorway showed small dark gray models of every kind of human-made air and space craft that had ever crashed back to earth and been left lying around: a lunar excursion module, an Apollo rocket launcher, and various models of airplanes.

What was the matter with our species?! Why was thinking before using so much to ask?! Apparently. Meanwhile, in conversations, whenever the subject of reproducing cropped up, people just gazed upon me as though I were a freak for thinking before wanting, and for not wanting what they all wanted: more, more, more of the same. More people.

For her part, my mother had a penchant for reading horrible stories in the news and showing them to me. So we each had a morbid habit. I had managed to partially train her out of her bad habit, and Grandmère had helped. I suppose that this was because my mother was a nurse; she was drawn to personal stories of tragedy, it seemed.

One story stuck itself permanently in my mind, however: it was about a woman who was HIV-positive. She was married, with 2 daughters, both miraculously conceived and born without being HIV-positive. Somehow, mysteriously, the husband wasn't infected either. The unfortunate woman had gone to Europe on a summer trip during her college years, stayed at a youth hostel – notoriously unsafe, unlocked places – and gone to sleep. A rapist broke in and infected her one night. She had been a virgin before the rape; lovely story! (Sarcasm!)

Well, my mother thought that this was just sweet – the unfortunate story had a happy ending in her mind. I had been in law school when she showed me this tale of disaster. Why had she shown it me? As an example of overcoming adversity? Yes – and a happy ending. What happy ending?! She got what she wanted, my mother said, as though she were addressing someone who had completely misunderstood what she had read.

Yes, I see that, I replied. But you missed something very unhappy – the daughters know that they mother will most likely die before they reach adulthood! Their mother won't see them go to college let alone graduate, or get married, or…fill in the blank. If I were one of those daughters, I would be a nervous wreck about that. I want my mother – a healthy mother with a warranty that offers a reasonable expectation that I will have her at least until I am 60something! The poor kids will likely be deprived of her soon, and then quite possibly get a stepmother – something that I would never be willing to accept, especially as a captive, not-yet-grown child!

That's the trouble with having kids – they get no choice in the matter, I concluded. That's why I consider human reproduction to one of the most knowingly selfish acts possible. Why would that woman do this, knowing that she had been infected with HIV, I demanded to know of my own mother, who – being a mother herself – could likely explain this?

She wanted them, was all that my mother could offer in the way of illumination.

Then she is hideously selfish. If I were one of those girls, I would probably spend half of my time crying in fear and half in a rage at her, knowing what was in my near future. I just wouldn't enjoy the time, knowing that it would be so much shorter than it ought to be. I told my mother this, and added that I was glad not to be near any tediously religious people who would tell me that I simply ought to be grateful for the time anyway, even if I was an anxious wreck. That wouldn't have made the slightest difference to me.

My mother showed me far fewer such stories after that. Later, she told me that she agreed with me about my assessment, and had changed her mind about it being a lovely story.

I am not at all patient with people who tell me how I ought to feel about things, or view a situation, or respond to it. And like my father, I am always doing my best to plan my way around problems, studying a situation before jumping into it. There are limits to what studying can do for problem-prevention, but I still believe in it.

It hadn't saved me from a poverty-stricken marriage with Hamish that kept us returning home to my parents, but at least I liked my husband. And at least we both liked and disliked the same things. I just worried constantly about making it on our own. As yet, we hadn't been able to do that, so despite the fact that we had a roof over our heads, it felt wrong because we couldn't pay for one of our own.

Hamish was home for now, but I knew it couldn't last.

Not having his own income bothered him endlessly, especially while having to stay with his in-laws and feel them watching him, wondering why he couldn't make money, while my father had made a killing for himself in international patent law, shuttling happily between Hartford, New York City and Paris. He had a small apartment in Chelsea, and had bought my grandparents' Haussmann-era flat in Paris. Coming and going was a simple matter for him.

And Hamish couldn't afford even one residence.

Neither could I, and I hated the thought that the days when an American could do so well financially and have so much fun as a result and accomplish so much and travel so much in such comfort were gone. Well, maybe not, and maybe not so for us, but since I had yet to see proof that it was possible for us, I just could not cheer up. I felt helpless, and hated to see anyone.

I hadn't called my friends much since getting married, and had hardly visited them. I just couldn't stand to see them with conventional lives and houses to live in while Hamish and I were in such a mess. Worse still were the concerned questions: didn't we want that? How stupid! Of course we wanted a home! We just hadn't made an income to fuel such a wondrous thing.

So I became progressively – or regressively, depending on one's point of view – more and more isolated socially and physically. I didn't want to be around people. My mother didn't know what to say anymore, and my parents both tried not to bring the subject up too much, even though it felt like a ticking time-bomb. Life was miserable, even though it looked, on its surface, pleasant enough. Looks can be very, very deceiving.

It looked fine as I walked around our neighborhood in the sunshine.

I went once around part of our street. Stoner Drive is rather long, and we lived about halfway down it in a large, rambling, slate-blue colonial-style structure with a huge lawn and garden, plus lots of shady trees. I stayed in the shade as much as possible. We were already in the midst of a heat wave and it was only June. We could chalk that up to global warming. How nice to just write at home and tell myself that I was not adding to it twice a day five days a week for an hour at a time…

It was a warm, sunny day. As usual, I kept to myself, waving to anyone I saw but not approaching, and keeping carefully to the opposite side of the street whenever I saw someone. I walked to think and get fresh air, not to socialize. I liked to walk fast, too, so I didn't want to get stuck with someone who went too slow, or who wanted to jog. I liked to think on these walks.

One thought that usually went through my mind in such nice weather was that global warming was so comfortable and so enjoyable, but not good for our planet. Yet people continued to love such days, at least in the northeastern part of the country. I saw little evidence that anyone even cared what that meant for our planet, as long as the nice weather continued. But there is usually a trade-off; if it's nice in one place, it's not so nice in another.

Sometimes I would rush back to my computer after a walk to write down whatever it was that I had been thinking about. Several short stories had resulted from this habit, and some science fiction novels. The novels hadn't made me rich or famous, but they paid a bit, and I was glad to have them because they would outlive me. I loved the idea that the Library of Congress would keep them on file forever, thanks to my having copyrighted each one.

Today I found myself thinking about Jacques and his friends. During the graduation party, I had observed them for quite a while. It was only natural; the party had been in their honor. It was all about parental pride and hopes for their futures. Jacques had someplace to go, and so did his friends. I had listened to them chatting about their colleges. Some kids hoped to study specific things, others wanted a good sports program so that they could attend the games, and others had admired a particular feature of their future campus, such as the library or a dorm.

Jacques didn't know exactly what he wanted to major in. He did say that he might like to follow his father into the family business and sell real estate after he finished, but that was as far as he had gotten with his future plans. One of the girls wanted to study political science and go on to law school. She had liked being on the debate team in high school. I didn't say anything about how there are over 800,000 licensed attorneys in the United States and not enough work for them. Too early to burst her bubble, I thought, and besides, the teenagers didn't want to hear from the silent woman at the next table.

One boy was very quiet, mostly just listening to his friends. I couldn't remember his name. He spoke up occasionally, but only to answer direct questions from his friends, who moved on as soon as he replied. I wondered why he was so quiet; he used to be as animated as the rest of them. He said that he was going to Boston University when Aunt Zoe stopped by to ask each of her son's friends where they would be attending college. When she asked what he would study, he said pre-med. Other than that, he never smiled and rarely spoke.

I almost sent Hamish over to talk to him about medical school, but he was busy talking about nanobots with someone across the lawn, and I never got the chance before we went home. It was probably just as well; most people who went to medical school did so because they intended to treat patients – not so that to do research. Hamish was on a unique career path.

It was nice out, so I was surprised to be able to wander around the neighborhood alone and think. But no one else was out walking, jogging, or otherwise visible. This was probably because it was a Tuesday afternoon. I would have met someone on a weekend.

When I came in, I went straight upstairs to play the violin, which Spock listened to intently. I could count on the cat to dash upstairs after me right on schedule. I love cats – they are creatures of habit and routine, and they set their own. If they love you, they have considered the matter carefully. I played something from *Indiana Jones*, then some *Star Trek* music, and then locked the instrument away.

I kept it high up in a cabinet with a key, which stayed on a key chain in my pocket whenever I was awake. That way, no one could mess with it. Sometimes, during a big family party, children might be visiting, and they would try to wander around the house, exploring everything. I took no chances. It's not that the violin was some million-dollar Stradivarius or Amati; I just wanted any restringing to be due to vigorous playing rather than kids with inquisitive fingers.

By 4 p.m. I was back in the kitchen, staring into the fridge and plotting dinner. If I couldn't make money, at least I could make a gourmet meal and do it often. It was better than nothing for staying with my parents, and they loved it.

But it was too early to make dinner; it wouldn't take that long to make a fish with orange sauce with asparagus and salad dinner. I went down to the basement to see how Hamish was doing. I didn't really want to see how he was doing again, because it would likely just depress us both, but I couldn't resist seeing my husband and chatting for a couple of minutes. I felt like a fly being drawn to honey sometimes.

I went down the stairs, turned left, and headed past the exercise bikes and television into a door by the laundry room. Spock followed me. Hamish was standing over a table, hovering near his chair but not relaxing into it, peering intently through a microscope. He wore glasses that had magnifying lenses mounted onto each eye-piece. Hamish had 20/20 vision, but nanite technology – robots with components the size of a microscopic nanometer – is invisible to the naked eye. Under the microscope, Hamish was manipulating his nanobots, and the ends of his tools looked invisible to me. He kept making notes on his computer as he worked.

After his time in the military, my husband was determined to do only good with his education. Nanites seemed a lot easier to make weapons out of than medical tools, but he was determined. I admired him for that, even though we had no money from his efforts yet.

"Hi Hamish! I love you!" I said.

He must have heard me coming, because he didn't jump.

"Hi Avril! I love you!" he replied immediately.

It was worth coming down here just to hear that.

Spock jumped onto the side table, keeping to the empty spot that Hamish kept ready for him, and settled into a crouch next to the open laptop computer to stare at us. Older cats knew not to step randomly on everything in sight – another plus about them as pets.

"What are you working on now?" I asked.

"More nanites, of course."

"I know that! I mean specifically what, not generally, and you know it!"

He loved to tease me and wind me up, and I was easy to annoy like that…

"Come on, what are they supposed to do?"

He put the glasses on the table and sat down, sighing. "Probe inside tumors, see the exact extent of them, see how they might be removed with as little tissue damage as possible – more of the usual," he said.

"Oh. Sounds good. I'm proud of you."

If only the pharmaceutical industry liked the idea. But time and again, his attempts to find a market for this sort of thing had run up against a brick wall erected by a powerful lobby that existed to perpetuate sales of drugs that brought in a lot of revenue from existing treatments – treatments marketed by big pharmacy, treatments that would be pushed aside if this caught on.

Hamish had lots of great ideas that would help people and improve human health and quality of life, but selling them seemed like a climb up Mount Everest. It sucked.

"Want to make out tonight?" I asked this from time to time, but always in a glum tone.

"When we get money. If something goes wrong, I'm not sure we can afford an abortion, or afford to find out fast enough to do it with a pill. I don't want you to have to have a surgical abortion. It would hurt and I would feel guilty. Besides, with no money, I feel like I've forgotten what it's like to have any libido."

Great…this was the one way in which my husband just did not resemble Craig Ferguson, who by contrast seemed obsessed with all things remotely sexual.

"So," I said, feeling miserable, "unless and until we get money, we shall enjoy nothing."

"Pretty much. We don't deserve to anyway."

"There are lots of people who find a way to enjoy life before they get money."

"Good for them."

This was our usual vicious spiral of mood-blackening banter.

"What if we had a safe, absolutely reliable method of user-friendly birth control that didn't require a sacrifice of spontaneity? And," I wanted to add this detail before Hamish could cut me off with his inevitable objection, "what if we had it while my parents were in Paris or New York and we were home alone together?"

"That's a lovely fantasy. Too bad it's not a reality."

I stared at him.

That was it. That was what he ought to be working on down here.

"Hamish – I've got an idea for us."

"I'm listening."

"You will have to do most of the work, but I can see your – and our – way to doing this."

"Okay."

"How about inventing a nanite system that lives in a woman's abdomen for her entire reproductive life cycle, if that's what she wants, one that can be linked to a computer system and manipulated from there, and is loaded with a life-time supply of super-concentrated RU486 that automatically sense hormone fluctuations and releases a dose each month, unless stopped?"

He stared at me for a moment.

I couldn't just leave it at that. "The benefit of it is that even though it would cost a bit more than condoms and birth control pills, it could be made affordable if paid for on a monthly plan, and it could become really popular without displacing the competition…"

He jumped up, started clearing some space on the table, and opening a new file on his laptop computer. Then he paused, turned to me, and hugged me.

"You're a genius!" He kissed me – on the mouth – a rare, romantic kiss.

We didn't get enough of those. All that effort at finding a soul mate and I hardly got to enjoy any of its benefits. Now look at him, I thought.

"So you want to try that?"

"I'm starting right now. Tricorders, surgical tools and cameras literally aren't cutting it."

I kissed him and left him to it.

I wouldn't get my hopes up, but at least it was something new to think about.

When I got upstairs, my father had come home early.

He was in the kitchen, looking for some red wine to have with some cheese before dinner, well aware that dinner wouldn't be appearing for a couple of hours at least. We liked to eat during *Jeopardy!* and shout out answers if we them. That meant cooking until about 7 p.m. No sense in eating too early, only to feel hungry in the middle of the night. My parents got a kick out seeing who knew what answer. None of us ever seemed to know the answers to the questions about sports, though. And I had married a man who didn't care about that either.

Dad was going to Manhattan tomorrow for some meetings, so he had brought his papers home to look over, and then he would go to bed by 9 p.m. He didn't want to leave suburbia and live in the city full time, and his firm liked to maintain satellite offices around southern New England, so he had what he wanted. So did my mother. Shopping was nice, but city air was mostly smog, she liked to say, and she could visit the shops occasionally without living right next to them.

She was going with him. Hamish and I would have a few days to ourselves.

I said "Bonjour, Dad!" and started taking stuff out of the fridge for dinner. Somehow, growing up bilingual, I had fallen into the habit of speaking French to my parents – to please them, I supposed, but calling them by American endearments. I called my mother Mommy and my father Dad, and it had been to avoid comments from other kids. My classmates had known that we were French, but I also liked using terms that sounded American. I was American anyway, born at Hartford Hospital. My mother had insisted upon it.

My father, being a lawyer, thought that this was eminently sensible and would ultimately both benefit and save me a lot of legal hassles later on. He was right. Dad was very logical in just about everything he did, and he didn't seem to mind the fact that I didn't do everything that he had wished for me exactly the way he did it.

My father had attended the Sorbonne in the 1960s, and then Cornell Law School immediately after that. He had played the silver trumpet all through lycée and into college, then quit to focus on the law. He met my mother when she was in nursing school in Paris. She had completed the program, then worked for a while in France until he finished at Cornell. Then they had gotten married and moved to the U.S.

They were a very conventional couple. She had promptly filed all of the standard paperwork to change her surname to his after they were married; I would never do that. He just accepted and expected it. I suppose the 1960s had something to do with that; the peace/hippie movement had completely missed them.

They were also a very attractive couple, and continued to be so. My father had never gone bald; he still had a very thick head of now mostly-white hair. He kept it short. I had a pet theory, totally unscientific, about why I had been physically attracted to Hamish: if a woman's father had a thick head of hair, then she wouldn't want a bald husband. Hamish also had thick hair with no sign of encroaching baldness. But back to my father; Dad was the opposite of Hamish in terms of his career and wardrobe. Dad followed a conventional, sure-thing path by practicing international patent law and made an excellent living from it. He also dressed up in suits almost every day, and in beautiful, casual shirts on weekends.

Not Hamish; he wore plain tee shirts and cargo pants most of the time, only dressing up for business meetings or social events. When he had to do that, it was clearly with trepidation and reluctance that he spiffed himself up. He would always complain when I spotted some detail that needed touching up, such as a hair out of place needing combing or trimming.

We were like twins; I didn't like being directed about my appearance either, and my mother was always wanting to do me over, trim my hair a few inches shorter, or add a piece of jewelry to my ensemble when we were going out somewhere special. I would consent to an occasional trim or a pin on my dress and that was it.

My mother was a thin, long-waisted, chic, elegant woman who would always be taller than me. (I was shorter than both of my parents and my husband – not that this was a big deal to me.) My mother's primary concern at any social event was to behave in a manner that would further her husband's status among whomever else was present. No wonder he was so successful. It bothered me that I had no clue how to do that for Hamish. Of course, some of it was up to Hamish…no, a lot of it was up to him.

I thought about all this often whenever I was getting food ready for dinner; especially if I was getting dinner ready while my parents were in the kitchen, which they were this evening. I got out some mixed greens, scallions and strawberries for salad. I put it all aside; I could assemble that while the fish was cooking.

I turned on the oven. Next, I put a saucier pan on the stove – a small one – and dumped a stick of butter into it. I turned on the heat. Then I grabbed a couple of oranges and juiced them, adding that to the saucier. Some fleur de sel, dried chervil and dill, fresh ground pepper, and that was it. The fish was in its package still, a huge pieced of red Sockeye salmon. I rinsed it and put it into a long baking dish. The sauce was ready, so I stirred it and poured it neatly over the salmon, added a few dried lavender flowers, and put it into the oven.

Dad sat at the kitchen table with his wine and cheese, silently watching me work.

The asparagus was in the vegetable drawer of the fridge still; I got that out and trimmed the ends – on a slant – and put the spears into a huge frying pan of water with a bit of olive oil and more dried dill. Then I started cutting up the strawberries and scallions.

I showed Dad what I had made earlier: a beautiful raspberry peach tart. He admired it as I popped the removable bottom up through the fluted side of the pan and put the whole thing onto a plate. Dinner and dessert were pretty much dealt with at this point.

What a life. It would be fine if only Hamish and I had our own money, but I dreaded the appearance of my husband onto the scene every evening. I dreaded the way that my parents would look at him when he came up the cellar stairs.

So did Hamish; he would come up and praise my food and smile at me every time, but we would both look over at my parents as he did so, absolutely convinced that they were finding us and our lives lacking. We knew what we lacked.

Tonight felt no different.

It should have, I told myself. I had just come up with a new idea and Hamish had adopted it with alacrity and enthusiasm. But then, I never felt sure of the value of my ideas until someone with a proven track record for generating an income had assessed them positively. And I needed it to be someone who might actually be willing and able to make it work for us, which we had never yet found, hence my glum outlook.

But tonight was different.

For one thing, Hamish came rushing up the stairs on his own, excited. I didn't have to go downstairs to get him and insist that he stop working and eat with us.

He just came up. And he was in an uncharacteristically exuberant mood.

My parents stared at him, watching and listening.

"Avril! I've got it all down. It's a rough sketch, but completely workable and compatible with long-term coexistence in the human body. All I have to do it write it up and build a prototype, and then we're ready for the development phase!"

"Great!" I said. Though, I thought, it would still be a long time before any funding for development came through, and then we would lose a lot in the deal-making phase. I wondered if we were ever going to profit from this.

"What are you working on?" Dad asked. He and my mother had stopped attacking the brie and were watching us like we were the most engaging episode of *Jeopardy!* I supposed that we were at that moment.

Hamish started explaining. "Avril came down to see me about an hour ago with the best idea for a birth control nanite system. It would contain a life-time supply of super-concentrated RU486, and it would have a release mechanism that would sense when a fertilized embryo was about to implant in the uterine wall, at which time it would dose the woman with enough of the drug to prevent a pregnancy. The user wouldn't have to reach for a condom or remember to take a pill in order to avoid getting pregnant. And if she did want to get pregnant, she could just contact her physician, who would go online, type in a pass code, and set the nanite to not release any RU486 for the next year or so…until the baby was born.”

Dad just stared at him for a full minute.

I began to worry that he thought it was the stupidest thing he had ever heard, and that a tirade about living in a world of science fiction fantasy was about to follow. He had yelled at Hamish on more than one occasion about his nanites, angry that it wasn't producing an income.

But then Dad spoke. “That's the best idea you've ever had. One of my regular clients makes RU486 – mifepristone – and I'll bet that I could get them to fund the development of this. I'll draw up an agreement between them and the 2 of you this weekend about profit-sharing. You will each get 5% of any profits from this device, for a total of 10%, and they will handle the production, development and manufacturing costs. No one gets deals like this, but I think you have a winner here. They won't be able to resist this.”

I stared at Dad in shock. This was a first. He was supporting Hamish's endeavors for a change. Of course, it was not lost on me that he was writing his daughter into it as a full partner solely on the strength of the fact that she had thought of the idea in the first place. After that, it was up to Hamish. But Hamish was running with it at full speed.

“Dad, why wouldn't they be able to resist this deal? I thought that big, wealthy pharmaceutical corporations would want to just sit back and let inventors pay for everything, then step in and steal their inventions out from under them.”

“You thought right – they would. But you and Hamish have a big, bad lawyer on your side, and an idea that would just keep on paying gazillions indefinitely.”

“Oh. Okay, if you really think so. I'm all for having an idea of ours actually pay.”

Nothing seemed real to me. It was more like a hallucination. It couldn't be that simple.

We sat down to dinner and ate.

Jeopardy! started, and soon we were all staring at the screen, suggesting answers to the clues. Even Hamish seemed to be cheerful enough to take an interest in it, which never happened. He was always too upset about our future.

I wondered whether this drug delivery device would lead us anywhere.

The show ended, and my parents turned back to us.

“Have you thought of a name for this invention yet?” My mother wanted to know.

Hamish hadn't; he was too excited about the logistics of making it happen.

That was fine with me.

“Well, you should think about it,” my mother persisted. “With a catchy name, and a good advertising slogan, you could be set for life.”

“I know that,” I said, “but we don't have one yet.”

“Come on Hamish – think of something!” My mother pressed, snapping him out of his reverie. No doubt he was mentally back in the basement workshop.

“Nae – I shall not.” Hamish was getting annoyed.

"That's it!" I jumped up, excited and grinning, and started getting the dessert plates out for the fruit tart.

My parents misunderstood for a moment; they thought I was mad at my mother for pushing my husband…I could tell from the expressions on their faces.

I turned to the three of them and said, "That's it – I've got the perfect name for it!"

Hamish actually snapped out of his mental calculations and turned around.

"What is it?"

"Nae-Née."

Hamish got it instantly and gave me a delighted grin.

"Nae-Née?" My father looked confused.

"Yes. Nae as in N-a-e – the way that Scottish people say no, like you just heard Hamish say it. That would be immediately followed by a hyphen, and then Née as in N-é-e with an acute accent on the first "e" – the French word for born. The name would literally translate as Not-Born, but it would reflect the cultural backgrounds of both of the inventors and sound like the same word repeated."

"That really is perfect!" My mother sounded absolutely thrilled. "What do you think, Henri? Isn't that perfect?"

"Parfaît!" He agreed, unable to resist lapsing into French.

Now we just needed a slogan. I was temporarily stumped, but Dad said not to worry; the advertising firm would handle that part.

My mother and I cleared the dinner things and we all settled into eating the dessert.

Somehow, it tasted better than ever.

It wasn't the raspberries; it was the feeling of hope.

Maybe it would improve people's lives – other than our own.

I liked to think so; I didn't want our success to be solely about me and Hamish.

Maybe the world didn't have to be crowded and miserable, I thought happily.

I was so naïve.

The damage was done already; Nae-Née would help future generations, but not this one.

Chapter 3

Inventing

Hamish spent the next 2 weeks designing and refining our new idea.

The night that we thought of it – well, that I thought of it – I had said to him: "Hamish, this really is it for us. This is THE idea that will get us out of this black hole of inertia that we are in. You've got to design this thing just so and demonstrate that it really can work. My father clearly can – and will – take it from there. And then you and I just have to keep going with it."

He agreed. This could make us financially secure and finally get us some respect from my parents and others. And that in turn would also help keep us safe. At least, that was the plan. Hamish wouldn't talk about his past much, so I didn't know what he wanted to be safe from.

Hamish couldn't stop thinking about the details of Nae-Née now; he was obsessed. Whenever he tried to sit still and relax for a few minutes, he just couldn't. He had to jump up and get his laptop going. Whenever he paused to take a break, he would load copies of everything to his memory sticks and ask me to save them to my desktop and laptop. I did it.

I wished that I could do more to help besides just protect the data, but having a doctorate in the history of women's medicine wasn't going to help much with making the idea a reality. It was all very nice that I had thought of it, but without Hamish, it would have remained just that: a really cool idea and nothing more.

At least I would be able to make it understandable to others, which was not Hamish's strong point. The title of my thesis was still worth more and more mileage on the lecture circuits at universities everywhere I went: *The Herstory of Medicine: Ancient Herbalist Wiccans and Midwives to RU-486.* Since graduating, I had re-written the whole thing in English and published it as a book, complete with photos wherever I could fit one in. Considering the fact that I had concluded the study with mifepristone, originally known as RU-486, it was not surprising that I had thought of using it in Nae-Née.

Most people still thought of the drug as RU-486. That was how it was first introduced to the world, so that was how people recognized it. At some point later, someone decided to give it a chemical name, which is typical, but it never carried the same recall status as the original one.

The trouble with using RU-486 solely as an abortifacient was the 9 to 16 days of bleeding and spotting. Thus, it would be undesirable to deploy it only after having clear and convincing evidence of a pregnancy. The Nae-Née nanobot had to be capable of measuring body chemistry levels and changes to confirm or deny the presence of a fertilized ovum, as well as traveling through capillaries.

The idea was to automatically release smaller doses as contraception, to ensure that the woman simply got her period each month. She should then pass every egg, fertilized or not, thanks to using the device. That was what was making Hamish's task such a complex one.

Condoms would still be necessary; like just about every other birth control device, it should not be used alone, and it would not protect against HIV or venereal disease.

The point of Nae-Née was to have a guaranteed guard against pregnancy, and to have that guard be so convenient as to negate any necessity for rushing to a hospital. Just go to a computer and cancel out the pregnancy, and no anti-choice fundamentalist would be able to force the woman to sit through videos or lectures in an attempt to change her mind. She would finally have reliable and quick control over her fertility.

Of course, a way would have to be found to make this cost-effective and within the financial reach of most women, or it would not be profitable. Dad had assured me that this could be done, and that nanobotic technology was now sufficiently standardized for that. Great.

My parents left for Manhattan the next day, and Hamish and I found ourselves home alone with Spock for company. The cat alternated between watching me and watching Hamish. We both worked steadily in our usual spots, so he kept up a routine between the basement and our bedroom. We met for meals, and of course we visited each other when we needed a break or to bounce ideas off of one another.

A couple of times I dragged Hamish outside for a walk, just to make him breathe fresh air and see sunshine. Other than that, I let him alone for a full week. My parents were gone for a week and a half, enjoying the city while my father attended some meetings.

After 8 days, however, I was itching to go out somewhere. We hadn't seen anything other than Stoner Drive for more than 2 weeks, so I insisted that Hamish come with me to the mall for dinner and a walk around the premises. Grumbling, he agreed to go out with me.

We didn't dress up; California Pizza Kitchen doesn't demand formality. We just liked the smashed pea barley soup and the pizza with applewood smoked bacon. It was a vice that we still looked forward to on occasion, especially after our time in the Islamic world, where bacon is not considered halal – the Muslim version of kosher. It was harmless food-fun, and after we had eaten, we went wandering around the mall.

It was a lot less stressful to go to a shopping mall with my husband than it was to go with my mother. Hamish would just joke around a lot, follow me in and out of stores, and mock-whine, "Can we go?" when I paused longer than a minute to scrutinize something. At least he didn't bug me about how I dressed.

Sometimes I would go out with my mother to shop, even though it bored me and I didn't buy much. She loves to inspect – at very close range – each and every single article of clothing on each and every rack. I look at a rack from a distance, spot perhaps one item that I want a closer look at, inspect that, and leave. To me, it quickly becomes Chinese water torture if I am expected to do more than that.

My mother typically responds to this by telling me what a smart person I am and that that's the reason for my lack of interest…at which point I remind her of how smart she is and how she routinely forgets that she studied for her citizenship test in English after learning it at her lycée (high school), then went right on to earn a double Associate's degree in nursing and English simultaneously. Only smart people do that.

She smiled sweetly at me whenever I did that.

Then I tell her how chic and elegant she is. My mother is flexible, and likes what is in fashion when it is in fashion. In recent years, however, she has actually complemented me on wearing more sophisticated clothing. Odd; I get annoyed at the fashion industry. I want deep, user-friendly pockets in all of my clothes for my keys, but that is hard to find. I want natural fabrics, comfortable styles, some floral patterns, a lot of pink and blue, and some black and white. I only want flat, rubber-soled shoes. They are comfortable, and silent, and enable me to sneak up on people! I know I'm an odd woman, but I just don't care.

The stores bored me, but I liked to people-watch and to get a fancy coffee with my husband, so we ended up sitting in the center court with our lattes and relaxing for a while. Hamish told me yet again that he felt lucky to have married me because I didn't love to shop and scrutinize every item on every rack of every store. I never tired of hearing this complement.

As we sat there, I spotted a kid sitting alone with a cup of coffee at the next table. He was sitting with his back partly facing us, so he didn't notice us. He was wearing cargo shorts, a tee shirt, and a lumpy jacket with an odd bulge on one side. And he was just sitting there, staring at his beverage, not touching it. He seemed to be lost in thought.

He was one of Jacques's friends from the party – the quiet one who hadn't said much.

"Greg!" I called over to him.

He looked up, dazed, and turned to face us.

"Hi!" I said. "How are you? The last time we saw you was at Jacques's graduation party."

"Oh yeah. Hi, Dr. Châtelet. Hi, Dr. MacDonall."

"Call us Avril and Hamish – we don't want to feel old."

"Okay." He still hadn't moved from his chair. He definitely seemed glum to me, but then teenagers tended not to want to chat much with people who were older than they were – or so I thought. Still, it would odd not to invite him to sit with us, so I went ahead and did it. "Come on over here with your coffee, or whatever it is you're drinking."

He got up and pulled his chair over to us.

"So Greg – I heard you say at the party that you intend to study pre-med in college. Hamish went to medical school. He doesn't treat patients – he researches nanite technology for medical use – but maybe you would like to ask him some questions about it."

The kid gave me an odd look. I was no good at interpreting signals from people's eyes, but this one just didn't match up with anything that I had ever seen after an invitation like that one. What was the matter?

Hamish spoke up. "I didn't do my undergrad studies here in the U.S. – that was in Scotland – but medical school was here. I'd be happy to share my experience with you if you want to hear about it. Just ask me whatever you want."

Greg looked really uncomfortable now. This was getting weird; I decided to ask some point-blank questions to see if I could draw him out.

"I heard you tell my Aunt Zoe that you are going to Boston University. Aren't you happy about it? Or were you hoping to get accepted elsewhere?"

Greg looked a bit defensive now, judging from his body language. It was as if he were trying to erect a physical barrier between the questions and himself. "I was hoping to get accepted somewhere," he said at last.

"Somewhere? But you were accepted to Boston University," I repeated, sounding as doubtful about this as I was starting to feel.

"No I wasn't. I just said I was."

Hamish and I glanced at each other. "Why did you say it then?" I asked him.

"Because all of my friends have been accepted somewhere. We all applied to several schools, knowing that there was a strong possibility that we might not be accepted to the school of our choice. Each of them got in somewhere, and only one of them – Janice, the one who wants to study law – got into her first-choice school, which was Brown. The rest of us didn't. And I couldn't let anyone find out that I didn't get in anywhere, despite sending out 40 college applications, a 3.9 GPA, a spot on the varsity track team and a role in a play each year, so I lied."

Hamish and I sat there, frozen. So it was happening already; overpopulation was affecting the kids of the present, not those of the future. I had to say something though, so I said, "I saw you in the play with Jacques, Janice and the rest of them. You were funny."

"Thanks."

"Where did you apply?"

Greg looked relieved to have someone to talk to about it. "Boston University, obviously, and Stanford, Colby, Bates, Columbia, Emory, UConn, Brown, U.C.L.A., U.S.C., Northwestern, UPenn, Colgate, Cornell, Union College, Trinity, Fairfield, Quinnipiac, Wesleyan, University of Hartford, UMass at Amherst, Rutgers, Drew, Pepperdine, Tulane, Columbia, N.Y.U., Bowdoin, Roger Williams, Middlebury, Ithaca College, Elmira College, Williams College, Hobart College, Amherst College, Lewis & Clark College, Thomas Aquinas, Wheaton, Willamette, and Bucknell."

Hamish said, "I've heard of all of those schools. It sounds like you applied to a decent range of them – reach schools, ivy-league, state schools, all sorts. And you are obviously qualified to attend any of them."

Greg looked at him. "I know I'm qualified. And so do they. The rejection letters they sent back all acknowledge that."

I spoke up. "What did these letters say?"

To our surprise, he suddenly pulled a large wad of envelopes out of his jacket. So that was what that bulge on one side had been.

"You've been carrying the letters around with you?"

"Yeah." Greg laid them out on the table among our coffee cups. Sure enough, there was one envelope from each of the schools. It was both disturbing and astonishing that not one of them had accepted this kid. I had heard enough about him to know that he was good enough and motivated enough to do well at any of them.

I considered my own academic achievements to be great accomplishments full of fond intellectual memories, travel stories and independence. It had always been something to be proud of. Whatever was going wrong with my life now, at least I could look back at my degrees and feel a permanent sense of self-esteem, plus know that my mind was an interesting place to live in. The dean had encouraged that when she spoke to us all on the first day of our first term at William Smith College. And now it looked as though this good kid would never have that.

It was suddenly clear when I looked into his eyes again. It was all over, they said to me.

The trouble with me is that if I don't show some evidence of a strong emotion, I appear not be feeling any. Most people get the mistaken impression that I just don't care. The way around that is to ask lots of questions. Hamish doesn't bother. I almost envied him the ability to just worry about his own difficulties, but I couldn't help thinking about other people's problems.

"Can we see some of the letters?" I asked.

"Sure, go ahead. I don't know what I've been saving them for. Maybe I just need to be reminded so I won't be in denial. But mostly I don't want my mother to find them."

I reached for the one from Boston University.

"How have you managed to keep this deception up this long? I mean, haven't you had to work at keeping your parents from finding these when you're asleep or in the shower?"

"They don't snoop. And I do my own laundry."

I opened the letter and read:

Dear Mr. Matthews:

After carefully considering your many and valuable qualifications, we have reached the unfortunate decision not to admit you to Boston University.

We give special attention to applicants whose families have a tradition of study at Boston University. We have extended this consideration in the evaluation of your application, but I regret to inform you that we are unable to offer you admission.

Please do not take this in any way as criticism. The problem is us, not you. We simply don't have enough spaces to admit all of the well-qualified applicants who approach us.

We wish you every success at whichever school does accept you, and in your future.

Sincerely,
Clifton J. Hyde
Dean of Admissions
Boston University

I looked up at Greg. "Did someone in your family attend Boston University?"

"Yeah. My uncle went there, and I have a cousin in her junior year there."

"Is that why you said that the place had accepted you? I mean, it seems to me that you could have chosen to say that any one of these places had. Why this one?"

"I got this letter last of all. By then I had posted copies of all the others on the wall of shame at school."

"What's a wall of shame?" Hamish asked.

I had heard of those. My generation hadn't had any; they had just appeared in the past few years. I told him, "It's a wall in a high school hallway where kids hang up their college rejection letters. Sharing the misery supposedly makes it easier when the dream school rejects a student, or when most or all of them do."

He looked appalled. Hamish hadn't had such problems. Despite coming from a rough neighborhood, he had held his own thanks to the ability to fight or, if the opponents were too brawny for him to go up against, to run. He had been bullied for his academic ability but pressed on and won scholarships and stipends, and thus escaped from Glasgow. He rarely went back or kept in touch with anyone there – except for his sister, Fiona.

Getting accepted to college or university just hadn't been the problem for him; the problem had been dealing with the reactions of his peers. He didn't care if it upset them; he just wanted to get away from them. There was that, and the numbers of applicants in both his day and mine hadn't been so overwhelming. When we were applying, being qualified had been enough to get accepted at least somewhere, and somewhere good – someplace placed at the competitive or even highly competitive level in the college rankings.

"Greg, I know that this won't fix the problem, but I'm going to say it anyway. This is not your fault. I don't know what to suggest next, but I really think that the reason for this is human overpopulation. Too many applicants applying for the same number of spots as when there were far fewer of them; too many parents who wanted too many kids."

"That's the first time that anyone has said that to me."

"I'm not surprised. What do you make of that assessment of academia?"

"It sounds about right."

"Do you follow the news much?"

"Yeah, and I've seen lots of stories about college rejections. I read it online, mostly. This is happening everywhere."

"How long have you been carrying these around, and how often do you look at them?"

"Since late this winter; I got the last of these in the spring. When I got the first few, I wasn't worried because I had several more colleges to go. I posted copies and just waited. I promised myself that I would not stop doing my best; that I would graduate without slacking off. I was hoping that Cornell or U.S.C., which both wait-listed me, would change their minds."

Both reach schools, to put it mildly. Wait-list purgatory wasn't going to come through. Especially not now; all applicants had sent in their registration fees before graduation.

I looked at the letters from Cornell and U.S.C. Yup – each envelope contained an extra, final letter of rejection, saying that all slots had been filled and the wait was over. No room for Greg at either school.

"Greg, did you at least tell your college counselor at Conard about this?"
"No."
"Why not?"
"Because I already know what she would say."
"How would know that?"
"I almost saw her once I got all of these. I was waiting to see her when I saw the kid ahead of me come out, crying, having been rejected everywhere that he had applied also. She told him to go to community college and apply again next year. That was when he cried. He said that the schools would just reject him again the next year in favor of the very best high school seniors that they could get – the pick of the litter. So I just left before she saw me there. She didn't notice; I hadn't made an appointment, so she wasn't expecting to see me."

"So what are you planning to do now? Did you get a summer job? Are you going to go to community college? Or apply to a college in a foreign country?"

He looked at me, startled. "A foreign country? No. I looked into that. The American University in Kuwait, and a few others. No way am I going to community college, and I couldn't find a summer job. There's nothing out there right now – no one's hiring. I have no clue what to do now."

Hamish looked up. "You looked at a school in Kuwait? I was in the war there. I've seen that school."

Greg looked up at him. "Interesting…but they don't have a life sciences department – it's mostly business. I don't know how I'm going to medical school. I just don't get it. I did everything right, including interning every summer at the UConn Health Center and Hartford Hospital. It seems like it was all for nothing now."

I looked at Hamish. "Do you know anyone he could talk to, anyone who might have some advice for him?"

Hamish thought about it. "I could contact some of my professors at Cambridge. Maybe they could suggest something," he said doubtfully. He wasn't one for social networking.

Greg looked irritated. "Look, thanks, I appreciate your concern, but they won't be able to save my wasted year that's coming up. And they won't be able to help me. It's too late."

"You've got to tell your parents. Parents are amazing; they always think of something."

He just looked at me.

I pressed on, "You can't seriously think that you can conceal this forever. Won't the summer be easier without the weight of a secret pressing on you?"

"Maybe."

"Please say you'll tell them soon."

"Okay, I will."

"My mother told me about a guy who couldn't get accepted to medical school in the U.S., so he went in Geneva, Switzerland. And that was in the 1960s. He's retired now. There's got to be a way. Don't give up just yet," I pleaded.

Greg seemed to be taking that in.

At last, he spoke again. "Okay, I'll look into all that…and tell my parents. Thanks for talking to me. I guess it feels better to have told someone. Just don't tell my friends."

"I'm not in touch with them. I almost never see Jacques, and you just asked me not to talk, so unless he indicates to me that he already knows about this, I won't say a word about it."

"Thanks."

"It's not your fault that they didn't accept you, Greg. You're qualified."

He looked like he might cry. I didn't want to cry first. This was his disappointment; I was just feeling awful on his behalf.

He grabbed up all of his envelopes, stuffed them back into his jacket, and threw his coffee cup in the nearest trash bin. "I've got to go. Thanks for listening."

"You're welcome. Here – take our business cards – you can call us if you want."

I handed him our cards, which I routinely made at home on our ink-jet printer. The cards looked impressive, except for the lack of institutional affiliation: names, degree initials, cell phone numbers, e-mail addresses.

He pocketed the cards and walked off.

I looked at Hamish, checked to make sure that Greg was out of sight, and dragged my chair over to my husband, where I promptly buried my face in his tee shirt. I wasn't crying, but I wanted a hug.

He hugged me.

"I hate this, Hamish. I know all about a terrible problem and can't help."

"I love you, Avril. But you can't help everyone."

"I just want to help the people I come face to face with rather than say something trite and stupid and leave them to continue struggling."

"We have to be able to take care of ourselves first, and we can't yet."

I sat up. "We will. Finish up with Nae-Née. I think we're on to something. The next question will be whether or not enough people have the sense to use it and refrain from reproducing…they need to have the foresight to not inflict too much life on the next generation."

Hamish laughed ruefully. "Too many people like kids for that to happen."

"They need to think past the baby phase of having kids. Even if we liked babies and little kids, and even if we became solvent – no, wealthy enough to pay for a kid to study right through the doctoral level of school – that wouldn't be enough anymore. I couldn't and wouldn't do that to someone. I am so glad that I don't want kids. I feel so bad for Greg. I refuse to ever let that happen to any kid of mine. So there won't be any kid of mine thanks to all of those reasons. It's too easy for us that way – no sense of disappointment for us. Just sympathy for others who will know what they are missing."

Hamish just listened.

"Say something!" I said.

"I don't know what to say – you're right about all of it!" he replied.

We finished our lattes and headed out to the car. On the way home, I couldn't just admire the sights and lovely smells of summer through the open car windows. I was too upset. If I liked kids, I knew that I would have been in worse shape.

I started ranting again. Hamish just let me.

"No one wants to say this because it sounds monstrous: we don't need all these people. There are too many people in the world. The planet would benefit greatly from a reduction in the human population. But how do we achieve that?" I was on a roll. "The reason that we now have this monstrous situation is that no one is even remotely willing to openly say that it is so. And so it grows and grows…worse."

Hamish said, "Okay, I'll bite. How do we get fewer people in the world?"

"By having fewer children, and by fewer of us having any at all."

"No one will ever willingly volunteer to be the ones who do that. Everyone wants to have what they want. They consider it to be their right."

"I know that. I'm just giving the realistic answer. The planet is full to the brim of people, and more and more of them are going to want educations – real ones, not community college ones – and the middle-class American lifestyle. The planet can't deliver all those orders. The world is already full, and no one is noticing."

"I know."

"I know *you* know – but people like Mindy – with 4 kids – are just contributing to the exponential human population explosion. It's a crisis. Greg's future is Sam's future – or worse. Those letters pretty much tell him to give up his dreams and become a menial slave – or to just die. I'm worried about that kid."

"Are you going to tell his parents?"

"No. But if I don't say anything to anyone and he kills himself, I'm going to feel guilty about it. I'm involved now that I know. That's the way it is, whether I like it or not."

For some unfathomable but convenient reason, my parents' place had a 3-car garage. Perhaps the previous owner had kept a recreational car. More waste and excess while other people on the planet had less than they needed to function…but back to obsessing about Greg…

"What's wrong with all these people who keep insisting upon having more and more babies?! Are they ignorant, crazy, in denial, mentally challenged, selfish, unable or unwilling to admit the truth about the planet's supply of resources to themselves? What is it with them?"

"Some combination of all of the above," Hamish replied absently. "Plus there are too many pro-lifers, anti-choicers, whatever you want to call them, who will scream and cry about all life being sacred regardless of its quality. That's why cancer patients get tortured and disfigured; rather than fund any innovative research, the medical profession just keeps serving up more poison because it's the accepted doctrine."

"That's not the only reason and you know it," I said irritably. "Big pharmaceutical companies don't want their profits threatened. I wonder how they'll like Nae-Née," I worried.

"The ones that sell RU486 will like it just fine. I'm going back to work," Hamish said.

He went downstairs to add some fine-tuning to Nae-Née. He had thought of some details while we were out, and he didn't want to forget the ideas. I knew he cared about what bothered me, but he couldn't help.

I worked the same way; I went up to my computer to work on a novel about people like Greg. It wasn't necessary to make this stuff up; reality was quite obliging with the details.

Chapter 4

An Eclipse – and Nae-Née is Born

What an oxymoron – to say that something that literally means "not-born" was born.

But it was.

Hamish finished the blueprint and the prototype for Nae-Née after 2 weeks of work.

He was satisfied that it was now time to run some tests.

This was just in time for our 8th anniversary, and a couple of weeks before an eclipse that we wouldn't be able to see, thanks to its geographic location: Easter Island, also known as Rapa Nui, in the middle of the southern Pacific Ocean. It would be a total solar eclipse.

Eclipses had always fascinated me. They were so beautiful, but just as when a man in ancient Greek mythology looked directly at Medusa, any human looking directly at an eclipse would burn their retina and go blind.

Both Medusa and an eclipse had to be viewed through a filter; with Medusa, it was a mirror, and with an eclipse, it was a box with a hole poked into it so that one could view a projection of the phenomenon on a piece of paper pasted inside the box.

I had tried to see an eclipse this way once when I was 9 years old, but the sky was overcast and the preparation had been a wasted effort. I still remembered how disappointed I was when I realized that the whole day would be gray and that I would see nothing new.

Photographs of total solar eclipses never ceased to impress me. The thought that the moon was directly between the sun and the spot of the Earth where the photographer had set up a camera just thrilled me. The flawless disk of black with a tendril of light – caused by a solar flare – here and there with the sun's corona showing around the moon was just so beautiful that I liked to save the images on my computer and go back to them from time to time.

Hamish and I hoped to go and view a full solar eclipse someday, when we had the leisure time and disposable income to spend on it. The thought of burning my retina by accidentally looking up at the wrong time frightened me, but he assured me that we could remind each other to be careful and just use the recommended viewing equipment. It would be fine…and really, really cool.

Then there were the superstitions about eclipses. Throughout human history, people have thought of them as omens, especially as related to battles or floods. Pick a society, look at whatever it fears, check to see whatever its cultural and spiritual beliefs are, and consider how that might affect it interpretation of an eclipse. People's fears will play a role in determining what they think an eclipse means…unless they are educated and have been taught the astronomer's explanation of the phenomenon.

It's just a cool thing to see, as long as you don't look at it…another oxymoron.

I couldn't help but wonder about the timing of Nae-Née and the eclipse. Would someone at some future date suggest a connection between the 2 events?

I decided that it was just too much fun to be a logical-minded, educated person who understood science well enough to know better. I was glad not to be involved in science at some fear-driven, unenlightened time in some past century.

We were simply creating a birth control method that would be very, very user-friendly.

For our anniversary, we went out to eat at a place called Belgique. Belgique was a beautiful place with the most delectable things to eat in Kent, Connecticut. It occupied 2 buildings on the southeast corner of the intersection of Routes 7 and 341. Both were painted butter yellow, which was entirely appropriate considering that butter is a common ingredient in almost everything Belgian.

The chef, Pierre Gilissen, was Belgian, and had cooked and baked at the White House, among other famous venues. He and his American wife, Susan, owned and operate the business together, which consisted of a huge, rambling Victorian house surrounded by well-kept gardens on a small lot, and a white gravel parking area in back that led to their Chocolaterie. The Chocolaterie is in a small, square-shaped building with a little cupola on top, and porcelain miniatures of it were sold as candy boxes inside.

The restaurant offered afternoon tea, a sit-down service inside the main building, or lunch, or dinner. Coffee, hot chocolate and patisseries were sold out back at the Chocolaterie. The parking lot had the most beautiful periwinkle-blue iris clusters all around it in the spring and early summer.

We arrived early, because I wanted to buy a few miniature cakes, some pâtés de fruits, and some of the handmade Belgian chocolates. I hadn't seen anything like this outside of Europe – not even in New York City, where one could supposedly get absolutely anything. I checked with Madame Susan Gilissen, and sure enough, she said that the restaurant would save them while we ate (the Chocolaterie closed at 6 p.m., when our reservation was set for).

Excellent; I bought some of the framboise pâtés de fruits, 2 chocolate hazelnut Dacquoises, a pear Charlotte, and one Arlequin. All of these were in small sizes and either round or paisley shapes. After that, we went inside and had an amazing dinner, the likes of which I normally expected to either have to make myself or find in Manhattan or Europe.

Hamish remarked that I was living up to the stereotype of being French by seeking out the most delectable meal possible, and added that this was just fine with him. Another dividend offered by the restaurant was that young children and babies were not allowed, thus protecting the romantic atmosphere for dates.

This was what we liked to budget our money for – delectable gourmet dinner dates.

A few days later, my parents came back from New York City and watched as Hamish put the finishing touches on his presentation. They didn't go down to the basement workshop and stare over his shoulder; they just listened and looked at whatever he showed us all whenever he brought the laptop upstairs.

We all looked at the images on the screen, and at the photographs he had shot through the microscope he used. Hamish was a clever engineer; using a digital camera – our more expensive one had been sacrificed to his scientific endeavors – and the microscope, and he found a way to link their microchips and interface the 2 devices. Thus, he could treat us to images of his nanobots. It was rather enthralling, to say the least.

My mother understood better than my father – she being a nurse and he being an attorney – when Hamish explained how the nanobots would interact with human flesh.

Now all that remained was to run some tests. It was time to contact my gynecologist. She could – and we had found out the previous week, would – help us with this.

Her name was Dr. Elizabeth N. Rowland, M.D., and she had an office nearby in Farmington, just down the road from the UConn Health Center. She was in her late 40s and anxious to add to her list of professional journal publications. If she could assist us in the development of our new invention, she could join the string of authors on the article that would undoubtedly be generated from it. But…nothing would be published until a patent was filed.

I had impressed this caveat upon Hamish early on in our relationship with no difficulty. However, he had worked with some colleagues in Kuwait who had not understood this, and so I had been enlisted to visit these men one day during our stay there. It was fun; I got to attend a diwaniya, which is an evening social gathering for businessmen.

There was no mistake when I said businessmen, not businesspeople. Women were not invited into the men's part of an Arab home as a rule. Women stayed in their own section, called the harim. The gathering of men took place in the men's share of the home, called the diwan, and was known as a diwaniya. The men would sit in a circle, along the perimeter of the room, chatting only about politics and social events, not business. They would enjoy a few treats, which varied from place to place. I had some wonderful heated cardamom-infused milk, some knar fruits, and some dates stuffed with pistachio nuts.

Hamish and his colleague had been busy developing a treatment for chemical injuries, and this Kuwaiti man, a Dr. Khalid, was not what I would call a cautious person. He could hardly wait to publish the data. Hamish was frantic that he would try to do so and spill the beans before the idea could be blanketed with legal protection. The other Kuwaitis involved were also concerned. Thus, his wife with the law degree was brought in to put a stop to such insanity.

The diwan was a beautiful, marble-floored room in a small palace of a mansion. The floor was covered by a huge Persian carpet, and all of the windows were heavily curtained so as to prevent anyone outside from seeing in. The sofas were cushions which were molded to perimeter of the room, all on the floor, with back pieces.

Men in dishdashahs with the traditional Arab headdress of a guthra and ekal sat clicking their prayer beads. Hamish told me that they were also involved in the project, and that some of them could write well enough to generate the much-desired publication. However, they preferred to do this with Hamish's involvement and me editing, so that the article could appear in a Western journal and in well-polished English.

Confident that I could convince them of the necessity of a patent before a publication, I went to meet them. It was all fine. I knew that my presence there was unusual, but I also knew that these men had traveled in the West and would not find my appearance odd, nor would they stare and stare. They had been socialized and therefore acclimatized to Western culture. And they had invited me into their inner sanctum. It was only a living room, after all – not a mosque.

I went in with Hamish, pausing unbidden to take off my Teva sandals. Sandals are just easier in the desert, and I knew to take them off inside homes. I was wearing my usual but elegant black linen pants with a colorful blouse. My toenails were painted raspberry pink, I wore makeup – considerably less than Arab women did – and my long hair was down.

But the Kuwaiti men didn't bat an eye. I was with my husband, and they had invited me. I had fun watching to see what would happen when, and tasting the treats that were served. I thanked the Indian men who brought out the trays of milk and fruit. The Kuwaitis didn't say a word to the servants, but they didn't react when I did so. Some time went by as we chatted about nothing of any particular importance before the big question was asked.

The question came from Dr. Khalid's friend and the host of the diwan, Dr. Ali. Dr. Ali ran the laboratory at Kuwait University where Khalid and Hamish were working.

"Dr. Avril, because you are an American lawyer, we wanted to ask you an important question: what do we have to lose by publishing our results and treatment recommendation before getting a patent for that treatment?"

At last, I thought, we have gotten to the point.

"What you have to lose is all of the money you might ever make from your efforts. I know that people become doctors to heal people, but doctors need to make a living at the same time. If you don't put a patent on your treatment – which is essentially an invention – before telling the world all about it, you might as well just grab wads of all of the money you have, go to the nearest toilet, and start flushing."

The men all stopped sipping, chewing and clicking their prayer beads to stare at me.

I looked at Dr. Khalid. He too was still. I was glad. One could spend hours trying to get his attention despite being in the same room with him, and he just wouldn't sit still and listen. It had taken the seriousness of a gathering with his professional colleagues to get through to him.

I looked back at all of the other Kuwaiti scientists. "Have I helped you with this explanation? I made it graphic on purpose, for the maximum emotional impact. Statements such as that one tend to have a lasting effect, and therefore make a permanent impression."

Dr. Ali spoke up first. "You have certainly convinced me. Dr. Khalid? Do you see now what we were all trying to tell you?"

He said he did. He looked a bit disappointed.

I told him that when the publication finally did come out, he would enjoy it much more knowing that his chances at earning profits were safe in addition to being praised for developing such a helpful treatment for chemical injuries.

He brightened up, thanked me, and passed me some of the wonderful puff-pastry sweets that are served in the Middle East: little bite-sized baklava treats of pistachio and honey.

So that was what the hold-up was on announcing our big hurrah to the world.

It didn't bother me in the least. Better to play it safe than jump the gun and ruin it.

Besides, I wanted to experience that test myself.

I would be the test subject. I wanted a reliable form of birth control without constantly pumping myself full of drugs or hormones of any kind. It wasn't in one's best interests health-wise to take birth control pills for one's entire reproductive life cycle; it could trigger cancer in an otherwise healthy woman who would otherwise never have had to worry about that.

I wanted to have my cake and eat it too: no babies, and no cancer.

It shouldn't be too much to ask out of life, I believed. So did Hamish.

We had been living without much sex because he refused to let me take hormones, and we hated it. Starting to cuddle and pulling away sucked. Enough said.

As for a vasectomy, Hamish didn't really want his testicles snipped – it was a fear of scalpels, surgery, accidents…he was a bit skittish about having any work done. He had never trusted doctors. It was one of the hazards of being one, he said.

Now that we intended to test Nae-Née out – on me – we were glad that he had never resorted to this. We would have had to enlist some other couple to try the device out, plus deal with lots of awkward, personal questions as to why we couldn't do it ourselves. Better this way…the only problem we foresaw was having enough libido on both sides of the equation with sufficient frequency to validate the device.

And Hamish would be checking his laptop after we…this was going to be weird.

Well…first he had to get the device sterilized, loaded with RU-486, and deployed in my body with the computer chip in sync with the computer. We would need it linked with a website. We couldn't just rely on Hamish's computer. What if it crashed? We would be out of luck.

Getting the website ready was quick; I had called a computer expert in and paid a lot.

This was funny. Most couples tried and tried to be able to make the announcement that the wife was pregnant. We were going for the opposite announcement: that the wife was *not* pregnant. It was going to our word against anyone's that we had even had sex, I realized.

So what. We would know what we had or had not done and when.

I called Dr. Rowland's office and made an appointment. The receptionist asked the purpose of the visit, and I was temporarily stumped. Why was I going to see her? After a moment, I said for birth control. That was true. I wasn't about to explain that we were testing a new method of the idea out for future use in the general population. She didn't need to know that. I hung up, satisfied with that.

The appointment was for next Tuesday at 4:30 p.m. I told Hamish, and he got his nanites ready. He was bringing 4 prototypes, all identical, just in case. He would check through his microscope at the last moment before giving Dr. Rowland the final go-ahead.

She promised to have some of the drug ready when she called us back that evening. The super-concentrated dose had existed for quite some time. The missing element had been a convenient mechanism that could serve as a delivery device. What was the use of a drug without a way to time its delivery just right?

Thinking back to the Kuwaitis, I knew that we were going through a similar routine for Nae-Née. The difference here was that Muslims would not have wanted it, or so I thought. Well, there were plenty of other markets. What did I know, anyway…maybe they would find it useful and want this…time would tell, I supposed.

Meanwhile, I had one other thing on my mind: Greg.

What would we do about him? What would become of him, and of others like him?

I found his phone number – his parents' phone number – through a less and less known method: the white pages. My parents, even though they kept a net-connected computer in the kitchen, still kept a land-line telephone and collected new phone books each year. I hated to think of the trees being killed for this purpose, but so many people still used them.

I called him and left a message without revealing why; his parents would have heard it.

He called back a day later, to leave a message on my cell phone. Now I had his cell phone number; I had to let the voice mail function recite it, but I got it.

I didn't keep my cell phone on all of the time. It wore down the battery, plus it tended to make me entirely too easy to reach, which also interfered with my writing. I couldn't have it distracting me while I was trying to type whatever creation was running through my mind.

So I called the kid back. "Greg, it's Avril. How are you?"

"Okay."

"So…have you told your parents that none of those schools admitted you yet?"

"Not yet."

"It's been 4 days since I talked to you. The sooner you tell them, the sooner they can help you look into going to college in some foreign country. If you find a good one, and you have enough qualifications to have a reasonable expectation of doing so, you ought to still be able to go to medical school in 4 years. You could even try transferring to an American college or university. If it doesn't work, it's not a disaster, but you could still try. Or you might decide that it's fine to stay with whatever foreign university. Your college counselor might talk with you now, even though school is out for the summer."

Silence, then, "This is very nice of you, but why do you care?"

"Because I had everything in terms of education and because I didn't have to face the hideous odds that you are facing. And because I feel involved now that I know that you haven't told anyone else. It's not okay for me to just go on my merry way, aware that a kid who should be heading off to college has been denied, and do nothing."

"Oh."

"Do you have regular access to the Internet?"

"Yes."

"Good. You can also contact your high school college counselor. Just go back there, to the office, and ask. The secretary should be there, and can get help you contact the counselor."

Silence again.

"Greg, are you still there?"

"Yes. I'm listening."

"Okay. I can't see you, so I have to ask when I don't hear anything."

"Thank you for all of your ideas."

"Will you promise me that you will first tell your parents what's going on, and second, start working on my suggestions?"

"Yes. I'll tell them."

"Will you call me in a few days and tell me how you are doing?"

Pause. "Okay."

"Thanks. I'm not trying to pressure you into staying in touch forever and ever – you don't know me – I just want to make sure that you're okay."

"Thanks. I'll tell them and then tell you."

"Okay. Good." I felt a bit relieved, but I would hold off on any celebrating until I heard back from him. "Okay – good-bye then, and good luck. Don't worry; it can still be okay."

"Thanks. Bye."

I rang off, and then went to tell Hamish about it. He thought I had done the right thing. He had advised against either telling my mother or worse, infuriating the kid by contacting his parents. Greg hadn't seemed suicidal, just unsure of his next move, Hamish thought.

I certainly hoped that was the case.

On another subject, my father actually seemed excited about Nae-Née. He had eagerly taken the specs that Hamish had given him and started to work up a patent application, which he would duplicate in various forms for the European Union, Japan, Australia, and wherever else.

Dad was obviously determined to protect the invention to the nth degree, so that his daughter and her husband would not lose any chance at having an income from it.

He was doing this each evening at the kitchen computer, with a memory stick and an external hard drive connected to it, his wine and cheese put aside until he took a break. I had never seen him bother with such backups before, but he had come home from Manhattan with these things and set them up with determination.

At work, he had a whole IT department at his bidding to handle this.

He must be determined to protect our trade secrets, I thought.

My mother joked that she had lost her computer, and we had both reverted to using our favorite cookbooks instead of checking for new recipe ideas online. We didn't care about not having the computer; I had built up a good library of gourmet books in our kitchen, plus one kitchen reference book.

My father and Hamish were getting along better than ever before, and they had been at arms' length up until now. A common purpose had united them.

Hamish couldn't just sit still and watch my father prepare the applications, though. He was available for consultation, as any inventor would need to be in order to the documents in proper order. Other than that, he went back to tinkering with his other nanites in the basement again, just to keep busy. He still hoped that someday they too would be put into service in human health care. Veterinary health care was a possibility, too.

I had never actually seen an attorney prepare a patent application, so I was fascinated and pleased to have the chance to find out how it works and how long it takes. I had to be careful not to seem too intrigued, however. The last thing I wanted was for my father to start suggesting that I make a career of it. Writing and observing with its constant variety of people, places and subjects was just too much fun. I didn't want to live in an office or courtroom and cater to the whims of rich clients. The money is so enticing that it can be hard to stop even if one hates the work. So I just watched while keeping my reactions to myself.

It took him about two weeks of work during his evenings and then he pronounced the application ready. Wisely, he wanted to wait until the device had been properly tested before sending it off. Skirting the awkward issue of his daughter's sex life, my father merely commented on the fact that this application was his gift to us, and that if we had hired an attorney – someone outside the family who would have charged us for this – the entire patent process would have cost us at least a million dollars…a million dollars which we simply did not have.

That is the dirty little secret about inventing today. In the 19th century, at the start of the Industrial Revolution, it didn't cost much to file a patent. Now, what with all of the filing fees required by the U.S. Patent and Trademark Office, plus those of whatever other governments around the world that an inventor files with, plus attorneys' fees, plus yearly maintenance fees, one can easily spend a million dollars just to introduce an invention. And that's not the end of it; there are still more attorneys' fees ever after to keep it going.

All of this combines to present a daunting obstacle to creativity and risk-taking.

But thanks to my dad, we could leap it on this particular creation.

Not so with university professors – another reason why Hamish hadn't been inventing while affiliated with some academic institution. If he had done so, whatever he created on university premises would automatically be deemed the property of that university. Hamish would get the professional accolades, and the university would get the millions of dollars. No thanks; he wanted the money too, so he could be independent and not answer to any authority figures. This was why my parents had not gotten along with him. They thought he should go for a regular income and thus be earning the money for a house for the two of us.

Maybe I was crazy, but I didn't like the idea of slavery to a boss with the possibility looming over our heads of sudden job and income loss thanks to budget cuts and downsizing. The idea frankly terrified and depressed me. Why spend all that time being obsequious to people who didn't give a damn about you only to lose out?

But almost no one agreed with me, so I just write my novels and said little about it.

On Sunday, Dr. Elizabeth Rowland paid us a visit to go over the details of the upcoming procedure. Hamish and I sat with her and his laptop in the living room while he explained the Nae-Née device, how it was constructed, how it worked, what he needed from her – which was a small amount of RU-486 to add on the spot – and how it would be deployed in a woman's system…mine.

Tuesday rolled around, and Hamish and I trundled down to the gynecologist's office with the Nae-Née equipment. Dr. Rowland was ready with the raw material – RU-486 in its purest, compacted form – for Hamish to load into the device.

She was curious to see how he loaded each nanite, and it wouldn't hurt to let her watch because she couldn't do this herself. Also, she ought to know exactly what she was about to insert into another human being's body.

She examined me while we waited, just to confirm what past appointments had told us: there was nothing wrong with me physically, nothing out of the ordinary about my body, and no reason not to go ahead with this procedure.

The doctor was excited about this for health reasons; she hated prescribing birth control pills. She told me that she privately considered them to be a health risk, a trade-off used to grant a woman some sexual freedom. The catch was that the woman increased her risk for certain types of cancers, each of which was likely to de-feminize her by attacking body parts and organs that made her female: ovaries, breasts, uteri, and so on. Dr. Rowland just didn't like the choices that were currently available to doctors and their patients, so she was excited to see a scientist trying to provide a better option to women.

Hamish worked for about 20 minutes, spending roughly 5 on each of the 4 nanites he had brought. Not bad for assembly time, I noted, imagining future manufacturing processes.

Soon he announced that the devices were ready. He had used a sterilizer – like a medical microwave oven – on each one before beginning. Still, loading the drug to the device hadn't taken as much time. The sterilization had been done while we waited to actually see the doctor.

Hamish had an injecting gadget – standard for nanites. It looked like a phaser from the Kirk-and-Spock television show of *Star Trek*, only a lot smaller. Funny how often science fiction became science fact, I thought to myself. People kept inventing the items in the stories.

Dr. Rowland, a slight woman with dark, curly hair tied up in a clip, watched, waiting for him to issue an instruction. They had gone over this in detail many times, by phone and in person when she had visited us over the weekend, but this felt different. This was the real deal.

Hamish loaded the injector with one of the nanites, and explained that if it were coming from a factory, they wouldn't have to bother with this step; it would come already loaded.

Then he handed it to her and said, "That's all there is to it – just point it as close to her reproductive systems as possible, then press the trigger down. She shouldn't even feel pain because the nanite is so small, and there's no needle. She should feel just a slight pressure."

He came over to me and held my hand. "I don't think I could go through with this if I thought it would hurt you or involve a needle gouging deeply into your body," he said. "It's more like a hypo spray, except that a nanite is going on, not only fluid."

I smiled at him.

Then I turned back to Dr. Rowland. She stood there, inspecting the injector, which was about 4 inches long, 2 inches high, and perhaps one inch across. It was made of steel. It was just your basic nanite injector, a thing that had been on the market for about 4 years now. Hamish had some connections at Harvard who helped him with research supplies. Nanite parts suppliers had cleared the legal hurdles necessary for supplying anyone with a medical license with whatever they needed; thus Hamish was in the clear for whatever he needed.

Dr. Rowland looked at us. "Okay – are you ready?"

"I'm ready," I said. "Go for it."

She placed the trigger mechanism directly over what I guessed was my left ovary.

Always squeamish about needles and other procedures, I looked away.

A moment passed. "Did you pull the trigger yet?"

"No – I thought you would want to watch, since you thought of this invention. This is your big, herstoric moment," Dr. Rowland said, using the women's studies term. I guess she hoped to relax me, maybe even make me smile.

I looked at her and smiled tensely.

"I'm aware enough – you know I'm ticklish and squeamish and a terrible patient. Just go ahead and pull the trigger. It's not like you're firing a weapon at me; I just don't like to watch medical devices in use. It's okay," I summed up.

"Okay," she said, and pulled.

I felt the faintest pressure, just as Hamish had said, and that was it.

"That was a lot of fanfare for something that I barely felt," I said, smiling now.

The nanite would move itself through my system on its own, he had assured me.

All I had to do was relax and let it work.

And it wouldn't be releasing any RU-486 unless and until a particular sequence of events had taken place:

1. I ovulated.
2. Hamish and I had sex after I ovulated.
3. The ovum got fertilized.
4. Hamish checked the chemical sensors in the device to detect the zygote.
5. Hamish confirmed the existence of the zygote in my system.
6. Hamish clicked on the trigger link in the computer program to release the RU-486.

Only then would I experience any spotting.

Actually, it would be more like just getting my period as usual.

The drug would simply prevent implantation of the zygote, it would pass out of my system, and out of my body; the perfect, user-friendly birth control system.

Once this had been proven to work, Hamish would set the sensors to automatically release the drug whenever they found a fertilized ovum in my system. And then we really could relax and enjoy the Nae-Née device, just as I had suggested when I thought of the idea.

It wouldn't even interfere with spontaneity.

Chapter 5

Clinical Trial: Nae-Née Ammo Locked and Loaded

Some women seem to go to great lengths to get some attention from their husbands.

Clearly, I fell into that category. My workaholic husband was always busy.

But now I had hit pay dirt: I was his work. And his work was suddenly to spend time with me on romance and fun and, well…the rest should be obvious at this point.

We drove home, having already signed an agreement with Dr. Rowland covering secrecy and plans for a clinical trial the previous Sunday – courtesy of my dad, again.

The clinical trial would take place in Dr. Rowland's offices. She had one in Farmington, one in Hartford, and one in Glastonbury; it was the usual array that Hartford Hospital doctors maintained to give themselves a change of scene and their patients shorter commutes whenever possible. [Too bad they couldn't get shorter waiting times for appointments.]

By now it was after 5 o'clock. Rush hour was underway, and despite the dismal employment levels of our state, there still seemed to be a glut of cars heading away from Hartford. We headed in the opposite direction, which moved along nicely until I turned left onto Mountain Road. Then we found ourselves stuck.

I drove the last quarter mile home through the rush hour traffic that I usually avoided like the plague it was. Whenever I had had a job within the city limits of Hartford, I had always arranged to be expected at 9:30 a.m., at the very earliest. That way, I left for work when the morning crush of cars was gone. Then I would wait until 6 p.m. to head home, to skip the evening rush hour.

Not today; Hamish and I sat there in a parking lot of cars on Mountain Road. Mountain Road had one lane in each direction, and no one seemed to want that number to increase – not me, not anyone else I had ever spoken to – but it took half an hour to get back to the house. So many people spend so much of their time sitting in traffic, using up so much fossil fuel, adding so much heat to the atmosphere.

I didn't envy them; it was better to not fit in with office life. Hamish and I didn't seem to fit in anywhere, and we had stopped caring long ago. We only cared about making a success of our own, unique efforts. It seemed like a waste of time to lament the fact that our skill sets just did not match up with the job descriptions that were e-mailed to me weekly. CareerBuilder.com, Monster.com, etc. – each sent job descriptions that would move me far away or else require experience and skills that I just did not have. Worried and stressed, I would escape to my writing projects and violin playing, not knowing what else to do about it.

Except that now we had Nae-Née to think about. If the clinical trial went as well as we hoped it would, we could be making money from that and stop worrying about jobs. We could do things like write and invent without feeling worried or guilty.

Inventors and writers who have yet to make money typically live with a sense of guilt and worry. They worry about making a living from their efforts, and felt guilty for not having done that yet. They also felt anxiety as people around them suggesting that they just give it up and get jobs. Lately, however, watching the grim employment news and looking around us at the state of the economy – plus reading about it in the news – all I could think was: what jobs?

Perhaps soon I wouldn't hear about that any more. Perhaps, after working a bit longer without pay, Hamish would have a successful human clinical trial under his proverbial belt and Nae-Née could go into production. Perhaps a market for this promising device could be identified, targeted, and fired upon with spectacular accuracy. Well, one could dream.

We were dreamers and always had been. Maybe the dreams were about to pay off.

Maybe I was hallucinating.

As it was, I was currently laboring under the impression that Hamish and I were about to have a lovely romantic time of it together for some months in order to prove the validity of a scientific hypothesis: that this user-friendly form of birth control would work like a charm.

My mother was waiting for us when we got in. The kitchen smelled really, really good; she was cooking coq au vin blanc, and she was almost done. She turned away from the Le Creuset pot and smiled at us.

"Hi Avril! I thought I would give you a night off of cooking, especially since you weren't going to be here anyway during cooking time. I made something you like a lot, too."

"Thanks – it smells delectable."

"So – did it work? I mean, does the device seem to be progressing as hoped thus far?"

This question was aimed at Hamish as well as me.

He looked a bit embarrassed for a split second, then shook it off. All we had done today was get the device in place, locked and loaded. He replied, "All set – but I brought back the 3 spares. I didn't want to leave them lying around the office for just anyone to see. So far, only Dr. Rowland has signed the confidentiality agreement, and agreed to do a clinical trial."

"That makes sense. Are you planning to invite her partners to participate as well? I think there are 8 doctors in that group. They don't all have to have their names on the journal article, you know. And they won't go on the patent. Just you and Avril get to have that."

Hamish looked relieved; he usually didn't think about such details. That would change now that something he had developed had progressed past the inception and inventing phases.

"That would certainly help to validate the clinical trial," he said. "I'll have to discuss that with Elizabeth."

I couldn't help thinking about political views inserting themselves into the equation. "Be careful about it, though. Some of the doctors may be anti-choice and dead set against anything that smacks of abortion. A lot of people – including some in the medical profession – think of RU-486 as a form of abortion rather than as pre-empting a pregnancy. I don't know what the individual views of those doctors are."

He looked at me. "You don't know? How come?"

"I haven't been asking my gynecologist about the other doctors at all. I read their diplomas on the way out just to see where they studied, imagining how much they had to move around in order to qualify as specialists, and that's it. The only things about Dr. Elizabeth Rowland that have ever concerned me are: she's a woman, so I will only have someone with the same anatomical makeup as myself for a gynecologist; and she is nice, so I feel comfortable around her and discussing my gynecological health with her. That's it."

That made such perfect sense to him that he just moved on. "So I will have to talk with her again soon about the clinical trial. Should we invite her over again?"

"Yes – definitely – and soon. Or to a restaurant – that might look better from a professional standpoint. But I would prefer to have her here, just for the sake of secrecy. No one will overhear anything if we talk here. Yeah, better make it here again."

"I'll e-mail her and then call to confirm."

"We should write that e-mail together, send it from your account, and have it copied to me and my father."

"Okay. After dinner, then. Let's not put it off."

"No. We'll get right to it."

I heard the garage door opening and my father's car pull in.

He walked in, tossed his keys into the basket on the windowsill, and asked, "How did the Nae-Née appointment go?"

Right to the point – that's something that he and I had in common – asking point-blank questions rather than beating around the bush. We had to find a topic embarrassing to do that, and not much embarrassed us. Well…some things did, and soon neither of us would be able to live without euphemisms to get the data collected. Perhaps a clinical trial about strangers using Nae-Née would be easier to discuss and allude to.

I looked up and replied, "Locked, loaded, fired, and ready for action. Dr. Rowland is very nice, so it was quick and easy, and thanks to Hamish's engineering ability, it was painless."

Dad glanced at Hamish with approval.

I went on to fill him in on our next move. He agreed that the meeting should be conducted at our home for secrecy's sake.

That evening, after dinner was over and cleaned up, we went up to my computer to send the e-mail. Once we were satisfied with the proposal, we hit "Send" and called the doctor at her home. She answered on the second ring.

"Avril? Is everything all right?" She actually sounded concerned.

I realized that she must be worrying about ill effects – why else would a patient whom she had just injected a couple of hours earlier be looking for her?

And it was highly unusual to have a doctor's home phone number…but then, so was this entire situation.

"Oh! Yes – I feel perfectly fine. That's not why we're calling. We just sent you an e-mail, and we're following up. We would like to invite you over again soon to discuss the details of the clinical trial that you will be doing at your offices. We wanted to have the meeting at home for secrecy's sake rather than at a restaurant."

"Oh, good." She breathed a small sigh of relief. "Good about it being all right. And – good about your plans. Yes, I would like to meet again soon. I presume that the issues you want to discuss are in the note?"

"Yes – secrecy, supplies of nanite guns, supplies of Nae-Née devices, willingness of doctors in addition to yourself to participate, patient participation forms, etc."

"I see – you would like to expand the trial, include more doctors, and are wondering whether or not any pro-lifers work in the practice."

"You guessed it."

"We do have one – he's older, and one of the founding partners."

"That figures," I said. "A man trying to control women's bodies and decisions."

"Unfortunately."

"Do you think he might try to derail the entire study?" I glanced up at Hamish as I asked this question; he looked panicked.

"No – just that he won't participate, and that his patients will miss out."

Hamish was waiting with bated breath to find out what she had said.

"Dr. Rowland, Hamish is sitting here with me, chafing at the bit to know what you just said in reply to that last question."

"You know, Dr. Avril Châtelet, you can call me Elizabeth if you want to."

I felt awkward; she was my doctor. I avoided the issue by saying, "Okay…thanks."

"You feel strange about that, don't you? I just said it because your husband has been calling me Elizabeth."

I laughed. "Don't worry; if this goes public, we'll probably all end up calling each other Drs. Rowland, MacDonall and Châtelet among strangers. We'll work it out amongst ourselves as we go along. Here's Hamish." I passed him the phone.

"Elizabeth? What about the study? Do you have a senior partner who would actually be able to stop it, and who would want to do so?" He was still tense.

The volume was on loud, and unlike my husband, I didn't have any hearing damage to contend with, so I heard her say, "I do have a senior colleague with considerable clout in the practice, but he can't tell the rest of us what to do. He won't want to participate, but he won't stop us. So only his patients will miss out. We'll still cover a lot of ground."

Hamish breathed a huge sigh of relief and sat down on the bed. He had been pacing up and down. He looked happier; his mood had improved. When he was happy and calm, he liked to banter with me or give an impression of a mad scientist with a maniacal laugh. He would put his hands up to his mouth and in a deep, warbling tenor tone give an echoing cackle.

After a couple more minutes on the phone and checking with me, a visit was set for the next Sunday afternoon. Dad would be available then – we had checked before calling. I didn't know why Dr. Rowland liked Sundays, but then I didn't know her family's weekend schedule. It didn't matter; the important thing was that Hamish and Dad had said that they could get commitments for supplies nailed down by then. They had already started the negotiations.

The call ended, and I planned on lunch and dessert for Sunday at 1 p.m. The doctor would arrive at half past noon and she planned on staying for about 2 hours. More, if the meeting needed more time to finish going over all of the details.

I turned on the television, looking for more forensic crime dramas. Who cared that they were all summer reruns; it was fun to see the characters interact with each other.

Hamish flopped on the bed next to me. We sat through the opening scene with Spock purring on the end of the bed. The credits rolled, and my husband suddenly started kissing me.

Wow. So that was what it took to get some attention, I thought – inventing a birth control device. Suddenly there was a loud purring in our ears. Spock had moved closer to us – very close. He was sitting a foot away from us, crouched, and staring intently at us.

"What does he want, cat treats? Are we that much more interesting than the show?"

I laughed. "Hamish, it's a rerun. And he likes you. You don't sit up here much."

Hamish rolled off of me and scooped the cat up. He started cuddling Spock and joking about nerve pinches, but the cat didn't care. He just closed his eyes and purred louder. I rolled over against Hamish and watched the show for a couple of minutes.

My mother knocked on the door.

I wondered how we were ever going to test Nae-Née out.

Then I got up and opened it.

She was standing there with the phone. "I just talked to Greg Matthews' parents."

"Is the call over with, or does someone want to talk to me?"

"They hung up."

"Who called whom?" I asked. "And what did you talk about?"

"You and Greg. His mother called here. It seems that you encouraged Greg to tell them about not getting accepted to any college, and that you gave him a suggestion about applying to foreign universities."

"That's true. Hamish and I found Greg at the mall, all alone, last weekend. He told us what happened and showed us his stash of rejection letters. He'd been secretly keeping them all and carrying them around. It was pretty depressing."

"Well – they are now busy looking at foreign universities, and very upset, but not at Greg. And they called to say thank you to you, but I said that you and your husband had gone to bed for the night, so his mother told me everything. I hope you don't mind, but I gave her your phone number. She still wants to meet you and talk to you."

I felt relieved; the kid was helping himself, his parents were helping him, and apparently no one was annoyed at me. All was well in the land of teenagers for the time being. I just hoped he would find a good school that wanted him and quickly.

"Does she think I'm going to have a magical hot tip on which foreign university is just right for Greg and will also admit him immediately? I'm glad she's not annoyed at me, but I was worried that the kid was so upset and isolated that he might hurt or kill himself. I thought of foreign universities because of your friend's father, that retired surgeon, but I don't know of a place that would be good…"

"No – don't worry about any of that. You always drive yourself crazy worrying about meeting people. She just wants to say thank you. I think she was worried that her son might have kept this to himself until it drove him to suicide, just like you were. As for finding a school, if you have an idea, great. If not, fine – those parents will handle it now."

"Hurray!" I said, but not loudly. It was a minor, not major cause for celebration as far as I could see. Greg still had no clear path toward becoming a doctor himself as yet.

"So don't worry about. Just wait for a voice mail and call her back. Take it from there."

"Okay."

"So what are you two up to now that dinner is over? You sent the e-mail and made the call?" My mother always wanted to know everything…

"Yes – all done. Sunday, lunch at 1 p.m., arrival at half past noon, long meeting with Hamish and Dad, etc."

"Perfect. What else can you do to prepare Nae-Née?"

I decided to see if I could induce my mother to catch on and leave us alone a lot.

"We can track when I will get my period, attempt to fertilize my ova and hit the trigger switch to release the RU-486 in my Nae-Née prototype, and just keep that up while recording the results while we wait for the clinical trial to get underway. Then, once it does, we'll have to keep it up. Hamish says that this device should last me the rest of my reproductive life cycle, so I'm all set. I don't have to fear a pregnancy. Once it's proven, he can set the device to release the drug automatically each time it sense hormone levels associated with a fertilized ovum."

My mother seemed to catch on. She looked like she was about to go back down the hallway when she thought of a detail. "Does the computer program just show chemical levels, so that only a doctor can monitor it, or could a layperson do this also?"

Nurses would think of this.

Hamish called over from the bed, where Spock was wriggling out his arms. "A doctor would have to do it. It will have to be built into a doctor's routine – to check on the patients' hormone levels."

"I see."

She paused, uncertain as to what to say next, while Spock dashed out of our room.

"Well – I think I'll go watch *Dancing with the Stars*. Good night."

"Good night." I shut the door. Alone at last.

Hamish was staring intently at me.

That was a change. Usually Spock did that.

"I thought she would never catch on and leave."

"Oh, she caught on," I said. "She just concealed it and acted like she had never failed to understand that we were trying to have some time alone. Remember, we usually spend all of the hours that she is awake with me in here and you downstairs. If I have company in here, it's usually just the cat."

"And that's my fault."

"Yeah, it is," I said heartlessly, "but you're here now."

I wasn't about to let that either slide or stop us from enjoying some time together.

Hamish grinned. He wasn't going to waste it either.

I went back over to the bed and lay down next to him.

We just sat there watching the show for a while, half listening for sounds that indicated that my parents were going into their room for the night, to sleep and not notice whatever we were doing.

After the credits for the next show rolled, I got up, went into the bathroom, brushed my teeth, and put on a pretty pink cotton summer nightgown.

Hamish watched me do all this from the bed; the bathroom was inside our room.

I got back onto the bed and the forensic drama continued. The jokes among the characters were amusing enough to keep us occupied, and Hamish as usual hadn't seen this show when it was first broadcast.

That gave me some time to think.

I thought that I must be hallucinating.

Lately, I was thinking this particular thought often.

I just wasn't used to having something that was potentially both lucrative and valuable to human health – one of my husband's inventions – moving along in a direction that suggested success and independence for us.

I also wasn't used to having my husband with me and relaxed enough about the future to want to be romantic.

That was what seemed so surreal about it all.

Was this actually happening?

Happiness had to be a hallucination, I kept telling myself.

Just as hallucinations are brought on by drugs, so is happiness.

But what would be the drug that brought it on?

Maybe it would finally be a success.

So we met again with Dr. Elizabeth Rowland to iron out all of the details, which included plans for yet another meeting with the other physicians in her practice. That meeting proved interesting, to say the least. It took place at 6 p.m. on a Wednesday evening the following week, and it had included all 8 of the gynecologists – including the anti-choice one.

He was everything that I had expected and worse, but he was only bark, not bite.

The anti-choicer's name was Dr. Gerald Farnsworth, and he was in his early 60s. He was tall, thin, white-haired, bald and bespectacled. He wore a lab coat, a bow-tie, and a disapproving scowl. He kept his chin inclined as he towered above me by several inches, not deigning to look me politely in the eye. His entire demeanor suggested that he considered any interaction with us to be beneath him and his sense of dignity.

I glanced at Hamish and saw that my husband was staring coldly at him as we were introduced. Dr. Farnsworth did not notice; he was still looking in my direction. Hamish looked as impressive as Farnsworth, and I was glad. After some fuss, I had persuaded my husband to wear chinos rather than jeans and a nice shirt with buttons on the collar, front, and cuffs. The small dark-and-light-blue plaid pattern set off his eyes nicely, and he looked professional.

But I was more interested in facing our adversary at the moment; I have never been the sort of person to just hold my tongue when someone talks down to me or otherwise condescends to me. I waited for my moment. I knew it would come.

Dad was there too, waiting for everyone to arrive with various legal forms: release forms, contracts, copies of the questionnaire that Hamish had prepared for the clinical trial – these had to be shared with the nanite and pharmaceutical companies as well as patients – and confidentiality agreements. He had prepared a special release form for Farnsworth, and he showed it to me now; it released Farnsworth from all liability for anything that might possibly go wrong, noted his objection to the idea of preemptive birth control, and acknowledged that he had been outvoted by the other physicians.

We met all of the other doctors, with Farnsworth being the last of them.

I already knew who he was; Elizabeth Rowland had warned me which one he was, that he was a Catholic anti-choice, old-school doctor who didn't like it when his patients made demands or asked too many questions. Apparently, each of his colleagues had had patients transfer out of his care and over to theirs. And he didn't care; he was nearing retirement. He liked to stay on mainly to ensure that no abortions were performed by any of the doctors in his practice. That was why he was still an active senior partner, she had confided to me.

Hamish and I met and shook hands with the other 4 women and 2 men in the room, chatted amiably for a couple of minutes with each.

Then Farnsworth stepped forward. He was tall, balding, grey, and held his chin up, staring coldly down at me with distaste and disdain. He loomed over me, shook my hand perfunctorily, and asked me one question:

"Your father tells me that you are 40 years old and don't want children. Why?"

Well, at least if intended to affront, he was getting on with it.

I looked up at him coolly and replied: "You mean, why don't I want a perpetually needy, misshapen, bald little creature that shits, pisses, drools, pukes, screams and cries but can't talk coherently and constantly demands total attention so that I can't spend time with my husband?"

The man actually lowered his chin and his mouth dropped open for a moment. "But you're getting older. Don't you want children so that your husband can pass on his name, and carry on your genetic line?" He stepped closer to me, deliberately looming over me.

I wasn't deterred from answering him as I wished; he had invited it.

"So you think I ought to pass on someone else's last name but not mine, do all of the work while my husband gets to do other things like sleep and meaningful work that he will be remembered for while I don't…oh, and age faster. And then what – watch the kid find that there is no room in the universities for her or him thanks to human overpopulation? Watch as she finds that the environment contains fewer and fewer species, and realizes that her parents didn't think it through? That they didn't care what would happen to her later, as long as she was born?"

"But every woman should want a baby." He was actually getting red in the face.

"Really? Tell me more about everywoman. This automaton sounds so dull and obedient. Do you know many of these clones?"

"What?!" he blew up at that. "You are twisting my words! What I'm trying to say is that all life is sacred! All life should be protected and allowed to exist."

"Interesting idea; so you think that even if a pregnancy will lead to a life of endless debt and no chance for a good education and a happy life – even if that person will never be happy and we can see all of the signs by looking at the parents – misery is sacred and should proceed?"

Now I had really gotten to him. He blew up at me. "You are unnatural! How can your husband put up with you?!"

I actually laughed at this point, and it was a good thing I did, because Hamish later told me that he was about to take a swing at the guy when I surprised him by cracking up. Hamish learned hand-to-hand combat in the British army, so he might have ruined the whole deal then and there if he had actually acted on that impulse.

I had noticed that the other doctors were trying to hide grins as we sparred.

"Is that how you argue your side of an issue? Attack your opponent personally, shout, and loom over them? That's funny." I waited to see what would come next.

He had one more tactic, and it seemed lame. "Using birth control so that women can just have sex is terrible; there should be some risk, some consequences for this behavior!"

"Such as the risk of getting pregnant, right?"

"Exactly."

"Spoken just like a man who would never have to worry about the pain, discomfort and physical distortion caused by pregnancy. Women should be able to enjoy their bodies as amusement parks, just as men do, with nothing to worry about other than venereal disease. And then both sexes should equally assume the burden of protecting themselves against that."

"That's unnatural!"

"So you want to see more cases of unwanted pregnancy with babies who will have awful lives because no one wanted them in the first place – and many of them do not get the fairy tale life of adoption by a nice middle-class, heterosexual, married couple – and more patients with venereal diseases. Aren't you just the dream gynecologist that every woman is clamoring for."

He was running out of ideas, so I brought up a point about Nae-Née:

We weren't doing abortions, I had pointed out, only pre-empting pregnancies. Did he or didn't he dispense any form of birth control? Yes, but only condoms and pills. The success rate wasn't one hundred percent, but that was just life.

Life?! Pregnancy is an unacceptable outcome.

Silence. Glaring and looming seemed to be his entire repertoire of debate skills. I didn't even like debates, but he was just making it too easy for me. The one time I enjoy a debate is when the facts are on my side; otherwise the exercise just seems silly.

"What do you think of countries with severe overpopulation problems? Do you actually think that condoms, pills, and pleas for abstinence change the situation there, such as in India?"

"No, but we can't force people to take our advice, thank God."

"No one is trying to force anything. Women want freedom. If you are either unable or unwilling to deliver what we want, then we have nothing further to discuss."

It seemed that that was all he had, because Farnsworth gave up. He asked my father for his release form, signed, and stalked out. The entire room seemed to breathe a collective sigh of relief. Hamish relaxed things by happily remarking that we could get some work done now that the resident self-aggrandizing, tin-plated jackass had left; everyone laughed appreciatively. That showed just another one of many reasons why I found my husband attractive.

So we were going forward with the clinical trial at this office; excellent. Hamish came up to me and gave me a sideways hug, and with a stage whisper told me, "I'm so proud of you."

Well, I had had my fun. I attended the meeting, noted what was being decided, and signed off on what Dad presented. I had agreed to the testing of my idea and my husband's efforts, and to be one of the patients in the trial. That was it.

Supplies came from the clients, who would be financing the trial and any future deals. We as inventors would get our ten percent of the profits, paid directly from the nanite companies. The trial lasted for 6 months, taking us all the way to Christmastime.

Nothing awful happened. In fact, nothing went wrong. Women reported that they were having a great time enjoying peace of mind; the gynecologists were diligent about tracking their nanites. There were no malfunctions, and no pregnancies. Plenty of fertilized ova were detected, and all of them were passed out of the patients' bodies without incident.

I was one of them; Hamish actually tracked 3 instances of near-pregnancy in me.

The patients in the clinical trial were so delighted that they wanted to keep their devices and have them set on automatic mode.

I put our own record down to a well-timed trip to Manhattan to see the musical *Wicked*, another weekend when my parents were away, and a trip back to my undergraduate alma mater to show Hamish where I had studied. Alone time with no parents walking about the house seemed to be the answer to the romance problem, as did a sense of economic hope.

Chapter 6

The Advertising Campaign

I must have been hallucinating again, I thought.

The clinical trial had been completed.

More were underway, just for good measure, but Dad's clients were ready to start the marketing phase.

His clients were the owners of a corporation that dispensed medical nanites to hospitals and doctors' offices all over the United States. They were also the owners of a similar company in France, which had subsidiaries all over Europe. And there were a couple of others in Japan and Australia.

Yeah, I had to be hallucinating.

No way could things be going this well for us.

But they were.

And now I understood why I thought that my husband resembled the comic Craig Ferguson more and more. It was because the comic was a happy, successful guy. My husband was starting to feel that way, and it showed. He was reverting to the being more like the guy that I had met and married several years earlier.

Hamish had been happy and hopeful about the future then.

And now he was that way again.

The patents were all filed, Dad told us – in the U.S., the E.U., Japan, Australia, and various other nations. Our work was protected. With that dealt with, Hamish wrote up and submitted the article for publication in *Obstetrics & Gynecology*. It would appear in the spring.

For Christmas, we got a great present: my father informed us that his clients were now ready to hire an advertising agency. We were to set it up and meet the writers after New Year's Eve in Manhattan.

They wanted to talk to us – me in particular, since I had thought of this idea, and of the name for Nae-Née. They were pleased with it, wanted to keep it, and were eager to show me and Hamish their ideas for the advertising campaign.

My parents and Hamish I were all going to the apartment in Chelsea together. My mother would hit the Eileen Fisher store for perhaps the hundredth time while the rest of us went to the meeting. We would get together later for dinner and tell her about it.

I checked my wallet; good…several one-dollar bills were in it. I didn't tell my parents this, but whenever I was walking alone in the city and saw a homeless person, I liked to put a dollar in their cup/hat/receptacle. Many people disapproved, I knew. They thought that the street-dweller would just spend it on drugs. But I wouldn't stop. It wasn't much money, and it might get spent on food – food of the beggar's choice. If there was one saying that I truly hated, it was "beggars can't be choosers." That idea just made life not worth living to me.

Choice represents free will to me. Without free will, I don't see what else there is. Even for homeless street people. But choice requires money. Money that they just don't have and can barely get; that's not necessarily their fault, and I don't have the time or resources to find out all about these people. So I give them a dollar when I can – directly into their hands – and sometimes, if I have the chance, I buy them a meal. If I can find out what a particular homeless person would like to eat, even better. That's my own little secret. I just can't ignore people.

And I get angry when more and more of them are thoughtlessly produced without a care for their future. This marketing business for Nae-Née was going to be fun. Just the idea of getting this thing on the market was exciting.

The meeting was set for Monday, January 3rd at 11 a.m. We would leave the evening before. Uncle Charlie was going to take us all to Union Station in Hartford, where we would catch the Sunday evening train. We would be in our apartment in couple of hours on West 21st Street, and eating at the corner café less than an hour later.

The ride was uneventful. We got out at Penn Station and trundled up to 8th Avenue with our small rolling luggage bags, where we found a cab. The cab crossed over to 9th – the odd-numbered Avenues ran south, and Penn Station is at 34th Street.

The place was crowded as usual, but not terribly so. People who left for the weekend were returning, presumably so that they would be back for Monday to Friday jobs the next morning. With the employment news that I kept reading, it continually fascinated me to see people who had such jobs in their own country coming and going to and from them.

The cab deposited us at the corner of 9th Avenue and 21st Street. We walked the last third of a block to our building, which sat across from P.S. 11 – the same school that has been seen in such movies as *No Reservations* and *Miss Congeniality 2*. It had large, brightly colored figures of children painted onto the concrete foundations. The playground was to the right of the building, directly across from our apartment house, which overlooked that yard.

Dad had bought this apartment in the early 1990s, a 2-bedroom, one-bath on the 2nd floor. Not everyone in the building owned their apartment, but about half of the tenants did. There was no doorman; just mailboxes in the hallway. The owner of the building was trying to phase out the rent-controlled apartments and refurbish them all. It was an old building, constructed in 1926. The practice led to a high turnover of tenants in the refurbished units as people found the rents too high. But the owner didn't care, Dad had told me – he wanted all units ultimately sold off to the tenants.

We lugged our stuff upstairs, dumped it, used the bathroom, and walked right back out to the opposite corner of 9th Avenue – to the Le Grainne Café. It used to be called Le Gamin Café, which literally translated as "street urchin," but it was under new ownership. That was the only change; the menu and the décor, right down to the ever-present, fabulous floral arrangement over the cash register, had not changed at all.

The building was a protected National Historic Landmark that dated back to the Federalist period. Its claim to fame was the Clement Clarke Moore had allegedly written '*Twas the Night Before Christmas* in the attic. He had also donated the land next door for use as the Episcopal Seminary, and it took up an entire city block.

All of us loved this place. We got a booth on the left, and I promptly found the 1951 LaRousse Français-English dictionary, complete with the currency conversion chart from that year – francs to dollars and back again. I could hardly wait to peruse that old, gray hard-cover book while waiting for our food to arrive.

It had been a while since we were all there together, and all eating out at once. My mother and I loved to cook and bake so much that we didn't go out unless it was one of our birthdays or anniversaries, just to stop us from doing all that work, fun though it was for us.

We ordered a glass of wine each, a couple of crêpes – there were salmon and goat cheese crepes – some seafood risotto with a ring of mussels around it, and one order of saffron mussels. Dessert was the most fun, though. Sometimes, Hamish and I would come here just for the crepes. There was a fabulous chestnut puree crêpe; there were chocolate ones, raspberry, and so on. They also had great café au lait, served in a little bowl so that it could be enjoyed French-style, tipping the cup with both hands.

The artwork in the place included the standard old French advertisements for black cat products and cabaret acts at the Moulin Rouge, plus some local efforts. The place was a bit dark, with a wooden floor, and each table had brown paper pinned across the top, which was replaced for each group of customers. On the table were metal bowls with packets of sugar-in-the-raw and a lit candle.

Some of the wait staff was French; another was from Ireland, and others were American. The busboy, as so many in New York are, was most likely from Mexico. The waiter brought out a wine bottle full of tap water and 4 glasses. I leafed through the LaRousse dictionary and pointed out the 1951 prices of things to my mother.

We would stay for a week while my father did his work. I intended to drag Hamish to a few museums, and he had said he would go with me. Not having his nanites to tinker with was going to stress him out, but since a lucrative deal for one of his creations was in the works, I figured he could cope.

After dinner, we walked back to the apartment and looked around, getting settled. My mother and I cleaned the bathroom – something that only happened when either of us was there – and dusted off the furniture. We fired up the computer in the living room and checked museum and store schedules.

After taking a quick inventory of the fridge, we made a run around the corner to the grocery store for breakfast items, then came back and put them away. We were officially ready for a week in the city. Then we both went to our rooms to watch television. The living room was full of lovely antiques that my mother had trolled the shops for, plus a huge bookcase and 2 comfortable sofas and a few gorgeous Tiffany lamps – but no television. The living room was for socializing, not vegetating in front of a box. A huge, red Persian carpet covered the floor.

New York City had a wonderful entertainment and communications company – Time-Warner. It supplied phone, Internet and television service, and I had set the whole thing up for my parents. One television in each room, complete with a DVD machine underneath, plus a small stereo under that. Each bedroom had yet more antiques.

The décor of my old room here, which could double as a guest room on occasion for someone else, was the opposite of my room in Connecticut. It was all in blues: carpeting, curtains, bedding. The bedding was a blue iris pattern, and the bed was pushed into the corner of the wall with pillows piled all around at the back and left side. Hamish and I liked to flop against these and watch movies.

This evening, I wanted to take a shower and then soak in the bathtub. The place had a huge, long, old-fashioned bathtub that had been in place since the building was constructed. It was the one part of the unit that the owner of the building had not seen fit to rip out and replace, and I loved it. I kept some lavender bath gel here just because of the tub.

My parents were still back and forth between their bedroom and bathroom for the time being, so I held off on the bath. I went into the kitchen and made Hamish a cup of green tea with honey and milk so that he would get sleepy. On second thought, I decided to have one also.

By the time we had settled in with our tea and yet another rendition of *Live Free or Die Hard*, Hamish was snoring next to me, his mug empty and forgotten on the floor beside him. I got up, checked our outfits for the next morning's meeting, and settled into the bathroom. 45 minutes later, I was ready for bed too. It was 1 a.m. I lay there looking at the street lights, glad that the curtain on the right-side window covered the brightest one, and listened to the cars, motorcycles and heavy trucks rush by. The building shook whenever a truck passed.

I loved it here.

The agency that Dad had hired was located in the Gramercy area, east of Chelsea. It was called *Issue-Spotters*, and it occupied several floors of a building just north of Gramercy Park, on Lexington Avenue. I had found it by looking up agencies on AdForum.com and then cross-referencing the ones I found with those who had won awards. There were several: the CLIO, Mobius and AAF-ADDY Awards, to name just a few. There was an international one given out at London International Awards, and there was even an Internet Advertising Award.

We were to meet Dad there at 10:30 a.m. If we got there first, we were to tell the receptionist that we had arrived and then wait, but Dad promised to be there. We ate breakfast at home to save time; I didn't want to go to a café and risk getting behind schedule.

Hamish suggested walking to the meeting, at which point I scolded him for trying to get exercise and save money. He had insisted upon wearing his navy blue suit and one of the beautiful ties I had given him. I wore a nice skirt, blouse and formal jacket; we could walk when the meeting was over, and preferably after going home and changing out of our good clothes!

He agreed. "You're right, you're right – we'll do that."

"We're taking a cab to and from the place. We can go out walking and exploring after."

"Fine; let's go."

We went. Getting a cab on a weekday on a street with a school meant walking to the adjoining Avenue; the entire street is blocked off during school hours, and the school uses the street as extra playground space. We walked to 8th Avenue and found a cab in short order. It was a quarter past 10 in the morning, so rush hour was over.

The cab dropped us outside the building and we found ourselves looking up at an early-to-mid 20th century place, about 30 stories high, with some decorative carvings here and there. The glass door led to a well-appointed lobby with a doorman who doubled as a receptionist.

We walked in and found a directory; before the doorman could ask us if we needed help I had found that *Issue-Spotters* occupied floors 10 through 15, with reception on the 12th floor. I smiled politely at the doorman and urged my husband toward the elevators.

The elevator doors opened into a reception room with a view of Lexington Avenue – no surprise – and several comfortable sofas. Dad was waiting on the one to the left of the desk. Before the efficient, elegant woman behind the desk could do more than look up from her multi-lined phone, Dad had gotten up and taken charge of us. She smiled and waved to the right; Dad led us down the hall to a conference room.

Phones rang in the sea of cubicles on our right as we passed; I suddenly thought of the one in my pocket, took it out, and shut it off. Hamish saw that and did the same thing.

The conference room had one long wooden table with padded armchairs on wheels all around it, some framed posters boasting of lucrative past and present clients on one wall, and a several windows opposite. Heavy curtains and blinds covered the windows. Glancing to the right, I could see why: a huge TV screen blanketed the smaller wall on the right. A table with coffee urns and cups and some fruit was at the opposite end of the room.

Dad led us straight in and introduced us to the advertising agency executives, 2 men and a woman in power suits with glued-on smiles. A Mr. Handler, Mr. Drake, and Ms. Shapiro stepped forward and shook our hands, congratulating us on the launch of our promising new product. Next, Dad introduced us to a Mr. Morse, the president of Creighton Enterprises, which was the manufacturer of Hamish's design for Nae-Née. Mr. Morse was a quiet, serious man whom we had met before. He dressed in dark suits with cool ties that suggested mechanical technology; today his tie depicted computer chips. He had dark hair with gray at the temples, steel-rimmed glasses, and listened much more than he talked. We liked him well enough.

Ms. Shapiro, who was wearing a deep purple suit and reeked of some sharp and expensive perfume, ushered us all into seats closest to the big screen. She insisted that I take the seat closest to the end of the table (no one sat there, and no chair was there) so that no taller person would block my view. I thanked her and sat in it.

I watched her. She let one of the men offer us coffee, which Hamish accepted and I declined. I didn't want to need a bathroom; I wanted to concentrate on the presentation. Ms. Shapiro, whose first name was Judith, wore heavy makeup and large, showy jewelry from Tiffany's. She was second in command to Mr. Drake, I realized, as I watched them interact. Her every move was correct and calm and she knew her job. I was both mystified and fascinated by her. I could never do what she did, but I didn't care. I just wanted to observe her.

Mr. Drake looked like an older version of one of the chain-smoking, suit-wearing executives in *Mad Men*, the show about advertisers, except that he didn't smoke. I was very glad about that; I hate the smell of cigarettes. He smiled when the moment called for it, but there was little warmth there. Perhaps that was why the firm was so successful. I had Googled it when Dad told that it was definitely going to be hired, and found that it represented several major pharmaceutical companies, some fast-food franchises, and a couple of well-known banks.

The meetings' agenda was simple and straightforward: we would be shown a 20-second video in multiple versions, plus some slides that would serve as printed brochures. We would be asked for our input, and then the final versions of each ad would be prepared.

I doubted that our input would count for much, but was willing to play along.

Mr. Drake addressed me before anyone hit the "Play" button, "I understand that you are a lawyer and a medical historian, yet the concept for Nae-Née and its name was your idea."

"That's true – all of it." Hamish and I answered simultaneously – it was like we were suddenly in perfect sync both mentally and physically. I glanced back at him and grinned. He grinned proudly at me.

Mr. Drake continued, "And you, Dr. MacDonall, just took your wife's idea and made it a reality in your basement workshop?"

"Yes," we both said at once, though this response was less of an accidental synchronization than the first had been.

"Well – that's incredible. Let's see if we can make it sell like the revolutionary concept that it is. Joel," he turned to Mr. Handler and said, "play the presentation."

The room went dark, and the screen lit up.

It was a computer graphics cartoon rendition of Nae-Née, set against a pink-and-blue background.

A voice-over by a woman calmly intoned the explanation of it:

Nae-Née is a nanite birth control delivery device with no side effects. Its name literally means "not-born." It consists of a nanobotic composite loaded with RU-486. The nanobot is injected into the woman's abdomen, at which time she feels only a slight pressure – no pinching or pricking thanks to Nae-Née's microscopic size.

Nae-Née works by sensing hormone levels in a woman's body, detecting when a fertilized egg is passing through her reproductive system. When this occurs, Nae-Née releases a dose of RU-486, ensuring that the woman simply gets her period as usual because the ovum is blocked from implanting itself in her uterine wall. Thus, a pregnancy is prevented.

Nae-Née must be used under the care of a licensed gynecologist.

Nae-Née will not protect against HIV or other sexually-transmitted diseases.

Nae-Née is a safe, convenient and user-friendly form of birth control that does not require the woman to sacrifice spontaneity with her partner.

Nae-Née: birth control, infallible, with nanites and convenience for all.

That was it. I rather liked it.

At this point, Ms. Shapiro added, "That last line is going to be the main slogan of the advertising campaign. What do you think of it?"

I looked across the table at her. She was smiling expectantly, confident that I would respond favorably. She was right, but I couldn't help wondering how much of this ad she had thought of.

"I like the slogan a lot; it comes across like the Pledge of Allegiance with the religious part taken out. I don't like religiousness, and I like the catchy beat that the slogan had adapted for its own use. Who thought of it?"

Judith Shapiro looked delighted. "A team of our creators did, led by me."

"So…was it you who came up with this specific line?"

She looked at me oddly. "Why do you ask?"

"Because when I'm not thinking of ideas such as Nae-Née I write. I love catchy, cool word combinations, so I was hoping to meet and thank whoever thought of this one."

Understanding lit up her face. "I see. It really was a team of us. I thought of the general idea of including those words in the slogan, and then my team – whom I would be happy to introduce you to – helped arrange it to sound like the Pledge of Allegiance. In fact, a woman named Darcy who recently graduated from Pepperdine University was the one who had the final flash of inspiration. I'll take you to her office and introduce you after this."

"Thanks! That would be great."

"Now let's just go over a few slides showing more versions of this ad, highlighting the slogan. The idea is, obviously, to convey a sense of greater freedom from using Nae-Nee."

She waved at Joel, who clicked through the rest of what now appeared to be a PowerPoint presentation. It showed more images like the first few, each with the slogan.

Nae-Née: birth control, infallible, with nanites and convenience for all.

It was almost mesmerizing, especially when paired with that hypnotic, disembodied female voice from the television advertisement.

I looked at Hamish. He said, "If you like it, I like it."

That was all that Dad and Mr. Morse were looking for from us.

We signed off on it, and Judith took us to meet Darcy and the rest of her team.

Darcy proved to be a woman in her mid-twenties who had just completed a Master's degree in advertising at Pepperdine, after which she had moved straight to Manhattan to take this job. What a life; some people still could live the American dream of college, graduate school, and then a job in their own country in a fun city. Fewer and fewer people could, but here was one who had done so. She was certainly enjoying her new career here; she talked excitedly about all of the advertising slogans from 20th century history that she admired.

After we had been shown out of the building and said good-bye to Dad, I told Hamish, "I want to call Bethany now that this doesn't have to be a top-secret project any more. Dad said that once the ad campaign gets underway – and he confirmed that signing on the line means just that – I can tell my friends."

Bethany was my best friend from college. She was fluent in Japanese and Chinese, had spent time in both countries, and we had explored our mutual love of cats and gourmet cooking and baking together on our school breaks and since college.

She lived in eastern Massachusetts now as a housewife with her husband, 2 cats, and 2 children. She had fulfilled her ambition of adopting a baby girl from China and had had her son with her husband by in vitro fertilization; getting pregnant had been difficult. We kept in touch by telephone.

Hamish was jubilant. "Anything you want! Let's go back to the flat and relax a bit for a while. You can call your friend, and then we can go out walking. It's not all that cold for January." He was grinning from ear to ear; it was wonderful to see my husband relaxed and happy for a change. He no longer looked like a depressed Craig Ferguson; he looked like himself – a happy version of himself, and the one I used to know.

Chapter 7

Success at Last

There it was again: that sense that I was hallucinating again.

I just wasn't used to feeling successful. My books had been few and far between, and they had never paid enough to enable me and Hamish to live independently. Now that was about to change.

But what did we want to do next, and when would be able to do it?

We didn't know the answer to either of these questions.

As it turned out, we didn't have long to wait.

Meanwhile, I hailed a cab and we went back to the apartment. [Hamish couldn't stop himself from calling it a flat, but I didn't care. What did I expect from a British guy, anyway?]

On the ride back, he said, "Soon I will be able to get you something. You got me that nanite microscope with your Kuwait book advance, and it's been bothering me ever since that I didn't have a way to reciprocate."

That had been last year. "Aren't you nice to have been worrying about that; I haven't."

"Well, I have, and I can't wait to get you something. I don't know what, but let me know if you can think of anything."

"Nothing comes to mind right now, and as yet we are still fantasizing about hypothetical money. Unless and until it actually starts flowing into our bank accounts, I have no intention of spending it. Let's just put that off for now. We'll go out and enjoy the city in some low-cost way later today."

He grinned. "Okay. I promise I won't sleep too long."

"Good. I want to get going by 3 o'clock."

The cab dropped us at the corner of 8th Avenue and 21st Street and we walked the last bit, past the nail salon, past the crossing guard, past apartment buildings and the renovated fire house with the huge red-painted door (also an apartment building now), and into our building.

The first thing we did was change out of our good clothes; then Hamish collapsed onto our bed with the TV remote in his hand. I turned on my cell phone to call Bethany.

Good – no messages. I could get straight to it.

Or not. It rang a moment later. My mother wanted to know how the meeting had gone. I answered and told her all about it, and that we were back and resting before going out exploring for the evening.

"So your father and I should get dinner without you two?"

I thought about that for a nanosecond, then said, "Definitely."

"Okay. While you're out, do you think you could stop by McNulty's and get some coffee? Your father seems to have used up all of our favorite coffee, and I'm nowhere near there. It's cold, too."

"Sure – we'll get some of everyone's favorite," I promised. "And it's not that cold, even though it's January. Strange weather we're having, but nice. You wouldn't be out shopping if it were that cold," I reminded her.

"True. Well, have fun. See you tonight."

"Thanks – you too. Bye."

Okay, time to call Bethany. I hadn't called her much lately. In fact, I hadn't called more than once in the past several months. I just wasn't good at lying or omission, so I had avoided conversations in which anyone might realize that I was hiding something. Granted, I would be able to tell her what was going on with us later, but I didn't want to jinx anything or ruin the deal by leaking any details, so I had dutifully not mentioned anything to her. Then I was left worrying that she could tell I was keeping something from her and would be annoyed. I hoped it was all just silly paranoia…

Bethany answered on the third ring. She was home and, as usual, she was pouring through her cookbook collection to plan the evening's recipes. She had to go out soon, because Phil, her husband, had used up all of the milk – again – without bothering to tell her. Plus she had to get her son Matt at school and her daughter Angelica at pre-school. But she was glad to get my call, and she didn't have to leave for another hour. It was only 1 p.m.

We went through the usual pleasantries, caught up on the holidays, and then I got on with it. "I have some big news," I announced.

"Oh? What's up, Avril?"

"I don't know whether or not you could tell, but something is definitely up, and has been for a little more than 6 months. I just couldn't tell anyone about it until today."

"I did sense that you were keeping something back. So – what's going on?"

I filled her in on the events of the past half year, idea, invention, patent, clinical trial, contracts, advertising campaign, the works. "So as of today, I can now talk about this. But I won't just randomly tell everyone in sight. For now, I'll tell my friends and family and leave it at that. What do you think of it all?"

"I think it's great. Just because I couldn't get pregnant without help doesn't mean that other people should have to keep every potential pregnancy that threatens to come into being."

Bethany was really cool that way – and ardently pro-choice. We had planned a symposium together in college about abortion, and our parents had come to it. It featured 3 events: a history lecture on the topic, a visit from a local Planned Parenthood physician, and a debate. Her mother, an active member of the League of Women Voters, had had some devilish fun following the anti-choice debater around afterwards, alluding to her miscarriages as "spontaneous abortions."

"So do you think that this could lead to you and Hamish being able to buy a house soon?"

"Maybe, but I refuse to think about it much unless and until sufficient funds are in the bank and a continuous income is rolling in from it."

"Not counting your chickens before they're hatched. That makes sense. So what now?"

"Now Hamish is taking a nap, and then we're going out wandering. Our only errand is to buy more coffee, so we'll just head into Greenwich Village, do that, and then see what strikes our fancy. We don't need a huge income just to do that, so it looks like an evening of mild celebrating is a safe venture for now."

"Cool. Well, I'd better get going. Phil certainly won't buy the milk on his way home, and we're out of cat food, and I have to get Matt and Angelica."

"Okay – well, it was nice to finally tell you my big secret and chat. Bye."

We rang off. It was only half past one. I went into the bedroom and found Hamish snoring away and clutching the remote control with the TV on. I slid it out of his hand and took over; I don't like to sleep during the day once I'm up. Hamish slept shorter amounts of time at night and then took naps. It drove me crazy; I wanted to just stay up and keep going, but at least I could watch some movies.

I found *A Room with a View* and zoned out happily in front of it until he woke up.

When 3 o'clock rolled around, Hamish, true to form, would not go out right away.

"I have to send some e-mails out," he protested.

"Can't you do it tomorrow?!"

"No," he said, sounding impatient. "It's the journal article that we prepared on Nae-Née – they're ready, and the reviewers are done editing them. Remember? Your father let us submit it in December, and they sent it back with revisions last week. I went over them all, and it's ready. It'll just take a few minutes."

"Oh, all right." I sat back down to look for another movie to watch later tonight. You could do that with Time-Warner cable, just scroll to a later time and see what would be on.

I thought about the week ahead. We would be staying until Sunday, so I would have plenty of time to go to a couple of museums and lots of bookstores. I knew that Hamish would just want to sit glued to his computer out in the living room, so we had brought his laptop, but I was determined to drag him away and air him out each day. This was New York, not quiet Connecticut. He was going to have fun, I had informed him. He had looked both pleased and cornered when I said that.

Half an hour passed. I went out to the living room to see what was going on.

He was sitting on the sofa, leaning over the coffee table, staring intently at the screen.

"Is everything okay?"

"What?" he looked up, startled. "Oh – yeah – I'm just addressing each point in a letter to go with the attached article."

I sat down next to him and looked at the screen. Sure enough, he was writing a novel to go with the attachment. "Are you almost done?" I asked impatiently. "I want to have fun – now, not hours later."

To my great relief, he hit "send" and powered the machine down.

"Just let me go to the bathroom."

"Okay. Don't drink anything – we're going to get something out, maybe at The Chocolate Bar. They have spicy hot chocolate with cinnamon and chipotle chili pepper in it."

"Fine – that sounds really good." He disappeared.

Hamish had taught me about spicy food – and I had taught him about it.

He had taught me that one could avoid various health risks, including cancer and inflammatory pain, by eating certain spices as a matter of routine. I had taught him how to find the most delicious spicy food. Because Indian food has ingrained itself into the British diet, it wasn't difficult. Hamish loved to go out for Indian food, or eat it at home. I liked to cook it.

From there, it was on to Cajun food, Mexican food, and whatever other spicy cuisines we could find and taste. We loved a good food adventure.

But Hamish was a terrible cook, so he kept something around to shake onto just about everything he whipped up, a spice blend that he ordered online called *ImmuneACTION*. It included the spices that he advocated using regularly, and he liked it because it was made for people who either couldn't cook well or didn't want to.

I just had to keep him from shaking it onto my homemade, gourmet foods. They didn't need it; they included plenty of healthy, great-tasting ingredients – including spices.

A few minutes later, we were off, walking towards 8th Avenue. We saw the old building superintendent as we went, Raul. Raul had allegedly been one of the Cubans who fought in the Bay of Pigs, which was a failure, and so the legend went that the C.I.A. had found him this job and an apartment in our building. He lived on the top floor in a rent-controlled unit.

Raul was a cantankerous old fellow with bushy black eyebrows and a very long beard. He was always seen wearing a panama-style hat and blue jeans. He understood English but spoke little of it. Hamish was sure that Raul despised him; I supposed that Raul was just frustrated by his Scottish accent, even though it wasn't all that thick. Hamish insisted that Raul just liked women better, and that everyone liked me.

I didn't believe him; that was my husband's bias talking. But Raul definitely greeted me with a friendly nod and smile every time we saw him. Today, he was trudging back from the corner store with a plastic bag. He was probably going to sit in his apartment; in warm weather he brought out a folding chair and sat outside the building, but he wouldn't do that in January.

We greeted each other and headed out to 8th Avenue and south to Greenwich Village.

Down 8th Avenue until it ran into Hudson Street, left at Abington Square by the wrought iron statue called *The Family*, past the former location of The Biography Bookshop and down Bleecker Street we went, breathing in the cold wind that blew sharpest on the wider streets and avenues. We passed various boutiques, and I wandered in and out of a few, browsing at a fast pace while Hamish whined, "Can we go?" He liked to whine, but he also liked to follow me around wherever I felt like going. He didn't whine in the old French antique ship, though. It was like a museum of antiques. My mother had pretty much mined it of whatever the Chelsea apartment could hold by now.

We turned right onto Christopher Street and went into McNulty's, which was about a quarter of the way down. Its sign read *McNulty's – Rare Teas & Choice Coffees Since 1895*. It was jam-packed with goods – the teas were all around where the customers could go, on a huge two-tiered table in little glass jars, and in boxes on the shelves to the left. The coffees had to be requested at the counter. A Chinese family had bought the place in the early 1980s, but kept on the Caucasian employee with the curly white hair, Tom. He knew everything about every kind of coffee, so he was indispensable. The little old grandfather stood to the back of the store, watching everything that went on while his adult son and grandson waited on customers.

Tom and the grandson were doing a brisk business behind the counter. I got in line and read the signs above: Toasted Praline, Pumpkin Spice, Sumatra Mandehling, Hawai'ian Kona, and so on and on. I ordered more of my parents' favorite version of French Roast, oddly named Java Mountain Supreme, plus some Pumpkin Spice for Hamish and some Toasted Praline for me, all finely ground and with no tape. The coffee came in white paper bags with metal twist tabs plus a sticker with the store's name on it and the flavor stamped onto the bag in red. If I didn't say anything about the tape, the bag tended to rip back home in the kitchen and spew the wonderful grounds all over the place, wasting the coffee.

Tom and the grandson were used to me, even if I hadn't been around much lately. I had been buying coffee from them for years, and occasionally I would bring my husband with me.

Today, Hamish was staring intently up at the top shelves, which ran all around the store. Tom noticed and told him, "There is a painting that runs across the wall on all 4 sides that dates back to the 1950s. It's a map of the world. You can't see it very well thanks to all the little cardboard boxes, but it's there." It looked beautiful, from what little we could see of it; pale aqua for the ocean and ivory for the continents.

The entire store was like a window into the past; all of the coffee bins had to date back to 1895. They were metal with painted wooden veneers that depicted Chinese people in Manchu dress, and other people harvesting teas and coffees. It was beautiful and we hoped it stayed the same for a good long time.

Tom handed me the order in a lovely white plastic bag – a thick one with McNulty's store sign emblazoned in bright green on it. I thanked him and called Hamish.

Out on the street, it was still late afternoon. With our errand done, we were free to do as we wished. Hamish took the bag – he liked to carry stuff for me – and said, "Where to next?"

"I don't know. Too late for a museum on a Monday night – most of them were closed today anyway. Let's walk around find a bookstore, find whatever else looks like fun, and then find a place to eat dinner."

"Sounds perfect."

We found The Biography Bookstore by heading back to Bleecker Street. I loved that place; there were always some dirt-cheap books and cards on the tables outside, and then more great stuff inside. The place specialized in biographical history, but there were also famous novels, some children's poetry books, and coffee-table books that showcased New York City. And the biographies were just the stuffy things of academia. There were biographies of rock stars like John Lennon and movie stars as well as politicians and authors. Hamish and I each ended up with something new to read for less than ten bucks apiece.

Doubling back but going north by one block we wended our way to another shop, one with beautiful wooden paneling throughout. It was very quiet in there, almost like a library – the opposite of the other place, where people chatted away happily here and there, including the staff. Not here; the women who ran it were middle-aged and very serious. Hamish and I felt the heaviness of the atmosphere upon entering by the corner door, but the books were too interesting to stay out. Travel books were at the back right, more history and biography toward the front, and some historical novels were placed throughout the store. There were coffee-table books here, too, but these were of a different variety – lots of historic house studies. I found something about a geisha, but didn't want to get carried away and thus have too much too carry around.

There were other exciting bookshops elsewhere in the city, such as the all-travel bookstore called Idlewild on 19th Street and the Strand on Broadway, but both were too far away; enough was enough for now. We were almost ready to eat, so we started thinking about where to go. I pulled out my *Michelin Guide to Restaurants for New York City*. I routinely carried that and *Manhattan Block by Block* around in the back pocket of my Vera Bradley bag, sticking up against my side. No doubt, I looked like a total tourist, but I just didn't care. Having that information available was just too convenient, and the books didn't weigh much.

We chose a Japanese restaurant, because we liked sushi and miso soup – and wandered among the beautiful Federalist houses and brownstone townhouses. Greenwich Village didn't have a grid layout to its streets or sky-high, modern buildings thanks to an outraged protest at the idea of razing the area in favor of urban renewal in the 1960s. As a result, the area had character and gorgeous historic buildings that were almost all beautifully maintained…at a high price. The area was no longer the lovely, affordable nook for bohemians that it once was. It had turned into a high-income, high-end neighborhood inhabited by the likes of the fashion designer Isaac Mizrahi, among other celebrities.

The Japanese food was great – green tea ice cream and all. My parents weren't into Japanese cuisine, so Hamish and I usually didn't eat this unless we were alone together in some city, usually this one.

When we got home, my parents were there, and Dad was just hanging up his suspenders. My father was the only person I knew who wore suspenders. The suspenders never had a design on them; they were just part of his persona. He looked elegant and debonair in them, with his thick hair brushed back and either a cravat or bow tie to finish the look. Dad dressed this way almost every day of his life. Only on weekends might he dress down ever so slightly. I was sure that he just liked to live in suits with suspenders. His ties were the focal point of his look; the most fun one I could think of was a musical-instruments one on blue. He liked cat ties, but saved them for special occasions. He wanted to look serious for court and meetings.

Hamish commented to me about the suspenders as we turned on our TV. "Your father looks like the sort of attorney that no one would mess with in those things," he said with a grin. "I don't know anyone else who wears suspenders."

“Hamish, we’re active in academia – sooner or later we’re bound to meet someone else who does. And other attorneys will definitely mess with any attorney. Lawyers are sharks.”

“Good thing your Dad is one of them. We need a shark on our side with Nae-Née.”

Chapter 8

Another Moving Experience

Things started moving faster and faster for us. It was weird, but I tried not to let it make me feel dizzy.

Hamish was getting job offers from universities and scientific institutes all over the country, and some outside of it as well.

Since my degrees were law and the history of medicine, I got invitations to lecture here and there as before, but now with a twist; I had become a part of the herstory of medicine. I really liked that word – it was so much more fun than just using the two words of "women's history" – and no one stopped me from using it anymore. Not as when I was in college, when fewer people were used to it.

And Nae-Née started to pay off in a big way. By that I mean it paid actual money, and more of it than I had ever thought of having. My mother advised us to visit a financial planner. I did as she suggested; soon we had it all organized perfectly, and I knew I could give homeless people dollar bills with impunity. I wondered what other good I could do with the money. Donate to charities that helped get girls out of prostitution, such as GEMS was one idea. The financial planner helped with that. Travel was another temptation; but not just yet.

We had to decide what to do next, as in where to go. We were still living in my parents' place, the house that I had grown up in, and I couldn't expect Hamish to just stay here forever. Now that we had an income, we had some respect, but I knew that they would expect us to go off and live our own lives someplace else. Visiting was fine, but they were watching to see how we responded to each offer.

Hamish was excited about each one. I was not. I don't like a change of environment. I had to accept some sort of change, and I was willing to do so, but it had to be one that I felt okay about. Simply moving to some completely unfamiliar place because we could afford to go and because we had been invited there was not enough of an inducement. I didn't see any rush to agree to anything, because the offers kept rolling in, and because they each came with plenty of time to reply.

It was mid-winter, and if we moved to a university, Hamish wouldn't need to be settled until late summer. If we moved to some scientific institution, we would be moving sooner, however. It presented a bit of a dilemma: what environment did we want to move to, how close or far away, university or institute, and what would I do there? I didn't like the idea of being dragged along by my husband's appointment or dutifully following even if I hated the idea.

I kept a lot of my thoughts to myself, except for the part about fear of change, having plenty of options and time, and wanting to like wherever we went. With Nae-Née and plenty of money at our fingertips, I couldn't see why that would be a problem.

We had moved several times and I had hated it, so I didn't want to move again unless we really liked where we were going. I had accepted moving back and forth in order to complete my education. I didn't want to live in an apartment with another girl after college or graduate school, either. That was an unstable situation; she would just leave and stick me with the rent or demand that I move so that she could have the place to share with a new husband. Forget it, I had decided; I would get married and live with my husband. Until then, I wasn't going anywhere. But I got lucky, as I saw it, and met my husband during law school.

It was when I was doing research on the legal history of medicine for a seminar that I met Hamish in the Francis A. Countway Library at Harvard. After that, he kept studying in the Law School's library, and at first I didn't understand why. I thought he had something to look up, but it turned out that he was just faking it so that he could follow me in the stacks. We were friends for 2 years before things changed.

Neither of us had realized what was going on. Everyone else around us could see it – except for us. We would banter and joke and sit together and go out to eat and study. But we were also very busy with other things – such as our degree programs – so we didn't realize that our favorite thing to do was spend time together until just before graduation. And our graduations were within days of one another.

So we graduated as a couple. We didn't get married right away, however, because life promptly led us in separate directions. But we didn't break up.

Hamish had a post-doctoral fellowship at Boston University that lasted for 3 years.

I went home to Connecticut, studied for the bar, took it that summer, and found out that fall that I had flunked it. I don't test well. After that, I swore I would never take it again. My father didn't push it. He remembered what my international law professor had said. I had taken a temporary job listing the contents of boxes for a toxic torts case rather than work in his firm; I didn't want a job based on nepotism that I knew I couldn't keep. Passing the bar wasn't something that I had ever counted upon.

I kept writing whenever I could, just because I love to do that.

Then I had to leave for a while. My grandmother in Aix-en-Provence needed someone to stay with her. She was my mother's mother, and she had helped raise me every summer when I was a kid. I used to go and stay with her and my grandfather and help them take care of the Chartreuse cats that they bred. We would pick berries, visit lavender farms, and go shopping at the local fish and farmers' markets. Now Nana was aging, and she couldn't stay home alone. She didn't want to go to some horrible nursing home, and I didn't blame her. She hated any change to her environment as much as I did. Going to stay with her felt like going to another one of my family's homes, so it felt fine.

Her husband, my Grandpère, had died while I was in graduate school. Grandpère had been a lot like me, quiet, not liking noise, and intensely interested in playing his violin. I missed him. We had all met in Provence for that funeral in my second year at the Sorbonne, and then I had returned to Paris to resume my studies, where I was staying with my other grandparents.

All that time – 6 and a half years – Nana had lived alone with my mother's sisters scattered across the country and her brother in the next town but busy with his spice store. I knew that no one else was going to stay with her, and I was the logical choice anyway, because my career seemed to be all about writing. When

I was invited away to give a lecture, which I could deliver either in English or in French, one of my aunts would take over. But Tante Chloe and Tante Lisanne were always glad when I came back to relieve them; they had kids to watch.

I was terrified by the thought of growing old all alone thanks to this.

Nana lived for 2 more years, and we had fun with her cats and the cuisine of Provence while I wrote and drew. As a result, I churned out a pretty children's book with pastel drawings about her Chartreux cats. The book detailed the history of the cats – covered in just a couple of pages – and then described my grandmother and her life. We stopped the breeding business when I moved in, and made sure that all of the kittens were adopted. Spock was one of them; I named and raised him, and brought him home with me when Nana died. My Oncle André took the remaining pets after Nana died in her sleep.

So that was why Hamish and I didn't immediately get married.

But when I returned, we got engaged. He gave me a beautiful heart-shaped diamond ring – and it was a pale rose-pink, which thrilled me. He had gotten it in a mine on a lecture trip to Canada, where there was a do-it-yourself mine. You could keep whatever you found in raw form, and get it cut later. Only then would you know what you had. It was the coolest thing; when Hamish asked me what I would like my dream engagement ring to look like I said heart-shaped, so that's how he had the stone cut. It was just under a carat, on yellow gold.

He gave it to on the evening of the Winter Solstice, so I wanted to get married on the evening of the Summer Solstice. That's what we did.

With that, the fairy tale degenerated into a normal, difficult and thoroughly real life. Hamish got a temporary position at the UConn Health Center, analyzing stem cells in a laboratory for a year. My parents were pleased; they were convinced that this would lead to a permanent position for him.

It didn't.

We had an apartment in Farmington with bad plumbing that lasted just long enough to complete the schedule at the Health Center. Spock got to live with us at least. Then we found ourselves on the road, moving from my parents' place to Austria to my parents' place to a faculty apartment at UConn in Storrs to my parents' place to Kuwait and back to my parents' place while Hamish bounced in and out of there.

So naturally I was sick of moving – sick to the point of more anxiety attacks at the mere mention of the idea. I figured that with healthy bank accounts, there was no need to make any hasty decisions.

Hamish had been wooed by the University of Southern California in Los Angeles, Saint Louis University in Missouri (a Catholic school), Emory University in Atlanta, Georgia, the University of London, in England, and several others, but these were the ones that Hamish was most interested in.

More offers came in, and Hamish told me about each one.

Next came an offer to teach at Kuwait University. I blew up at that one.

"No way am I moving back to Kuwait!" I said, outraged. "I'm done living in the Islamic world. We'd just have to move again after I couldn't stand it for more than perhaps a semester."

"Okay, fine," said Hamish. "But if I got an offer from a place in France, would you be objecting?"

"Actually, yes, I would," I replied. "All of my grandparents have either died or moved out, and my aunts and uncle aren't that friendly with us. And I really don't want to live in any other country than this one."

He looked rather tense.

"I realize that you are chafing at the bit to get out of your in-laws' house, but I have no intention of jumping the gun just because of that. Whatever we decide, it should be something that we both love so that we won't have to keep moving. I hate moving. Aren't you sick of it too by now?" I asked him.

"Yes. I am. I just want to accept something before the offers dry up and there's nothing left to accept."

"It's only been a couple of weeks, Hamish. You're getting overly anxious. I thought that getting really anxious was my job."

He gave me a wry grin for that.

We were sitting in the bedroom on Stoner Drive on a gray afternoon in late January. Spock was staring at us. My parents wanted to keep him. Another change that was freaking me out. They said that Hamish and I should get our own cat – together. I could see their point; a new cat would be our first pet together.

"What about U.S.C. or Saint Louis University?"

"I don't want to go to either California or Missouri."

"Why? They are in the 48 contiguous states."

"One is in earthquake hell. We would get settled only to either die in some accident or have all of our stuff destroyed, and I don't want different stuff. The other is in a flood zone – similar outcome threatened – at a Catholic university. With our attitudes about abortion and birth control, two pro-choice people at an anti-choice place, I would expect trouble. Sooner or later one of us would have a disagreement with school policy that would affect our research or lectures. And neither of us would accept that."

He hadn't considered that. "Okay, I concede your points. What about Emory?"

"Hurricane zone. And floods. Don't you watch or read the news?"

"You know I do."

"Not climate reports. I watch and read with 2 things in mind: one is to see what's happening. The other is to imagine what it would be like to live in each place. Then I tell myself that in most cases, I wouldn't want to leave this area."

"What do you want to do?"

"I want to go someplace that doesn't require a plane ride to get back here for holidays. Some volcanic eruption will just make that impossible at some random yet thoroughly inconvenient time, or a blizzard will do that – or it would be overcrowding on airlines. I hate waiting in line; I'm not about to sign up to do it as a matter of routine. That's one of the reasons why I would never just get an apartment across the country from here and then have to trundle on back in order to be here sometimes. And I didn't want to go away on a permanent basis to begin with. I like travel and adventure, but you also know that I only like it on the condition that I can come back when the relatively short adventure is over."

"What are we going to do, then?" Hamish sat on the bed, twisting his wedding ring around, staring at Spock, who was washing his tail.

"We are going to calm down and see what else happens. There is still a lot to settle, and Nae-Née was my idea. Now you are getting lots of offers because you have the skills to bring the idea into existence. I refuse to just tag along dutifully and obediently even if it makes me unhappy. Of course, I would probably refuse anyway. I want to go somewhere that pleases us both, or not at all."

He had to concede those points as well; they made sense to him. A lot had happened in 2 weeks; more could happen in the next 2 for all that either of us knew.

And it did.

Something really quite nice happened the next week: Hamish got an offer to do research at the Rockefeller University Institute in Manhattan – as did I. That second part of the offer seemed really odd to me, however. I wasn't an engineer or life scientist. I didn't do the sort of research that was usually conducted there. What did the place want with a medical historian?

My father cleared it up for me: they wanted prestige. They wanted the husband-and-wife team who had created Nae-Née. They were the only institution that had jointly invited us rather than just wooing Hamish, and they were in New York City – familiar territory to me.

My mother pointed out that we could go and stay in the Chelsea apartment, check out the Rockefeller Institute, and decide whether or not we liked the idea. Then we just stay there while we looked for a place of our own in the city.

She and Dad talked like they already knew what our decision would be.

They were probably right about that; Hamish and I were both acting like it was either Christmas or a trip to the most entertaining and intellectually stimulating vacation spot that we could imagine.

We discussed it further and decided to go and see what the officials there had in mind.

We would leave on Friday, which was in two days.

Chapter 9

The Rockefeller University Institute

We arrived in Chelsea at 8:10 p.m. on Friday and walked from Penn Station to the apartment. We preferred it that way when we went there without my parents. It wasn't that far.

We had come deliberately at the start of the weekend so as to have plenty of time to settle in before the meeting on Monday morning. We were due to arrive at 9:30 a.m. to meet the President, tour the premises, and hear his proposal for our positions there.

I could tell that Hamish was very glad that I was even starting to seriously consider moving somewhere alone with him, and that he was equally glad to have it be Manhattan. We both loved it here, and this really was the most attractive offer yet to come our way, because it included something that treated me as a partner in the Nae-Née invention rather than as a wife who would be packed up and brought along with him. He had even said so to me.

That was what had really sold him on it. It was more than he had expected to get from any institution, having me included jointly in an offer was what he had really wanted. To have it come from a place that I would actually want to go to made it doubly enticing.

All we could do now was hope for the best on Monday.

We got settled, went out for Japanese food, and came home.

Instead of joining Hamish in front of the TV, I fired up the living room computer and read all about the Rockefeller University Institute on the Internet.

Founded in 1901 by Rockefellers Senior and Junior, it had been the home base of lots of Nobel Prize winners. Lots of great science had come out of the place, including methadone treatments for drug addicts, proof that humans have a natural immunity to tumors, and so on. Now they wanted to be in on user-friendly birth control, apparently. No doubt, they also wanted Hamish's tumor-tracking nanite research added to their list of credentials. He was fine with that.

The place was located along the East River on York Street between 62nd and 68th Streets, and abutted the Cornell University and Sloan-Kettering Memorial Hospitals. It was a medical and research neighborhood. It would probably feel exceptionally cold, I thought, thanks to being right next to the river, so we would have to bundle up and get inside quick.

Too bad; I would have liked to get acclimated to the campus by looking around at the outsides as well as the insides of the buildings. We had been promised a tour of the place after the interview.

Other than leaving the apartment at 9 a.m., dressing nicely and wearing winter coats, hats and gloves, no other forms of preparation occurred to me. The President had received our CVs, copies of our academic scientific journal publications, including the one pending, and was also in possession of a published copy of each of my books. Whatever else he might want, we couldn't guess, so we weren't worrying about it.

I figured we could easily get there on time in a cab just after rush hour ended. If possible, I intended to make 9:30 a.m. a standard arrival time once we were settled into faculty appointments there, if all went well. I didn't want rush hour to be a part of my everyday life.

The weekend passed quietly, and that was fine with both of us. I walked down to Chelsea Market with Hamish tagging along on Saturday to shop for the weekend's groceries. He liked to see all the gourmet food shops in there, eat some lobster bisque with me at a tall side table in the hall outside The Lobster Place, and then get some tea and cookies at either Amy's Bread or Sarabeth's Kitchen. If it were summertime, we would have gotten gelato at the place near the Bowery Kitchen Supply store.

I got fresh produce at the Manhattan Fruit Exchange (must pay cash there) and some Spanish mackerel and Cajun catfish at The Lobster Place, which was a fish market that offered all sorts of fabulous fin fish and shellfish, plus sushi and fish sandwiches. If all went well on Monday, we planned to come back and eat dinner at The Green Table, which changed its menu each season according to whatever the local farms were selling to its chefs.

Hamish commented to me that not only did I know how to lay low when we didn't have any money and needed to be careful, but I also knew how to have fun when did have money. And we weren't getting ourselves into any trouble; partying and booze and drugs held no appeal for us. Overeating seemed sickening. We wanted to travel, study, explore, and have gourmet food adventures. We could treat our palates like amusement parks without ruining our health.

We stayed in and I cooked each night that weekend, except for some walks around the neighborhood for hot chocolate or dessert out. We also saw the neighbor girl from across the hall. She lived with her parents in a one-bedroom, rent-controlled apartment.

She had gotten a tattoo on her hip, which she secretively and proudly showed us in the hallway. Her name was Jordan. She already had dyed her dark hair yellow with bright blue streaks and had several piercings in each ear. Her next one would be on her tongue she confided. I was revolted and said so. Hamish advised her against it; he warned of cracked molars and infections. Glancing into her family's place, it appeared to be packed with stuff to the point of claustrophobia. It was the only place they had to put their things, so naturally they hoarded a bit.

Jordan was supposed to take out our trash and recycling in return for $20 each week. My parents had made this arrangement with her as soon as she was old enough to do such chores. There weren't very many ways for a kid to earn money, and they had wanted to help. She and her parents had a key to our place, and they would check to make sure that all was well in our absence. My father also gave Jordan tickets to museum exhibits and Broadway shows several times each year.

Sometimes I would take Jordan to the movies with me, and I was in the habit of bringing her gifts for her birthday or for Hanukah. But lately, she was less and less interested in us. We had little in common, and she wanted to hang out with her friends in all of her spare time. If we saw her alone, her thumbs were always busy, texting her friends nonstop.

She took off with some of them each evening, and I wondered when her homework was being done. I had gotten her a Wi-Fi gadget to use with her laptop for that express purpose. We realized that this had opened up the world of social networking to her, but blocking it was like trying to hold back the tide. We just hoped that she was working.

On Monday morning, we got up at a quarter to eight and got ready to go. We ate in the apartment and drank our McNulty's coffee, then got dressed. Predictably, Hamish suggested taking the subway, but I said absolutely not, we weren't risking being late for an important interview. We could take it on the way home and see how long it would take to get back. I was nervous enough as it was; I don't interview well.

The cab ride got us there in plenty of time. On the way, Hamish's cell phone jingled with his Bach's *Fugue in D Minor*, an ominous one that he had insisted upon. Mine jingled a minute later with Mozart's *The Magic Flute*. Hamish wasn't planning to check his voice mail until I suggested that it might relate to the interview, so we both listened: the interview was now set for 10 a.m. thanks to some unspecified delay. I suspected that the delay was getting going in the morning, but didn't say so.

That gave us some time to explore the area a bit, and look around outside. Fortunately, the wind wasn't too sharp as we walked around. I had my black velvet ribbon-covered hat on, so the wind didn't seem too fierce. Hamish just toughed it out, ignoring the cold as his ears turned red. I tried to wrap his scarf around his head, but he pushed me off, looking furtively around as if a stray interviewer might be hiding and watching our every move.

We saw the general layout of the campus, with its original main building, Founder's Hall, which had opened in 1906. The place had a dormitory for graduate students, a café, a dining room, a club for faculty and students, a Philosophers' Garden that no doubt looked a lot better in the spring than it did now, and a tennis court.

After seeing all that, we headed inside to warm up and find the rest rooms before announcing our presence. We still had time to spare after that.

Suddenly I just wanted this to be over. Hamish saw me staring into space at nothing as we waited and hugged me. The receptionist had left her desk, so there were no witnesses to my minor anxiety attack. I was okay. Everyone got like this before an interview, I told myself. At least I didn't have to go on 20,000 of them in order to get one job that would only last a short time only to repeat the cycle a few months – or worse, weeks – later. That was the lot of so many people now in this ruined economy.

The President appeared a moment later, apologized for setting the meeting back, we excused it like it was no imposition at all, and he led us into his inner sanctum to chat. As expected, the office was like a formal but very comfortable living room with his desk over at the window in its own nook. The computer was running, and a Starbucks cup sat next to it.

Ironically, his last name was Nurse. So we were being interviewed by a Dr. Nurse, I mused silently. That was the advice of career counselors to job-seekers, I told myself: imagine the interview in his or her underwear and you'll calm down.

This was some approximation of that. My mind wandered – a defense mechanism against stress – and I wondered idly whether he was related in any way to Rebecca Nurse, one of the accused in the 1692 Salem witch trials. Irrelevant; I forced myself to pay attention to the conversation at hand.

We were seated on the long sofa and Dr. Nurse sat in the wing chair across from us, then offered us coffee. We declined, truthfully explaining that we had had some with breakfast and come straight here. On the table between us sat printed copies of our journal articles, our CVs, and my published books.

"Our appointments committee has reviewed your work, of course. We wanted to invite both of you to locate here because we know that both of you invented Nae-Née."

It was as I had guessed, and I was pleased. I started to relax a little, but only a little. What did these people want me to do here? This was a place for scientists, not medical historians.

I asked Dr. Nurse this question. "I am delighted to be acknowledged, but I keep wondering what use you would have here for a medical historian at an institute that focuses on medical and scientific discoveries and innovations."

"I thought you might be. What we are hoping is that you can be an Associate Professor-in-Residence and lecture several times a year about your area of expertise. Scientists and physicians should be educated and informed about the history and current events of their fields."

"So you would want me to keep up with my research as usual and share it as it relates to current work with the doctors and professors here."

"Exactly…and give lectures every couple of weeks, and publish books that are collections of those lectures."

Oh. I could do that. Cool. "That sounds great," I replied.

"I'm glad to hear that. And your husband could continue his nanite research on tumor tracking here, with our laboratories and equipment at his disposal."

Just as I had guessed; this was great. Hamish would be able to work in a state-of-the-art environment instead of a basement in a private home. Not that my parents would be dismantling the room down there. They were having too much fun showing it to their friends and telling people about how Nae-Née had been created there.

I looked up at Hamish and smiled. He gave me a grin back, then turned to Dr. Nurse.

"That sounds like the start of wonderful arrangement. Tell us more."

"Well, naturally, the Rockefeller University would take a substantial portion of the profits derived from any of your future research, leaving you with your annual salary as a full professor here. But you would still get a percentage to yourself."

"How much would that be?" Hamish asked.

"2 percent, plus your salary. We're prepared to offer you $140,000 to start with."

This was slightly more than the other sums we had had quoted to us through the grapevines at other places, so it was all the more tempting…especially considering cost of living expenses for New York City.

"That sounds good. What salary are you going to offer to Avril?"

Dr. Nurse turned to me. "An associate professor-in-residence makes considerably less than a professor, so we were thinking of offering you $65,000 per year."

I tried to look like this sounded normal to me. "That sounds fair."

Dr. Nurse was looking very happy; he was about to reel in a prize catch.

"Do you have any other questions? Benefits package, health, retirement, etc.?"

I said, "Yes – we'd like to hear about that also."

He ran through the standard litany of 401Ks, IRAs, health care packages, and then handed us each a packet full of contracts and details to take with us.

"Any other questions?"

"Where would we be working – could we see our prospective office area or areas, laboratory, and so on?" I asked.

"Certainly. If it's all right with both of you, we had picked out a shared office suite for the two of you to share. It has a private office for each you that adjoin a central reception area where your shared secretary's desk would be. You would each have access to the University's library, with the accompanying borrowing and interlibrary loan privileges, and Dr. MacDonall would have a laboratory down the hall."

We completely failed to keep our expressions neutral; the lure of a shared office suite together was what did it. Our jaws dropped open slightly, and then we glanced at each other and grinned like we had just entered Willy Wonka's chocolate factory. Then we forced our faces back into neutrality so we could say, both at once, "That's definitely all right with us."

Dr. Nurse was enjoying himself now.

"Well – great – let's start the tour, then."

And we were off, whisked on a whirlwind walking tour of the building, the campus, and our future/prospective offices. It was the chocolate factory as far as I could see. I loved the idea of it all, which made me suspicious of everything. Before signing on the dotted lines, I intended to take the packages and contracts home, show them to Dad, and go over the details with both of my parents to make sure that I wasn't naively rushing into a trap or a big mistake.

I was sure that both Hamish and I, with our limited experience in the real world of business and our noses perpetually buried in our academic pursuits, sorely needed to double-check a deal such as this one rather than just blindly plunging in.

The research building, where our offices would be should we in fact decide to accept the posts, was conveniently reachable without going back outside into the cold. Several of the buildings were connected, so we just walked south to get there while staying warm. We left our coats and the packets in the President's office, and got them back a couple of hours after looking around and meeting some other professors.

Our next stop was to the faculty dining area with several of these people plus Dr. Nurse. The conversation was mostly about life at the Rockefeller University

Institute, with some about our careers. I answered a few questions about Kuwait and France.

Before we left, Dr. Nurse just had a few more questions. He was curious about us. "How did you come up with this idea?"

Hamish smiled and looked at me. I answered, "I just wanted a user-friendly, reliable form of birth control that took little or no effort on the part of women to live with. It just came to me in a sudden bit of inspiration – and I knew that Hamish could bring the idea to life. Fortunately, he saw it too, got really excited about it, and had the whole thing written up a few hours later."

Dr. Nurse was intrigued, but had another, different question, just for me. "And you – you write about things that have nothing to do with your degrees, and you still find time to practice your violin. What makes you do these things, things which seem to be so time-consuming yet external to your main field?"

I was taken aback for a moment. Then I had an answer. "I don't want to live my life with regrets: regret that I never did whatever it is that I love to do, such as keep playing the violin, or regret for not doing other things that I always really, really wanted to do, like publish fiction and at least one children's book with beautiful illustrations, so I just go ahead and do those things."

Dr. Nurse stared at me for a moment, and then said, "A lot of people would envy you that, including me. Good for you."

We shook hands, and I wondered what it was that he wasn't doing with his life.

And then it was over, and Hamish and were heading out to York Avenue.

When we were sure that we were clear of the place and unobserved, we breathed a shared sigh of thrilled relief.

We knew we wanted the posts.

Hamish agreed to be cautious and go over the papers with Dad before signing, and handed his over to me for safe-keeping.

Suddenly I didn't want to take the subway home. I wanted to clutch those packets tightly until they were safely and securely deposited in the Chelsea apartment. Hamish agreed. There was plenty of time for exploring the subway route to and from our new jobs later.

Back at the apartment, I stashed the packets in the bureau drawer. I stood there for a moment, staring at the piece of furniture once it was shut, as though it was somehow announcing that it had something valuable in it. Normally, I didn't really think of the apartment as being full of valuables, but this was different.

Suddenly I was glad that Dad was arriving tonight. I called my mother and told her how it had gone, and asked whether she was coming tonight as well.

"I wasn't going to, but Aunt Zoe just said that she would feed Spock, so yes. We should be there around 5:30. Do you want to get dinner with us?"

"Yes! And I have to show you the contracts. We didn't sign yet; we didn't want to seem foolish or naïve, so we want to show the stuff to you and Dad first, then sign."

"It sounds like you're being careful but planning to ultimately just sign."

"Well…yes, that's our current plan."

"We'll talk about it tonight, but it sounds really exciting."

We hung up.

"Hamish – take me out for hot chocolate!"

He turned around from hanging up his suit and looked at me.

"Come on – I'll just switch this nice jacket for a sweater. Please? Let's make a fancy date of it to celebrate. Let's go to Rockefeller Plaza and get something at La Maison du Chocolat!"

He smiled and hugged me. "Okay."

He squeezed harder. "Looks like we're about to have a nice life together at last."

I twisted my head up to look at him and gave him a big grin. "Yes – at last."

An hour later, I sat there with my husband, leafing happily through the dessert recipe book while we drank the wonderful, thick dark chocolate drinks with the complimentary dollop of whipped cream on a plate between us and little individual-wrapped chocolate squares on our saucers. "We could do this every week or so," Hamish said to me.

We had great afternoon.

My parents arrived shortly after we got back and we went out to Chelsea Market for a fancy, celebratory dinner at The Green Table, just as Hamish and I had planned, but now with all 4 of us. The menu featured fresh food from local farms, so it changed with each season.

Dad looked at the packets when we got home; they were similar, but not identical. After about an hour of reading and comparing, he pronounced the deals to be fair to the point of generous, definitely acceptable, and obvious plays for the latest and greatest hot items in our fields: us. We were wanted, and badly enough to offer us slightly more money than was standard. He gave us the go-ahead to sign the papers.

And so we signed and brought them back the next day. We could start at any time; Hamish would be assigned some graduate students to supervise, but otherwise he could continue with his nanite research. We said we would start in two weeks time, on a Monday.

Meanwhile, my mother said that we should just stay at the Chelsea apartment while we took our time and found a place of our own and bought it. She said we should go right ahead and get a kitten, too. No reason not to have one in the apartment. I knew she just wanted to keep Spock all to herself and Dad, but this had been long expected, so I agreed.

I asked Hamish what sort of place he wanted. He said he was willing to go along with whatever sort of place I wanted.

At the moment, I wasn't sure of much except that I didn't want it to be high up in some modern building. And that I wanted it to be in lower Manhattan. It was something that I had always considered to be so out of our price range as to feel like it was just an unreachable dream. Not anymore, according to our accountant. We could get a place there if we wanted to, and still have a huge income from Nae-Née.

So we would be able to drive or take a train back and forth between Connecticut and Manhattan. No plane rides on holidays and ending up sleeping through a blizzard at an airport, no big change, no hassle. We could even take our time getting settled yet still start showing up for work fairly soon.

This was nice. Maybe I wouldn't have to be confronted with yet another view of anxiety. Maybe I wouldn't have to deal with that haze obscuring my vision for days on end. I was quite certain that if we had in fact gone elsewhere – someplace really far off and unfamiliar, and a long plane ride away – that the haze would not have cleared in a mere 4 days. It would have lasted much longer, and I couldn't guess how long that would have been.

I so wanted to skip that altogether.

If something was going to make me anxious, I was ready for it to be something else. A change in what I was to do on a daily basis would be good for me.

I wanted Hamish to be around for the rest of my life – I wasn't fool enough not to be careful what I wished for – but a change of some sort had to be faced.

I wanted some control over my life while still making a change. It looked like we had found it together.

Was I hallucinating? I asked myself yet again. Life wasn't supposed to be happy, or so I had come to believe after bouncing from one place to another only to dig my heels in, barricade myself into my old room in Connecticut, and deciding to just write for a while.

Well…apparently not. Maybe it was okay to believe that now we would be happy.

I would try to enjoy it.

That looked easy; the reports from the company that manufactured Nae-Nee kept rolling in with glowing accounts of customer satisfaction. I could hardly believe it – we had created something useful and user-friendly that met a constant need.

We contacted a real estate agent to help us find a place to live.

The idea of never moving again but doing some recreational travel was extremely appealing. We had a long list of places we might like to visit once we were settled into a routine and knew when we would take off: Paris (Hamish had yet to go there on a romantic visit with me); Hawai'i; India on the Orient Express train; Japan, including Kyoto, which had pre-World War II buildings, a rare thing there; New Zealand, where *The Lord of the Rings* trilogy had been filmed, Hamish's favorite movies; Venice, Florence and Pompeii, Italy; several places in the Netherlands, including the World Court at the Hague, the Secret Annex in Amsterdam and Vermeer's sites in Delft; Belgium, mostly for the food but also for the art in Bruges…

But first we had to get a place of our own.

I looked forward to it.

Chapter 10

Life on Our Own

Hunting for a place to live was fun. I suppose any kind of shopping is fun when you know that you can buy whatever you want, even if you don't know precisely what that is until you actually find it. The point was that we could buy it when we found it.

Dad surprised me the next morning by handing me a release form.

"Get every real estate broker or agent you deal with to sign off on this before you look at even one piece of property with them," he insisted.

The form required the signee to promise never to tell any member of the media what we bought, the point being to make it difficult to find us at our new home.

I looked up at him, startled. "Is this really necessary?"

We were sitting in my parents' room, which was all in pale greens. All four of us were home, drinking our coffee and not ready to go anywhere just yet.

Dad grabbed the remote and turned the TV on. He channel surfed for a moment, then said, "There – look at that."

The ad for Nae-Née was running. He flipped around to a few other commercial channels, and hit it just right – the shows were on break. The ad appeared on each one within a few seconds of each other.

"The ads hit the media 2 weeks ago. Haven't you been watching?"

I felt ridiculous; commercials were when I ran to the bathroom or checked the Internet for whatever I had either thought about on my own or wondered about thanks to the crime shows I was watching. I had completely missed my own advertisement.

"No," I confessed. "I run to the bathroom during ads, and Hamish and I keep watching movie channels in Manhattan."

"Oh. Well, that clears that mystery up. The secret is out – Nae-Née is on the market, it's for birth control by nanites, and soon the public will find out that you and Hamish are the inventors."

"How soon? What do you know?"

"A reporter from *The New York Times* called my office looking for you, so soon."

"When was that?"

"Yesterday. Expect a call from them today. I gave them both of your cell phone numbers."

I sat down on the bed, stunned. As I mentioned before I don't interview well, but when someone has already made up their mind before they've even met you, as Dr. Nurse had, it doesn't matter. This would be different.

"Thanks for the release form, Dad. Do you think anyone will actually sign it?"

"Anyone who wants to work with you will."

Huh. "Okay, thanks. I'll use it." He had given me 20 copies. I put them in my extra bag, a Vera Bradley tote with a notepad. Now I would have to carry it around while house-hunting.

My mother walked in, sipping her coffee. "Can I come with you on a few of these house tours?" She loved to shop, and she also loved to go on house tours back in Connecticut, just to compare notes on the perfectly decorated and furnished homes with her friends.

"Okay." I hoped Hamish wouldn't mind having his mother-in-law in tow for all of this. But it didn't matter; we were moving out of her house, she wasn't moving in with us.

"This is going to great fun!" she gushed. "Once you have a place picked out, we can go to the French antique shop on Bleecker Street and look around!"

Obviously, visions of home furnishings and décor were swirling around in her waking dreams. She was in house-heaven. Well, that was fine. It would be fun, once the house was chosen. The odd part of this was that I considered this to be partly a chore, whereas it was total fun to my mother.

An hour later, after dropping off the signed papers at the Rockefeller University Institute, yet another cab dropped us off at a real estate office in Midtown. I sincerely hoped that we weren't going to need all 20 release forms. That would mean a tedious process of meeting 20 strangers and getting used to all of them only to find that they wanted to sell out our secrets, such as they seemed, to more strangers.

It wasn't that bad. We met a woman named Leah Rothstein, an elegant, tough-as-nails businesswoman with lacquered, blood-red nails and tinted glasses who liked to wear spike-heeled pumps. She was friendly enough, with a steely smile, and she had no objection to signing the form. My mother later told me that she was probably used to such things, and didn't mind as long as she could make money on big sales commissions.

We told her what we were looking for: a 3-bedroom place with at 2 full bathrooms plus a half bath, a laundry area, a nice kitchen for a gourmet cook, and a living and dining room. We did not want to be high up, and we hoped for a place in Greenwich Village. Also, a place for one car would be nice. She grabbed several files with keys to each place, and we were off.

Leah brought us to several places that I just did not like, and I wondered whether she was willfully not listening to us, or just laboring under the mistaken impression that we would go for whatever she showed us.

We saw a place that towered over Central Park and came with 2 parking spaces underground. The garage was dark, creepy and forbidding. She gave us an odd look when I was visibly turned off and had an attack of vertigo looking out the window of the unit.

"You weren't kidding about heights," she remarked.

"Yeah," I said, "I told you so. I don't like to have my head in the clouds unless I'm enclosed in an airplane. Flying is fun, but this isn't."

"Okay…on to the next place."

The next place was an ultra-modern apartment in a trendy new building. I hated it.

I looked at Hamish, who looked like he couldn't imagine relaxing with all that glass that passed for an outer wall. Never mind that it wasn't far from my parents' apartment in Chelsea; I could just imagine stones raining through this glass house, be they hail stones or otherwise.

Ms. Rothstein started chatting with us in the car. "Tell me what your previous residence was like, just to give me an idea of what you find appealing." Good; she was catching on.

I thought for a moment. "Not too many windows, not new – maybe dating from the early to mid-20th century, nothing modern or contemporary. No underground garages. Nothing high up. A quiet, out-of-the-way location, not on any main drag of a street. Plenty of wall space for bookcases and art."

She listened this time. "Are you and your husband professors?"

"We're about to be. He's a doctor-engineer and I'm a writer and medical historian. How did you guess?"

"I didn't quite guess; I've seen the ads for your invention at my doctor's office – your photos are on the brochure. Plus you want space for bookcases."

"You've seen those ads before I realized that they were on TV," I said.

She smiled as she pulled onto a quiet street in Greenwich Village.

At last – we were going to see something in the area we had requested.

She parked and we walked halfway down the street. We weren't far from Christopher and Bleecker Streets, I noticed. We stopped in front of an old firehouse. But it wasn't a firehouse any more. It had been converted to a private residence, and it was for sale.

I stared at it, walking up and down in front of it, looking up at the windows.

"This place is actually for sale?" I asked, sounding as incredulous as I felt.

"It is," she said, smiling as she put a key into the lock.

Hamish was staring up at it like it was the coolest thing he had seen in a while. I recognized that look. It was the one he got whenever he saw an intriguing nanobotics tool.

My mother was watching us, gauging our reactions. If we looked too eager, she would scold us later for not being good shoppers. I stayed quiet and followed Leah inside.

Soon we were walking through the building, which looked better and better the more we saw of it. There were bedrooms upstairs – 2 guest rooms with a shared bathroom on the next level – plus a laundry room conveniently located on that floor – and another bedroom on the top floor with its own bathroom. Both rooms stretched from front to back, with the bathroom opposite the staircase, which went up the front right side of the building. The half bathroom was on the ground floor under the staircase, which wound up through the firehouse – no pole.

The ground floor had a garage – that was behind the huge door that used to house the fire engine – and the front door was on the left. The doors were both painted a dull off-white, but that could be changed. Going straight back from the front door one walked into the kitchen, which was finished with stainless steel appliances and a pretty pink-black-silver-blue granite for countertops. A window looked into the backyard, which had a patio that was walled off from the other yards. A pair of French doors led out there from the dining area, which continued seamlessly into the living room.

There was no furniture. The firehouse was completely empty.

"What made the previous owners give this place up?" I found myself asking. Not that I actually expected to find out.

Leah Rothstein just said vaguely, "They wanted a grander place, something trendier. They bought this one in a hurry, and changed their minds once they got to know New York."

I wasn't about to ask who they were. If we bought this place, we would find out at the closing.

I loved the place, but let Leah show us a few more just for good measure, and because my mother was obviously having a great time seeing the insides of lofts, brownstones, and whatever else the broker had to offer us. After that, I hoped my mother would be willing to stop, if we were in fact able to get this wonderful firehouse.

We had forgotten to eat lunch thanks to such an engrossing tour. It was after 3 p.m. when I suddenly realized this. Hamish was getting antsy, pulling out his cell phone to check the time (neither of us would put on a wrist watch for any amount of money, so I had a pretty little pocket watch and he checked his cell phone if we wanted to know what time it was). When I heard his stomach growl, mine promptly followed suit and it was loud enough that both my mother and Leah Rothstein stopped chatting and stared at us.

I grinned sideways with a wry expression, said we had forgotten to eat and couldn't wait much longer, and thanked her very much for showing us so many interesting places.

With that, she dropped us near home and took off for her office, leaving us with the literature on the firehouse and a loft. We were on Greenwich Avenue, and facing one of our favorite restaurants, a Belgian one called the Café de Bruxelles. It specialized in mussels – a whole page of its menu was devoted to Moules à Fill-in-the-Blank. We went right in. By now, my mother realized that she had seen enough for today and was ready to eat as well.

We all ate until we realized that my father would be unable to get us to eat dinner.

I told my mother that I had a beautiful salmon cake from The Lobster Place in the fridge, plus some potatoes, salad greens and cookies. "Good," she said. "We'll feed him that and stay in. Tomorrow we'll have to stop looking in the middle of the day and eat."

Hamish and I looked at each other over the frîtes. We loved that firehouse. We had often dreamed of living in one whenever we were out walking together on past visits to Manhattan. And now that we had seen the inside of one, it had lived up to our fondest fantasies.

My mother saw that. "What? Did you two fall in love with a place today? Which one?"

I looked back at her. "The firehouse." I added that we had dreamed of having one.

She looked crestfallen; no more house tours. "We'll tell your father. No doubt he'll insist upon appraisals and who knows what else. We should look around some more in case it doesn't work out." But she knew that getting us to look further was going to be difficult if not impossible. Unlike her, I approached shopping for just about everything but books with the idea that I would go in, get what I came for, and get out.

So did Hamish. No wonder I breezed through stores with him in tow; he knew already that he wouldn't be trapped in there for long, and if it was a bookstore, it was fun for him, too.

I tried to distract her from the disappointment. "You look great in that new outfit. Is it from Eileen Fisher?"

"Of course it is." She looked at me unhappily, wishing I would look around more.

Not to be deterred, I continued, "Your hair looks good in that new style, too." She had just had her wavy, salt-and-pepper hair cut in a bob; it was chin-length. "Were you sick of tying it up? Was this easier?" My strategy was to distract her, even though I knew that she would see right through it.

"Yes." She wasn't going to be deterred either. "Can't you look at a few more places, just to make sure you're happy?"

"Only if the appraisal finds some structural problem or there is a discrepancy that crops up in the title search," I replied.

She gave up.

I, for one, was elated by the sudden realization that Hamish and I could foot the bills for both of those things, plus buy the firehouse and make whatever changes we wanted to it.

Dad was going to Paris soon for a round of meetings about Nae-Née and whatever else he was involved with, so when we told him about the firehouse, he called Leah Rothstein right away to express interest and arrange for the appraisal. She called back the next day with the news that the owners had agreed to hold the sale pending the appraisal. Apparently, the firehouse had been on the market for a year without selling.

So Dad went away for a week while my mother stayed at the Chelsea apartment.

I got a call from the Rockefeller University Institute a few days later.

"Could you come in and have a look at some decorating plans? The curtains, carpets and furnishings in your new offices need replacing, and the Institute wanted your input." It was the head secretary for the faculty. I agreed to go in the next afternoon, a Friday.

This was nice; I would have a say in the aesthetics. I spent about an hour, looked at samples and chose a floral pattern for my office in pinks, blues and lavenders, and a plain one for Hamish's office, picked out desks, carpets, etc., and that was that. Supposedly, all would be in order when we started work: phones, Internet, computers, everything.

I wasn't going to move my desktop computer from Connecticut. Hamish and I had everything copied onto our laptops. A new external hard drive was enough for now, and then we would get a new desktop computer for our kitchen to share when we actually moved.

Never, ever, would I just keep my whole intellectual life at any place of work. I would save everything to memory sticks every day, then take it home and copy it to our computers. I wanted my writings available to me any time, any place. That was the trouble with having a law degree and being an author, I mused; it made me very cautious and protective of my efforts.

With a week of down time, I insisted that Hamish come with me to several museums. Grumbling about missing work time, he accompanied me and then predictably had a great time once we were there. We visited the Frick, the Metropolitan Museum of Art, the Museum of Natural History, and the Morgan Library & Museum. That last one was a museum in both the library and the exhibit areas; it even had a hidden staircase behind the 3 levels of stacks to the left as you entered the huge, early 20th century room.

Hamish went to the Rockefeller Institute the next week to get familiar with his new laboratory and came back very satisfied. He was a bit frustrated at not being able to start in the office sooner, but it was in an uproar with the renovations. The head secretary had been very nice and soothing about it; she and our future, shared secretary, Patsy, seemed to have the matter well in hand, so I just stayed out of their way. I had met Patsy when I picked out the curtains.

It was obvious to us that we would be starting work while still staying in the Chelsea apartment, but that didn't concern us or my parents. Soon we would be on our own.

We would really be on our own, able to support ourselves alone, living together and working and enjoying life like a normal married couple. I could still see my parents and cat – they weren't far away.

Oh…we were supposed to be getting our own cat.

The weekend before we were to start, I dragged Hamish up to the American Society for the Prevention of Cruelty to Animals. It was the place that appeared on the Animal Planet channel with the blond cop – the one with bangs and a long ponytail – who rescued animals. They were brought here, healed if necessary, and adopted out if at all possible. It was on East 92nd Street between York and 1st Avenues.

They had kittens – kittens that were actually neutered or spayed, vaccinated, and almost ready to go. We had to sign a form promising never to declaw the cute little creature, and never to let her out, before being allowed to look at prospective pets. It was okay to just get one kitten, unlike at Petco, where they wanted people to take an adult cat with every kitten or no deal.

We looked around for a female with a long tail, shorthaired, and friendly. It wasn't difficult; pretty soon we had found a little girl kitten who fit that description. She had green eyes and black fur with some flecks of orange and white – she was a tortie calico. We named her Eowyn for the heroic princess in *The Lord of the Rings* who slayed a Nazgul – an undead, evil king. Hamish was a huge fan of that trilogy; I had read the whole thing after we met.

But the people in charge said that we would have to wait another month; she was still too little. Her mother still wanted her. The cat family had been found in an abandoned apartment in Brooklyn and brought to 92nd Street shortly after the kittens had been born. So we filled out the adoption papers, paid the fees for her care, and left her with her mother.

We were having a great time, though. We stopped at some pet shops on the way home, where we found a cat carrier, a bed that fit inside it, another bed for home, some toys, dishes, a litter box, litter supplies, and I got canned and dry kitten food – Wellness brand – only the best. When Eowyn could come home with us, she would already have everything she needed.

Monday came, and we went to our new offices. I had memory sticks loaded with our research data, our writings, the works – 2 for each of us, just in case.

We settled in, and Hamish took off for the lab like a racehorse being released from the starting gate. It was fun to watch him go, go, go…off down the hall. I sat down in front my computer looking over my files, organizing, and noticed that I could request interlibrary loans from any library in the country without leaving my desk. I could hardly wait to inspect the library, however. No sense bothering the librarians if a book I wanted was already here.

We each had a window that looked out at the East River. My desk was sideways to the window, which had a sofa under it. I could read there, and go to the desk to write, just like I had done at home. The rest room was down the hall. My door led to the reception area, now being staffed by Patsy, our secretary. I would have to get to know her, I decided.

Having a secretary to do my bidding was a new and odd experience. I could ask her to make calls for me, get books from the library for me, answer my phone, hold calls, make excuses to people for me so that I could just keep working, make reservations at restaurants…how weird. I thought about what was reasonable to expect. There was no way that I would ask her to make a reservation for a non-work related meal. It had to be a business lunch or dinner. Other than that, I wasn't sure how to live with a secretary.

Let's see…don't be obnoxious or rude, don't have her do personal things for me beyond taking phone messages and telling me who called and what they wanted, give her a bonus at Christmastime, find out her birthday and get a card and some flowers – and maybe a gift – take her out to lunch on Secretaries Day (when was that?!), which I would have to look up, take her out to lunch to get to know her…

I went out and invited her to lunch for the next day. For the first day of work, I wanted to eat on my own or, if a boss or co-worker intended to whisk me away, be available so that I wouldn't seem unreachable or unsociable.

And what about Hamish in this equation – what should he ask of her? He ought to be sociable too, not that he would think of that on his own. I headed out down the hall to talk to him in his new laboratory.

He was already setting up his nanobots and microscopes and other tools.

He looked up when I appeared, seeming as happy as Charlie in Wonka's chocolate factory again. His graduate students were there, helping him set things up. There were 2 men and a woman, all in their late 20s, wearing lab coats. Hamish was wearing old clothes – navy blue cargo pants and a solid-colored, long-sleeved green tee shirt. He didn't believe in wearing lab coats; the loose sleeves could catch on something.

"Hamish, we might have to go to lunch with our department head or something. I hope you're ready to do that on the first day, just in case."

"Uh-oh. I said I'd go with my new graduate students. This is Jason, Erin and Ron."

I greeted them, shaking hands and introducing myself as the new medical historian.

"Will any of you be coming to my lecture the Thursday after next? It's at 4 p.m., and it's going to be about birth control over the past 3 millennia all over the planet." I was sticking with old stuff for now; the Institute wanted a lecture right away, and they were happy to get familiar with what I already had while I worked up some new stuff.

Erin spoke up; she had a lovely, musical Irish accent. "I'm coming, and I think Ron is, too." Jason said something about an appointment he had made weeks ago, but added that he looked forward to the next one.

"Great – so I'll see you then." Hamish and I decided that we would go to lunch with our boss if he requested it, otherwise it would be the grad students, who would show us the dining facilities. I didn't say it, but I was hoping to just eat with them and get used to this new experience quietly. I got my wish, as it turned out.

With that over with, I felt more and more at ease with our new surroundings, and thrilled that this institution had seen fit to summon me as well as Hamish and recognize my career too.

I went back to my office and Patsy told me I had a phone call. I wasn't expecting one.

It was Dr. Nurse; he was inviting me to join a little chamber music group of professors and doctors at the Institute. "I play the cello," he said, "and although we're not Carnegie hall material, we're okay. Hamish tells me you're pretty good, too."

I laughed and accepted, adding, "I'm not ready for Tanglewood, but – this will be fun."

Time to check out the library. The Rita and Frits Markus Library was a beautiful place. It had white walls, wood paneling, and state-of-the-art electronic research equipment. The librarian at the reference desk came out and showed me how to access everything, and left me to peruse the stacks. I could take out several books at a time. Perhaps I wouldn't be asking Patsy to do any of that; she couldn't go into the stacks and drool over the books for me. That would be like asking someone to eat your food for you.

There was a section on herbal medicine, and I considered preparing a lecture on Wiccans and how the local wise woman in the Dark Ages would prepare remedies in her cauldron outside and often at night during the summer. At last, I could do what I had wanted to do since graduate school but had been unable to access the research materials for: write about exactly what was in the cauldron and what it did for patients. Since leaving university life, I had not had borrowing privileges at a medical library, which would make such a project much, much easier.

Gleeful and happy, I took several books off the shelves and headed back to find the librarian. She set up my I.D. card with the borrowing data I required, and checked them all out. I thanked her and went back to my office.

Patsy was sitting there looking at me as I walked in with 9 books in my arms.

"Oh – let me help you with those!" She grabbed 6 of them and rushed to my office.

I followed with the rest, feeling bad; she must be wondering what to do on the first day, worrying about seeming sufficiently busy, and I just didn't have a pile of work for her to do yet. It was too early in the game for that – no one's fault.

She moved toward my desk and I asked her to put them on the coffee table. I followed suit, and explained how I liked to work; read at the sofa, type at the desk. She nodded.

"Don't worry about not having a regular workload on Day One," I said to her. "Neither of us knows what that will be as yet. Have you worked here long? For other people here, I mean?"

"No," she said. "You're my first bosses here."

"Oh. Well – we'll get used to each other and our jobs soon enough," I said, smiling in what I hoped was a friendly and encouraging manner. "I think I'll start reading now."

"Okay," she said. "I'll just be at my desk if you need me."

She went out. Thus far, I had observed that her demeanor was extremely conventional, that she might be close in age to me, that she was a few inches taller than me, and enormously overweight. She had long, dyed blond hair and a pretty face, and wore a turquoise pants suit.

As soon as the door closed, I went to my computer. I wanted to find a nearby lunch restaurant and make a reservation. For taking my secretary out to lunch, it seemed to me that I should be the one to call for a reservation, not her. I was the hostess and she the guest, so I should do that.

Luckily, I hit pay dirt by using the Google map function; there was a Le Pain Quotidien nearby. It was a wonderful Belgian chain with places all over Manhattan. We could get soups, salads, open-faced sandwiches, café au lait, dessert, whatever. And it was first come, first served. There – done. I knew where I was taking Patsy tomorrow. I hoped she would like it.

I flopped onto the sofa and opened one of the books.

This was going to be fun – the work, the area, everything.

I started reading, determined to prepare a great lecture and future book chapter on the herbal medicines provided by ancient European witches – really just harmless, goddess-worshipping, single women or widows with pet cats.

Chapter 11

Patsy Warne

The next day, at lunchtime, I put down my books and went to the outer office.

Patsy was there, sitting at her desk, typing a letter that Hamish had dictated. She had headphones on.

Apparently, he had dictated lots of memos, letters, and whatever else to go out through his e-mail account, plus a couple of formal things to go on Institute stationery. Hamish was a hunt-and-peck typist; he had labored slowly over his Ph.D. thesis and professional journal articles, never learning how to speed up. I thought it was easier to just memorize the keyboard and get used to moving my fingers around, up to the left and down to the right, but logic got nowhere fast with Hamish on this point.

I didn't want to startle her, so I walked right up to the desk – slowly – and stood quietly in front of her until she looked up.

She looked up right away, without jumping or otherwise freaking out, and gave me one of those looks that formulaic, corporate culture-trained people give, raising her eyes and eyebrows and smiling with exaggerated politeness. Then she took the headphones off.

"Hi Patsy," I said, smiling pleasantly. "Remember I invited you to go out to lunch with me today?"

"Oh! Yes – I just had so much typing to do that I forgot," she said. "Your husband gave me 20 dictations to type, and said he needed them done by 2 p.m."

"Really…did he give any order of priority for them, or just set a blanket preference for the whole batch?" I asked, mildly annoyed at Hamish. 20 dictations – no way to finish in the time requested, I thought. "And when did he give them to you?"

She looked up at me. "45 minutes ago."

"45 minutes ago." I repeated this mildly. "How reasonable of him; I did tell him that I was taking you out to lunch today. He might still be in his lab. Get your coat; we'll stop by and I'll tell him what we're doing, so he won't be laboring under unrealistic expectations."

She stared at me for a moment, then went to the coat hooks along the wall by Hamish's office door and got her turquoise one off of it, plus a huge sage-green felt hat. I got my raspberry pink coat and black hat and led the way out.

Sure enough, Hamish was still in his lab, peering into a microscope while holding the intricate pair of tools that adjusted the nanites under the lenses.

I usually walk rather quietly, and with rubber-soled shoes it was easy to move without announcing my presence, but I wanted him to know we were coming. This was a place where someone's work could be ruined if you sneaked up on them – one false move could cause a mistake in the set-up of an assay in one lab, a broken nanite component in another, or a forgotten idea if someone was startled out of writing the data down.

So I rustled and trod heavily and said to Patsy, "Here he is – good, he didn't go to lunch yet." It worked; Hamish let go of the tools and straightened up to look at us.

"Hi Hamish! I'm taking Patsy out to lunch now, just as I told you I would last night. She'll resume typing all those things that you just gave her when we come back. I don't know about 2 p.m. for a deadline, though. You might want to leave her a note while we're out telling her which things absolutely have to be done by then."

He looked at me as though I were waking him out of trance. I'd seen that look before, whenever he hadn't thought a request through from any angle other than his own. Typical tunnel-vision in an absent-minded professor, I thought.

"Oh! Right…I could tell you now – the letter for Dr. Rowland is the one that needs to go by 2 p.m. The ones that go on Institute letterhead that I have to sign can be ready for 4 p.m. so they can be mailed by 4:30, and that's about it. Sorry – I should have explained all that."

Patsy looked relieved, and I looked bemused and mildly annoyed at him. I knew what we were dealing with, but a new secretary who had just met us must have wondered whether to expect trouble from us and been a bit unnerved by a demand to rush, rush, rush with a ton of typing on her second day. Well…at least one of us had given her something to do. Yesterday she had been stuck sitting there with nothing, looking worried about that.

I kissed him good-bye and led Patsy out.

Outside in the cold wind, I tried to chat amiably but achieved little more than communicating our destination as we tucked our heads into our scarves and tried not to feel the bitter cold wind too much. New York City's grid pattern made it easy to feel the icy breezes.

At least it felt normal; we just walked in what felt like a good mood for a couple of blocks. I found out that Patsy had never been in a Le Pain Quotidien. She seemed up for anything, though, so described it: Belgian, lots of fresh wheat bread, hazelnut spread, 4-berry jam and apricot jam on the tables, vegetable pureed soups, open sandwiches… She started to smile at me and said I was making her hungry. Good, I said; me too.

We arrived at the place and eagerly unwound our scarves and unbuttoned our coats. The wait staff told us to go ahead and sit, and a tall thin girl ushered us in with menus, pointing out the blackboard specials of the day.

Patsy looked around at the wood-paneled place, and stared at the jars of hazelnut and other spreads for sale. She opened the one on the table and took a sniff, then inhaled deeply. I enjoyed watching her; French and Belgian food is wonderful, and I always got a kick out of introducing it to someone who wasn't used to it.

"What is this stuff? It smells wonderful!"

I told her to try it on the bread that out lunches would come with.

When our lunches arrived, each bowl of carrot-ginger soup came with a huge slice of wheat bread, so she took my advice. She couldn't stop going on about how good the hazelnut spread tasted.

I smiled and kept eating my soup. This was going well; she was getting relaxed.

One of the things that I had hoped to find out during this meal was her work history. If I could lull her into a sense of enjoyment, she might just tell me more than what I could discover from reading her resume…which I hadn't asked for yet. I hoped I could do that subtly.

"I'm glad you like it here. There aren't a lot of places near the Institute to eat at what with 3 hospitals clustered around the nearest intersection," I replied. "So – tell me about yourself, and I'll tell you about myself. I wanted to use this visit to get to know you a bit."

She looked up at me warily; I could tell that she was the sort of person who had spent her life gathering more social skills and logging more social interaction time than I ever would. If she wanted to hold something back, she would know how. If I wanted to find it out, I would have to be patient. But for now, I would be satisfied just to find out some basics simply because I was starting with next to no information about her.

"What would like to know?" she asked.

I smiled, and then asked, "Well, I haven't yet seen your resume, so naturally I am curious about your work history, how you came to this particular job – not that that would be on it – and about your life and family. Just regular stuff, and I'll tell the same sorts of things about me. It seems strange to work together and not know anything about each other, don't you think?"

"Yes, it does. I'll give you a copy of my resume when we get back – it's on my computer."

"Thanks. So – since I can't wait to see the general ideas of it – where did you work before you came to the Rockefeller Institute, and how did you end up here?"

She took a bite of her turkey sandwich. She chewed, looked away to her left for a moment, then swallowed. I wondered how truthful she would be; looking to left was supposedly a sign of insincerity, I had heard somewhere.

At last she spoke. "I was in California, in L.A., working at Paramount Pictures for 4 years. I just came back to New York last October."

Wow – I loved movies. I told her so. She smiled. "Really? Me too – and television. That's why I thought it would be fun to work there."

"What did you do for Paramount? Did you like it?"

"I was in charge of a department of secretaries who worked for some television producers. We made their travel and requisition arrangements. It was fun, and I loved it."

"What made you leave such a great job?"

"They cut my position. I couldn't find another one out there, so after a summer there, as much as I love L.A., I had to come home. My mother lives in the Stuyvesant apartments, and my dad lives in the city too. They said to come back and stay with my mother until I could find a job, since I couldn't keep my apartment out there any longer."

That sounded sad; I knew what it was like to have to move out of a place and come home.

It was like a defeat.

I wondered why they would cut her position, though. It was odd. "What do your parents do?" I asked, deciding not to press the issue of the Paramount job.

"My father is a city social worker for homeless people and mentally ill types, such as hoarders, and my mother is a retired nurse."

"Really – my mother is a retired nurse, too." Actually, she had retired when I was little, but kept up with the profession by reading and maintaining her license, always telling me to keep my work skills current, just in case I ended up in need of a job. So I had.

Patsy looked at me politely.

I continued, "What area of nursing did your mother work in? Mine was a triage nurse in a gastroenterologist's office."

She looked at me in alarm. "I don't know – she was a hospital nurse, taking care of patients, but I don't know what branch of medicine she dealt with."

"Oh. I was just curious. I love details. I work with details."

She nodded as if she had just figured out a piece of the puzzle that was me. "I see. I hate details. My boyfriend gets frustrated with me when we go to museums because I can't stand to stay for the whole lecture about whatever it is we're seeing. I keep making him leave before it's finished."

I was appalled but kept my expression neutral. "What museums were these? And tell me a little bit about your boyfriend, how long you've known him, and where and how you met – I love stories like that," I encouraged her.

She seemed to like that. "We met in a bar in Brooklyn. He's from Scotland, like your husband, he repairs boilers and commercial fridges, and we met last November, about a month after I came home. We went away for a weekend to my grandmother's old house in Hyde Park, and Jim wanted to see the FDR museum. But it was so boring, and the tour guide just kept going on and on and on about how FDR built his own wheelchair out of a kitchen chair that I couldn't stand it. I kept wandering around, staring out the windows, so Jim agreed to leave."

I listened, incredulous. "I love historic house museums; I used to do tours in the Mark Twain and Harriet Beecher Stowe Houses in Hartford. The FDR home is the exact one that I intend to drag Hamish to as soon as we get into the swing of things here, and I want to be there in the middle of a week, because the Culinary Institute of America – the "other" C.I.A. – is down the road from it. On Wednesdays, the students open the restaurants to customers and try out their skills, so that's why I want to visit then."

She listened politely, but said nothing. It was clear that we were opposites, but then, she was a secretary and I was a professor. What else did I expect?

I brought the conversation back to her. "So you met Jim at a bar, and started dating. Tell me more. What's his last name? How long has he been in the U.S.? Does he like it here? What sorts of things do you have in common with him?"

"His last name is Wallace, we like to go out drinking, we like movies, shopping, driving around together, and my cat stays at his place. He likes it here, he has a house in Brooklyn, and he's been here for 20 years. He just got his citizenship last year, so he will have to get used to voting soon. I'll go with him and show him what to do."

"Wallace – just like the character in *Braveheart*. Any relation? Do people ask that question a lot?"

"No relation that he can prove, and yes," she grinned, "people ask all the time."

"Hamish is studying for his U.S. citizenship now," I added.

"Cool."

"And you have a cat? Tell me more – I love cats, and Hamish and I are adopting a kitten soon. We can't take her home yet because she's too little, but in a couple more weeks, we can."

"Really? That's great. I got mine in a shelter in L.A. She's 6 years old, fluffy, black with a white belly, and cranky, so I named her Rosalie, like the unhappy blond vampire in the *Twilight* series."

"Do you carry a picture of her with you?"

"No, but I'm going to bring one for my desk."

"Great! I'm going to have one of our kitten too, when we get her. She's a shorthair, mostly black with a little orange tortoise patterning here and there on her. We're going to call her Eowyn, for a character in *The Lord of the Rings*."

"I saw all 3 of those movies. But I don't remember her. Which one was she?"

"Oh, she was the human princess of Rohan who slayed an undead, evil king – a Nazgul. It was really cool; the magic spell granting him immunity in battle had one escape clause in it: that a woman could kill him. He banked on the idea that only men would go to battle, and lost. She put her sword through his helmet after he fatally injured her nice, father-figure uncle, the king of Rohan. It was a great moment."

"That *is* cool," Patsy said.

"So your father is a social worker. Does he like what he does?"

"He loves what he does. He went to Harvard, and my grandmother expected him to be a stockbroker or investment banker because he majored in social and political economics, but he said he would never do that. So he taught for a while at N.Y.U., and then got into social work."

"Wow. And he lives in Manhattan?"

"Yes – in the West Village."

"And you live with your mother?"

"For now, though I stay in Brooklyn a lot with Jim, too. I want to see my cat, and she wasn't happy with my mother's cat, so I put her there. Jim is crazy about her now. She climbs under the covers with him and purrs."

"That's great. I love it when cats show affection like that."

Patsy smiled at me. "So – what about you? How did you become a professor of medical history? I haven't seen your resume, so I don't know much about you either."

My turn now…it was time to make good on my promise to tell her about myself.

"My CV should be on the Institute's website in another hour or so, or so the Technical Services people led me to expect. So will Hamish's CV. I gave them to them last week, and they made us sit for I.D. photos. But I'll tell you a bit now."

"What's a CV?" Patsy interrupted.

"It's an academic resume that goes on for more than a page; it stands for curriculum vitae. Mine goes on for 3 pages, and Hamish's goes on for 6. He's 10 years older than I am, so that makes sense. He was in the war in Kuwait with the British army as a chemical weapons officer."

"Oh."

"So…let's see…the story of my professional and academic life…I went to William Smith College, majored in history and women's studies, graduated after 4 years, then attended the Sorbonne University in Paris where I got my Doctor of Science degree in the history of medicine, concentrating on women's health and birth control, and then went on to law school right after that. I met Hamish there, while he was in medical school. He had just finished his Ph.D. engineering and started medical school a year earlier."

"Wow. Where was this?"

"Harvard Law School and Medical School. Hamish did his Ph.D. at M.I.T."

"When did you guys get married?"

"In the summer of 2002, late in June."

"Why so long after graduation? Didn't you both graduate in 1999?"

"We did. I had to help my grandmother in Provence, in the south of France. She needed home care, and no one else in the family was available. My aunts and uncle didn't live in the area, and I am a writer, so I was able to stay with her. I even got another book written during that, time, a kids' book about the Chartreux cats she used to breed."

"What's a Chartreux cat?"

"It's a solid gray one with a round head, and French. She and my grandfather used to breed them, and I used to stay with them in the summer when I was a kid. He died while I was working on my D.Sci."

"Is that like a French Ph.D.?"

"Yeah, pretty much equivalent to it."

"What was the book you wrote?"

"Just a fun one about the lavender fields and the cats and my grandmother; it gave me a chance to include some colorful pastel drawings that I had been accumulating whenever I visited her. The book is called *Mielle: Chatte Chartreuse, Reine de La Maison*. It features my grandmother's queen breeding cat, Eponine, who pretty much ran the house. She was a hilarious cat, and very friendly. It's probably the only children's book I'll ever do. I like to write science fiction and history – well, herstory – of medicine more."

"Why do you also write fiction? I mean, you're already really busy with history – herstory – of medicine lectures and books and articles."

"Well…I like to play goddess, and the best way to do that is to write fiction, because fiction isn't real, so if anyone gets hurt in it, neither are they. I'm such a witch that way."

"What do you mean, you're such a witch?"

"Do you know much about Wicca?"

"No – I thought it was devils and stuff like that – evil."

"A lot of people do. That's because they don't know anything about it – only the superstitious nonsense that they grew up hearing from religious fundamentalists. Wicca is a revival of the ancient European, goddess-based, nature-worshipping pre-Christian religion that included herbal medicine. People who were sick used to go to the local wise woman, the witch, when they weren't feeling well."

"Are you going to lecture about this? And what was this Wiccan woman like?"

"Yes, I am. She was typically a single woman, often an old widow who wore black in mourning for her husband, with no one for regular company except her pet cat. She brewed herbal potions in her cauldron, and in the warmer seasons of the year, she did it at night, the coolest time of day – hence the eerie yet familiar image of a lone witch stirring potions – or she would be doing her laundry. Everyone had a cauldron then – it was during what was known as the dark ages, the time before universities were founded, when Christianity had not yet shed its "light" on everyone."

"But what about being such a witch in some way – what way?"

"One of the basic philosophies of Wicca is that you may do whatever you want as long as it doesn't hurt anyone else…unlike Christianity. That religion did its work so well that by the time it had spread all over Europe, only one woman was left alive in every village, and it wasn't the wise woman. Also, not too many cats survived. They had to go – they were in cahoots with the wise women. And then…in came bubonic plague, the Black Death. That's because there were no more cats to control the flea-bearing, plague-transmitting rodent population. That's what came of messing with the environment and projecting religion onto the natural world."

"You sound anti-Christian. Don't you worry about how people might take all that?"

"No. Objectively speaking, this is all fact and has been proven a long time ago – especially the environmental parts. As for the herstorical side of it, this is a very good time, an open-minded time, in which to explain the rest. I heard it all in college from a male history professor over 20 years ago, not just in women's studies classes from feminist professors. The Christians have plenty of good ideas. No religion is all good or all bad. The worst religious idea is that one's own religion is the only good one, the only one that counts, and that all others are therefore monstrous and should be stamped out in their entirety."

She stared at me for a moment, then nodded. "That makes sense."

I grinned. "Well – I'm glad you think so. Do you want dessert? I was thinking of getting a little raspberry tart and coffee," I invited her.

"Sure – thanks. I'll have a chocolate pear tart. Those looked little, and interesting."

We caught the waitress's eye and she took our order.

The conversation turned to Nae-Née, which I had expected it to do sooner or later. Patsy told me that she was pro-choice, and though that the nanite sounded like the best birth-control method she had ever heard of. She added that anti-choice protests annoyed her. At last, I thought; something in common!

After lunch, Patsy resumed her typing and finished it all by 3:30. I was glad I had pointed out to Hamish that he had to think about the person who would actually do his typing chores while showing our secretary that we were reasonable people.

My books were waiting for me, but first I read the resume that Patsy e-mailed. She did that just before diving back into Hamish's dictations.

It was a page of densely-packed information. I was used to short entries that listed many items. Something puzzled me about this document: Patsy had finished her Bachelor's degree in 1999, the same year that I had finished my formal education. Since she had mentioned that we were the same age, I was confused by this. Her father had graduated from Harvard, her mother had been a hospital nurse, and yet she would have been 29 years old when she completed her undergraduate work.

That mystery would have to wait, though. I needed to get a feel for my new job, so that I would know typically how much effort it took to crank out a new lecture every couple of weeks. Back to the history books and the computer I went, reading and making notes, outlining a talk on hygiene and its effects on patient care and medical practice.

I peeked out at her once when I needed some post-it notes; she was staring at her computer screen intently. She looked startled, so I asked her if she was okay.

"Oh, yeah – I was just reading your CVs, taking a few minutes to slow down since I got the 2 o'clock stuff typed and ready."

"Oh. Well – good. I'll just go back to reading. See you later."

I went back to work.

The day ended on a positive enough note, I thought.

That evening, I managed to extract my husband from the lab by 5 o'clock. We decided to learn the subway route back to Chelsea as long as the freezing wind was still in the air. It was easy – we took the 6 south to 5th Avenue, switched to an E train, and rode it to West 23rd Street. The difficult part was waiting for trains and cramming ourselves into the crush of people commuting back from wherever at the same time. Welcome to rush hour, I thought, promising myself to rearrange my routine or walk in order to avoid this in the future.

We got to talk a bit while we waited.

"How was lunch with Patsy?" Hamish asked.

"Good. I found out a few things about her, and after lunch I looked at her resume. This is her first job at the Institute. She was in L.A. for 4 years working at Paramount. She loved it."

"That's nice."

"A couple of things about her don't make sense, but maybe they will after a while."

"Like what?"

"She had never eaten in a Le Pain Quotidien before today – didn't even know what they are – yet she's a New Yorker. She was here for most of her life, and only in L.A. for 4 years. Plus, we're the same age but she just graduated from college, from the New School, in 1999."

"Maybe she flunked out and had to change schools. She might have partied. And she's so huge that she'd have to lose half her body weight to be healthy, so it's no surprise about the restaurant chain. They sell delicious but healthy foods there, not junk."

I looked at him, surprised, but thought, that could be it.

I guess I would find out one way or the other as we settled in.

Chapter 12

Our Firehouse – and Fame

Dad got back from Europe and said that the appraisal had found nothing wrong with the firehouse; soon he was brokering the sale with Leah Rothstein. He seemed to be a really good mood about it, and I told him so.

"Bien sûr!" he said, lapsing into French. He glanced at Hamish and switched back to English. "My daughter is going to have her own home with her husband and you two will have your own cat, but not be too far away from us. What's not to be in a good mood about?" he said, as the four of us headed yet again to Le Grainne Café. Hamish spoke some French, but wasn't fluent. Dad didn't like leave Hamish wondering what was going on.

My mother grinned at us. She was excited too – this was exactly what she wanted, too.

"We get to keep Spock, you're getting Eowyn soon; this will be perfect!" she sounded thrilled. "I'm staying around while you get settled in. We can shop for things together, like furniture and carpeting and curtains, and I can be there while you're at work to meet the movers and carpet installers and whomever else. You'll be all set up in no time."

Dad looked at us. "In that case, I'm going to do most of my work in New York for a while. I don't want to stay home alone in Connecticut. Zoe can feed Spock until we get back."

And so it went. Evenings and weekends were spent with my mother, trolling the antique shops and boutiques, and the corner of the living room became a temporary storage area for tablecloths, bolts of curtain fabric, and new bedding once I had found the perfect canopy bed for our room on the top floor.

The closing on the firehouse happened 2 weeks after Dad's announcement.

Carpets had been chosen and measurements made – I didn't want cold bedroom floors in the winter – so two days later, on a Friday, the carpets were laid.

That evening, Hamish and I spent the evening hailing a cab and toting all the stuff over to the place. The beds and other furniture for all three of the bedrooms would arrive the next day, when I could wait with my mother. I didn't like the idea of her waiting alone, but Dad and Hamish didn't think the moving men would be any threat, so I had let her oversee the carpet-laying that day. The mattresses, however, wouldn't arrive until Monday, which was when the moving van with our stuff from Connecticut was coming.

I had hired a professional seamstress to make curtains out of the bolts of fabric. The walls were all painted in nice shades of pastel blues and ivories, so I saw no need to redo the walls. All this moving would be over with soon, I hoped.

My mother was in her element, having a great time. She loved waiting for people to bring home furnishings and watching it all get installed. It must have been fun for her to imagine us living happily on our own once it was all finished, too. She certainly said so often enough.

"Soon your father and I will be able to come over for dinner here!" she must have said 10 times as we unpacked the kitchen things Monday evening. We had gotten lucky; the sofas had arrived that day, too. I had gotten some comfortable, tapestry-cloth covered ones – a 3-seater and a loveseat – from Jennifer's Convertibles. With the exception of a huge, rectangular Persian carpet that Hamish had somehow managed to bring home from a trip to Iran in 2000 (a scientific conference), the whole place was done up in floral patterns. Come to think of it, the Persian carpet was a floral too – a pale ivory covered with flowers and birds, an Isfahan pattern, bought at the Tehran bazaar.

Dad and Hamish were on the sofa, sated with Indian take-out food. It had been a while since my parents had wanted Indian food, but they knew we could get great food in New York.

It was quiet; the new flat-screen TV wouldn't arrive until Wednesday. The curtains would be installed tomorrow. Soon there would be nothing to do but add little details here and there, the sort of thing that everyone did after settling into a new home – gradually, and over time. Hamish and I were staying here tonight.

My mother said that her work here was finished. Any further changes were up to us. She and Dad were going back to Connecticut this weekend. They were so pleased that they kept grinning from ear to ear, satisfied beyond all belief to see us settled someplace together, alone together, and near them in a home that we would likely keep for decades.

We got Eowyn on Thursday. I was glad that it had worked out this way, because I hadn't wanted to put her in the Chelsea apartment and then move her again after every last fussy moving event was over with. She couldn't reach the curtains; I had ordered the kind that ran across the tops of the windows, and used the white blinds.

The kitten was thrilled with her new home, and she drove us crazy, racing around the rooms, leaping onto everything, and then falling asleep, purring loudly, up against one of us. Hamish was in cat heaven over her every antic. I had fun getting her smile at us, sweet-talking to her and staring at her with my eyes almost shut (that's how cats smile). She smiled back at me every time, and rolled around on her back near me. She wasn't even wrecking the furniture thanks to regular nail-clipping and lots of scratching posts placed throughout the house.

The cable company was easy to deal with; the firehouse had outlets for phones, television and Internet in every room, so I walked to East 23rd Street that Saturday, waited in line, and brought the cable boxes and parts home. Hamish was sitting at the dining room table typing on his laptop when I walked in, lugging two big orange bags of equipment. He saw me and jumped up to relieve me of the load.

I certainly felt relieved. Hamish followed me all over the house, carrying stuff to wherever it belonged. Soon we had a television set up in the living room, facing the kitchen – as I mentioned, one could see straight across the back of the ground floor of the firehouse. There were cable outlets more elsewhere, one in each bedroom, so we got smaller TVs for each one. We didn't want land line phones; we had cell phones. The Internet adapter was in the kitchen, at the desk, and we had Wi-Fi all over the house.

Time to buy more food; Saturday was easier for that because Whole Foods wasn't too crowded. The worst time to go was during and just after rush hour, when it would be literally choked with commuters. Lines stretched all over the place and shoppers could barely move among the aisles to select goods. Hamish accompanied me to both Whole Foods, which was at Union Square, and Trader Joe's after that. Too bad there was no SAM'S club.

Now I had every herb and spice necessary to work with, plus vinegars, oils, dry goods, etc. Hamish helped me carry it all, and he had fun wandering among the aisles picking out other gourmet goodies.

It was a great place, and we soon had fixed it up to our taste and specifications.

We had hardwood floors in the living room with the standard American fixture of a flat-screen TV, artwork on the walls commemorating our travels around the world, and wooden bookcase lining the walls. Our own personal combined library, representing our many interests and intellectual curiosities, filled them.

That fabulous kitchen was absolutely perfect for an at-home chef, and I made good use of the place whenever I get the chance. This was fueled by many trips to Williams-Sonoma stores, of which the island had many, and a constantly increasing collection of cook's tools, bakeware, and French cookware. I suppose it was inevitable after the training that my mother put me through, combined with a lot of leeway to cook and bake whatever thrilled me. I was in cook's heaven with the Whole Foods stores, The Lobster Place, Chelsea Market, and sometimes Chinatown's unusual ingredients.

On the top level, we had a beautiful bedroom. Our low-to-the-floor four poster bed was made out of beautiful carved cherry wood. It had filmy white fabric draped over the top with a rose-and-iris patterned canopy that matched our curtains. It was the focal point of the room. I insisted on getting wall-to-wall carpeting so that we wouldn't feel so cold in the winter.

The bathroom was a fun room. It looked out to the back garden, and the huge paned window was draped with lace and filmy white curtains for privacy. There was a good reason for this: a huge white marble tub with room for two is right underneath it. There was also a shower stall with a sliding glass door.

At last we had what we had so desperately needed for our marriage: total privacy.

We made good use of it.

But I'm not the sort of person who likes to describe her sex life for total strangers, so that's all I'm going to say on that subject.

I was just as bad about love letters. When I'm dead, I don't want anyone to read whatever Hamish and I wrote to each other, even if some graduate student or professional chronicler is hoping to enter the data into a historical record. Tough.

I would do what Bess Truman did: memorize everything when I'm old, then destroy the letters, cards, and whatever other evidence of our emotional correspondence.

She burned hers. But we had moved into a firehouse, which ironically meant that there was no fireplace. The whole purpose of this place had originally been to prevent and eradicate fires, not start them. I bought a shredder and put under the desk in the kitchen, by the computer. For now, I just used it to prevent identity theft, shredding junk mail, outer envelopes from bills, and whatever else seemed worthy of obliteration.

Hamish and I had quite a collection amassed already: anniversary cards, birthday cards, little notes from whenever he gave me flowers, little cards in boxes of earrings plus the ones with my engagement ring, and so on. And then there were the e-mails…I would have to delete those when I got really old. And all of this assumed that I wouldn't get hit by a truck and not be able to do this first…

Enough obsessing.

We were enjoying our lives in the firehouse, and so was our new kitten. She was so cute, racing around and around, up and down the stairs on the right-hand side of the house, then falling asleep next to us as we watched television. Eowyn didn't care what we did as long as we spent some time with her in the evening, letting her run all over the house and then sitting still so she could sleep up against one of us. She was a great kitten, and was growing at a great rate, gobbling food with enthusiasm and swatting her toys under the furniture.

I thought about the firehouse on Valentine's evening as we sat in the huge tub, soaking and sharing strawberries after a great dinner at Jubilee.

"Only one more thing to do to this place," I told Hamish.

"What's that?"

"When it warms up, I'm having the garage door and front door painted a pale blue. I don't like that beige-to-off-white color."

"Okay. Whatever you want," he said.

"And I found a door-knocker online that looks like an iris for the front door. I have it, and I'll get it put on after the paint job."

"Okay."

There was a wisteria vine that grew over the front of the building; Leah Rothstein had told us it had purple blossoms. I was thrilled, and looked forward to the warm weather.

The only thing left to do was get our car. We didn't need to use it right away, but in the spring I wanted to drive Hamish to Hyde Park for that museum and restaurant trip. I told him about the idea, and he looked really excited.

"We've been planning to do that for years," he said. "After we get the car, let's reserve the time in our schedules – tell the Institute that we want to go away for a week."

"Or just make sure we can do it over spring break, if ours doesn't coincide with the one at the C.I.A.," I suggested.

"Oh – right. You're the logistics officer in this marriage," he said, grinning.

The next day, that reporter from *The New York Times* called our office. We had been expecting to hear from him sooner or later, and now he had gotten back to us, wanting to conduct a joint interview and get our story out. He had a deadline of Friday morning.

His name was Jason Bridges, and he had been doing this for years – human interest stories, usually about New York City professionals. I guessed every reporter had a specialty.

He arrived the next day in mid-morning with a photographer, who spent about 45 minutes right away posing me and Hamish in our offices, together and separately, plus in Hamish's laboratory (that was just Hamish). Then we sat down with Jason Bridges, a man in his mid-forties with wavy, sandy hair, grey eyes, and a nondescript outfit of khaki pants, tan belt and blue oxford shirt under a wool sweater and overcoat.

We talked for another 45 minutes or so – I didn't watch the clock, but that's what it felt like. He drew the entire story of our lives out of us, both separately and together, asking about life since we were married, professional frustrations and disappointment, and finally the flash of insight that inspired and spawned Nae-Née.

After bringing the tale up to the present and hearing how we had ended up in our current posts together – plus where else Hamish had been offered a position without me – Bridges was satisfied. He saved his notes on his laptop, saved the recording of our interview on his portable audio recorder, and packed up.

"Well, thank you both very much for your time. I've got to go back to the office and write this up. The presses are waiting to roll as we speak."

"Thank you for interviewing us." Hamish and I sounded like a pair of twins in sync again. Bridges looked like he was taking mental notes.

We showed him out and said good-bye.

The next day, the story appeared, both in print and online. My mother rushed out to the local stores in Connecticut and bought as many copies as she could find. I just saved a digital copy. The story was called "Husband-and-Wife Team Create Birth Control Nanite System; Settle in Manhattan." I looked at the tiny lettering across the bottom of the online version. It said that the story had appeared on page A4 of the print edition.

It ran for two pages online and included a photo of me and Hamish. We were looking at it on my office computer screen; I was seated, scrolling through the document, while Hamish stood over me, peering at the content. Fortunately, it did not give our address at home; it merely alluded to the fact that we had found and moved into our dream home in Greenwich Village. Good; I didn't want to be bothered coming and going from home like some celebrity. I didn't want to be a superstar. I didn't want to have to duck into the nearest obliging alley or shop as I tried to walk about, and I didn't want to feel lots of eyes trained on me.

Hamish assured me that no one was all that interested in scientist and a medical historian. We had developed something that would revolutionize birth control – streamline it, even – and we would soon blend into the background after having had our 15 minutes of fame. I hoped so; I wanted to enjoy living in New York City and, and get used being on our own.

We really hadn't had time yet to settle into any particular routine; the past month and a half had been nothing but upheaval, change, moving, getting used to new jobs, and excitement as we sculpted our environment to our liking and adopted a kitten.

I wondered when I would play the violin again, and work in some fiction writing, and figure out how to fit in trips to museums. Maybe I could play the violin a couple of evenings each week and on weekends; with a job, my routine had to change. The museums would fit in according to exhibit schedules, I realized, and in the evenings and on weekends as well. The romantic trips alone with Hamish would be intermittent.

Soon after the interview ran, I decided to make a garden on the roof of our firehouse. It wasn't so much about growing food – though I did plant some strawberries and raspberries – as it was about contributing my own air-scrubber and heat-reflector to the city's rooftops. Hamish helped me for an entire weekend in late May, lugging soil and grass seeds home and up to our roof. Soon we had a lawn that covered the firehouse, with the exception of the skylight.

As for Eowyn, she would be a bit older when we started going away. I had spoken with Jordan about her. The teenager loved cats and kittens, and so did her mother. Eowyn could stay across the hall at my parents' apartment in Chelsea whenever we went away, so that they could feed her and check on her.

I was surprised at how easy it was to arrange to have a life. It must have been because my parents were in the area first, and we already knew some people, I told myself.

Time started to go by faster and faster.

Chapter 13

Patsy Warne, Continued

While I got used to my new duties as a medical history lecturer and Hamish dived into his new laboratory and teaching activities, my mother and I had finished getting the firehouse ready to live in. In just under a month, it was over and we were all set. When we brought Eowyn home with us, I took lots of photos of her.

I brought in a pair of identical framed photos of Eowyn lolling and smiling in her ring-pillow bed and let Patsy see before putting them on my desk and Hamish's. She took the frame and starting loudly oohing and aahing about it.

"Ooh! How *cute*! Is she a lot of fun? Does she climb all over you and try to dive under the covers with you? Does she get everything she wants?"

I was a bit taken aback. I continued to smile and look pleased, but Patsy was so loudly effusive that I found her insincere, even though I knew she liked cats.

"She's loads of fun. I don't spoil her like Hamish does – he doesn't discipline her much – but I did get her lots of scratching posts and pads. She can't reach the new curtains, so yeah, we're having a great time with her. She doesn't go under the covers, though. And we're glad."

Patsy stopped shrieking and handed back the framed picture.

"So," I said, hoping I hadn't offended her by not being on the same cooing wavelength, "did you get a photo of your cat yet? Hamish and I would love to see."

Hamish was putting his coat on the hooks near his office door. He looked up at us, nonplussed. I knew he wanted to take off for his lab after checking his e-mail, not chat, but he didn't want to be blatantly rude, either. Besides, it was a chance to see a cat photo.

We looked at Patsy. She was wearing a dress today, an ugly, brown-and-blue-patterned thing. Her hair was down long, and she towered over me by several inches. Hamish loomed silently over her by a few more.

"Um, yeah, I have one, but I didn't get it framed yet. It's in my desk drawer."

She took out a little zip-lock bag from her upper desk drawer and handed it to us. Inside was a photo of a beautiful green-eyed, fluffy black cat with a white chest and white paws.

"Wow, that's a beautiful, elegant-looking cat. Look, Hamish – this is Patsy's cat, Rosalie. This cat goes under bed covers, and purrs for Patsy's boyfriend, Jim. He loves having her with him."

Hamish took the photo and smiled. It was good to see him being sociable toward our secretary; she must have thought that he seemed utterly disinterested in everything about her up until now, dashing off each day after giving her a bunch of recordings to type up.

"That's a lovely cat. Where did you get her?"

"In L.A., at a shelter. She was 3 months old, spayed, and yowling at me as I walked by. That was it; I wanted her as soon as she called out to me."

"That's terrific," Hamish said. "How did you get her back here?"

"On the plane. I hated to let her fly in the cargo hold, but summer was over, and I couldn't get her into the cabin. She still seems upset; she hides under furniture more than she used to."

"That's terrible! Avril has used Air France to bring cats home from Provence, and they let cats fly in the cabin. What is it, 8 small animals per flight for $50 each?"

"Yes," I answered. "But I think Air France works with Delta Airlines in the U.S., and they don't do the same thing. That's another reason why I was worried about moving across the country, so far away from everything we know. Nothing familiar out there, plus a travel problem for any cat of ours."

Hamish stared at me. "I hadn't realized that. Well, we're here now, and this is the perfect place for both of us. Plus they want us as a team – the Nae-Née inventors."

I grinned at him. "Well, we won't keep you. You probably want to get back to your next quality-of-life-improving nanite development."

He looked relieved; he said yes and ducked into his office.

I turned to Patsy. "How do you like it here so far? Have you found some friends to hang out with at lunch? Do you like this area? Is it fairly easy to get back and forth from home?"

She walked back behind her desk and put the photo away. I was still standing there holding both of our new ones, framed. Maybe I could get Patsy a frame for hers as a surprise, I thought to myself.

"It's not bad," she said. "It takes an hour to get to Jim's place, and just a half hour to get to either of my parents' places. And the other secretaries are nice. There are several of them who are my – our – age. I keep forgetting, we're both 40 years old."

"That's good. I'm glad. Well, I'll just put these photos on our desks and get going with my work." I went into Hamish's office first and put the Eowyn photo on the desk. He picked it up and grinned.

"This is great. She's the best kitten ever. I love you!" and he suddenly grabbed me by the waist and squeezed me.

I squeezed back, putting the photo down just in time.

"So – where do you want to go for Valentine's Day?" Hamish asked. It was on Monday, and this was only Wednesday. We had a bit more work to do in order to settle into the firehouse, but we were almost through.

I thought about it for a moment. "How about Jubilee? We loved that place, and it's not too far away."

"Okay," he said. "I'll get escargots again."

"Great – I'll call right away and make a reservation." No way was I going to wait for Hamish to do it; he was too absent-minded, and as a result, we had almost missed eating at the Boom in Kuwait for Valentine's Day a few years earlier. But that was another story…

I took my new cat photo and went back out past Patsy and into my office.

By now, I had another day before I was to deliver my second lecture. Hamish had attended the first one and reported that the people around him seemed interested in the material and impressed with my delivery of it. It was an old one, though, and I had had plenty of time to perfect it and try it out on audience after audience. This was new. Oh well. Time for another topic; I was almost through polishing it off, and I decided that I would do a practice run of it with Patsy as my captive audience.

I went out to her desk and explained what I wanted of her.

"Patsy, as you know, my job is to write totally new lectures to deliver every other Thursday. There's something I would like you to do for me – something I don't know if you've ever done before."

She looked up at me, obviously wondering what was coming next.

I continued, "I would like to print out and read what I have to you with a red pen in hand, to spot errors and awkward phrases, to make sure that it flows well without typos or other problems. There's nothing worse than a dry, dull lecture full of choppy sentences that run on and on without a break. I just want to test it out the day before and make sure that it's easy to follow along with."

She looked a bit surprised. "Okay," she said. "When do you want to do this?"

"After lunch, I guess. I'm putting the finishing touches on it this morning."

"Okay. That's perfect; I should be through typing whatever your husband wants by then."

Hamish appeared 20 minutes later as I sat at my computer, tabbing through the document, looking for problems.

"So you've recruited a captive audience?" he said, with a devilish grin.

"She told you?"

"Yeah – she wanted to make sure that I wouldn't mind if you monopolized her this afternoon, and made a regular, pre-lecture practice of it."

"Did she put it that way?"

"No, of course not. And I said it was no problem. She's our secretary, not just mine, and you don't demand much of her. I told her as much. She seems worried that we won't be satisfied with her."

Huh. "Neither of us have lots of experience directing a secretary. In fact, you've only had one, and that was in Austria, where it didn't do you much good. I've had none. I just hope we seem polite and don't lapse into asking her to do anything personal for us. Oh – I made the Jubilee reservation, by the way. It's for 7 o'clock on Valentine's Day evening."

He smiled at me. "I'll get you some roses. How's the new lecture coming?"

"Good – I think I like it. Are you coming to hear it?"

"Of course." He kissed me and left, already thinking about his nanites.

I looked at my lecture for another few minutes, then printed it up.

Patsy's resume said that she had majored in some sort of television production area before switching to general studies. I wondered about that; the New School for Social Research had other programs, such as art, design, liberal arts (which meant a variety of possible majors), and of course social research. Why had she switched from such a specific area of study to one that was so bland after being excited by television? And that was another odd thing; the New School didn't offer any majors about television...more mysteries.

I took a book with me to lunch in the dining room, in case I didn't find anyone to eat with. Several times, I had sat with Hamish and a group of 4 other scientists from different departments whose work intersected with nanites. They were all male and all in their 50s with well-established academic careers. They seemed nice, and welcomed me into the group.

I was used to listening to scientists talk, and could follow along with their discussions. It was nothing that I could write about on my own, but I understood thanks to having married my own personal science encyclopedia. Hamish was always willing to satisfy my curiosity about whatever came to mind, which typically led to fun conversations wherever we were.

But Hamish wasn't here. Later, I found out that he had had to write a detailed graph for an article, and had asked Patsy to order him something from a Chinese place to eat in his office.

So I got some soup and spicy shrimp and rice and found a seat by myself. It was just as well; I was looking forward to flipping through this book. It was a large one, full of medieval prints, hot off the presses on glossy paper. Basically, it was a coffee-table book for medical historians on hygiene methods throughout the ages – both for doctors and patients.

Definitely not something you wanted to be perusing with company…some of the tales and illustrations in it were a bit gross. I placed the huge book – about 4 times the size of standard hard-cover book – on the table in front of my tray, facing me, and opened it with 2 hands. I flipped to a spot that I wanted to look at, and settled in.

What I was hoping to do was to find a few more photos to add to the PowerPoint presentation that was my new lecture, and click and drag them in from the book's CD. I already had a lot, but I was polishing it off, and at this point it was just fun. The idea was to make it entertaining as well as educational, with some bizarre and shocking images as well as the expected and merely intriguing ones.

As I started to eat, I noticed Patsy walk in with 3 other secretaries. They were all her age.

The Institute had lots of secretaries, all managed and overseen by a Human Resources department, and of varying ages and experience. Patsy had obviously found herself a group that could meet at the same time and chat about things of mutual interest. Good.

I ate my lunch and smelled the pages of the book – glossy, new, and smooth. I liked that smell. Soon I found some photos that looked promising. With any luck, they would work well in the new lecture.

A few more minutes went by, and the secretaries reappeared with their trays full of food. They sat down together a couple of tables away from me. I was eating at 1 o'clock, so there weren't a lot of people in here – just a couple of older men in a corner and few graduate students by the far window.

The secretaries were a bit noisy, but I managed to tune them out while I ate most of my food and read the blurbs with the photos.

Then I started to hear bits and pieces of what they were saying.

It was mostly about boyfriends, husbands, babies, sex, chores, commutes, and work.

The husbands didn't help with chores, the commutes took too long and were too crowded, work was dull, babies were fun – they lost me there – and they were going to go shopping for the latest fashion trends at T.J. Maxx or Marshall's, then move on to the Gap or Macy's. They wanted to spend the weekend looking at clothes or taking kids to play groups.

Kids? Patsy didn't have any, and I perked up without turning around. I realized that one of the secretaries had a new baby, and another had a niece and nephew she was going to babysit for. So only one of the four had kids. Two of them, including Patsy, kept referring to boyfriends, sometimes just by their names, so it took a few minutes to figure out that the other two were married. The one with the niece and nephew wasn't married.

Maybe I could get Patsy a picture frame at T.J. Maxx, I thought. There were frame shops everywhere, but that place tended to have the most interesting ones.

It was the story of my life; I preferred to hang out with men, and not the kind who liked team sports. I realized that I was sitting apart from yet another group of women, doing my own thing while they talked about clothes and reality shows, but I had no interest in joining them.

I was glad I had Bethany. When she and I got together – or just chatted on the phone – we talked about gourmet food and books, or travel...never about fashion. We might mention shopping for new clothes to replace old ones, but we didn't care about trends. What counted was what we liked, and then we moved on.

No wonder I only had a few female friends. Oh well.

Patsy suddenly appeared at my side.

"Hi Avril. We saw you over here, by yourself, and wondered if you'd like to join us."

I looked up at her, nonplussed. Then I smiled. "Thanks! But I'm almost ready to go back. I was looking through this book to see if any of its photos would work well with that lecture." The book was open to an illustration of a black, 19th-century, man's tail coat.

"Oh. Okay, I'll be up soon. What's that?" she asked, pointing to the picture.

I looked at the caption. "It's a typical 19th-century American surgeon's operating coat. They hardly ever washed them in the early part of the century, so the guys liked to wear black. This one was owned by a surgeon that Dr. Elizabeth Blackwell, the first woman doctor to get a medical degree, interned with. He never washed his jacket, and bragged that it held its shape when he took it off, thanks to all the blood and pus-spatters."

She looked revolted. "That's disgusting."

"I know – that's why I told the dean that my lectures should not be delivered during meals. And why I was reading this while I was alone. Don't worry – the next lecture will be about something else...herbal potions of ancient European witches, I think. I'll get the books for that one out tomorrow, when the ones I ordered from Interlibrary Loan arrive. I wanted to do that lecture first, but realized I have to time the preparations with access to books from other libraries. At least it gets me planning ahead."

She looked a bit overwhelmed by my reply. I had the habit of saying an awful lot whenever someone asked me a question. Finally, she nodded.

I stood up, shut the huge book, and tucked it under my arm so I could take the tray away.

"See you back there – enjoy the rest of your lunch. I won't be ready for the test run for another hour, so no big rush," I told her.

She smiled and went back to her friends.

As I headed out of the dining hall, I heard giggling at that table. It reminded me of high school, where I had had a couple of friends from time to time, but mostly had avoided cliques of popular girls while doing my own thing at the all-girls Ethel Walker School.

I shook off the feeling and walked out.

Patsy listened later, sitting on the sofa next to me as I droned on and on, trying to sound interesting, showing her the photos that would be projected with every other slide. Her eyes glazed over repeatedly. It was nothing like practicing the stuff on my husband or parents.

I was worried. My husband and parents were biased listeners who were always complimentary of my efforts. Did I suck? Was I boring? What was wrong? I didn't have too many people to practice on.

Despite the disturbing test run of the lecture, the real thing was well-received the next afternoon. People kept coming up to compliment me on detail, content, delivery, the choice of photos, and how it helped them to make sense of their own projects.

Maybe I was worrying about nothing.

But I had noticed a couple of typos in the draft as I read it off to Patsy, who hadn't spotted a single error.

At least she had been there physically, enabling me to pretend that I had a live audience.

Chapter 14

Sound Bites and News Flashes

I followed the news as usual, sitting glued to the websites for *The New York Times*, *National Geographic*, *Discover*, *Time*, and others each morning until I had seen the most recent news of women's issues, the environment, reproductive and population issues, and politics.

Following a routine of finding, saving and reading the stories, plus checking the photos, I archived them all. When I was in law school, I did not have the Internet constantly available to me, so I had had the onerous chore of collecting a stack of paper photocopies as well as books in order to assemble research. Thanks to computers and flash drives, I was now doing a lot of that work in advance, even before I knew what project it was for, and saving trees, too.

The days blurred as I followed a routine: arrive at the office at 9:30 a.m.; read the news; perhaps go to the Institute's library, perhaps just read what I had; write bits and pieces of a lecture; break for lunch, either on campus or off, usually at Le Pain Quotidien to do some people watching; back to the office for more work on lectures; out at 4:30 p.m. Wednesday evenings were for the chamber music group, with concerts once a month. Hamish never missed one.

I would walk home if the weather permitted. It was a long way, but I liked the exercise and the chance to people-watch as I went. My route home varied, but not much. I would go down York Avenue and then cut west to Lexington, Madison or 5th Avenue, passing the ritzy stores and observing the shoppers. Many of them were from foreign countries, while lots of others were American tourists or New Yorkers. From there, I would head south through Gramercy Park and on to Union Square, often stopping at the Barnes & Noble headquarters on the north side. In the summer, the farmers market would be there, with locally grown, fresh fruits and vegetables.

Hamish tended to stay a bit later than I did, supervising his graduate students and improving his nanites, but he would always come home by 8 p.m. at the very latest. When I first started walking home, he panicked. He hadn't realized what fun walking was for me. He called me on my cell phone, and once he even called my mother when she was staying in Chelsea. I had to train him to realize that I was fine, and was just enjoying myself and getting some exercise.

To short-circuit his worries, I got into the habit of leaving him messages with Patsy as I walked away from the Rockefeller Institute. Within the first few blocks out, I usually knew what I would do – walk or take the subway. After explaining the problem to her – Hamish freaking out and calling everywhere for me – she expected this as part of our end-of-the-day routine.

Life started to resemble a DVD player on Fast Forward, it seemed to move so fast: news-reading, writing, lunch, writing, walking or subway – over and over again. The news reports punctuated and differentiated individual days, while 2-week time-blocks were mapped out by lectures. The one exception was a trip to Hyde Park, New York, where we spent 3 lovely nights at a bed-and-breakfast near both the historic Roosevelt Estate, and ate in a restaurant at the Culinary Institute of America. The DVD show seemed to slow down to Play mode during that week. Other than that, it was a steady routine, set on Fast Forward.

This was a welcome change from the past, when life had been seemingly jammed on some travesty of a slow-motion setting as we had felt ourselves continually and painfully aware of our lack of financial ability to function in the world and our failures to advance our careers without getting stuck on Pause whenever a post at some university expired.

For Secretary's Day, I took Patsy out to lunch. I found a place called Sel et Poivre (Salt and Pepper). Hamish sent her a dozen white roses with a note: "Happy Secretary's Day from Hamish and Avril." She seemed sincerely delighted, even for someone who typically made loud, absurdly emoted, drawn-out fusses over gifts.

I gave six new lectures before summer: *Surgical, Medical and Patient Hygiene through the Ages*; *Herbal Potions of Ancient Witches*; *Prosthetic Solutions to Disease and War*; *Injuries from Environmental Tampering throughout Time*; *Traditional Lore vs. University Medical Training in Medieval Europe*; *Traveling Microbes and Plagues Exported to Indigenous Peoples*.

Patsy continued to trot into my office and sit for test runs of each lecture with her eyes glazed over. She only snapped out of her stupor when I showed pictures and photos, showing disgust or fascination, depending upon what she saw. I was intrigued; whatever the reason for her inability to pay attention – unwillingness, mental deficiency, lack of interest – her behavior served to warn me that some people just could not be reached if they were required to think.

The news reports were intriguing. I got into the habit of checking C-SPAN to see debates in the Senate and House chambers of Congress. Every day, something came up that seemed to vaguely point to a shift in the social and political consciousness of people everywhere. Maybe it was the choice of topics, maybe it was something more, but it was definitely there.

Sometimes I would watch to see which senators were sparring over which issues – it helped at voting times – and just to observe what they looked like and how they moved, particularly what their vocal inflections and emotive gestures were like. That revealed a lot about their personalities…much more than whatever words and phrases they chose to use. Politicians lied so much that I figured I could read them a bit better by watching them in action.

One of the anti-choice men, a Republican Christian from Tennessee was particularly entertaining to watch. He was a caricature of himself, right down to his name: Lance P. Boenher. It was pronounced exactly as it looked: "bone-her." He had married a former beauty queen from his high school who had gone on to lead Bible study classes at their church; they had 6 kids. Boenher was known for having lots of extra-marital affairs, and had even been quoted by his mistresses as thanking Nae-Née for keeping out of "trouble" – no further explanation needed. The senator was tall, powerfully built, and had a perpetual tan. He devoted a significant portion of his speeches to family values, though he never defined the term.

I often switched from C-SPAN to reading articles to get a sense of what was being discussed or argued about in Congress, and what was being done – if anything. Debates could go on and on and stall almost any effort at change or progress. If I had sat through all of the debates, the trend that I was sensing might have been clearer. The trend was a convergence of issues that combined reproductive rights, environmental pressures, resource supplies, and economics. Something was fueling this, and it was cropping up elsewhere besides the United States.

Once, Patsy asked what fascinated me about all this. She seemed uneasy.

"I like to people-watch, and politicians and intellectuals give me a sense of our future quality of life," I told her. "What's the matter?" I asked.

"It's just that your lectures seem to be about the past, but you are focused on the present and the future. How does your work relate to that?"

Interesting; she hadn't paid any attention at all to my practice readings. It was like her brain had turned off during them all, and now I was getting confirmation of that. "The lectures explain the connections; the lessons of the past are meant to caution us about our behavior now so as to protect our futures, and I say that in them."

"Oh." She went back to her desk. I went back to work.

Species depletions fascinated me. One that I had described in my graduate thesis – which had morphed into a book about the herstory of birth control – was an herb called silphium that had grown in Europe during Roman times. It was brewed into a tea, and it grew wild, but no one thought to cultivate and preserve it. It had a vaguely heart-shaped appearance, and died out because of overgrazing, which turned the lands it grew on to desert. Biodiversity loss thanks to human overconsumption was nothing new; it was just getting worse and worse now.

Today, the existence of many other species was threatened; life as it was currently known changing so drastically and so fast, because so many people had reaped what the planet had to offer. It made me angry to think that so many wonderful things that humans had enjoyed for so many millennia were disappearing thanks to the thoughtless overconsumption of that same exponentially reproducing human species.

The list went on and on: bees, which aided in cultivating flowers and berries; tuna, being depleted through excessive hunting; tigers, killed by the Chinese for their aphrodisiac properties; the tropical rainforest of the Amazon jungle, rapidly being replaced by farm and pastureland, destroying its air-scrubbing trees, plus countless plant species that were the sources of pharmaceutical and nutraceutical solutions to illnesses; coral reefs dying off due to overheating, leading to the loss of habitats for a myriad of underwater species.

There were more wonderful but vanishing things, but these were just a few. Why were humans just using the planet up with such reckless, parasitic abandon?! I had an answer almost as soon as I had thought the question when a quote from a Tea Party member summed it up nicely: "I read my Bible; God made this Earth and the things on it for us to utilize." Great...the answer was in religion and religiousness. I don't like religion and religiousness. Fill in the blank with any particular religion; whichever one you choose, I will not change my mind.

Only the Native Americans seemed to respect and appreciate the environment, but they had the least political clout. The Navajo tribe favored wind and solar energy, saying that the tradeoffs of mining – asthma, bronchitis, heart attacks and a dwindling supply of potable water – weren't worth any benefit from it, and that it was far wiser and better to save the land. They had it all figured out: to them, digging into the land was like cutting into one's own skin.

Droughts were killing crops now, permafrost was melting, and people were dying of heat exhaustion across the southern United States. The mistakes of the past were already haunting us as people saw the climate of the south becoming the climate of the north. Wealthy, developed nations were coming to the unwelcome realization that they were not immune to climate change.

Climatologists blamed all of the severe weather that the planet was experiencing on the combined emissions produced since the Industrial Revolution. I was almost mesmerized by the reports and the damage wrought by the storms, both here at home and around the world.

In September, mini-tornadoes wreaked such chaos on the subway system that we rode cabs to work and then walked home together just to observe their effects. The damage wrought was the sort that people still thought of as normal only for the Midwest, but the fact was that such storms were now occurring yearly in New York City.

Elsewhere, there were floods, storms and earthquakes that destroyed infrastructures. Lost people stayed lost due to a lack of resources with which to find them, and homes were not rebuilt. Homeless hordes spread out, angry and disenfranchised, further exacerbating the strains caused by the initial disasters. It all suggested that the Earth was trying to fight back against the relentless consumption of humans.

There was even a comic strip (I liked to read those) about the effects of overpopulation. It said that the next generation, the one that was currently in its teens, would be the first to have a lower standard of living than its parents had. It was depressing, but not surprising.

All in the while, politicians who wanted things to stay the same – anti-abortion, religious, establishment-minded politicians – were more strident than ever. It seemed that they were anxious about something that they would not name. Strident speeches and arguments tend to indicate resistance to a change in the social order, and seriously worried that it is coming.

The voices of logic and reason were not so loud, but when someone is right, they tend to speak in more modulated tones. The politicians and intellectuals, many of whom were based at think-tanks and universities, spoke in normal volumes and patient tones as they pointed out the state of the planet, the economy, and discussed the future of life in a hotter, information-saturated, and increasingly populous world.

I didn't see either side coming right out and saying what was going on behind the proverbial scenes; I just saw that something was in fact brewing. Whatever it was, the media would find out soon enough, and so would the rest of us. I wondered how we would all feel about it when it happened.

Chapter 15

Andrew Warne

The mystery of Patsy, such as I thought about it, continued.

I had plenty of other things to occupy my time, but she was there every weekday, so it was inevitable that we would interact, learn more about each other, and be puzzled by our differences. I was probably more intrigued than disturbed, while the reverse could be said of her.

Summer came.

Now that the academic schedule was in recess, I found myself with no lectures to do, but I still had to show up at my office to answer e-mails and respond to requests for information on medical history. To fill the extra time, I did what I had been planning to do: I started to convert my collection of six new PowerPoint presentations with lecture notes to six new book chapters. The finished product would be longer than that, and would be added to as I produced more lectures in the fall. The Rockefeller Institute was hoping as much.

That left me alone in my office, occasionally admiring the sunny views of the East River, but mostly glued to my computer screen. Patsy did in fact end up trotting over to the library for me as I requested the same books again for the re-write process. She was an adequate secretary; a fast typist, very good on the phone, good with people, and getting comfortable with us.

She began to talk with me more and more, and tried to include me at lunch with her friends, the other secretaries. I sat with them a couple of times, but soon started bringing the most off-putting (to them) books that I could, complete with photos, to enable me to eat alone, or else taking off for Le Pain Quotidien on my own.

The first time I ate lunch with them, Patsy introduced me to her colleagues. There was Kirsten, the other single girl, a short, plump, pretty brunette with lots of rings on her fingers. She had a fiancé, and she showed me her engagement ring, a standard Tiffany-setting of 6-prongs on a round diamond. She had a Master's degree in health management, and worked as an administrative assistant to the dean.

The other 2 women were both married. Their names were Jen and Colleen. Jen was the one with a niece and nephew, ages 4 and 6, whom she liked to baby-sit. She had no kids of her own. Colleen had 2 boys and a girl, and was constantly tired because one of the boys was only 6 months old and he kept her up half the night. Jen had a medium build, and was somewhat pretty. Colleen had the look of someone who was once the same way, but had lost her figure to pregnancies and never bothered to lose the weight or watch her diet, too busy with child care to pay attention to her appearance…or health.

Jen and Colleen were joined at the hip. They talked of little else besides their kids. I asked about their husbands; Jen's worked for ConEd, and Colleen's was a corrections officer on Riker's Island. Kirsten's fiancé was a bartender in Brooklyn, and he owned the place. That was where Patsy had met her boyfriend, so it was a pleasant surprise to find a connection when she came to work at the Rockefeller Institute.

I didn't talk much during the first lunch. I felt as though I didn't belong there, but I was determined to be polite, so I sat with this group. Because I had come to the dining hall without a book, I realized I had left myself no other option barring blatant rudeness and the appearance of snobbery. Hamish was off with some oncologists at Sloan-Kettering, planning his next journal article on tumor-seeking nanites, so I was on my own.

Colleen needed no further urging than a suggestion from Patsy to take her baby photos out of her purse. All of the women had huge, bulky handbags shoved under their chairs. I had my usual small, compact Vera Bradley one, all cloth and easily slung over my neck and shoulder, tucked neatly to my side.

"Look at my kids," Colleen said, passing me a leather case jammed full of photos.

I took it and opened it up. Almost every photo was of a child, which confused me for a moment. "You have 3 kids? Are all of these of your kids at different stages in their lives?"

The others exchanged glances. I must have looked as though I were making a study of a curious new lecture topic. Colleen paused to think about it, then said, "Yes – I like to keep them all. Jack says I'm going to have to buy a bigger wallet soon."

I let her show me which kid was which, then flipped all the way through, hoping to find a photo of Jack. I didn't see one. "Is there one of your husband in here?" I asked.

She laughed and said that there was, but that she had covered it up with another photo of the baby. I asked her to show me – I was curious to see what he looked like. She took the wallet back, tugged at the contents of one of the pages, and pulled out a tight pile. Then she passed me a photo of herself and her husband, dressed up for some formal occasion.

My eyes widened slightly as I was able to recognize the man's features in those of the older children. He had a mustache, dark hair and eyes, and was a couple of inches taller than his wife. Colleen stood next to him in a pretty dress, smiling. She looked much thinner.

"That was our engagement photo," she told me. "Jack still looks the same."

"You look beautiful in it," I replied. "When was this taken?"

She looked at me, and I couldn't read her expression. "8 years ago. I'm 40 now, and after having 3 kids, I don't look the same."

"You still look really pretty. And you have a nice family." I passed the wallet back.

I repeated the same routine with Jen as she showed me her niece and nephew. Apparently, Jen was trying to get pregnant. She and her husband Fred had just gotten married 2 years earlier, and they had just started trying a few months earlier. She looked at me as though expecting a response after she told me this, so I said, "Oh, well – good luck. I hope you get what you want."

"Thank you," she said, smiling.

Conversation turned to me next. I hadn't cooed over any of the baby photos, and I suspected that they were wondering why not. I wasn't about to just announce, unbidden, that I wasn't into babies and reproduction. I felt like an outsider, a guest, and wondered where this would lead.

They asked about me, about Hamish, got the stories of our lives out of me – not that I had any objection to sharing it with them – and then the inevitable interrogation followed. I strongly suspected that Patsy had put them up to this.

"So, how old are you and Hamish?"

"I'm 40 – my birthday was in December, on the 21st. He turned 50 in September."

"Are you going to have kids? You're running out of time if you want them."

Talk about a set-up, I thought. Well, they asked for it, they got it.

"We don't want kids. We want cats, and we just adopted a kitten when we moved here."

With that, I ignored the exchanged glances and brought out my own wallet of photos, and showed them Spock, Eowyn, and my adult relatives and Hamish's sister Fiona. So what that other things mattered to me that whatever did it for them. There was nothing wrong with what I loved and wanted in my life.

They complimented me on how handsome Hamish was, said my kitten was beautiful, asked a few polite questions about my family, and that was that.

Once again, I didn't fit in with a group. I hadn't cared when I was little, when I was a teenager, or now. I had fit in while in graduate school, but I wasn't going to stay on in Paris and neither would my classmates, and so in law school I was back to being a loner. I was the only one in my class who didn't argue, and that was strange in a lawyer. If the facts weren't in my favor, I just didn't see the point in arguing for them, I once said. The class had stared at me as though I were speaking Vulcan.

That was in the international law class. Oh well…

Now I stuck out like a sore thumb, but I had expected this. I was used to it, I had experience with it, and I had 2 graduate degrees and was sitting among a group of secretaries. If I could just eat my food without deeply offending them I would be satisfied. They couldn't seriously expect me to have much in common with them anyway.

The questions kept coming, but at least they weren't about kids.

It was Kirsten this time. "So…I read that article about you and your husband in *The New York Times* last February. What was the name of that birth control thing you two invented?"

"Nae-Née."

She actually seemed interested in it. "How does it work? And what does its name mean?"

"It's a nanite – microscopic robot – loaded with RU-486, the abortion drug. It's injected into a woman's abdomen, and it moves around in her body tracking hormone levels. If it detects a rise in those levels, indicating the presence of a fertilized egg, it releases some of the drug so that the egg doesn't implant in the uterus. It just passes out of the woman's body, and she gets her period as usual. A doctor monitors the device to make sure that it's working properly, and if the woman wants to have a baby, she tells the doctor, who enters a code that stops the device from releasing the drug until after woman has had one."

"And the name? What does it mean?" This was Patsy. She actually was paying attention to what I was saying even though, as usual, I had given a long, involved answer.

"It literally means "not born" – I thought of it because Hamish is Scottish, and he says "nae" rather than no when he gets excited, and "née is French for "born" so that became the other half of the name. It just seemed perfect, because we're co-inventors. I thought of the idea and the name, and he brought it to life."

The women exchanged glances. "What made you want to create such a thing?" Jen asked. "I mean, there are condoms and birth control pills and other contraceptives."

"Well, those other methods have a lower success rate than Nae-Née, and they either build up a level of synthetic hormones in a woman's body, thus putting her at a greater risk for certain kinds of cancers, or else they interfere with spontaneity. Nae-Née is more user-friendly and poses almost no risk – the worst thing that can happen is it won't turn back on after a pregnancy, though we haven't heard of any computer chip failures yet. In that case, the device could be extracted and replaced at no cost to the patient, who paid for a fully functional one."

"Avril, I'm just curious," Patsy went on, "I've been working for you for 4 and a half months, and I still don't understand what it is that you do here."

So that was what she had wanted out of this invitation. Okay. Fair enough.

"My job is to produce medical history lectures that are relevant to the work being done here at the Rockefeller Institute, and to choose topics that relate not only to ongoing but also future projects by following the news reports. So I spend the first hour or so of my day here reading the news online, saving articles that cover health, environmental and women's issues, plus I watch for political trends that may affect policy decisions for those things. The rest of the time, I prepare and deliver the lectures, which will eventually become a book."

"And that takes up all of your time here?"

I looked at her, wondering what she meant by that. "Yes."

"Oh; just wondering."

Recently, I had been invited to visit Columbia University Medical School and deliver one of my lectures again, and more invitations were rolling in from other schools in the city. I had no intention of traveling all over the country to do this, however. There was plenty to do here.

The next time I ate lunch with Patsy, it was just her and Kirsten.

Chatting with Kirsten was fun; she was a happy person, and she didn't look at me as though I were somehow abnormal. She accepted me, and we even talked about school experiences, which temporarily left Patsy sitting quietly. Kirsten had enjoying her studies.

Kirsten had worked on her master's degree at the University of London, and had taken some of her classes at the famous London School of Economics, so she knew a few things about social and political pressures shaping events.

We enjoyed hashing out current events and I felt a brief longing to have Kirsten as my secretary instead of Patsy, but squelched it as quickly as the idea came to me. Kirsten worked in the dean's office; she seemed well set there, and Patsy had done nothing to warrant this. I finished my lunch, excused myself, and went back to the office.

Patsy followed 10 minutes later.

Knock, knock. She was at my office door. I had just sat down at the desk.

"Come in."

The door opened, and she came in. She sat down next on my sofa. She was wearing a dress that came down to her knees; it was too short, and her legs showed under it, huge. Closing them was physically impossible for her, but Hamish wasn't around, so I didn't worry about it.

She seemed to be thinking something over; she was quiet after a session of loud giggling with her friend, which was how I had gotten used to seeing her when she was with any of them.

"Avril, I think you would enjoy meeting my father."

That certainly piqued my interest.

"Oh? What's he like? Would he want to meet me? Could Hamish come too?"

She still looked completely serious. "Of course Hamish could come. And I think he definitely wants to meet you. In fact, he mentioned that he read about you at the U.N., where he volunteers on environmental issues. You and your husband were mentioned in the paper, and some office at the U.N. picked that up and added your story to a report he was looking at. He's a great guy, always interested in who he can help next."

"And he volunteers at the U.N. in addition to being a social worker for the homeless and for hoarders. Sounds like a busy and involved guy. I'd love to meet him. What's his name?"

"Andrew Warne. He did his master's degree in the 1990s, just because he is so interested in global warming, and then started going to the U.N. in the evenings after work once he was finished with it."

"Where did he study for his master's degree?" I wanted to know.

"Right here in the city – at N.Y.U."

"Cool."

"You remembered that he works with homeless people and hoarders? I told you that months ago, when you took me out to lunch."

"I know. I have a scary memory. I can't help it. If it's interesting to me, I just remember it, whatever it is."

"Huh."

"So – when can we meet your father?"

"I'll ask him about it. He lives near your parents' place, off of 9th Avenue, so you probably know the area well."

"Great – let me know. I'll tell Hamish."

"Tell me what?"

We both jumped; we hadn't heard Hamish walk in. Patsy realized that her legs showed, bare and enormous on the low sofa, and stood up suddenly. "I'm going back to my desk," she said, edging out.

Hamish came further into the room to let her pass. She shut the door.

I told him about the invitation, and what I knew about Andrew Warne.

"So would you be interested in meeting him? Would you come with me out to dinner when the visit is set up?"

"Definitely – it sounds like a great idea. He sounds so different from his daughter, too. Maybe we can find out more about that."

"Maybe. I'm kind of curious about that. But I won't count on discovering much about her on this visit. It'll probably be mostly about him and us, exchanging notes about our work and interests."

"That's fine."

Hamish went back out, saying he needed to check his e-mail for a file.

I answered a call from the painter about the blue doors on the firehouse; the job was done, it seemed, the door-knocker hung, and the bill due. I paid it when I got home, which was about when Hamish arrived thanks to great weather and a long walk. I had a bagful of berries from the Union Square farmers market, too.

We started planning for our departure, which was in a couple of days. We were going to Paris for a week and a half, which would include our anniversary. The timing of this trip was set to coincide with the late spring season in the Tuileries and other gardens around the city, so that we could enjoy those as well as the museums and historic sites…and foods.

Our honeymoon had been a brief trip to Virginia, driving around the Blue Ridge Mountains and touring Monticello, so this was a long overdue romantic interlude for us.

Patsy knew we would be away, so she didn't mention meeting her father again until we returned from our vacation.

She said that her father had been excited to get the invitation, and gave us his cell phone number, urging us to call after 4:30, so we did. Hamish came into my office and sat on the sofa while I punched in the number.

Mr. Warne answered on the second ring; I guessed he wasn't phone-shy, like me. I usually kept my phone off, and checked the voice mail.

"Hello! Andrew here," a man's voice said brightly. Wow – cheerful, I thought. He doesn't even know what to expect, but he's glad to answer.

"Um…hello. Andrew Warne? This is Avril Châtelet."

"Yes – hi – my daughter said you would be calling me. Good to hear from you. I've read all about you and your husband."

"You have? I thought there was just the one article in *The New York Times*." I must have sounded nervous. Little did I know that I didn't need to be.

"Yes – I read it. And I looked up your CVs on the Rockefeller Institute's website."

"Oh – now I understand. Patsy's told us all about you, too. I can hardly wait to meet you. You sound fascinating, and you must be very nice, being a social worker."

Pause. Oh great, another social blunder, I thought, worrying. Probably the wrong thing to say…

But then he spoke again. "Wow – I haven't even met you yet. Patsy must have said something really complimentary."

"Not particularly…I'm just giving you my assessment after an objective listing of the few facts I have about you. Plus I saw a photo of you on her desk. You look like a nice person."

The photo was of a smiling, white-haired man with magnifying-lens glasses.

"Well! I can't wait to meet you. How about Friday evening? I have some meetings at the U.N. this week, plus some paperwork from my day job, so I can't get away until then."

I checked with Hamish, who nodded.

"Friday's fine. Where would you like to meet?"

"How about Gascogne, on 8th Avenue? You like French food, don't you?"

"Well, I am French, so yes."

"That was a joke – I knew you would. Have you ever been there?"

"Yes, we've been there a couple of times, with my parents. I like the garden."

"Excellent – shall we say 7 o'clock, then? I'll make the reservation," he added.

"Okay," I said.

"Great – I'll see the 2 of you then," he said, and rang off.

I shut my phone and looked at Hamish. "Well, that was easy," I said, feeling a bit stunned. I needed to get out more, I thought.

Hamish came over and kissed me. "Don't worry. You like meeting intellectual men. It would make me jealous, but this guy is someone's dad and I've seen his photo." He left.

Friday rolled around, and we headed out early so as to arrive on time. This was a new experience, my husband closing up shop at the same time as I did, I thought.

We didn't dress up, but I cleaned up, made sure I had a nice blouse on, and made Hamish wear a nice shirt with buttons and a collar. He grumbled as usual, but complied. We fed our kitten, and then took a cab so that we wouldn't arrive all hot and sweaty. It was early July, and hot and humid.

Andrew Warne was waiting in the doorway. He looked exactly like his photo, and was wearing beige Dockers pants, a plain brown belt, matching, thick rubber-soled leather shoes, and a dark blue polo shirt. He smiled and waved as we entered.

"Hey – it's great to meet you both!" and he shook our hands with a big smile.

We smiled back and shook his hands. He seemed like the exact opposite of his daughter, though I could see the family resemblance in his face.

"I asked for a table out back in the garden – you said you liked it," he told me.

I was really pleased, and grinned back. "Thanks! I do."

The waiter led us through the narrow passages, down the steps and up again into the small garden that resembled a piece of small-town France transplanted into a Manhattan backyard. There were vines on some of the walls, and shuttered windows, and wooden tables with candlesticks and white cloths.

We got settled quickly, perused the menus, and soon were chatting away about politics, the environment, social pressures, and population pressures. It turned out that a lot of his interests were fueled by a concern about dwindling resources and competition for them amongst an ever-increasing human population.

Hamish and I stared at each other when he said this. It was exactly what we had been thinking and saying to each other for a long time.

"Really, Mr. Warne – we say this sort of thing to each other all the time. It's one of the reasons why we don't want kids, but we don't tell other people this very often because the moment that they find out that we don't want any, they seem to judge us, and negatively, like we're demons or something."

"Call me Andrew, not Mr. Warne. It's too formal."

"Okay, Andrew," we said, in sync as usual.

"And they shouldn't judge you. More people should think about the life that their potential offspring will have before just rushing to reproduce."

I stared at him, and then at my husband. I was starting to relax significantly with this man; he was just accepting of us as we were. And he was a thoughtful person.

Andrew had another question. "Why do you get the sense that people are judging you?"

I described the lunch with Patsy's baby-loving co-workers, and the abrupt change of subject after I answered their question as to why Hamish and I didn't have any kids and didn't plan on it. "I didn't say that I don't like babies and little kids, but it was probably obvious to them because I looked at the photos of their babies, and I didn't ooh and aah over them, give silly little smiles, or say that the babies were cute. I don't find them cute, and won't lie, and so I said something else, something truthful, and hoped it sounded pleasant. I said that the woman with the babies and little kids had a nice family. It was easier after I saw the hidden photo of her husband, which she had covered with a new baby photo."

Andrew cracked up. "I love it. Too many people are insincere. There was nothing wrong with that answer. And by the way, my girlfriend doesn't like babies either, but she's a great person."

I gaped at him for a moment, then smiled. "Thank you – it's so nice to meet someone who just accepts this about us without taking offense at it or deciding that we are monstrous, selfish people."

"Quite the opposite; I think that people who just want things without caring about the consequences inflicted on others by their choices are the selfish ones."

"I wish there were more people like you. Can we stay in touch?"

"I'd be delighted."

We exchanged business cards – all 3 of us. Hamish was having a good time too – I could tell, even though he didn't come right out and say it.

Andrew was more of a phone person than I was, and he didn't use his e-mail except for work, but he was going to get a laptop soon. He asked me what I thought, commenting that he remembered Patsy saying that I had set up mine and Hamish's machines.

Somehow, I wasn't worried about faux pas in either phone or face-to-face conversations with him. Dinner and dessert passed with lightning speed, and I realized that this was because we were just having a really, really, great time talking to Andrew.

As we headed outside, Andrew asked me if I could meet him at Best Buy on 6th Avenue the following week to help him pick out a laptop, along with whatever else he might need.

Time to walk and talk with him in a really informal setting, I thought. I was up for that.

"What day is good for you?" I asked him.

"Are you free on Saturday? We both have to be in at work the rest of the week."

"Yeah, I am. How about 1 o'clock?"

"I'll be there."

"Great."

Hamish and I walked home, thrilled. "He's like a dad," I said, once we were out of earshot. Andrew had headed off in the opposite direction by then, and city was plenty loud enough to mask our conversation from his receding form as I got smaller and smaller, heading for 9th Avenue on 14th Street.

"He is a dad, Avril."

"I know, but most dads don't seem like easygoing, approachable, accepting people to their own children, let alone other people."

"I see what you mean. You should try to visit with him some more, then, not just for the computer shopping trip."

"But he's our secretary's father. What if that doesn't work out well? I'd be sorry to lose a friend over that."

"I think you're worrying too much about something that may never happen."

I disagreed, but went along with what he said.

Saturday's meeting was fun; I helped Andrew pick out an Asus laptop, Microsoft Office, Norton Internet Security, and a memory stick. He bought a printer to go with it, and I insisted on carrying it for him while we went around the corner for coffee. There was a great place on 23rd Street called Madeleine Patisserie with plenty of room, comfortable chairs, and not much noise – perfect for setting it all up for him.

We went in and found seats on the sofa, put the stuff down to save our spot, and came back quickly with little financiers, round sponge-cake cookies with chocolate chips, and café au lait. I started sorting blank DVDs – for the backup – programs, and the computer case. Soon everything was loading nicely. I even had a memory stick with me full of National Geographic wallpaper photos, which I shared with Andrew.

He couldn't gush and thank me enough. "Thank you – I would never have known how to set all this up. I'm spoiled by the tech support people at the office, and then I keep going out into the field, away from all this technology."

"Do you think you'll know how to use it?" I asked. "I can go over it with you if you want."

"Maybe just a quick once-over, but then I should be okay. I know how to get at my e-mail and attachments, which is what I need this thing for – for U.N. stuff – but I was intimidated by the selection and set-up process. You've taken a huge load off my mind."

I smiled. I loved being helpful, and didn't get too many chances to do such things for people – especially such nice ones.

I got the disk out of the HP printer box and loaded the software for it to the laptop, then showed Andrew how to work the whole thing, and described how to plug the stuff in at home. "And don't forget the surge protector – you don't want all this stuff fried in the next lightning storm, and it's summer."

"Good point."

We sat back on the sofa, happy with the afternoon's work.

"So, Andrew…after 4 and a half months with your daughter, and then meeting you, I can see the family resemblance, but that's all. You too seem so different."

He sighed. "We are."

"I keep trying to understand her without firing a bunch of personal questions at her, but I feel like she's figured me out while I still don't understand her very well. I guess that's why I like to watch people. I love puzzles, and people are hard for me to figure out. I can't read their expressions – especially in their eyes."

Why was I telling him all this? I usually didn't trust anyone, but I trusted Andrew with my innermost thoughts, it seemed. That was something that I felt with Hamish, and few other people. There was nothing romantic in this, and I could tell somehow that Andrew knew that.

He suddenly told me all about his daughter.

It was like having months' worth of curiosity satisfied all at once.

"Patsy likes to party. I assume you've seen her resume, since she's working for you."

"Yes. I wondered how she could have studied television production at the New School. They don't offer a program in that."

He looked at me. "Sharp observation. She started college at N.Y.U.'s Tisch School of the Arts. That's where the television production program is. She partied, fooled around and flunked out. She took a couple of years off here and there, working and trying to figure out what she wanted to do, seemed more interested in rock concerts and waiting in line to see celebrities than in getting serious about anything, and finally I helped her get her papers in order at the New School. By then, she only had time to do a major in general studies – nothing specific. That's how she became the secretary she is today."

"Oh." What to say…well, this wasn't my fault, and he was confiding in me. "She seems to like Sheryl Crow a lot."

"That's the one. She's liked her, and Cyndi Lauper, since high school."

"I liked Cyndi Lauper's music, but I like orchestra music even more – especially movie soundtracks."

"Patsy mentioned that you play the violin. It's nice that you kept that up on your own."

I smiled. "It's still fun. What kind of music do you like?"

"Classical – symphonies, that sort of thing. I go to Lincoln Center now and then."

Hamish and I were planning to get into that, but we hadn't found the time yet. We would soon, I reminded myself.

Something else nagged at me, and I didn't think that I would get another chance to ask this, so I pressed on. "Patsy talks about her life in California with such fondness; it seems like she's really sorry that it ended. She got a cat that really loves there, too."

"Rosalie's a nice cat. A bit ornery, but nice. Patsy had a good run there, but she had some trouble on the job. They had to let her go."

"She told me that they cut her position."

"Don't say anything to her, but they didn't. She was accused of bullying one of the people working under her. I offered to help her sue, but she turned me down. She didn't want me to spend the money, and let me send her to a weight loss program instead. I'd been wanting to do that for her for a long time. She lost 100 pounds, and came home looking a lot better than she had for a long time."

"That's great. I won't say anything to her about the Paramount thing."

"Thanks. I helped her get the Rockefeller job – someone who owed me a favor at the Altman Foundation helped us out with that. She's not supervising anyone, so I doubt anything will happen. She's smart, and has good work skills, so this seems like a good fit for her."

"She's doing a good job for us. We're perfectly satisfied. She comes into my office every couple of weeks, when I'm about to give a new lecture, and plays test audience for me."

"Really? I wouldn't have thought that she would be able to pay attention. She's intelligent, but has attention deficit disorder, and has never disciplined herself to pay attention to details."

"So that's it," I said. "She doesn't pay close attention, but she does what I need; she sits and lets me drone on and on until I've gone through it for a living human being at least once. She told me that she doesn't like to listen in museums when her boyfriend wants to go."

"I like Jim. I hope they get married. But Patsy has put on more weight since she came home. I suspect that she's eating recreationally, or to relieve stress, just like she did in college, when she lived with me."

Why was he telling me all this? I was sure I would have to ante up some payback data soon. Sure enough, he had some questions for me.

Why wasn't I practicing law if I had a law degree?

I explained about not liking debates, not seeing the logic in arguing a point when my side was in the wrong just because I had a side to represent, and not wanting the standard, formulaic pattern that was the expected thing for most people to follow. And about not testing well.

He nodded, and asked me to continue, saying that he could appreciate all that, because he had had to tell his mother that he had no intention of being miserable as a stock broker just because he was a Harvard man. "She was disappointed that I wasn't headed for life as a rich businessman, but I wanted to go out among people who needed help, not shut myself up with a bunch of suits and scurry for a senior partner."

I grinned. "My dad thought that I would follow him into international patent law, but I could never make it work. Fortunately, my international law professor helped get that idea out of his mind, and it was a total accident. It was just what I needed; but my father is happy with me as I am. I finished the graduate degrees, and I write. He has enough to gloat about, I suppose."

"So he doesn't want you to follow him into his law practice now."

"No – fortunately."

Andrew looked like he was hoping for a longer response than that, so I went on for a bit. The last thing I want is to lead an ordinary life, following society's formula for happiness that is recommended to, and often expected and required of women. Women are expected and required to like and want this formula: earn a Bachelor's degree at some respected academic institution, marry a guy who has also accomplished this task, get a mundane office job, a mortgage, and car loans, cell phones with those accompanying bills, learn basic computer skills and then built upon those, and reproduce.

After this setup is in order, the woman is then expected to take maternity leave from her cubicle – to which she may or may not return after that interval has elapsed – and then begin to raise her kids amid much noise, chaos, mess, dull routine, and invisibility on her part.

Saving money for retirement is the next Herculean task…or more like one for Sisyphus, as expenses continually exceed one's income. As that money is saved and then dipped into as the bills continue to crop up – both recurring and unexpected for things such as medical emergencies and car failures – one will glumly be reminded that it will all be worse for the children when it is time to pay for college or university educations.

There won't be any savings for that in most cases. The kids will have to pay for their educations by either getting loans, or scholarships, or both, and hope that their parents can help with the rest. If mom and dad do that, they will have to mortgage their home, thus undoing whatever equity they have managed to accumulate over the preceding couple of decades.

There will be no retirement, no vacations, no relief from debt, and no sense of one's offspring going onward and upward.

It used to be different, but that changed when a drunken fraternity brother whose most notable anecdotes as President included dropping his pet dog on its head and choking on a pretzel while watching a football game had looted the U.S. economy.

All the while, caught up in this endless struggle to survive and make ends meet, the woman who chooses the role of mother finds herself in a vicious cycle of career stagnation at best and utter invisibility at best. When she dies, she will leave behind vague memories of bringing order and efficiency to chaos and confusion.

This being said, I ought to add a dirty little secret about myself: I don't like babies and little kids. Teenagers, if they are presented one by one and are interested in studying and achieving something intriguing, are a different thing. But babies are constant mind-numbing noise, mess, stink and sleep-deprivation. One can forget being able to focus and concentrate on developing a career with babies around, and although they will grow out of that phase of life, they rapidly find new ways of being a time-suck: "Mommy! Mommy! Mommy! Mommy!"

while tapping and demanding attention. I've seen it happen; it's normal and to be expected.

What most people don't realize is that reproduction is optional, not inevitable, and that even more astonishing to them, there's nothing wrong with this attitude. We are not all supposed to like babies and have them.

"I have been called selfish more times than I care to remember or enumerate by conventional thinkers who believe that one must like babies – especially if one is female."

"What an outrage," Andrew commented, smiling.

I don't know what got into me, but I blurted: "Here's the socially unacceptable, honest truth: I hate babies. I can't stand the way that people act around them: "Ooh! What a cute little baby!" This tends to be followed up with stupid cooing sounds and clown expressions, followed by deliberate lisping to the infant in question. No wonder most kids take so long to start talking clearly and coherently. Babies are ugly, oddly shaped, hairless, drooling creatures that puke, shit and piss and often let out high-pitched shrieks that pierce one's ears. I just don't like them."

Andrew laughed and said, "My girlfriend, Cathy, says that they're like pets in many ways, except for one: they have the ability to progress beyond this state. She doesn't stop there; she also says it's a good thing they do, because unlike kittens, who grow into wonderful purring, smiling, quiet cats, they start off being so much more work for so much less enjoyment."

I couldn't believe this. It was great. Could I keep him for a friend? "I like quiet," I said. "And you're girlfriend sounds nice. What does she do?"

"She works with animals – horses, mostly – helping out at the New York City police officers' stables."

"Wow – that's a neat job. I've seen those horses on walks around the city. The cops with them seem to have different job descriptions, like a cross between caring for a pet and public relations. People come up to them and ask them about the horses – their names, ages, personalities, the works. I've done it, too."

Andrew smiled.

"How did you and Cathy meet?"

"At a cat show here in the city, believe it or not. Cathy has one bossy, 14-year-old grey cat named Sassy, and I helped her picked that cat out from a group of Russian blue kittens at the show. Someone had abandoned them."

"That's terrific!" I told him about Eowyn, how we had gotten her the ASPCA, how I had chosen her name, and then about my grandmother and her Chartreux cat-breeding business back in Provence, and how we had had to gradually shut it down towards the end of her life, so that the cats would all end up in good homes.

He thought that was all just wonderful. "I'd love to get an autographed copy of your book for Cathy," he told me.

"I'll get one ready – and I'd love to meet her. Could we go out sometime with her and Hamish?"

"Sure – though I'd have to check with her about scheduling. I think she's going to be pretty busy for the next couple of weeks."

"Maybe Patsy can bring it to her, so she won't have to wait. Does she visit with the two of you much? I could bring the book to the office."

He looked uncomfortable. "Actually, Patsy doesn't like Cathy much. Their personalities are too different. I'm surprised she's been doing so well with you, because you and Cathy seem an awful lot alike. I guess it's because you're not Cathy. Patsy's fine with having divorced parents, but she doesn't like Cathy. It's because Cathy is in her mother's old place in my life."

"Okay then, I'll just get the book ready and save it for when we meet."

"Good. Has she said anything to you about France?"

"France? No – why?"

"I've been worried about that since she signed on with you. She went to France in high school with her class, and again when she started college."

"She went with her high school? She never let on that she could speak French!" I must have sounded excited, because he held up his hand to calm me down.

"Don't say anything to her. She went to the Pomfret School in Connecticut, and went wild in Paris and drove the teachers crazy. She learned very little French, and they called me, worried about her behavior. She and her friends had been able to buy wine and they got drunk in the hotel room, then ran wild as soon as they were allowed to visit the Galleries Lafayette and whatever other shops."

I stared at him. "I won't ask her about it, then. I was wondering why she didn't say anything whenever I mentioned Paris."

"That's another story. She went back to visit a classmate who was studying at the Sorbonne, and the girl had become very serious and focused. Their friendship broke up over that. Patsy spoke English in shops, and the Parisians got angry with her when she wouldn't learn how to count out francs and centimes – she just held out a handful of coins to them several times, and couldn't understand why that would annoy them."

"That would annoy anyone working in a shop. It puts the burden on them to honestly take the right amount, and leaves them wide open to criticism if the customer forgets how much money she or he had in the first place."

"Exactly. Well – tell me a little bit more about why you do what you do for a career before we go."

Oh. Okay, I thought, why not. This stuff was harmless enough, considering who I was chatting with.

"I want to work on my science and play my violin in peace and quiet, so that I can concentrate and create and hone my skills and knowledge base. While I live, I want to be visible, not invisible, and when I finally die, I want to die memorable, leaving my own imprint of achievements that benefit others in some lasting, valued way."

"So that's why you focus on publishing books."

"Yes – it's someone I am good at – writing, I mean – so I concentrate on that. I am constantly terrified of dying forgettable, which is probably why I work so hard. And I don't see anything wrong with my attitude about that, or about babies."

Apparently he agreed, because he said, "The world is already overpopulated, so why add more people to the mix unless: 1. You will love and want the child; and 2. You will be able to afford your retirement and its education. Otherwise, to me at least, reproduction seems to be the ultimate selfish act."

"Wow. Someone who agrees with me. But you had one kid. Of course, the world wasn't so crowded 40 years ago."

"No. And my wife really wanted at least one child. I like kids, but that doesn't mean that I should have 10 of them. I've discussed this at the U.N. with my colleagues. We ask ourselves things like: Why do so many people do this? I've heard lots of answers, none of which convince me that much thinking or consideration of the child's benefits or future life and happiness went into the decision – if a conscious decision was in fact made – to reproduce."

I said, "Here are some of the responses that have cropped up at baby showers and elsewhere:

1. I want someone to take care of me when I'm old;
2. Kids are cute – I just want one;
3. Babies just come when they come (always incredible with condoms and diaphragms!);
4. They don't need to go to college.

This last excuse really wins the idiot prize. Seriously…the nerve of someone to substitute their own judgment on this point in advance of their offspring's awareness of the value of an education! The kid will – in more instances than one wishes to contemplate – near completion of high school and realize that despite qualifications, desire to achieve something, and willingness to work toward it, realize that financing this goal is like Mount Everest."

He smiled at me. I went on:

"I refuse to do that to someone – inflict a life of soul-crushing problems on another human being while giving them no choice in the matter, and then demanding that they just make the best of it and take care of me when I age. The hell with me if that's all there is for the poor hypothetical offspring, and the hell with what I might want. Either I take care of my own offspring, or go it alone if I can't do that."

"That is refreshing," he said. I wish more people thought as you do."

"Really?"

"Really."

"Huh. Okay…so…the hell with people and what they want."

We laughed, picked up his computer stuff, now all sorted, organized, and set up to his satisfaction, and carried our empty dishes over to the side table. Soon we were on the curbside, and I had hailed a cab and put the printer box on the seat for him.

"Are you sure you'll be able to maneuver all this stuff yourself?"

"No problem," he assured me. He leaned over to hug me. "And look – thanks a lot, don't let anyone tell you and your husband to do things any differently, and we'll be in touch to arrange a visit with Cathy. Maybe sooner – I've got some people at the U.N. who might like to meet you both as well."

"Okay," I said, feeling kind of excited. Maybe a social life would happen for us. That would be a new experience.

I want quiet, and that isn't hurting others, but I wanted some friends to go to concerts and dinner with sometimes, too. Now that Hamish and I had achieved financial independence, perhaps we could have that. Andrew seemed like a good start to that.

He was so nice – he didn't expect me to be different.

I'm such a witch – Wiccan – I believe that one ought to be able to do whatever one wants as long as it doesn't hurt anyone else. And I can arrange to live that way, so I resent being called selfish for doing so. Quite the opposite: I consider myself selfless in my decision not to reproduce. It means that I won't have someone on layaway to take care of me when I'm old.

And he found nothing shameful or offensive about that.

All I had to do, it seemed, was get along with his daughter and not create conflict with her. I hoped that I could keep up my end. What if she couldn't keep up hers?

Well, I would take Hamish's advice for now and not let that worry me.

Chapter 16

Religion and Politics

That evening, I told Hamish in detail about the visit with Andrew Warne.

"Why would he just tell me everything I wanted to know, and then agree with me about population issues? I'm not used to people accepting me, agreeing with me, or thinking that there is nothing wrong with not wanting kids. I feel like trusting this guy, but I so seldom find any reason to do that that I'm wondering if I'm being stupid to do so. Do you think maybe he likes me but is worried about what will go wrong with his daughter?"

"Yes to all of that. Go ahead and be friends with him, and meet his girlfriend. I'll come with you."

"Really?"

"Yep."

"Wow." I hugged him. We were watching a movie on cable TV in our bedroom, with the kitten snoring quietly and breathing deeply on top of the covers. She kept twisting around, showing us her chin and whiskers as she slept.

"What about you, Hamish?"

"What do you mean?"

"I mean, are you making any new friends?"

"At work? No. I get along with people, but it's just professional. And I haven't been out meeting people. As much as you think that you lack social skills, you try harder than I do, and you bother more than I do. But don't worry about it; I'll be friends with your friends, and if they fall through, I won't want to deal with them either."

That sounded like potential trouble, but I guessed I would just enjoy it and try not to worry. Neither Hamish nor I were great experts. We were stuck being polite and hoping to be lucky with people. If it worked out, great, if not, we went back to being loners.

Regardless, I was hoping to meet some nice friends who live a long time, not insist on a life that revolved around team sports or kids, and then have some fun visits. But great friendships are rare and hard to find. Maybe everyone has to rely on luck.

A few evenings later, we were watching the news and eating at home when Hamish said to me, "Have you been following the news lately? I mean the stuff that's going on in the Senate." I had just taken a couple of days off to go to some museum exhibits, so I was sure that I was missing something.

"A little bit. Why?"

"That tanned Republican with the phallic last name – whatever it is…"

"Boenher?"

"Yeah, him. He's been arguing for an amendment to the Constitution banning abortion. It's hilarious. His arguments are all about religion. I don't have a law degree, and I'm still studying for my citizenship test, but it doesn't take much to know that it'll never work. It won't, will it?" he suddenly wondered, sounded almost worried.

"It won't. He would need to rally most of the Senate, and then get the President to sign off on it. It's too much of a long-shot. Why? You weren't actually worried about Nae-Née and future sales, were you?"

"Yeah, I was. But not that much."

I got out my pocket copy of the U.S. Constitution and flipped to Article V.

"Here it is, Hamish. Two-thirds of both the House and Senate – both parts of Congress – must propose and pass an amendment. Or two-thirds of all state legislatures must call a convention of Congress for that purpose – which has never been done before, by the way. It certainly sounds much more complicated. Anyway, after that, the proposed amendment has to be ratified. That's another hurdle that isn't so easily leaped. That requires a three-quarters majority of either state legislatures or of conventions in all 50 states. When this law was written, in 1787, there were only 13 states, but I'll bet it felt nearly as difficult then as it sounds now to get an amendment through. Getting enough people to agree to such a significant change is a really unusual occurrence."

"Yet slavery has been finished with an amendment, and black men can vote thanks to one of those, and later women, and then the voting age was lowered through an amendment."

"That doesn't seem so astonishing to me. It was hard, but ultimately, it was the right thing to do. What seems amazing is the fact that Prohibition ever passed. Getting rid of it isn't surprising; it was such an unrealistic idea in the first place. Trying to control people to that degree and do their thinking for them is probably why it failed."

"Interesting analysis. Is that why you think that an amendment about abortion wouldn't get passed?"

"Pretty much. Telling people whether or not to stay pregnant, or how many kids to have, seems unworkable. People will just keep doing whatever they want, even if it destroys them. It's their choice."

Hamish thought about that.

"Not if the Senate has anything to say about that. Big Brother seems to be hovering around it."

"What do you mean? I thought it was mostly full of pro-choice Senators. They won't let Boenher push them."

"Not that. I mean something else. Those same pro-choice people are also in favor of population control measures. They just started talking about it yesterday."

"Seriously? What are they suggesting?"

"Well, right now it's just mandating birth control classes and secular sex education in schools. Abstinence wasn't a realistic thing to teach, but the General Accounting Office and some other think tanks have been publishing some statistics about population growth, and yesterday the Senators started discussing it. I think they were talking about it in the House, too, as though it were something to be alarmed about."

"Really?" I got up from the sofa, leaving my dinner on the coffee table, and rushed to get the computer out of sleep mode. I didn't want to wait to see a report on this. I wanted it now – this was significant news, even if nothing was yet proposed.

The website for *The New York Times* had a story on the main page about it. It was huge: "Senate and House Alarmed Over Population Growth – Politicians Say the U.S. Can't Afford It" the headline screamed.

Wow.

I read it through; it was just what I had been thinking all along.

I saved a copy for my records, wondering what I was going to do with it. A lecture on big government trying to control citizens' decisions? China's one-child policy? There was plenty of medical historical material there. But how would it seem coming from a co-inventor of a birth control device?

And what happened to going green, I wondered. I re-read the article. There it was, mid-way through: going green wouldn't be enough, even if we all stopped using fossil fuels. There were simply too many humans on the planet right now, and it was getting worse every day. Despite this, the anti-choice protests and other efforts continued, in Congress and elsewhere. It was as if the religious-minded people didn't care about their children's future, or were simply in mind-numbing denial about it.

Still, what was I going to write about at work? Wouldn't I seem self-interested in every talk I prepared from now on?

I shared my concerns with Hamish. He suggested that I visit Dr. Nurse and talk to him about it. "Don't worry about it. See what he wants. He hired you because he thought that the Rockefeller Institute could benefit from your lectures. As long as he still thinks so, you have nothing to worry about."

Okay. I went back to thinking about politics again.

"It seems incredible to think that our government would actually be able to check the rate of human population growth," I remarked.

"Yeah, that's what I think too, but if something isn't done, our reasons for not having kids are going to be validated in a big way during the next few decades, and we'll see the results."

"Well...that will certainly be interesting."

"Yeah."

The next day, armed with a printed copy of that article, I asked Patsy to call Dr. Nurse's office and make me an appointment, and to see if he was free that afternoon.

He was. I went to see him at 3 p.m.

That feeling that I might be hallucinating was back. I hadn't had it for a long time, but it was back again. This time, I couldn't decide how I felt about it. Of course, it was hard to feel one way or the other about a thing that was essentially still very much up in the air.

It was just a debate, not a decision.

But facts were irrefutable: the population of the United States was growing past the limits of capacity – capacity of the land, the water, the resources, the schools, the universities, and the economy to accommodate it. And now the elected representatives of our government were thinking about that.

But next year was election year for those same people.

Realistically, nothing was going to change until after that.

Whatever happened in U.S. politics over the course of the next year and a half would be aimed at job security, not future national security.

By national security, I meant financial and quality-of-life.

If we actually grew past capacity, our security would be threatened, because civil liberties cost money. Without a stable economy and a sense of hope, the social order could break down anywhere, I thought to myself…even here in the nation with the best legal system yet to exist.

I knew that our system wasn't perfect, but I still thought that it was the best one.

No wonder Hamish was willing to become a U.S. citizen and commit to living here with me for the rest of his life.

I went into Dr. Nurse's suite and said "Hi" to Kirsten and the receptionist, Annie, as I arrived. They smiled and greeted me back, and Kirsten told me to go on in.

"Come in," he called when I knocked.

I went in.

Dr. Nurse was sitting in the wing chair as when he had interviewed us, but today his TV was on, tuned in to C-SPAN. He looked up at me.

"Let me guess: you're here about this." He gestured at the screen.

Senator Boenher held the floor, arguing relentlessly about the natural order of things and the right of men and women to perpetuate their own DNA with impunity and thus keep their lines alive, claiming that it was a God-given right and how dare anyone say otherwise.

I paused to stare at the scene, then remarked, "I guess he's not in favor of free speech after all. So much for his oath to protect the Constitution."

Dr. Nurse laughed mirthlessly. "We're going to see a lot of that for a while. What's on your mind, Professor Châtelet?"

I took the seat on the sofa that he motioned and said, "Call me Avril."

"Only if call me Jeffrey."

"Okay, Jeffrey. I am in fact here because of these debates. I'm worried that my lectures will seem self-serving, that they will reflect badly on this institution, and that people here will be angry with me over Nae-Née now that Congress is hotly debating human population growth as if it needs to be controlled. If birth can be controlled by a nanite, how long before someone in Washington gets the bright idea of controlling human reproduction rates with it? Granted, we're looking at an election year, but then what? So that's what motivated me to come visit you."

He sat there looking at me for a moment. "I see."

I waited.

Jeffrey spoke again a moment later. "I don't want you to leave. Your lectures are contributing a great deal to the reputation of this institution. I like to say that those who don't study history will repeat the mistakes of the past – and I'm paraphrasing to avoid plagiarizing that quote – but scientists don't have time to study history. You're filling in that gap for us, and I'm looking forward to the book that will result from your lectures in another year. That's how many more lectures you will need to prepare before you have enough for a book, isn't it?"

I stared at him for a moment, then said, "Yes – I was hoping for 18 chapters, and a coffee-table sort of book full of photos."

"Well go back and do it! And don't worry about Nae-Née being any impediment. If some radical religious right-winger wants to rant and rave about Nae-Née changing the world, some leftist will balance that one out, and so on and on. Just keep doing your thing."

"Okay. Well – thank you for setting my mind at ease."

"No problem. I'm looking forward to this fall's lectures."

He grinned at me, and I stood up, smiled, and walked out.

Well…back to work, then.

First I went to find Hamish and tell him about it. He was back in his office, checking the pie charts on some test results. The charts looked like the positive results of the nanites filled most of each pie.

I flopped onto his sofa and waited.

Soon he came over and sat on the floor in front of the sofa and hugged me. "How did it go?" was all he asked.

"Fine. He wants me to keep doing what I've been doing, doesn't think the debates will reflect badly on this place, and doesn't seem impressed by Boenher's rants. He was ranting on C-SPAN on Nurse's TV when I walked in."

"What did he say about that?"

"He said 'Let me guess: you're here about this,' and invited me to sit down."

"Sounds about right."

"We also started calling each other by our first names. I started it by objecting when he called me Professor Châtelet. It's cool, but it feels awkward coming from my boss."

Hamish laughed. "I've been calling him Jeff since we got here."

"You're both guys."

"Whatever. I have to finish this pie chart."

I got up. "I'm going to read for some more lecture topics. I hope I can get a list ready so that I can map them all out, then just read the material and write them up faster and faster."

"Good luck – you can do it." He kissed me and turned back to his desk. I chased him, kissed him back, and left.

Patsy was at her desk, watching for me. "So – my dad says that you 2 really hit it off. He likes you – I can tell. And he and his girlfriend have a cat," she added.

So maybe there was no problem about this as yet. I wondered why she had introduced us. Maybe she thought it was a good idea on some level; maybe her father had been intrigued and bugged her about it; maybe he wanted to check me out to see how things might go with his daughter's job – gauge the future situation. Probably that was it, I decided.

"Yeah – he got a new laptop this weekend, and asked my opinion about what to get."

"I know – he told me about it. I'll probably see it this weekend. I have a computer at home, but it's a desktop, so I can't show it to you very easily."

"What kind is it?"

"A Mac. I like to be able to look up a lot of graphic sites – fan magazines, stuff like that – and Macs make it easier."

"Do you do any writing on it?"

"No. I don't have the Word program for it, so I don't bother. It's just a toy."

"Oh. Well, I'm going to get back to work," I said.

"Okay. See you later."

I did get a lot of work done, and a list made of potential topics that pretty much outlined the rest of the book and therefore 12 more lectures, taking me into the next summer. It was a good last hour.

When I left, Patsy was typing away at something Hamish had dictated. He would meet me at home later. I walked part of the way, wandered through Tiffany's just to browse and enjoy the air-conditioning, then wimped out and took a cab home. I had everything we needed for dinner except for some fish, so I went back out and visited The Lobster Place in Greenwich Village.

When I got back, I paused at the door with my keys. It felt as though someone were watching me, which made me feel paranoid on a city street with random passersby.

Still, I nonchalantly let myself in as fast as I could and locked the door, then looked out through the peephole.

Across the street, a tall, thin blond man was pacing with a cigarette in his hand, glancing around at nothing in particular.

He was wearing jeans, sneakers, and a tee shirt. He looked like he was in his 30s or 40s, and there was nothing out of the ordinary about his appearance.

As I watched him, he suddenly stared right at me.

I froze.

He couldn't possibly know that I was still there, or hear whether or not I had stayed right behind my front door.

I looked at him a moment longer, and then stamped out his cigarette and headed up the street, walking what appeared to be a normal pace.

Maybe I was paranoid. But Hamish liked to say that just because you're paranoid, it doesn't mean that they're not out to get you.

When Hamish came home, I was finished cooking, and sitting with the cat on the sofa, watching C-SPAN. The debates hadn't changed in topic or intensity.

And now religion was playing a role in them, too.

Hamish picked up the remote and flicked to a few other news channels, just to see what else was up. He went to CNN, Fox News, and our favorite, MSNBC. Keith Olbermann was starting soon.

The scenes were the same on each channel.

Protestors were camped out daily outside the U.S. Capitol building, and also around state capitol buildings around the nation, showing picket signs proclaiming outrage and quoting the Bible. "We want our children!" They shouted.

I told Hamish about the guy who had stood outside.

He looked concerned for a split second, then sat on the sofa with me and said, "I think you're worrying about nothing. Just relax." He reached across and petted Eowyn, who was rolling around on the sofa next to me, going crazy with a catnip toy. "She's high. How long has she had that mouse? Isn't there a pouch of catnip in its belly?"

"About 20 minutes. I let her run around and go crazy so she'd get tired." I snatched it from her a moment later and put it in the coffee table drawer with the coasters and the rest of her toy collection. Spoiled cat – I loved giving her new toys. I glanced at the collection and decided to stop that for a while. This cat probably had a lifetime's supply by now.

Hamish kissed me. "Something smells delicious; is it Cajun catfish and sweet potato fries?"

"Yes – and salad and sautéed okra with garlic. And a raspberry tart for dessert."

"I love you!" he said and started kissing me. I laughed and kissed him back.

We ate, and watched a movie on the DVD player, then sat in our huge tub for two.

Soon I had forgotten all about the guy in the tee shirt and jeans.

Fall came, and with it the summer heat wave started to die down. I resumed my walks down the length of lower Manhattan, sometimes wandering over to Broadway to see the Ed Sullivan Theatre. Sometime I wanted to go there on a weekday with my digital camera and see if David Letterman would appear, but I refused to make that my only reason for going there.

Broadway was a fun place to see once in a while, despite the hordes of tourists meandering through Times Square. As long as I wasn't here at New Year's Eve, it seemed like fun, I thought – I hated crowds, and failed to see the appeal of spending hours in the freeze just to watch a ball drop down a pole.

Hamish and I met Cathy in September and I gave her a copy of my cat book, autographed and addressed personally to her. She and Andrew and Hamish and I had a fun evening at a Japanese place called Monster Sushi, and they promised to go out with us again soon.

We met a couple of times at the Angelika Theater, which showed a lot of independent films that we would have had a hard time finding back in Connecticut. Andrew seemed to be showing me what a great intellectual playground Manhattan was without even trying.

The lecture series continued to go well, including the one on China's one-child policy. Looking at it after a few decades of use had fascinated the audience, which included some guests from other universities and hospitals, and some people who had visited China. The result was too many adult males with too few adult females to marry, and not all of the women wanted to get married. There was a lot of jealously and resentment among the men who couldn't find anyone. The Chinese government's efforts to promote daughters as desirable had been partially pursued through bribes and advertising campaigns.

The most upsetting part had been the tales of formaldehyde being injected into the heads of babies that had been born without a license. Government doctors were somehow willing to murder newborns in the delivery room, right in front of the mothers, just to enforce the one-child policy. Someone commented to me –

one of Hamish's colleagues from the Medical Sciences and Human Genetics lab – that those doctors were being monitored by the totalitarian government. It was the illegally born babies or them, apparently.

I was glad to be in the U.S. in that case. I couldn't think of a worse method of population control. Nae-Née seemed so tame in comparison. It pre-empted babies rather than hurting any who had been brought into existence. Perhaps there was nothing to worry about; no wonder Jeffrey Nurse had wanted me to go ahead with this lecture.

He had attended, and he met me and Hamish afterwards to say as much.

"See? Your invention gives people hope that there is a much better way to manage the numbers of human beings that many that have been used elsewhere. I'm glad you went ahead with this lecture. Keep up the good work."

So I did.

Patsy seemed to want to be in on associating with me; Andrew must have been mentioning our visits to her from time to time.

She invited me to go with her to something called The Big Apple Circus. I had never heard of it. When she told me that it was in a tent on the Lincoln Center grounds every year, I was surprised.

"Yeah, it's really there. I go every year. Come with me this year," she insisted.

"Okay – when is it?"

"November – at least, that's when my tickets are for…on the 1st, a Tuesday."

I checked my calendar. "Okay – no lecture until the next week."

On the evening of the 1st, I left work early and found a bagel shop. I got a smoked salmon bagel – they had a long list of smoked salmon choices – and a bottle of water, plus some chips. I was sure that nothing at the circus would seem healthy, and I didn't want to be stuck eating fat, salt and sugar. I could have some popcorn to be polite, I decided.

Then I headed over to Lincoln Center, walking up the middle of the square, facing all 3 of the buildings – ballet, opera and symphony halls.

A huge banner was draped across the Metropolitan Opera building, announcing that Mozart's *The Marriage of Figaro* was playing through December. It had already started.

And here I was, heading for what was…a kiddie circus. Hordes of little kids – toddlers and kids under the age of 10 – were being led towards a huge white tent that loomed to the left of the opera house.

What had I agreed to?!

Too late now.

I approached the gate and saw Patsy grinning and waving to me. She handed me a huge ticket and I followed her in.

"What's that?" she asked as we went into the tent. A clown – male, but dressed like an old woman – waved us in. It turned out that he was the Circus's signature character, a Grandma clown. Red and yellow decorations were everywhere, and a concessions stand was straight ahead, just before a right turn that led into the seating area.

"It's a bagel with smoked salmon. I didn't want to rely on junk food for dinner, so I brought this. I'm looking forward to popcorn, though."

She looked a bit surprised, but nodded and got a huge, long hot dog and slathered it with ketchup and mustard from red and yellow squirt bottles, plus a lemonade, pink cotton candy, and popcorn. "We can share this," she said, handing me the popcorn and pink sticky stuff. Then she ordered me a lemonade. "Don't worry, it's all part of the ticket," she added. "You can get as much as you want – take some candy bars!"

"Are you sure?"

"Yes! I do this every year – well, I did before I went to L.A., and I did it again last year."

"Oh." I took a couple of Hershey bars and the lemonade. It came in a huge, gaudy, plastic cup with a straw attachment that bent up and down. The top was transparent, fluorescent green, and the cup itself had the Grandma clown painted onto it.

"The cup is a souvenir. I've got several of them," she told me.

Lovely. I smiled and said I would keep mine and show Hamish.

We went in and took our seats, which gave us a decent view of the ring, halfway up and a third of the way around the ring from the performers' entrance.

The show started, and I wondered about the trapeze artists. Perhaps there would be some death-defying feats. I liked the idea as long as there would be a net. But when the time came for acrobats, they didn't go up very high at all; in fact, the men merely carried the women around the ring while the women twirled around a few times.

There was a dog act, but that wasn't remarkable. The dogs didn't seem to do anything too fascinating either. And so it went.

I watched the kids around me, bewildered. Their parents kept grinning at them and encouraging them to clap and smile. I recalled being a child with no difficulty; this would not have impressed then, and it seemed utterly inane now. But then, I was a strange child, only impressed by a good story or something that I could learn – a bit of science, art or history.

What was particularly unpleasant was the constant touching of my legs and shoulders by sticky little hands as the toddlers balanced against everyone and everything that they came in contact with. Their parents did nothing about it.

I had been inadvertently and unknowingly lured into this situation. I just had to get through the rest of the evening, I told myself, and then I wouldn't come back if they paid me to.

As we sat there, with the inane circus act going on interminably in front of us and with toddler kids ambling and brushing all around and against us, Patsy suddenly said something to me that put her interest in this dull spectacle into perspective.

"I want a baby."

I looked at her very seriously, keeping my expression as deadpan as possible. Frankly, I was appalled. Another baby in the world – on top of all these around us….and from a woman who seemed utterly unfit to be a parent, from what I knew about her thus far.

A moment later, I found my voice again.

"A baby?!" I said, without raising the volume of my reply. The tone had conveyed my disapproval on its own. "But the world is overpopulated. There aren't enough resources for everyone to enjoy a happy, comfortable, and interesting life."

Her reply was as thoughtless as it was instantaneous: "But I don't care about everybody else," she said with a careless giggle and a huge grin, "I just care about me, me, me."

I didn't attempt to continue what was apparently supposed to pass for conversation.

She was easily the most selfish and self-absorbed individual that I had ever met.

At least she had the one redeeming virtue of being honest about it.

I was disgusted, however. It was now abundantly clear that we had nothing in common, were total opposites in every way, and that there was absolutely nothing on which to base a friendship. I wondered why she and I had tried. Curiosity, perhaps, but that would now end.

Her comments about reproduction proved to be a defining moment for me, although I did not realize it then. I found myself thinking: so this is how our species came to be in the situation in which we currently found ourselves: short-term thinking led to the overpopulation that now strained the planet's resources. It was then that I stopped caring about the disappointment that people like her might feel if they were somehow unable to have children. Our species desperately needed long-term attitudes and we needed them now. Party time was winding down.

It was then that I realized how population control could be implemented, and that this was the only way that it could be implemented: by assigning the task to people who did not feel the urge to reproduce. No way – not unless hell froze over – would any of the others make a move to do so. No one who wanted the party to continue would sacrifice for the future of all.

When at last it was over and I was free to go, I didn't. I didn't want her to know what I really thought of the circus. I walked with her instead to a record and poster shop on Broadway, where we actually had some fun browsing for *Wonder Woman* and *Duran Duran* paraphernalia. I didn't buy anything, but I definitely had fun.

I was glad that we did that, because this was a person I would have to spend time with on a daily basis for the foreseeable future. Eventually, we had seen enough and hailed a cab after Patsy bought an old Sheryl Crow poster. She got out on 14th Street, and I continued on down to Greenwich Village.

I was reminded of something that had happened a long time ago as I rode the last few blocks.

Once, early in my first year of college, the R.A. of my dorm, a nice Italian-American Catholic girl in her junior year told me that there were two things I should never discuss: religion and politics. I had immediately responded, outraged, with the retort that there was nothing else that interested me. She had looked disturbed, and made no reply.

I thought of her again now. I hadn't changed my mind, but it occurred to me that there were an awful lot of other people out there who thought as she did.

No wonder I kept to myself and only chatted with a few people. I couldn't find very many who wanted to talk about interesting things.

I was glad I hadn't brought that up at the moment that Patsy told me she wanted a baby.

When I got home, Hamish was snoring in front of the living room TV with the cat on his chest. She had gotten big. Not fat, just nearly full-grown; she covered the length of his torso. I kissed him and he woke up with a start, looking upset.

"What's the matter?" I asked. "You're acting guilty for falling asleep."

"I wanted to meet you at the door." He got up and kissed me, carrying the cat as he did so. He put her in her bed on the poufy chair near the stairs. "So – how was it?"

"Awful – riddled with sticky-pawed toddlers who kept touching random strangers to keep their balance, inane circus acts that wouldn't have impressed me when I was a kid myself – though I was an odd kid, so that's no reason for the show to have been any different – and disgusting, unhealthy food. I brought my own, so I don't feel sick. All that salty, sugary crap was included in the ticket. I hope Patsy couldn't figure out what I really thought; I tried to hide it and just act polite, but I wasn't extremely enthusiastic, so who knows what she thought."

He looked at me seriously as I described it. "I don't envy you that evening."

"Oh, and to top it all off – although this was something I noticed as I approached the tent – right next to it was the Metropolitan Opera at Lincoln Center. They're playing *The Marriage of Figaro*, and there I was going into the most inane rubbish…it made me miss you."

Hamish rushed over and hugged me when I said that.

"Did you have dinner?" I asked him.

"Oh yeah – I stopped on the way home at a Korean joint and tried something that you would have hated, complete with kim-chee."

"Ugh. Glad to have missed it."

I spent the next couple of minutes relating the "I want a baby" interchange, then followed it up with the part about browsing in the record store.

He looked appalled, then pleased. "At least it ended on a good note," he observed. "We don't want to offend our secretary. I've been careful not to have her type up anything about obesity, although I have wondered what I could do with nanites and fat cells once the tumor-seeker project is completed."

I stared at him. "I realize that I don't know what I'm talking about, but that sounds like a bit of a stretch to me. Isn't fighting obesity still mostly about diet?"

"It is, but I keep wondering if nanites can't give the problem a bit of a nudge. It may not be anything I can work on, but I feel as though I can't efficiently look into it with Patsy fielding e-mails and calls."

"Great."

Late that night, at 2 a.m., I noticed that I was alone in our bed. I got up and looked around for Hamish. Eowyn wasn't in the bed either, so I figured she was with him.

They were both downstairs at the kitchen computer; the cat was sitting on the built-in desk next to the monitor, staring at the mouse pointer as Hamish moved it around the screen. He kept holding her back as she stuck her nose and whiskers too close for him to see what he was doing. I picked her up and asked, "What are you doing up?"

He grinned at me. "Buying us tickets to that Mozart opera. I got them for Saturday afternoon, the 3rd of December."

"Really?!" I was absolutely thrilled. "That's terrific! I love you! You're the best husband in the world!" I put the cat down and hugged him. He squeezed back.

The next day at the office, Patsy asked me if I had had a good time. What a loaded question, I thought. But I had to give a decent reply.

"Yes – it was fun to spend some time with you and get to know you a bit more. And thanks for showing me that shop on Broadway. I had forgotten how much I enjoyed the 80s rock groups and Wonder Woman – I liked that TV show a lot, too. So we have something in common," I concluded.

She seemed to like that. "Good! I was wondering what you would make of it all."

"Patsy – did I not notice when you got engaged or something? Am I being an oblivious boss, not noticing important stuff like that?"

"No!" she sounded shocked. "Why would you say that?"

"Because you said you wanted a baby. Are you and Jim getting married?"

"Oooohhhh. I see. No. I want to get married, but he doesn't see any reason to do that unless we have kids, and he doesn't want to do that unless I can lose more weight, which I have a really hard time doing. He thinks the baby wouldn't be healthy otherwise."

I looked at her for a moment, wondering how to respond. Well, at least I gotten some more information politely enough, but now what? "Have you talked about getting married?"

"Yes. I'd go down to city hall right now if he called me with a ring."

"Really…interesting…I'd drag Hamish out of his lab and we would be your witnesses if necessary. You need 2 of them to make it legal. But wouldn't you want a white dress and a reception?"

"Yes and no. At this point, I feel as though it would be a miracle to just get married. I'm forty years old and no diet seems to work."

"Do you go out walking much?"

"Not really. Jim took me to the street fairs near my dad's place, but it was so hot and humid I could hardly stand it. I haven't been out for a walk since last summer."

"I did Weight Watchers after law school. It encouraged half-hour walks each day, and lots of fresh fruits and vegetables. I lost the 30 pounds that I had put on from some anti-anxiety pills – plus I quit the pills. Better to be anxious and able to write and be thin, I decided."

"I envy you – I don't like fruits and vegetables as much as I should, and I get too hungry without bread. I can't stand it. Plus, I do take anti-anxiety pills."

"Really…you would have to stop those if you wanted to get pregnant – they're bad for a growing fetus. Any doctor would tell you that."

"I know. I have to make up my mind soon, before I get any older. It's harder to lose weight when you're older, I keep reading. I read all the weight loss articles I can. Maybe it's time for some diet pills," Patsy said.

Hamish had come out of his office in time to hear that. "No – don't do that. Diet pills will ruin your liver."

She looked up at him unhappily.

I chimed in, "Listen to him – he's got a medical degree. Just do diet and exercise to lose weight. If you join a Weight Watchers group close to where you live, you can find some friends to do the exercise with. You're a sociable person; you could do that easily. I had to just go it alone, walking between the meeting place and home, but I did it."

"Maybe I'll do that. At least I don't have any delusions about praying the weight off."

"What makes you mention that idea?"

"There's a weird woman who lives across the hall from my mother who keeps suggesting that I do that. My mother tells me every day that I've got to lose weight, and that it's disgusting how heavy I am, but even she laughed at our neighbor. Faith won't fix this. I have to do it."

Patsy was just full of information today; it had been almost a year since we had started working together and I was just finding out her views on religion. What about politics? "Have you noticed the debates about U.S. population growth in Congress? They've been going on for a few months," I asked her.

"Yeah. But it's an election year. Nothing's going to change for a while. And I really can't imagine that the government would try to stop people from having kids."

"Me either – birth control methods are one thing, insisting that people use them rather than merely encouraging it is quite another."

"Exactly. You say things so well – you sound like a book sometimes."

"Oops." I laughed. "I get that sometimes. I try to sound a bit informal to avoid that."

Chapter 17

Attorney Lakshmi

Andrew Warne called me that Saturday.

He wanted to introduce me to someone. Hamish was invited also; in fact, Andrew wanted both of us to meet her.

Her name was Lakshmi Jasmine Rahni, J.D., Ph.D. She was an attorney, and she worked at the U.N. Department of Economic and Social Affairs, in the Population Division.

"When can we get together?"

"Why don't I give you some possibilities from our schedules, and then you can take them to her and figure it out, and then get back to us?"

"Sounds good."

"Let's see…Hamish is taking his citizenship test on Tuesday, then he gets sworn in – if he passes, which I'm sure he will – 2 weeks later, on the 22nd, so that day is out…and we're going to the Opera on December 3rd. Oh, and we'll be in Connecticut for Thanksgiving, leaving on Tuesday afternoon and returning on Saturday. So any evening other than those dates would be good, if that's the time-frame you had in mind."

"That was it – okay, I wrote it all down. I'll get a hold of Lakshmi and get back to you soon. She likes gourmet Indian restaurants – and knows them all – are you two up for that?"

"Are you kidding?! We love Indian food! This already sounds like a fun evening, and it isn't even scheduled yet."

I could almost hear Andrew smiling as he said, "Perfect. I'll get back to you soon. And tell your husband good luck with his citizenship test."

"Thanks – I will. Bye."

I turned to Hamish and explained, and passed on the good luck wish. He was intrigued by the invitation.

"I wonder what we'll talk about? If she's a lawyer for the U.N., maybe she can tell us some of the inside scoop on how they deal with birth control and overpopulation issues."

"Maybe…or maybe, because of attorney-client privilege, it will be really vague and just a great discussion of hot issues."

"That would be good, too."

He paused a moment, then asked, "Why can't we wait until Wednesday to drive to your parents' place? I could get more work done at the lab."

"You get plenty of work time, you workaholic! We're better than solvent, and I want to make 3 homemade pumpkin pies and buttery crust for them, which means the day before Thanksgiving, I already have to be there. My mother is hosting the dinner, which means cooking and baking for a ton of people whom we haven't seen in a while. And there is no baking of pies the day of Thanksgiving, because the oven is booked for the whole day – by the entrée."

"Oh, all right," he said, knowing when a battle was utterly lost.

"At least Dad will be happy that we're driving our car – it hasn't gotten much use since we moved to Manhattan. It probably won't get much use again until Christmas."

"Oh, we're not going back to your parents for Christmas. I'm taking you to Hawai'i."

Hamish stood there grinning at me like a cat who was waiting to be told it was good for killing a mouse.

I stood there for a moment, stunned. I was having another hallucination – the best kind.

"You are?" I grinned, then my face fell. "My parents will be disappointed. Did you already arrange for tickets and a hotel, or is the trip flexible?"

He looked determined – intractable – but I was willing to go with him for Christmas. I just didn't want to upset anyone, and I told him so.

"The trip is set. I've been planning it for a month, and I wanted to surprise you."

"Well, you succeeded brilliantly. I'm totally surprised…and thrilled. I'm going to call my mother now." I took out my cell phone and hit the speed dial for my parents' place. It was evening, so they might be home.

My mother answered on the third ring. One more and the answering machine would have kicked in. "Hello?"

"Mommy – Hamish just dropped a wonderful bombshell on me. He's planned a trip to Hawai'i for us for Christmas. But I'm worried that you and Dad will be upset about not having us there for the holidays."

Silence.

Then she said, "Are you kidding?! You're married! Go! Besides, I helped him plan it."

Now the silence came from me, but just for a moment, and then I started laughing as I looked at Hamish, who had leaned in close enough to hear what she had said and was laughing it up too.

"I see. I've been tag-teamed. And it's an oddly pleasant experience," I replied.

We chatted about citizenship tests and pie-baking, Hamish said a few words to her, and then said good-bye.

Then I started hugging my husband and talking about what we could do there.

"Let's find a black sand beach! I read that there are some of those in Hawai'i – I'm not sure which islands, I think Kaua'i and Mau'i – and see a Kona coffee plantation, and the museums about Hawai'ian people, like Hulihe'e Palace, and try some poi. Where are we staying?" I finally stopped talking.

Hamish pulled me onto the sofa and hugged me. "I found a great hotel and your mother showed me how to book it. It's called the Turtle Bay Resort, and it's on O'ahu."

"Wow. I feel like I'm having a really great dream. Don't wake me up."

He grinned mischievously and pinched me. "We're still going!"

I laughed. Then I jumped up and raced upstairs.

"Where are you going?" he wanted to know, following me.

"To make sure I can find my bikini. I know it's here somewhere – I saw it when we moved in – I just have to check."

"You have a bikini?" Hamish sounded fascinated. Cool – I had piqued his interest.

"Yeah," we were in our bedroom now, "in here somewhere…" I routed around in a drawer. "Here it is!" I held it up; it was a medium pink, all cloth with ties at the hips and on the halter top, with a white heart pattern. "I got it on sale a few winters ago hoping that we would eventually find a reason to enjoy it, and you did it!" I pulled his swimming trunks out of one of his drawers…also unused.

"Try it on." He sat down on the edge of the bed and waited for me to model it.

Andrew called us back on Monday evening. Attorney Rahni wanted to meet us on December 6th for dinner. I checked with Hamish, and then said okay. Dinner would be at a place midway between the Rockefeller Institute and the United Nations buildings, at a place called Dawat. We looked forward to it.

Meanwhile, I had started another lecture, this one on the history of plastic and reconstructive surgery. I decided to bring it up to the present by showing cleft palate surgeries and reconstructions of Afghani women whose husbands had mutilated their faces.

Hamish walked in on me as I went over a collection of photos for the presentation and paused on one of a beautiful woman whose nose had been sliced off by her husband. He had chased her when she fled, held her down, and cut it off, thus inflicting a literal disfigurement in return for the loss of his figurative nose. Afghani husbands have a belief that if one of their wives leaves her husband, then his nose has been cut off, so he decided to make her more miserable than he had been made by her departure.

Hamish stopped and stared angrily at it and asked what had happened to her. I told him. "That's not a husband – that's a monster! I don't care how ethnocentric I sound, either!" he roared.

"What a nice husband you are," I said. I kept saving photos. The lecture was already shaping up rather nicely. It would be my last one before the Hawai'i trip. I had somehow gotten ahead on my work, and was speeding through it, able to work on editing chapters from the lectures. I hoped to have a book ready to go to press shortly after the end of the next semester.

Time started to move in Fast Forward mode again. Hamish passed his citizenship test. He and I went to his swearing in ceremony, where I had trouble seeing him in the room full of new citizens. There were so many of them. We celebrated by finding a nice American restaurant, one called Vynl on 8th Avenue, which had informal dishes and old records glued to the ceiling, plus dolls of famous American rock stars in little alcoves built into the left wall.

One dividend to living in the city was the fact that driving wasn't an issue, so I could drink a Daiquiri or a Margarita and not worry about feeling tipsy for a while afterward.

Thanksgiving went well. I drove up to West Hartford and back, and we brought Eowyn with us. My mother had us lock her in my room and let Spock have the run of the house. He gave me an outraged look, but let me cuddle him. Aunt Zoe and Uncle Charlie wanted to hear all about the nanites and my book, and Grandmère wanted to hear about our summer trip to France and our upcoming trip to Hawai'i. I heard from my mother that Greg had found a college in Australia, of all places, and was doing well.

Then it was time to attend the Metropolitan Opera, which was as fabulous as we had hoped. We sat on the side of the mezzanine and laughed as Figaro attempted to measure a space for his future bed with Susanna. The singer-actor did a hilarious job of pantomiming the dilemma.

And then it was time to meet the U.N. attorney.

She was waiting for us just inside the restaurant, Dawat, on East 58th Street just off of 3rd Avenue. The restaurant was owned by the famous Indian chef Madhur Jaffrey, so we were happily anticipating a delectable meal. We were not disappointed.

Lakshmi was wearing a beautiful dark blue skirt suit, and her hair was up in a clip with waves and curls pinned her and there around the bun on the crown of her head. She had sparkly eye shadow and lipstick on, and some gold bangles on her wrists. And she wore a bhindi on her forehead, just between her eyebrows, a Hindu indication that she was married.

The first thing she did was to tell us to call her Lakshmi, as we were all close in age; in fact, she was 45 years old. She had asked whether we liked Indian food and I was replying that we love it, and that I cook it at home often, and had several cookbooks by both Chefs Jaffrey and Julie Sahni when Andrew appeared just behind us.

We were promptly led to a booth straight back from the entrance, which the host proudly pointed out was their "celebrity seat" because of its horseshoe shape. No chairs were on the open side of the table, which was rather small. This caused the diners to sit facing each other, thus able to carry on a conversation, but with their faces fully visible to everyone else in the room. I had never seen a seat quite like it before. But we were not celebrities, so I didn't worry about photos of us chewing ending up in some news publication.

"So how are you enjoying living in New York City?" Lakshmi asked us once we were all seated. She and I were in the middle, with Hamish next to me and Andrew on the other side.

"We love it here – it's possible to find just about any ingredient for any recipe, which is terrific because I like to cook and bake at home – and it's like one big playground of an island what with all the museums and shows and music concerts available here. I just hope that it doesn't suddenly turn into a pumpkin in another decade or so and become New Venice rather than New York as we know and love it. Sea levels are rising, the earth is warming up, and no one is willing to change the way that they live. People just want more, more, more. I don't want things to end, and it seems like they will – and soon."

She listened to me gravely during this rant of a speech, and then nodded.

"That's why I tell my two daughters that they shouldn't have children. Get married, yes, enjoy life, yes, but don't inflict future disappointments on another generation. I'm trying to make the world better for them, but it seems that more people are bent on using it all up."

I liked Lakshmi; she was a realist. There were so few of them in the world.

"How old are your daughters?" Hamish asked. "Are they still in school?"

"They are both at the United Nations International School, here in New York. I find that it's easy for us to be together. They are in 10th and 12th grades. My oldest has been accepted to Columbia University, so I'm very happy; she will be near me next year."

"That's terrific. What are their names?" I asked.

"My oldest is Harapriya, and my youngest is named Devasri."

"And what would they like to do for careers…or do they know yet?"

"Harapriya would like to study medicine and practice gynecology. I think she listens to me talking to my colleagues about women who cannot control their own fertility even though they would like to, and to have a less exhausting life of childbearing and rearing."

And Devasri?" I asked, still curious.

"Devasri wants to follow in my footsteps, but practice law in India and help women who need more autonomy in their lives. She wants to either join or set up a legal clinic for women who need to get away from husbands and in-laws who demand big dowries, and for prostitutes who have escaped from their pimps."

"That sounds terrific," Andrew said. "You must be very proud of them."

"I am, but time will tell if they can do all this. They will have to not only study hard but be accepted to good schools, and that isn't easy any more. Their father and I worry that all of their hard work might not be enough."

I told her about what had happened to Greg back in Connecticut, about his high GPA, his extra-curricular activities, his dream of going to medical school, and how no college had accepted him, despite all that. I added that he was in Australia now, having found a good school there, but he had intended to go to a school in the U.S. At least I was able to end the tale on a positive note; I had worried about his sanity for a while, until I heard the outcome.

Lakshmi listened gravely, nodding and shaking her head as the facts warranted. Andrew looked appalled, but never surprised, and then relieved when I concluded with the part about Australia.

"All the way to another country to college, because his own was full," he commented sadly. "I think that that will start to happen with great frequency as time goes on. All these kids have been raised with expectations – their own and their parents' – that they will attend a respectable 4-year college and go on to do great things. But if they all expect to do great things, a lot of them will fall by the wayside, disappointed."

This was getting utterly morbid, but we were all too fascinated with the subject to drop it.

Hamish jumped in next. "What about your husband? What does he do?"

She smiled. "Anand is in business. He is the CEO of a spice company in Mumbai."

"So he lives there?" I asked, with a tone of amazement and empathy.

"Yes. He visits often, though. His business brings him here frequently."

I told her that Hamish and I had had a lot of experience with being apart.

She smiled then, realizing why I had seemed so interested and upset about that.

We ordered several appetizers to share because Lakshmi told us that we could watch the chefs in the corner to our right make them. Two Indian men in white chef outfits were visible from the waist up behind a glass enclosure there, working over an open oven that was built into the counter in front of them. She insisted that Hamish and I get up and have a look into it, so we did. The chefs paused to grin and wave at us, and we waved back.

The waiter left us to discuss our dinner orders while he put in the appetizer order. I started to worry that we would get too full to try dessert, but Lakshmi just laughed and said to get doggie bags and go ahead. We had a thali of sauces and rice and vegetables, some shrimp and basmati rice, and chicken biryani rice, followed by carrot khulfi and cardamom-infused, almond rice pudding with chai tea.

Meanwhile, we talked about Nae-Née and population explosions. She wanted to hear all about our invention, how it had come about, who thought of what parts, and how cost-effective it was. I could almost see her as she recorded mental notes about it.

I asked her if she knew whether or not Nae-Née was being used much in India, and if she was wishing that it could be used a great deal there, or if the idea hadn't caught on. I knew that some of our sales came from India, but not precisely how great a percentage of the population was benefitting from it.

"Actually, quite a few people use it. My aunt is a gynecologist in Mumbai, where I am from, and she is finding that a lot of her patients want it. They find it is the easiest way to handle family planning, and the most reliable method yet presented to them."

Hamish and I exchanged delighted glances.

"Does your aunt say whether other doctors are finding similar thinking elsewhere?"

"Yes, she does – she told me that she attended a medical conference in New Delhi recently, and there were 2 lectures that dealt with it. One of those speakers even expressed a hope that it would be the salvation of India. No one is concerned that people would not have children, you see – only that they would inadvertently have too many. With a remote-controlled device such as Nae-Née, that problem would be eliminated. The government is even looking at it as a means to keep India's numbers from outstripping its resources."

I was floored. Nae-Née must be selling like mad there already. No wonder Hamish and I weren't concerned about buying opera tickets and paying for trips to Hawai‘i.

Lakshmi gave me a big smile then. "You didn't realize what a big thing it is, did you?"

"No. Only that debates in the U.S. Congress seem to be heating up about population growth in this country. I have yet to hear Nae-Née proposed as a solution to the dilemma."

"Just wait; I'm sure it will be. It's entirely too tempting. You and your husband have created a nanobotic miracle that could go a long way towards saving the planet."

I just looked at her for a moment, so she added, "You should see your face right now."

"I'm just glad that we're not real celebrities in this seat. I would hate to have a photo of my face with this doubtlessly stunned expression preserved for posterity."

Andrew burst out laughing. "You like to keep your hands at your sides and your expressions neutral, don't you?" he commented. "Are you sure you aren't Japanese?"

I gave a wry grin as Hamish laughed with him. "I'm sure, but my best friend from college has pointed that out about me before. She majored in Japanese language and culture."

Hamish spoke up now. "As a member of the U.N.'s Population Division, you must see a lot of data from studies of the subject, detailing the situation of nations all over the planet."

"I do. The studies are getting alarming, especially when compared against resources. The problem with these studies is that people try to make objective scientific facts political, which only serves to postpone dealing with the issue. Maybe I should say "problem" rather than "issue" here," she commented. "In any case, the data on nations' population policies is broken up in categories of projections, called too low, satisfactory, and too high. It is further broken into region of the planet: North America, Europe, Asia, Africa, Latin America and the Caribbean, and Oceana – which brings to mind George Orwell's *1984*, but is geographically elsewhere! – followed by most, less and least developed countries, lumping groups of them in together namelessly. I am explaining all of these because you are a scientist, and I know that if I try to leave this out, you will just ask me." She gave a wry smile.

Hamish grinned and thanked her.

"But what about the problem part of it?" I asked, trying to bring the conversation back to the point as quickly as possible.

"Ah yes…the point of it is that when politicians see the categories of extremes couching a happy medium on the charts, they start suggesting that the problem isn't as dire as scientists would have us all believe, and that we are talking like alarmists, upsetting the public, and so on."

"So they would like us to all live in a state of denial until a crisis of epic proportions forces us to face the music?" Andrew asked.

"That is exactly what they would have us do."

"Well," I said, "that won't work out very well, to put it mildly."

"No," Lakshmi agreed.

"Of course, I don't see governments forcing the use of birth control on an entire planet, or licensing births like the Chinese have been doing. It flies in the face of civil liberties. Religious fundamentalists would start screaming foul, and there would be uproars everywhere. Plus, enforcement mechanisms would be difficult to carry out, both logistically and otherwise. Also, how would everyone be reached? The planet may be more connected than ever, but some people are still quite isolated by geography or a lack of technology."

Lakshmi looked at me. "You are very well informed about the state of the world today, and very articulate about concerns that we spend most of our time thinking about at the U.N."

"Thanks. I just love to keep up with it all, and my job facilitates that. When I get to the office, the first thing I do is research current events in order to think of topics for my history of medicine lectures, and also for material that makes them relevant to today's practices and issues."

"I see."

"So how do you think the future looks – both the very near future and that of a decade from now?" Hamish asked her.

She said, "With the way the human population is expanding, and the droughts, floods and other impediments to growing sufficient food for everyone, I don't see how there won't be a bloodbath somewhere, sometime within the next few decades – or sooner – over basic resources. I hate to think of it, but I actually believe that someday soon, if humans don't sacrifice on having more babies, people will start dying of starvation in some places and killing each other in other places due to insufficient supplies."

Andrew looked horrified. "Are you really sure that will happen? It seems terrible to think that we can sit here in our comfortable, developed country, enjoying fine food and company – dinner and a show in the corner over there – while a tempest of discontent and dire distress is building up to a catastrophic detonation elsewhere in the world."

Lakshmi listened to him, and then provided some historical background on U.N. population studies.

"Since the early 1960s, governments around the world have been paying attention to human population growth rates. There was concern as early as 1958 that rapid growth would wipe out any economic advances in countries such as India by diverting resources from investment to consumption. That is starting to happen everywhere now."

"So it's like a ticking time bomb."

"Pretty much," Lakshmi answered. "I don't see how our children can afford to have children, frankly. They would be well-advised not to do so without carefully considering the future of those children, their chances at access to a good college education that include the arts as well as the sciences and foreign languages, and regular access to fresh fruits and vegetables."

Andrew listened to her soberly. "In my day, we didn't have to consider such things. If we wanted children, we had them, and that was it. I hate to say it, but I really think that those days are over."

Lakshmi nodded. "They really are. If we can't afford to provide this, and if our children can't bring themselves to think it through first, I hope that many of them won't insist on having children anyway. It's so unfair to the innocent children. It means dumping a barely – if at all – manageable problem on them just to make parents happy in the short term. I have told my daughters this, and I think that are listening."

Andrew looked at her without a trace of his usual cheeriness. "I have to have a talk with my daughter, then. She is very self-absorbed, love babies and little kids, and tells me that she wants one. But I know that she isn't up to this. If she were the age that she is now 40 or 50 years ago, it wouldn't matter, but this is now, and it does matter, very much."

I looked at Andrew. This was the first time that he had given such a blunt assessment of Patsy's character. I knew he meant Patsy; he only had one child. Andrew reminded Lakshmi that his daughter was our secretary – that was how we had all met here, after all. She nodded.

"Did she tell you about the Big Apple Circus?" I asked him.

"Yes. She said that you seemed to have a good time with her, but that she suspects that you don't like little children – toddlers."

"What did you say to her?"

"That she had figured you out, but not to say anything to you about that. We don't all need to reproduce, and you're better off not wanting something that the world has way too much of anyway."

"Wow."

"I'm glad you said that," Hamish told him. "We've been very careful not to tell her how we really feel about political and population issues. Somehow, we can just sense that she wouldn't agree with us on many points."

Andrew smiled. "You're doing fine, and you're doing the best you can. If it doesn't work out with my daughter at your office, I won't hold it against you."

I hoped he was right. One never knew what the future might bring.

Dinner ended on a sober and thoughtful note, but we were all delighted to have met.

We exchanged business cards with Lakshmi and promised to stay in touch.

A couple of weeks later, the academic term at the Rockefeller Institute drew to a close and Hamish and I were free to go off on our second romantic trip together in the space of a year.

We had a wonderful, romantic time in Hawai'i and did in fact see a Kona coffee plantation. We also went to a luau and tried poi, which was white and pasty. It served the same purpose in the traditional Hawai'ian diet that rice and potatoes did elsewhere in the world. We also tried a wonderful dessert called haupia, which was a chilled coconut gelatin, cut into small bars. We saw plumeria flowers, which are used to make leis. Everything about the trip was memorable.

One thing that was memorable in a sobering way, however, was the climate. This is not to say that the weather wasn't nice; it was absolutely perfect. So perfect, in fact, that everywhere we went, we encountered residents of the islands who lamented the changes in Hawai'i's forests, the greater frequency and severity of hurricanes, and general biodiversity loss.

Hamish insisted upon sending an old war acquaintance a postcard, on which he had written an old joke: "The weather is here – wish you were beautiful." Insert drumbeat here.

Another thing that gave us a laugh – a significant one – was meeting some geese that were native only to the Hawai'ian Islands. The geese were black and white with striped necks and wings, and they had a name that was pronounced precisely like our invention: nene. The only difference was the spelling. We were so intrigued that we told our guide about Nae-Née. He loved it; he thought it was amazing how the world's languages make similar sounds to mean such different things.

What was beautiful about the weather was constantly emphasized to tourists as a sign of the global warming that we kept hearing about as we toured the islands. Some people complained about having to be educated while on vacation, but not us. We welcomed it. We went on a tour of the mountains and were shown some beautiful reddish birds with down-turned, narrow beaks. They were called i'iwi honeycreepers, and they lived in the Hawai'ian mountains.

Climate change was raising the temperature of their natural habitat, bringing disease-bearing mosquitoes to the honeycreepers. The honeycreepers lacked natural defenses in their immune systems to fight off illnesses that had been introduced due to higher temperatures, which had been induced by higher levels of carbon dioxide in the atmosphere.

Our tour guide informed us that the people of Hawai'i were suffering from this as well; mosquitoes were bothering them also. They had to adjust to using bug repellent at these higher altitudes, which was at best a nuisance and at worst, a real problem when it came to staying healthy. The native Hawai'ian people were particularly upset by the changes to their lands.

But global warming was menacing yet another of the planet's beautiful species, and it was the fault of humans, it was not a natural occurrence, and now humans were feeling the change. There were too many people in the world, using too much fossil fuel, and destroying too many trees. The native Hawai'ian guide told us how frustrating it was to hear complaints about this fall on deaf ears, at both the state and federal government levels.

Meanwhile, parents at Hawai'ian high schools were very angry over a clash between enjoyment of football games and an endangered bird on a list of environmentally protected species. It was called the Newell's shearwater, or the ao by native Hawai'ians, and it was a beautiful little creature with a smoky-grey back and a white breast. The chicks would hatch and fly toward the ocean, only to get confused by bright lights pointing skyward as they flew over nighttime football games. Some lived on the Big Island, but most were on Kaua'i.

We heard parents arguing about it with a federal prosecutor one night in a restaurant, and eavesdropped. The problem was that the birds mistook the lights for the moon and stars, flew in circles until exhausted, at which point they fell to the grass where they became sitting ducks for cats and other predators. The parents didn't care. They wanted football at night so that no human would suffer heat exhaustion during a daytime game, rather than during the day on a weekend.

Hamish and I looked askance at each other as we heard a complaint that the government had chosen the birds over their children. "It's like they refuse to see that if they don't choose the birds, they are throwing away their children's future just for a passing thrill," Hamish griped.

I had to put in my own two cents. "It's one thing for an indigenous species to be threatened by a planet-wide use of fossil fuels; it's quite another for it to the fault of the residents."

The prosecutor looked trapped over his dinner with the parents, three couples whom he had obviously agreed to meet in order to reason with them and explore alternative solutions. I felt sorry for him, but admired his refusal to back down about the lights. When I heard him give the parents an ultimatum – either ante up funds for lights that pointed downwards or deal with daytime games – I grinned at him. The man actually perked up at that.

The next day, I saw a story about that in both *The Star Advertiser* and *The Hawai'i Tribune-Herald* in our hotel's lobby and actually bought a paper version of a newspaper – well, both – so I could read the whole story. "If I know you," Hamish said with a grin, "you won't want the trees for those issues to have died in vain, and you'll keep those copies for ever after."

"Stop teasing me, I'm trying to read," I said, settling closer to him. The story detailed the whole situation rather grimly, complete with a photograph of the beautiful endangered shearwater bird. At least it left some hope of saving it with the downward-pointing lights.

But it was getting worse and worse, because we as humans just weren't willing to scale back on our greedy use of resources to save the earth or ourselves; not if it impeded our current comfort levels. Just realizing that as I looked at the i'iwi honeycreeper gave me a sense of speeding toward a cement wall with no brakes.

Chapter 18

Shakeup in the Senate

The news reports over the course of the next year continued to heat up along with the sense that global warming was making itself felt more strongly with each passing year.

January was one of the snowiest months that I could remember in my lifetime. Canada, in contrast, had a record-breaking, mild winter. It was as though we had switched climates with our northern neighbors. The climatologists and nay-sayers had a field day debating what that meant.

I had spent my birthday, the 21st of December, in Hawai'i, so I had not noticed the difference until I came home and felt the stinging bite of icy winds whenever I walked down one of Manhattan's wider streets or an avenue. Somehow, the cold felt colder than ever before.

My collection of medical history and herstory lectures (it really was both) was almost in order by late spring. I loved my job.

Time had raced by all winter and spring; we didn't get back to Connecticut much. There were a couple of weekends when I drove us back there, parking our car in the garage and letting my mother drag to me to every mall in the area without complaint, but Hamish felt hemmed in tinkering in the basement after enjoying the gadgets at the Rockefeller Institute. He went running around the neighborhood, and down to West Hartford Center and back, but that was about it. He wanted to get back to Manhattan, where we had our life together, and my parents seemed perfectly happy to see us on their not-infrequent trips to Chelsea.

Soon it was early summer in the city, and I was inhaling the blossoms on the wisteria vine that grew over the front of our firehouse, and wandering on Saturdays in search of chocolate shops and browsing just to enjoy a good walk. Hamish felt secure enough in his progress at the laboratory to follow me around, whining "Can we go?" if I paused too long. I teased him for following me, saying that he knew what he was getting into. He said he just liked the whole routine, including the whining; he was just teasing me when he did that.

We went away for three weeks at the end of June again, this time to Belgium and the Netherlands. There was another list of things that we wanted to see: Bruges, Belgium is full of medieval art, and Brussels, the capital, was full of attractions, plus the food was the best in the world – even better than in France, I grudging told Hamish. We actually went to the Netherlands first, because we wanted to end the trip with that great gastronomic memory.

The Netherlands – Holland – had its own lures: the World Court, a.k.a. the International Court of Justice (ICJ) was based in The Hague, and as a lawyer I was curious to see it. The Secret Annex in Amsterdam was another important stop, as was Delft, the hometown of the painter Vermeer. We looked at his paintings in several places, not just there.

But we timed our anniversary for a meal in Belgium, and it lived up to the quiet hype that I had found in the literature about the country's cuisine. We had endives, moules, frites, Brussels sprouts that tasted wonderful – not the stuff that American kids complain about having to choke down after their parents have microwaved or boiled the color, vitamins and taste of it – and a chocolate tart with the most wonderful buttery crust imaginable.

We didn't pay attention to the news for 3 weeks; we just coasted along, oblivious to the world's news and other minor events, and enjoyed our vacation. I knew that I would be able to catch up on it all when we got home; the medical history book had gone to press, and I could just sit with the news reports for a week if I chose to.

That, in fact, was exactly what I chose to do.

I walked in to the office the Monday after we got back from Europe after having slept off the jet lag with Hamish – though it took more sleeping on my part than his to get my energy level back up to speed – not having checked the news reports yet. My parents had dropped off the cat last night, but we had talked of nothing but our trip and they had just told me that Grandmère was fine, and so was everyone else in the family, so I really hadn't heard anything new as yet.

As we arrived, Hamish just said "Hi" to Patsy and made a beeline for his own office.

I paused to chat before continuing into my own; it didn't seem very nice to just keep going without so much as a "how are you" to her.

"Hi Patsy. How are you? How has your summer been going?"

She looked up and smiled pleasantly enough. "I'm good. I waited in line for hours Friday night to meet Sheryl Crow, and cried. The heat wave had finally let up a bit, so it wasn't too hard to do, plus I was standing with lots of other fans after a big rainstorm, so…" She had an annoying habit of not finishing her sentences, but I got the idea.

"You waited in line for hours to meet a rock star, then cried when your turn came? Why would getting what you wanted make you cry?" I asked.

She stared at me. "Don't you cry when you get to meet someone that you admire?"

"No – never. I say I'm glad to meet them, and ask them whatever is on my mind from reading their work or whatever their fame is about."

"Wait…you don't get excited when you meet someone famous? What about rock stars?"

"Well…yes. I like rock music, and I still listen to a lot of it, but the one time I attended a rock concert, with my high school classmates and chaperones, I just sat listening carefully, enjoying the lyrics and listening for the familiar words and tunes. It was a bit hard to see from halfway up on the side. People around us were shrieking, but I would never do that. How can they pay attention to the music if they do that?"

She was looking at me as if I were speaking another language. "They're shrieking because they're thrilled to be in the same room with the rock stars – even if it's a huge arena."

"Oh."

"What kinds of concerts do you like?" she asked me.

"We're meeting my parents at Tanglewood in August, for Tanglewood on Parade."

"I know that place – my dad took me there when I was thirteen. He wanted me to hear opera, but I find soprano voices irritating."

Interesting, I thought. "Oh. Well, I like soprano voices. If I could sing like that, I would have fun doing it, but I can't. We're going to hear some Mozart, Debussy, and best of all, John Williams is going to conduct some of his movie soundtracks. That's really my favorite."

"Huh."

"So you said that it's been really hot here? I have to confess, I haven't checked the news yet. Hamish and I just went to museums and restaurants for 3 weeks, and paid no attention to what was happening in the world. A real vacation."

"Well then, you've missed the headlines: June had a nasty heat wave in New York City, and the power actually went out for one night a week after you left. Some elderly people in a nursing home died."

"Really – I hope I can find that story."

"You'll probably find several – people are still talking about it. Jen's grandmother was one of them."

"Oh no – I'll send her a card. Do you think she'd like it if I did?"

"Oh, definitely."

"Good. How is everyone in your life – your father, mother, Jim, Rosalie the cat?"

"All good, thanks."

"Great. Well – I'm going to spend who knows how much time catching up on all sorts of news reports now. See you later." I went into my office.

I fired up the computer and checked everything over – all in order.

Then I clicked on the Internet and set up the tabs: e-mail page; Google search engine page; *The New York Times* page…that was the third one.

When it came up, several headlines practically leaped off the screen at me:

1.   Heat Wave of Epic Proportions Killed Tens of Thousands of Elderly in June;

2.   Infrastructure Literally Cracking from Extreme Heat – Talk of Burying Power Lines;

3.   Polar Icecaps Melting, Expected to Disappear in Another Year;

4.   Senators in Washington Debating about Birth Licensing in Special Session;

5.   Presidential Campaign Focuses on Population Growth and Going Green.

I started opening new tabs for each article, suddenly feeling terribly impatient for them to load, even though the delay was only an instant per article.

The phone rang in my office.

Patsy knew that I hated phones and the noise that they made, and that the ringing typically startled me, making me jump a mile and then fall into a very bad mood for the next half hour – especially if it were for something that she could have me read a message for and then call the person back about.

It must be important enough to put straight through, then.

It was – the caller I.D. said it was my mother.

I picked up. "Hi Mommy!"

"Hi Avril. I went over to the firehouse to see Eowyn again – and I forgot my book."

And then she called me? What for? Was something wrong?

"Is everything okay there?"

"Oh yes, fine. The cat's fine, I got the book, the house is fine, I'm fine."

"But something is up. What is it?"

"Well, I came out, and I noticed that, for the fourth time, a strange man was staring at the door as I went in. I acted natural, let myself in, shut the door, and then looked out the peephole and across the street. He was still there, and staring straight at me. I realize he could no longer see me from there – no x-ray vision involved, since this is real life and not science fiction – but it felt like he was seeing me right through the door."

"Mommy, it couldn't be anything more than a coincidence," I thought, recalling the blond guy with the cigarette from the year before, and hoping that it was nothing more than someone admiring an attractively renovated firehouse. "Was he there when you came out?"

"No, he was gone. Maybe he was just admiring the house. He was dressed nicely. Maybe he scoping out Greenwich Village for a place to live."

"Unless you think you were being followed home, or around the city as you went about your business, I wouldn't read too much into it. But tell Dad. And I'll tell Hamish."

"Okay. Maybe I'll stop by. I've never seen your office, or Hamish's, or his lab, or met Patsy, or seen the Institute. Do you think they'll let me in?"

"I'll tell Patsy you're coming, provide a copy of your photo, and she'll make sure that they let you in. When are you coming?"

"How about noon – we can get lunch at the nearest Le Pain Quotidien. You keep mentioning that there is one near there, and we like those."

"Okay – perfect."

We hung up and I took care of the arrangements with Patsy, then took off down the hall to tell Hamish about the guy outside.

"What did she say he looked like?" he wanted to know.

"She just said he was well dressed. I'll ask her more when she gets here."

"I'll come with you for lunch; it'll be nice to get out of here, and I can ask her myself."

"Okay. Well, I have a lot of news to read. I had just set it up when she called. The polar ice caps are about to totally melt away, the Senators are debating about human population growth levels, and so on."

He looked intrigued, but torn between that and his nanites. "I had the news on last night for a couple of minutes, but not long enough to find out any details. Fill me in at lunch?"

"Definitely." I kissed him good-bye and went back to my office to read.

The article about the Presidential campaign wasn't that fascinating; I was just reading it to be a well-informed voter. The one about the heat wave was a shocker, though: the heat wave had stressed electrical power grids around the nation so badly in June that there had been several outages. Elderly people had died in their homes and in assisted living facilities and nursing homes as transformers blew up, and some electrical workers had collapsed of heat exhaustion as they worked to repair them. The tally for June alone, with the rest of the summer still to go, was astonishing: 25,000 people. Some of them were not elderly people, but the majority of them were. All of these deaths had been attributed to the heat wave as air conditioners failed.

Perhaps I could do a lecture on deaths and health problems related to heat waves and cold snaps, and the history of treatments for such problems. I wondered how exciting that could be, feeling a bit sarcastic as I thought about it. Well...maybe it was still a good idea. I set up a folder to devote to it and moved on.

The polar ice caps story was just as shocking. It covered the reasons behind the heat wave, describing yet again how pieces of ice were sliding into the ocean – icebergs, glaciers, ice shelves breaking up, etc. – and melting as they floated in the salty ocean water, just like ice cubes in a glass. Sea levels were rising, and small island nations were dispatching delegates to the U.N. for a special summit meeting to discuss the increased use of fossil fuels, which was causing the meltdown. Not surprisingly, politicians from nations whose territories were not likely to be underwater anytime soon kept arguing that there could be other reasons – though they didn't offer any – for the meltdown.

And then there was the uproar in the Senate. The crux of the debate was the economy plus population growth in the United States. Several prominent Democrats, some from the committees on the Energy and Natural Resources, plus others from the one on Environment and Public Works, were presenting the findings of climatologists, environmentalists, and population experts to support their arguments in favor of a policy of licensing human births.

I had to re-read that statement. Licensing people to reproduce? I thought back to the previous December, when Attorney Lakshmi Rahni and I had laughed off the possibility that the government – especially the U.S. government – would ever even consider requiring its citizens to scale back on...themselves.

I read the whole thing, and saved it carefully. The last time that I had even heard of this idea combined with my own country was in the movie *A.I.*, in which this exact scenario had led to this exact course of action. Polar icecaps had melted, ocean levels had risen, people had fought over resources, and when all was said and done, if anyone wanted to have a child, they could only do so after being granted a license each and every time that they wanted one. Most couples only got one license, and if the child died due to illness or an accident, tough; that was their one chance to reproduce. The first minute or so of the movie had laid out these facts, which I suspected many viewers had quickly forgotten. But I had been riveted by them.

Now it seemed to really be happening. But what about the fighting?

I started looking around at other reports, not listed on the home page of *The New York Times*. Sure enough, there were some stories of riots in Bangladesh over living space and food supplies. That was easy to find; Bangladesh was a nation whose territory was largely on a river delta, and rapidly diminishing as sea levels rose.

What about those little island nations in the South Pacific, I wondered, scrolling through the site and clicking on more areas. There it was: Nauru.

Nauru, a tiny island nation northeast of Australia, was a little more than 8 square miles. Its irregular, roundish shape was mostly flat, and it had exhausted its phosphate resources decades ago. Lately, its only survival income had come from being a tax haven and from illicit money laundering, thanks to the demise of Air Nauru. This was the nation that was now mostly underwater. Unless its people started building every last structure up on stilts, they now could not claim that they actually possessed any territory any more. Nauru was gone.

What about Greenland? Denmark claimed ownership of this arctic island, and climatologists had been collecting ice samples that recorded the state of the Earth's atmosphere going back hundreds of thousands of millennia for freezers back in Copenhagen. More and more of its coating of ice disappeared each year.

Going, going, going…almost melted. Of course, during winter some of it might come back, but the gains wouldn't be enough to make up for the loss of eons' worth ice and snow. No wonder islands were disappearing and territory was shrinking elsewhere. Perhaps New York actually would soon become New Venice. I hoped not.

And the original Venice seemed to be expiring, too. It was such a great place; but it was built on marshlands, and those structures were rotting and old at the bases. Well, maybe the engineers who were working on that underwater levy system would be successful.

The Netherlands had a great system that we had seen in motion; massive gates could enclose the coastline of the lowlands when it was deemed necessary. They had been closed while we were there, but we hadn't paid much attention to them. We were busy touring and hadn't scrutinized the dikes. We knew what they were for, and we had long ago seen a documentary which explained them, but that was all.

So human activity had melted the ice and caused higher sea levels, and now that the air was too hot and too few trees could scrub the impurities out of it and the ozone layer was wider than ever and more people than ever before were adding to the problem by wanting to consume more resources per person with a middle-class lifestyle – now that the situation was dire and quite possibly irreversible – the Senate wanted to hit the brakes.

The car was half off the cliff at this point, it seemed. A little slow on the pedal, I couldn't help thinking. It was making me anxious and irritable.

I turned on the television after reading and saving all this in time to see the Senate floor debates on C-SPAN. There was a shouting match going on between Boenher and a group of Democrats. I had to listen carefully for a couple of minutes, but then I saw what the screaming was all about: licensing for births. Well, licensing women to get pregnant, to be more precise.

Boenher was against it, of course.

The group of Democrats – 4 of them who were trying to get a word in edgewise as they explained the data in support of their position – included 2 women and 2 men, from Connecticut, California, Pennsylvania and Louisiana.

Interesting – a state from the Deep South, and one with a lot of coastline to worry about.

Senator Amy LaRosse of Louisiana was presenting the data of climatologists from NOAA – the National Oceanic and Atmospheric Administration – that explained how the Earth was heating up to levels that would effectively ruin quality of life for the next generation and any that followed. The solution was obvious, but grossly inconvenient, to paraphrase a familiar, Nobel Peace Prize-winner alumnus of the Senate: have fewer children from now on.

Boenher was red in the face, raging about people's God-given right to have as many children as they wanted. "You want to force people to ask permission to have children!"

Senator LaRosse was trying to point out – from what little she was able to say as she struggled to make herself heard – the problem of future quality of life for any of those children. "I do not *want* to do that. What I want is to ensure that those who are born have a chance at a good life, as our generation had."

"Survival of the fittest! If they can't make it, the best will win out!" Boenher brayed. "Besides, that's God's will; we shouldn't interfere with natural reproduction processes."

"So we should respect God's will." LaRosse spoke those words in flat, deliberate, bland tones. "As we do when a doctor intervenes in a failing childbirth to save the baby rather than let nature take its course, like with your sixth child."

"You are twisting my words – that's not what I meant!" Boenher roared.

"And you are a classic example of the pot calling the kettle black. The fact is that humans have been altering nature for millennia. That is how we got to this point. We have succeeded so well at advancing our technologies that there are now too many of us in relation to available resources. The solution is obvious: maintain those of us who already exist, but have fewer children."

"That is just wrong! People have a right to have as many children as they want to, without big government stepping in and regulating them. As I said, survival of the fittest! Let nature take its course!"

"What do you mean? That we should just sit back and let our children kill each other over resources as we all age past the point of being able to do anything about it?" she countered.

"If that's what it takes to protect civil liberties, yes!"

Senator LaRosse stared at him for a moment, then said, "So we should ensure the same situation until it grows beyond our capacity to accommodate it financially or through the education system, so that our kids can't find jobs to feed themselves even if they are well-trained and willing to work, and then watch them get desperate because we insisted on having too many just because it made us happy?"

"Yes! No! I mean, civil liberties are what makes this nation great! We have to protect them at all costs!"

"Even at the cost of our children's future." LaRosse made her reply in a flat tone, like a statement. She seemed to be finishing Boenher's reply for him.

"I don't see any cost other than that the government will be licensing itself to conduct searches and seizures of women's bodies, and all to prevent rather than allow pregnancies! Life is sacred and should always be respected and preserved!"

"That's interesting," LaRosse said. "You left something out: the word "unreasonable." We are debating about *reasonable* searches and seizures – seizing a woman to inject a nanite, and then monitoring her on a regular basis to protect both her convenience and that of the rest of the human population. Convenience is continued comfort on a planet with as little biodiversity loss and land loss as possible. Anyone who claims that life is sacred and that it ought to be respected and preserved should consider its quality. If someone insists that even a miserable life is a sacred one, they are not respecting life. True respect for life would take quality and happiness into account, and think long rather than short-term. We all have the right to be happy."

He stared at LaRosse for a moment, got redder under his tan, and then lunged at her. It happened so fast that at first, no one moved. They went down in a heap, with him on top, and her unconscious underneath.

He had punched her in the jaw, this fortysomething woman who was physically half his size. He had his hands around her throat and was throttling her. She was turning red.

The next thing I knew, several other male Senators had jumped up and rushed over to help LaRosse, pulling at Boenher's hands and punching the huge ex-football player. It was a mix of Democrats and Republicans, the voice-over noted. Good to see that our political system was intact, I thought wryly, as paramedics rushed in, followed by the Capitol Police.

I found myself thinking in disgust: Who did this guy think he was, Preston Brooks? The last time that anything like this had happened in the Senate chamber had been 1856, when Brooks, a Representative from South Carolina, had severely beaten outspoken abolitionist Senator Charles Sumner of Massachusetts, pinning him on the Senate floor under his desk, which was bolted to the floor. Sumner suffered a severe head injury and ended up with PTSD, but was re-elected as a symbol of the cause for which he had spoken. Sumner had been personally insulting towards Brooks' relative, Senator Andrew Butler, in the 3-hour speech he had made, which was what had provoked the attack in the first place.

Senator Amy LaRosse, by marked contrast, had been polite as she had verbally sparred with Boenher. She had not been near her desk; both Senators were front and center on the Senate floor, looking at the reports and other data that had gone flying around her as she fell. Her opponent had not premeditated his attack – it was perpetrated in the heat of the moment.

Boenher was dragged from the Senate chamber by the Capitol Police as the paramedics worked over LaRosse. The camera showed everything in the immediate area of the attack, and it was possible to see Senator LaRosse's wavy, shoulder-length red hair and mauve skirt suit as they worked, placing an oxygen mask over her face and fitting a neck brace onto her. Someone had loosened her hair; she had been wearing it up in a clip.

As I watched, she shifted one of her feet, and a cheer went up from the other Senators still in the room, as well as from the spectators who were watching from the upper tier of seating. Good; I would hate to think that the lunatic had paralyzed her.

She was moved onto a stretcher and carried out, waving to the others, with one pause to grip the hand of the other woman senator who had been holding some of the data that supported their arguments, Senator Darcy Sheffield of Pennsylvania, and to remark for all to hear that rights came with responsibilities to others. This elicited a round of cheers, and then the medics carried her out. The voice of the reporter who was explaining what was happening said that she would be checked out at George Washington University Hospital, and that Senator Boenher was under arrest.

Good. It would be interesting to see what became of him.

My mother arrived just then; I could hear her in the outer office, and went to greet her and introduce her to Patsy. I left the TV on.

I quickly made the introductions, and then asked them both to come into my office and watch C-SPAN, explaining what had just happened. They gasped and rushed in after me. I took out my cell phone and called Hamish's lab to tell him what was going on at the Capitol. He appeared a few minutes later and joined us as we all stared at the screen.

"What brought the attack on?" my mother asked. They all looked at me; this was breaking news, so they hadn't heard any of it yet. I explained the reasoned debate and the apoplectic, violent shouting that had preceded the punch-and-throttle assault and battery.

Patsy just stared. "They want to make people get licenses to have babies?"

Was that all she had gotten out this, I thought to myself with more than a touch of sarcasm. Of course; she wanted a baby. And she didn't care whether or not there was any reason not to do so – she just wanted one, and that was that. There was no point in discussing it.

So I just said, "Yes – it appears that a majority of the Senators are in favor of it, and they were explaining why, armed with tons of data – see those papers scattered on the floor plus the ones that Sheffield and the others are holding – to support their position. They're worried about the future quality of life of any children born from now on, plus those already in existence."

"But there must be something in the Constitution to stop this!" Patsy looked frantic.

"There is something about the right to be secure in our persons in the 4th Amendment that would help fight the idea, but there is also the Preamble, explaining the overall goals of the document, about insuring domestic tranquility. Senator Boenher just broke his oath to uphold the Constitution on that count."

Hamish took a deep breath and smiled wryly. "And here I thought I was becoming the citizen of a civilized nation," he said.

"Cheer up, Hamish," I said. "They arrested Boenher. I'll bet he won't be back."

Although our country's claim that we were above such barbaric behavior had just been ruined...now we had brawling in our legislative assembly in common with Taiwan and various other places...

Patsy looked really upset, and not about the assault; I wondered whether she was still taking those anti-anxiety pills. She began to hyperventilate, so I suddenly doubted it.

"Patsy?" My mother was looking at her too. "Can we get you something? Do you need some water, or food? What's wrong?"

"I want a baby. I don't want a Nae-Née device."

My mother tried to soothe her. "Try not to worry about it unless it actually happens," she said. "Most likely it will be put to a vote first, and you can register your objection."

"Mommy, it won't be put to a vote – it's not an election. This is a single issue. The politicians will vote on it. If Patsy is determined to take action, her only real option is to write a letter to her Senator and Congressional Representative." As long as I had Patsy working for me, I was determined to make every effort to get along with her. So I offered, "If you want to, Patsy, we can look them up when I get back from lunch with my mother. Then you can write them a letter stating your position. I'll even check it over for you if you like."

"You will? But if the majority of them votes to put a Nae-Née device inside of me, it's all over. I can't imagine being granted a license at my age, and with my weight." She looked red and was breathing heavily – more so than usual.

"Patsy, I don't see how having a Nae-Née device will achieve what they are suggesting. Granted, the government can grab any patent out of the national databanks and make whatever it sees fit regardless of the inventors' views, but even so, the device still allows each woman possessing one the choice to deactivate and have a baby. Try to focus on that."

"I will; I'm okay. I just hope this doesn't happen. I'll just go back to my desk now." She got up and went back out there.

To be perfectly honest, I hoped for the sake of the child and its health that she wouldn't have one, but I intended to do nothing to either prevent it from coming into existence nor to enable that to happen. Patsy annoyed me with her quest to reproduce. She cared nothing for the child's health or education, and she wanted to use it for both an end in itself – because she liked babies – and to entrap Jim into marriage. Marriages like that couldn't last. It was terrible.

After a couple of minutes more, we shut off the TV and headed out as well.

It wasn't until halfway through lunch that Hamish brought up the question of the man outside our firehouse that my mother had noticed this morning.

"Oh, right – I'd almost forgotten about that. It scared me, but at least he was gone when I was ready to leave; I looked out the peep-hole before opening the door."

Damn, I thought…he could have been waiting just to the side of it, out of view if he really meant to jump someone.

"What did he look like?" Hamish asked.

"Tall, heavy build, dark brown hair, thick except for a little thinning area on the crown of his head – I saw it when he tied his shoe – hair was combed back on the sides, dark sunglasses perched on his neck…and that was odd, they were resting on the back of his neck, not the front. He was wearing a Ralph Lauren shirt, nice trousers, a belt, and black sneakers that matched his look. He was clean shaven with no particular marks on his face, and I don't remember any tattoos, either."

"Wow, Mommy, let's summon you as a witness for a police lineup! That was really specific," I said.

Hamish looked oddly relieved, then asked, "What's a police lineup?"

I laughed. "How could you not have learned that by now? You've been here for how many years? More than 15? It's an identity parade. Good thing I watch public television."

My mother cracked up, too. "We saw that on an episode of *As Time Goes By* – Dame Judi Dench's character had to go to one of those because she made up some tall tale for the cops. It was hilarious."

We all laughed, then I got serious again. "So Hamish – do you think someone is stalking the firehouse or my mother?"

"No. Greenwich Village is full of guys like that – well-dressed, well-groomed – it's not that far from Chelsea, and sometimes random strangers ask me about the area. They're shopping for apartments and houses. I just tell them it's a fun place to live and they should move there."

So that was that.

Until that evening, when Hamish did something out of character: he walked home with me. All the way down the length of 5th Avenue. He closed up his laboratory early on the first day back and walked with me, pausing patiently everywhere I wanted to stop.

I took advantage of the situation by pulling him into first La Maison du Chocolat and finally the raw foods vegan place called Pure Food and Wine when we were almost home. He just followed me like a cute overgrown mountain lion all the way home.

As we sat at a table on the back patio near the bar, I brought up the topic of the man in the Ralph Lauren shirt again.

"Leave it to my mother to note the brand of shirt that he was wearing," I said. "But you know what a police lineup is. What's going on?"

"I hired that man and others to watch both our place and us. This afternoon, I called them again and asked them to watch your parents as well, both here and in Connecticut."

I stared at my husband in shock for a few moments, speechless.

Then I asked, "How did you choose them?"

"They are old war buddies of mine, former C.I.A. They started their own business after the war when they left the agency. They wanted to be civilians, but found that they couldn't quite leave that life behind – lucky for us, and for their other clients."

"Well…here's hoping that none of their other clients want to know about us or do us in. Can I meet them, or is that too dangerous?"

"I'd better just show you some old photos for now. We'll see about a meeting, but if I can just point them out in public, or from behind our front door, that would be wiser."

"You could point them out from behind our front door?"

"Yes. There are 4 of them, and they change shifts every morning."

"How long have they been tailing us?"

"Since you saw that blond guy outside last summer. None of these guys are blonds."

"And how will they watch my parents?"

"They won't. They have employees whom they have vetted through their hiring system. They're very adept at choosing people who can be trusted after working for the C.I.A."

"Okay, if you say so. Wow. Life as a potential target…totally plausible after what I saw on C-SPAN today."

"Indeed."

With that, I ordered some hard apple cider; I suddenly needed a good buzz.

Chapter 19

The Treaty

The election campaign dragged on throughout the summer and fall.

The arctic icecap completely melted, as did more of Greenland's sheet of ice.

Another heat wave hit New York City and other places around the planet.

And another 40,000 people died of heat exhaustion-related causes throughout the United States alone in July and August.

That was what put the Kyoto Climate Treaty back on the table for the U.S., the last nation that had not yet signed it. We signed onto it at the very end of August, without so much as a peep of protest from the Republicans in Congress.

But there was another treaty in the works, as I would soon find out.

I read all the reports and recalled that the previous summer, just as things were looking up for me and Hamish with Nae-Née's clinical trial, wildfires had spread smog and choking haze over much of Russia, ruining forests, wiping out villages that would not be rebuilt, killing firefighters and residents, and causing most others to go out and about with surgical masks on.

And now I knew that I was being followed by professional ex-C.I.A. buddies of Hamish's. Had he really gotten protection for himself? I demanded to know this in the middle of the night after the evening that he had told me about this.

I woke him out of a sound sleep, rolling him over so that his good ear would pick up every word. "How do I know that you have protection too? Will I see any invoices to prove it? Will they detail who is being watched and for how much – not that we can't pay for it – and against what threat? What are you worried about, anyway? Anti-abortion religious fundamentalists? Angry have-nots who can't find jobs? Separatists who might want to make an example of anyone who enables easier birth control?"

"You've pretty much covered it – all of the above," Hamish replied sleepily. "Now you see why I don't like it in Connecticut any more – we're wide open yet hemmed into your parents' house there. And I'll show you the contract and some invoices – I really am on the list of people in this family who are being tailed. Don't worry; I'm not planning to carelessly or otherwise turn you into a widow and leave you alone."

"Really?"

"Really. Now go to sleep. I'll wait until you're ready to leave for the office tomorrow and go with you so you don't have to get up earlier. I want to come with you, just to spend more time with you. And I'll show you the invoices and contract before we go."

With that, I was able to go back to sleep, wondering whether some highly-paid man in civilian black were waiting outside, watching the firehouse as we slept comfortably inside.

The next morning, Hamish had in fact shown me some convincing documents, and then we had looked at the company's website online. It was called Blackout Security, and it was based in Virginia, but it had another office in Manhattan. Hamish said it was a small service as far as such things went.

"And you told Dad that people were tailing us?"

"Yes. We'll have to tell your mother soon. She's smart and observant, so she's started to notice things."

"How good are these guys at what they do? I mean, if they can be noticed by my mother…"

"Your mother is smarter than most people. And so are you."

"So are the bad guys, whoever they are."

"We'll see. I don't know what else to do."

"Just don't suggest leaving the country and living elsewhere. I don't want to, and I doubt that we couldn't or wouldn't be found anyway; might as well be happily in familiar places."

"I guess." He sounded less than thrilled, but resigned. He could see that our fame had pretty much cornered us. For once, I was glad to be recognizable. It meant not having to move. People had recognized me and Hamish in restaurants and done double-takes, and chatted with us in lines at movie theaters, asking if we were the ones who had invented Nae-Née. We had given up on attempts at denying it months ago.

My mother was less than thrilled to realize that unmarked cars were following her to grocery stores, malls and wherever else, complete with guys who would get out and follow her around the aisles as she chose cereal and mustard. Were our homes bugged, too, she asked when we were walking through Chelsea together?

No, Hamish told her, but he had ordered cameras – tiny, nanite-sized, mobile ones to the tune of a hundred thousand dollars – to handle surveillance of the firehouse, the Chelsea apartment, the Connecticut house on Stoner Drive, and our cars – mine, my mother's, and my father's. We had all been warned not to be passengers in other people's cars. Terrific.

I followed the news, wondered what threat we were guarding ourselves against. Life didn't seem all that different, and Hamish had assured me that I could walk home when I felt like it. Senator LaRosse recovered from her full-throttle attack and returned to the debates, but she was clearly suffering from the aftershocks of what had happened. She looked okay – that is, she looked the same, with her hair swirled gracefully back into its clip, her bright blue suit looking elegant and her makeup flawless, but her eyes were anxious. Still, she bravely argued as necessary for human population control measures such as licensed births.

She wasn't letting anyone stop her.

The Secret Service protected all officials of the U.S. government, so why hold back? U.S. Senators, members of Congress, Supreme Court Justices and the President were all followed by professional, government-sanctioned thugs and intelligence experts wired into the nation's top-secret techno-telepathy equipment, which was constantly updated: those squiggly white wires that seemed to grow out of agents' ears and into their shirt collars being the most visible examples of that.

And Lance Boenher was gone; the other Senators had voted for his departure that very afternoon – unanimously. He had disgraced them, said Senator Leahy, one of the men who had jumped into the fray to loosen his grip on LaRosse's neck. Charges had been filed, of course. Meanwhile, Boenher's attorney had posted bail and his client had returned to Tennessee, where he had a huge estate near Memphis.

It was odd to go out to the movies and dinner with Andrew Warne and not tell him about the guys who were following us, but we did several times over the course of the summer and fall.

One evening, as we ate at The Green Table, I finally felt comfortable to ask him something that had nagged at me for a long time. Cathy and Hamish were busy chatting about how nanobots could help diagnose and treat horse ailments, so they weren't paying attention.

"Your daughter is a very good secretary. I think she can tell that we have almost nothing in common – except for having been teenagers in the 1980s and liking a few of the same TV shows and rock groups. And kids are often interested in different things than what their parents like. But I keep wondering how she could be so dramatically different from you. You're terrific, by the way. She really admires you, yet she differs from you so much. How did this happen?"

He looked at me for a long moment, then said, "When I decided to leave her mother, she did her best to keep Patsy to herself and poison her mind against me. Her mother was very angry and abusive; she had an alcohol problem at the time. Patsy did stay with me occasionally on school vacations during high school, but that was years later. By then she had spent a lot of time alone with her mother. She was 9 years old when we got divorced. It got better when I sent her away to the Pomfret School. The education was better, and it got her out of her mother's place."

"So years of exposure to her mother contributed to this?"

"That, and her own decision to just ignore anything upsetting and concentrate on having a good time. Unfortunately, that spilled over into her studies. She chose to have a good time with her friends rather than discipline herself, which is how she flunked out of college and became a secretary. She tends to live vicariously rather than through her own efforts, coasting along."

"Thank you for explaining her. It's been nagging at me; I can't just read people by watching them. The expressions in their eyes are an endless puzzle that I can't solve. I worry about the outcome of working with her."

"What do you mean?"

"I mean that I don't want to stop being friends with you, and I worry that if something snaps at the office with Patsy, she will make sure that you cut off contact with me, or that you might decide to do so, and I will never know how you feel about any of it, and just obsess that you are angry with me. Over what, I don't know, because nothing has happened yet. But she's very upset about birth licensing, so I sense a storm cloud of some sort hovering over us."

"Oh – well, don't worry. If she gets mad and leaves, I'll still talk to you."

I hoped that would prove to be true. I wanted to keep my friends; I really liked Andrew. After a moment of thoughtful silence from both of us, during which Cathy and Hamish turned to look at us, Andrew suddenly said, "Lakshmi sends her regards to you. I saw her at the U.N. a couple of evenings ago."

"Oh – please tell her we said "Hi" and that we hope everything is going well with her and her family," I replied.

"I will," he said. "And on that pleasant note, I have to pass on something else that she told me the strictest confidence."

We all sat facing him very seriously and very quietly, listening with rapt anticipation.

"You must promise not to tell anyone this. She gave me strict instructions to tell you this much and no more, and not to pass it on. Don't tell your parents," he said, looking at me.

Interesting opening, I thought. "Okay…I won't. She wants you to tell us this?"

"Yes. She wants you to know that a treaty is being drafted at the U.N., and that it deals with human population control through licensed births. Nae-Née will likely be the mechanism for carrying this out. It could be ready as early as December."

"So that is why human birth licenses are being debated in Congress and elsewhere?" I had noticed that the U.S. wasn't the only nation whose legislative assembly was heatedly discussing this issue. Everywhere I looked, it seemed that nations were absorbed by it.

"Yes."

"Wow."

"And that's not all. She wanted me to tell you that if she makes no move to contact you directly for a while, it's for your benefit, not hers. She would really like to know you better, but she doesn't want you to have to take any more negative attacks than you will already be likely to experience once this goes public. People will be very angry if this treaty is signed and ratified, and they will be quick to take it out on the inventors as much as the lawmakers."

Hamish and I looked at each other, then back at Andrew.

Finally, I spoke up. "At least I still have a friend. I'm glad you told me that last part. Especially that last part. And thanks for the warning about the treaty. I really appreciate it."

"Don't talk about it, though."

"I won't."

"What are you thinking about?" Cathy asked me.

"I'm thinking that it will be amazing if such a legal change is actually made. I've been glued to the reports about this issue, and heard the other side shrieking about civil liberties and the right of every person to reproduce as much as they wish to. This all seems so much like some intellectual's wild novel of the early 20th century that I have a hard time imagining that it could actually happen. It would certainly change everyone's lives."

That it would, they all echoed.

It seemed inconceivable – the idea that it could actually happen – but it did.

November came, and the President was re-elected to a second term. With that, the political equation changed significantly. A President on his second term is less concerned with public opinion than one who still hopes to win that second term. Now those controls had been disabled. He could focus much more on his legacy.

That was when the debates in the U.S. Congress changed their tone. The Senators and Representatives behaved as though they knew that they could soon reel in a huge catch.

The existence of a treaty on this divisive issue of human birth licensing was announced.

On December 21, 2012, the day that prophets of all sorts had predicted big changes would occur, the U.N. Convention on the Global Application of Medical Human Population Control was opened for signatures at the headquarters of the United Nations in Manhattan.

The U.S. Senate had debated this issue for precisely 6 months, the pundits informed us, since the 21st of June. Listening to C-SPAN and quizzing the Senators on the issue whenever they left the Senate chamber had not produced any clarity as to the outcome of the debates.

A vote was taken in the Senate chamber, broadcast live on C-SPAN, on whether to advise the President that he had the consent of the Senate to sign the United States on to this earth-shaking treaty. It seemed that not only were the Senators concerned with voting to keep their current jobs, but also with the future of the nation. And it was as though those who had decided how they would vote were wavering until the last minute, unsure whether or not they might actually go through with a vote in favor of signing the treaty.

Perhaps that was why the vote was not cast, counted and announced until the eleventh hour, on the very morning that the President needed a decision on the issue.

Not that the President had left the public in any doubt as to what his course of action would be; he had assured the American public from the moment he took his second oath of office that he would sign the treaty if the Senate authorized it.

And so it happened that on December 21, 2012, at 9:45 a.m., the U.S. Senate advised and consented – by a vote of 81 Senators – that the President affix his signature to the document.

The signing ceremony took place just 15 minutes later, stunning news-watchers world-wide. The stunning part was the fact that a representative from each and every nation on the entire planet had come to sign it.

It was hard to comprehend that the deed had truly been done, and what life would be like after that. It would certainly be very different from what everyone had previously known.

The treaty signing was, as expected, all quite orderly, civilized, efficient, polite, and neat.

What transpired outside the U.N. building, however, was anything but.

Crowds of supporters and protestors had managed to congregate on the sidewalk and street in front of the building, accompanied by the standard contingent of newscasters. Thus, one could see it all live on television, both inside and out at the United Nations headquarters, and then watch it replayed ad nauseam ad infinitum for hours afterward.

Professor Martin Justin Peabody, Ph.D., the most outspoken proponent of the use of Nae-Née and a member of the philosophy faculty at Stanford University, was simultaneously shot by an angry imam from Saudi Arabia and stabbed by an alleged Bible-belt fanatic from Tennessee. He bled out on the sidewalk in front of the United Nations grounds.

The imam was caught in seconds, but somehow the Bible-belt fanatic got away undetected. News clips failed to capture so much as an image of his face. All that witnesses could offer in the way of a description was a sketchy image of a blond man with long, stringy hair in his face, a dirty white cap over his eyes, and heavy winter clothing. He disappeared into the crowd, having dropped the knife from his gloved hand. The knife revealed no fingerprints.

It took the N.Y.P.D. a couple of hours and several cases of tear gas to restore order.

I watched it all from inside my office, having taken a cab to get there and recommended that the driver use a circuitous route. Hamish had gone on ahead of me, very early, anticipating the crowds also. As the cab moved through Manhattan, up 8th Avenue to 81st Street and under the footbridges of Central Park via the 79th Street Transverse, I suddenly looked behind me. A car was following the cab, a blue Hyundai, and it had two men in it. They had dark glasses on. Their expressions were neutral, and they stared silently ahead as they drove.

I didn't know that the treaty would actually be signed that day; I only knew that it might happen, thanks to the news coverage of the crowds of protestors. Hamish and I had watched *Countdown* on MSNBC the previous evening (and many others in the past few months) just to see what sort of spin Keith Olbermann would put on it. Infotainment as usual, plus his opinion that it would change life as we knew it was what we heard; he didn't seem opposed to it, as far as we could tell.

I paid the cab driver, a Sikh whom I had seen a few times at the 9th Avenue take-out place that sold delicious, spicy five-dollar dinners and chai tea for a buck. Taxi drivers would pay the meter nearby and line their vehicles up in the evenings, and hang out watching Bollywood movies on the TV screen hung in the top right corner of the shop. He wore a dark purple turban, and he remembered me. "Don't you live near the take-out restaurant on 9th Avenue?"

"I used to," I replied. "Nice to run into you again."

He grinned and waved, and took off.

I wondered whether it was coincidence that he had driven me or not, but headed inside.

Patsy was there, sitting at her desk in a highly nervous state.

"Did you see the crowds on TV? Or on the way here?" she wanted to know.

"Not on the way here," I answered. "Just on TV; I took a cab and the driver went through Central Park to avoid the traffic jams."

"Oh. I hope you don't mind; I was watching it on your office TV."

"No, I don't mind. Come in there with me and we can check C-SPAN and MSNBC to see what's going on."

She jumped up when I said that, obviously thrilled by the invitation. I just couldn't leave her sitting there like that, in such a frantic state, and pay no attention to her. Indifference is the worst way to treat someone, I thought.

Almost as soon as we got settled, Hamish came in. "Everyone is so obsessed with the news that no one can concentrate on their experiments," he explained, sitting next to me on the sofa. "I figured I would put everything away for a while rather than mess something up and waste anything."

I grinned and leaned against him on the sofa, flicking between MSNBC and C-SPAN. After a couple of minutes, I realized that C-SPAN was where the primary events were unfolding; the Senate was busy voting and then counting the votes.

We all gaped at the screen as the announcement came: 81 votes in favor of signing the treaty, 19 against it. Patsy gasped, and started to cry. I pushed a Kleenex box towards her and switched to MSNBC. It was time to see what was happening downtown at the U.N.

Reporters were stationed inside and out, watching the proceeding via remote cameras and narrating it all for their viewers. At the front of the room, the treaty was laid out, and delegates from all over the planet – at least, from the array of cultures represented by the imaginative and colorful clothing on many of the people present – were lined up around the room, waiting to sign the document.

A copy of it was available online, including on *The New York Times* website. When I heard that, I jumped up to save one. Then, uncharacteristically, I printed it out to look at on the sofa with Hamish.

Suddenly, as I tried to read while glancing continually at the TV screen, the MSNBC announcer informed us that the U.S. President was at the table, raising his pen to sign. We all stopped and watched history play out for a moment. That was all it took; a few strokes of a pen, and the deed was done.

Hamish had been sworn in as a U.S. citizen the previous December, and commented that no matter which country he called home, the legal situation would be the same on Nae-Née now.

The march of the signatories went on and on for a while longer, however. There were a total of 195 nations on the entire planet, so it took a while to finish the process.

The Vatican did not sign in the end, but because that nation was populated by people who did not reproduce anyway, it did not seem to matter to anyone. A little enclosed city of nuns and priests wasn't going to change the overall effect of this document. The Cardinal who appeared at the signing ceremony simply announced the Catholic Church's opposition to this event, and then returned to his seat.

Patsy was having a hard time with this. The level of Kleenex in the box was going down as she sat there, and Hamish and I had no clue as to what to say to her. Finally, I asked, "Patsy, can you get Jim or your father on the phone? You shouldn't just be upset with no one to tell. And we already know."

"They're both at work. I might be able to get Jim on the phone, but my dad is probably walking around somewhere with his cell phone turned off, busy with his work."

"Well...it looks as though we've seen all that's going to happen for now. Let's go out to Le Pain Quotidien for some hot chocolate and a chocolate dessert. This isn't the time to diet; you need some comfort food," I invited her.

Hamish chimed in, "Yeah – get some phenylethylamines into your system."

She gave him a confused look.

"That means mood-boosting chemicals, which chocolate has a lot of," I clarified.

We didn't know about the murder of Professor Peabody until hours later, thanks to that decision. For all I knew, that stringy-haired blond murderer could have been looking for me at the Rockefeller Institute. But we weren't there.

Hamish came with us, and from there we had hailed a cab, handed Patsy two twenty-dollar bills, and told her to go straight home. Then we wandered over to the Metropolitan Museum of Art, where we spent the rest of the day, looking at the artifacts and paintings in a state of semi-shock.

That evening, Hamish took me out to the Café de Bruxelles for my birthday dinner. We had a lovely time, and he surprised me with a beautiful pair of Mikimoto pearl earrings and a dozen pink roses.

When we came home, I called Andrew found out that he had had his phone on after all. He had spent the morning at home, glued to the television, and had called in to work to say that he could barely get through the city thanks to the uproar. Then he spent the day at a café with his U.N. buddies who volunteered on environmental issues, discussing what this policy would mean for the future of the planet.

I told him about Patsy – he wasn't surprised – and added that unless someone figured out how to make nuclear fusion work as a power source and also how to mass produce it, the planet might just be past redemption.

"You could be right, though I hope not," he said.

Hamish and I weren't going to stay in the city for Christmas, and we weren't going on a big trip anywhere either this year. We were going to Connecticut. I drove us there the next day, bringing Eowyn with us.

Oddly, despite the chaos of the day before, the city seemed back to normal.

Driving north to the Henry Hudson Bridge and up through New York State to I-84 wasn't any more difficult than usual. I had insisted upon leaving around 1 p.m. to enjoy some daylight driving time. We pulled into my parents' garage by 4:30 p.m.

Hamish shut the garage door before letting me get out of the car, gripping my arm as he hit the remote control button.

Chapter 20

The Speech

The next evening, in a special, televised address to the nation, President of the United States explained how and why what was now being referred to as the Planet-Wide Birth Control Treaty was signed.

The speech was presented in the House of Representatives, as a State of the Union Address. It certainly felt like one. Well, it was one; it didn't have to only occur in January and never at any other time.

All of the major news stations carried the speech: ABC, CBS, NBC, MSNBC, CNBC, Fox News, and CNN. Other broadcasters around the world picked up his speech, plus those of other leaders, and commentators. The reactions ranged from disagreement by the naysayers, who spoke out of wishful thinking and nostalgia for easier times, and agreement by the academics of the world in many countries, including the United States. These were, as usual, the people who faced reality and said what wasn't liked, but what was true.

The speech was televised live on December 22, 2012, at 9:11 p.m. It lasted 20 minutes.

It had a catchy title:

On the Urgent Need for Human Population Control...

The President was announced with customary pomp and volume by the House Majority Floor Services Chief, and in he marched, smiling (but not happily), waving, and up to the Speaker's podium. He carried with him a sheaf of paper, which he soberly placed on the podium.

As he typically did whenever he was about to say something important – which was often, since we were currently lucky enough to have an intelligent, reason individual in office who respected the data of scientists and economic experts rather than trying to put his own spin on it – he locked eyes with the camera, and then with many others in the room with him during what was most ironically a pregnant pause. And then he began to speak:

"My fellow Americans: I stand here before you tonight to explain why we as a species will benefit from a treaty such as the one that representatives from every nation on the planet signed this afternoon.

"Global warming is upon us. It is here now, the effects are being felt around the world, and going green will only get us so far.

"If we are to pass on any meaningful future to whatever children we have, changes must be made, and they must be made immediately.

"This will anger and disappoint many people as they discover that what they took for granted can no longer be a part of their lives.

"The quality of life that we leave behind for the generations that follow us matters. It matters more than our right to have children. If we cannot guarantee a decent environment for the people who follow us, we have no business producing those generations.

"We have a responsibility and a duty to see that whatever can be done to protect our children's future is done.

"For too long, humans have enjoyed the benefits of living off of our planet's resources without taking cost into account. It is time to face the cost of living as a hard reality.

"Up until now, we have been concerned about certain stressors on our planet: climate change, global warming, a diminishing supply of natural resources, threatening or even looming extinctions of multiple species, and a lack of universal health care, to name just a few.

"All of these problems add up to threats not only to quality of life but also to national and international security. This is because where quality of life is threatened, so is the security of the people who depend on that quality.

"Now we have realized that there is another stressor on our planet, one which is likely driving the others that I just mentioned: human overpopulation.

"The latest U.S. Census Bureau statistic on the world's population is 7.6 billion. Of that, over 390 million are Americans. The numbers are only going to increase if nothing is done about that. Current projections say that human population will surpass 9 billion by 2050. That is an unsustainable number for our planet. We are already operating way beyond its capacity to support life – over 30 percent beyond it. We cannot continue on this path of self-destruction.

"We need to face facts: less is more. To be specific: 60 percent less is more – more room, more resources, and more opportunities for those who come after us.

"Once a child is born alive and well, it matters. Its future and quality of life matter. And that child will want a share of whatever life has to offer. But there won't be a share for all of our children if we keep going the way we have been.

"We do not need to have, and we must not have, all of the children that we will certainly have in the future – the very near future – if our desires go unchecked and unregulated. There is a huge difference between what we want and what we need. Right now, in the present, we need less. As time goes on, this will only become truer, and more urgent, than it already is.

"Thanks in large part to medical advances such as vaccines and disease cures, the children that we have can be expected to live to a ripe old age. But without sufficient resources and educational opportunities to accommodate them all, their lives may become a misery rather than a gift, an impossible burden rather than something that they enjoy.

"Unfortunately, even with all of these medical resources at our disposal, children in this country are already experiencing the negative and even dire consequences of human overpopulation. Those who live below the poverty level cannot access even a minimal standard of dental care, and some have died when untreated infections have spread to their brains. This is not the fault of dentists; it is the fault of a strained Medicaid system that cannot carry the financial burden of pediatric dental care. Other nations around the world are also finding that they cannot afford to provide care for everyone who needs it. This is unnecessary and preventable, but beating this problem will take more than just managing our money carefully. It will take managing our wants more carefully as well.

"It is time to consider something other than what we want, and what will happen to the children that we do have. Will they have the opportunities to succeed and to enjoy the same quality of life that we have enjoyed access to? Will they be happy? If not, we shouldn't reproduce just to make ourselves happy, or with a view toward having someone to take care of us when we are older.

"Many children move geographically far away from their parents in order to secure employment and make a living, thus negating that possibility, yet people continue to reproduce in the hope that their children will return to take care of them. It is time that we recognized that this is often not possible or desirable, and is even selfish on the part of parents.

"For many, tradition drives their actions. We should consider the origins of these traditions and the reasons that they were instituted. Often, those reasons are the same as the ones that I just mentioned: to impose a duty on someone else to give up their own plans or dreams and take care of the person who placed this burden on that individual.

"Rather than acknowledge the inherent selfishness of this attitude, the long-standing practice has been to label any adult children who balked at this burden or who could not afford to fulfill it as selfish, thus shifting the burden and censure back onto the offspring once again, a generation that had no choice in its destiny.

"It is not fair or reasonable to have so many children that they will never be able to access higher education due to a lack of sufficient capacity to accommodate the ever-increasing numbers of applicants, nor is it fair or reasonable to then blame those children for not beating those impossible odds and gaining admittance to those same competitive colleges and universities despite this. As if that weren't enough, today's young people are saddled – no, crippled – with the financial burden of ever-escalating tuition rates and interest rates on their student loans, and treated as lazy or ungrateful if they can't find sufficient employment to tackle this and support themselves financially outside of their parents' homes. This is unreasonable, and it is caused by human overpopulation.

"It is also not fair to have so many people aspiring to the same middle-class comforts and conveniences with the same fossil fuels that have enabled this since the Industrial Revolution – which is more than a century and a half – that we push the Earth over the brink into such terrible biodiversity loss that our children will have no fresh fruits and vegetables to eat, and nothing to appreciate that makes life worth living.

"We as Americans started the Earth on this path, and we as Americans have a duty – a responsibility – to lead the way out of it. While scientists in places all over the world work on alternative fuels such as fusion, we don't actually have a viable alternative as yet.

"But we must act now to protect our children's future. We cannot afford to wait, or to put off any action that will do that for a moment longer. What we have now is Nae-Née, so we must use that now. When we have fusion power, or whatever fuel source will help our planet's environment and biodiversity, we shall add that to our efforts. But for now, we must use what we have to save the future. If we don't, our future will mirror Easter Island.

"To preserve a decent, reasonable quality of life for the next generation, many of us will have to sacrifice by having fewer children…maybe just one or two…or even none at all.

"To this end, I am creating a new Cabinet post and a Department of Demographics Oversight to administrate the requirements not only of this treaty, but of the future well-being of this nation: human population management and control.

"That is the inconvenient and unpleasant reality that we are presently facing. If the human species is to survive and thrive, we must reduce our numbers.

"We would like to achieve that without violence, and the treaty that was signed today in New York City by leaders from nearly every nation on this planet, and in fact by every nation that has children, aims at doing just that.

"Henceforth, this nation shall require that each and every citizen who wishes to have a child file for a license to do so. Religion shall not be allowed as an excuse for an exemption.

"The act of filing for this license shall in no way guarantee that it will be granted. Many, if not most of these applications will be denied.

"There will be no limit upon the number of times that a person may apply for a license to have a child. However, after someone has been denied an application, there will be no appeal. The maximum number of acceptances that may be received shall be set at 2, but that is by no means any guarantee that any applicant shall ever receive even one acceptance.

"The criteria for acceptance of any birth licensing application shall be as follows: the age of the mother; the economic ability of both parents to support the child; the health of both parents – including an obesity analysis – as well as habits such as smoking and eating habits.

"Factors which will not be considered in this process shall include, but not be limited to: the economic status of the two parents; religion; culture; level of education attained.

"Any woman who is now pregnant – even one who just became pregnant – shall not have the device implanted until she gives birth. No after-the-fact, retroactive laws are valid in the United States.

"Now, as many of you may have noticed, the ideal method of carrying out the terms of this treaty exists already. Perhaps you have seen the advertisements for it on television. It is a nanobotic device called Nae-Née, the creation of a husband-and-wife team of inventors. It is loaded with a lifetime's supply of RU-486, and monitored by a physician.

"As the advertisements run, the name of the device is explained. It quite literally means "not born" and says so with a Scottish Nae followed by a French Née. It was intended by its inventors to be a user-friendly, convenient device that would not interfere with spontaneity.

"The inventors, I must emphasize, were not consulted about this treaty or the actions of any government. We have taken their device and added on to it. They were not consulted as to the use of this device as a human population control management mechanism. They knew no more about this than anyone else following current events and news.

"The advertisement campaign that runs with Nae-Née has reflected the views of the inventors: Birth Control, Infallible, with Nanites and Convenience for All.

"That was what was run when its use was optional. Now that the government will be dispensing it to all of its female citizens, the slogan will be somewhat different.

"Nae-Née: Population Control, Inescapable, with Nanites and a Greener Future for All shall be its new slogan.

"To carry out the massive logistics of this undertaking, a supercomputer will be used, with backups at undisclosed locations around the nation. A physician will be placed in charge of each one, and the identities of these individuals shall each be treated as a state secret.

"This physician, who will be known only as The Operator, will oversee the activation of each woman's Nae-Née device, ensuring that no fertilized egg implants itself in her uterus without the woman and her partner having first been granted a license for that express purpose.

"For those who anticipate the effects of living with this policy, be that with pleasure or disapproval, keep in mind that birth control is an entirely separate issue from sexually transmitted diseases. With that to consider, sexual promiscuity still carries with it such consequences as HIV infections, gonorrhea, syphilis, Chlamydia, Herpes, and whatever other diseases one can contract from sexual contact.

"The computer segment of the device shall have a few things added to it that the inventors did not include in their original design, however:

1. The tracking system that is integrated into Nae-Née shall have not only a computer that allows a doctor to monitor a woman's hormone levels, but also a GPS tracking device. This will enable The Operator to ensure that the device is not removed, which shall be illegal;

2. The government-issued version of Nae-Née shall also include an enforcement mechanism that will make its removal impossible without a code. The code would disable the nanobot's ability to resist removal. This enforcement mechanism will be a combined method of hiding from any retrieval and removal device, and if found, it shall attach itself to a spot at random, and immediately move once the retrieval gun is withdrawn.

"The method by which each citizen shall receive a Nae-Née device is painless – having a nanobot injected causes nothing more than a slight sensation of pressure. To ensure that I would have first-hand knowledge of this, I myself underwent such an injection this fall. Perhaps you saw the broadcast of that event.

"As I speak, the factories – and there are many more than one around the world – which produce Nae-Née are working overtime to produce enough of these devices to go into each and every female citizen between the ages of 10 and 60.

"Once those are ready, the government will collect the stockpiles and add its own modifications, which I have just described.

"From there, nurses and other health care professionals who have been put out of work by the ongoing recession will be hired to assist in the distribution and injection of the Nae-Née campaign. In short, no woman will be left behind, to paraphrase my predecessor.

"And that is the plan that my staff and I have put together to carry out the terms of the treaty that I signed yesterday morning at the United Nations building in New York City.

"I take full responsibility for it, and hope that in time – probably not until our grandchildren are adults – I will be thanked for it. I don't expect happiness and celebrations over it. Not in the remainder of my term in office as President of this great nation, and quite possibly not in my lifetime.

"But this is what must be done if we are to preserve and protect the future of this planet and that of our descendants.

"We must sacrifice today or there will be no tomorrow. The party is over. The Earth will not give boundlessly without forcing us to scale back.

"We saw this last summer as flooding and drought induced massive human migrations around the globe, further stressing areas that were just getting by with the resources that they had. The places that the survivors moved to could not handle the influx.

"With the melting of the arctic icecap and the rapid shrinkage occurring over Greenland right now, land masses all over the world are decreasing. We cannot afford to wait until there are more and more human beings crowding out those who were already there. That will lead to a breakdown in the social order, chaos, and violence as people become desperate for life-sustaining resources.

"The enjoyment of a civil society is not entirely contingent upon the possession of an excellent legal system. That element is a crucial part of it, yes, but not the entire picture.

"Looking at the big picture, the harsh reality of having a civil society is that it requires resources – financial, environmental, and lots of room to grow.

"We have just about used that up. We cannot wait until we are standing closely up against one another with nowhere else to go before we wake up and smell the rising saltwater.

"The United States is by far the biggest offender in terms of pollution and resource use. We simply must scale back now. We can no longer put it off or take it upon ourselves to place our own interpretations over those of the best climatologists and population experts in the world.

"People, I understand that you each want certain things.

"Things that will enable you to enjoy comfortable, happy, educated and interesting lives: electricity, fresh, clean water, heat in the winter, air conditioning in the summer, fresh fruits and vegetables, decent housing, transportation, good schools, college educations rather than just a teasing promise of a chance at admission to a good university or college, freedom of speech and information access, entertainment, art, sporting events, and a voice in your government.

"We all want those things.

"But each of them is in limited supply and will continue to be that way. Each of those things costs money, and supplies of each of those things can only be stretched so far before we find that there just isn't enough to go around.

"Then what?

"How do we tell our children that they will miss out because we failed to plan, because we didn't want to face facts and think ahead, because we didn't want to face reality and see that if we just continued on our current path of having several children per family, then they wouldn't be able to enjoy most of the things on that list? That having children would be an impossibility for them because we had used up all of their chances in our own generation's lifetime?

"How could we do that to our own children?

"I don't want to ever have to say such a thing to my own children.

"I don't want to have to say that the world is full, there's no more room for them, and there are no more chances for them. That they cannot go onward and upward because humanity has reached a brick ceiling on possibilities, resources, living spaces, choices, and its future.

"I want there to be a future for them, and I have no doubt in my mind that each of you also wants that for all of our children.

"That is why I asked Congress for its advice and consent to sign the United States on to this new treaty. And that I why I will be asking it to draft and ratify an Amendment to our Constitution to protect the future of this momentous and critical decision.

"People of the United States, I thank you very much for the trust and confidence that you have placed in me, and for your time this evening."

With that, the President gathered up his notes and stepped down to sober but steady applause. He headed out of the Senate chamber immediately, pausing as he went to shake the hands of several Senators, including Senator Amy LaRosse. She gave him a solemn smile.

And then he was out the door, leaving it to the pundits.

He had not so much as mentioned the holidays in his speech. It was almost as thought the subject might be too volatile to follow up with holiday wishes. They might have come off as trite, had he ventured to offer them.

The President's remarks were promptly, sharply, and widely condemned by many.

Despite the fact that the U.S. Senate had advised and consented to it by a vote of more than three-quarters of its members, thus significantly exceeding the required percentage of a two-thirds majority, several charges were leveled against him for allowing the signing of the treaty.

Not surprisingly, a majority of the outraged remarks came from the Republican right.

However, many also came from liberals whose family plans were now to be disrupted.

The most commonly heard complaint was that compliance with this treaty would not affect him personally, thus it was easy to authorize the signing of it by the United States.

Specifically, he already had 2 children and was satisfied with that number.

The White House issued no comment on the matter.

Queries and outraged reviews of the speech ensued for the next couple of hours.

When it became obvious that this litany of complaints was to take up the next foreseeable block of air time – meaning the rest of the evening – I hit the "Mute" button on the remote and sat back on the sofa to think. My parents had abruptly left the room when it was over, stunned.

Hamish was quick to interrupt my musings.

"Well, a couple of things are for certain, and another leaves me wondering."

"Okay, I'll bite. What are the ones that are for certain?" I had to ask. No wonder my father used to call me an amalgamated woofer-snapper when I was a kid.

"One: we will make more money than we know what to do with," he said.

"That we can figure out how to handle – I'll just hire an attorney, set up yet another charitable trust, and we'll work with an accountant and the attorney to manage it and give chunks of it away. If we tried to keep it all, it would just be a waste, and we'd get taxed into oblivion for doing so. Plus we'd be jerks. We really ought to give it away hand over fist to environmental projects, so that greener forms of fuel can be developed. All this talk of global warming is getting scarier with each passing day. Education in the arts is another idea."

Hamish listened to that, almost started to argue until he heard what I had in mind for the money, then heard the rest and thought better of it.

"That sounds about right. Want to hear the other thing?"

"Sure. But I think I can guess: when the world finds out that we invented Nae-Née, we shall have no peace, and possibly less security – physical security, I mean."

"You guessed it."

"Well…won't that be fun. We'll have to cross that bridge when we come to it, because I don't know yet how to handle that. It sounds like a damned nuisance, though. I thought that not reproducing would bring more peace to our lives, not less of it."

"Life's little ironies coming back to haunt us…"

"So, Hamish – what's the thing that leaves you wondering?" I couldn't resist asking.

"I'm wondering how they intend to enforce this. How are they going to make sure that a Nae-Née device can't be removed, and can't be resisted?"

"Hamish, I'm surprised at you! You've watched *Star Trek* and read some of Michael Creighton's novels. The answers are all there. The difference is that Borg-like methods and the mentality that accompanies them plus nanobotics will be incorporated into our invention."

He twisted around on the sofa to stare at me. "Go on."

"Okay. Remember that opening scene of *Star Trek: First Contact* in which Captain Picard is having a nightmare, remembering his time as Locutus of Borg? He is still dreaming when he thinks he has woken up. He goes to the sink to splash some water on his face and a nasty, round, toothy metal flower of a Borg implant pops out of his face. THEN he wakes up, utterly freaked out."

"Yeah…I remember that part, vaguely. So?"

"So…imagine a Nae-Née implant, nano-sized as it is, with something like that popping out of it if anyone attempts to remove it, burrowing into someone's flesh, remotely operated by a secret government supercomputer with a shadowy, unidentified operator."

Hamish stared at me. After a long moment, he said, "If I didn't know you better, I would say that you have read and watched so much science fiction that you can no longer separate fact from fiction. But after what just happened at the U.N. and what we know we have invented and successfully put on the market, I think you've hit the nail on the head."

"Me too – all of what you just said."

He suddenly pounced on me, kissing me. "I'm so proud of you – you're such a genius!"

I enjoyed this, but gave a mirthless laugh. He was right, for all the good that this would lead to for us. I anticipated trouble in our near futures, a lack of privacy, and a lot of anger at us.

If I had it to do over again, I told myself, I would do it all again.

The planet *is* overpopulated by selfish humans who just want more and more.

We didn't need all of these people. Wanting more people was not good for us.

Enough was enough.

Hamish agreed. When I seemed too quiet a little while later, just before we went to bed, he asked what I was thinking about.

"A classic *Star Trek* episode called The Mark of Gideon," I replied.

"What was it about?" Hamish asked.

"A planet with no disease, and apparently few accidents; all sorts of deaths had been eliminated, and no checks on reproduction had ever been imposed. It was so crowded – so overpopulated – that the inhabitants were desperate for some space to themselves. Kirk saw them out the window when he was kidnapped for a disease phage that was latent in his system; they had almost no room to move, and were silently jostling their way around one another."

"I guess our planet's governments are thinking ahead, unlike theirs," Hamish replied. "I wonder how that must feel," he mused.

"Just go to Whole Foods at Union Square during rush hour and attempt to shop," I said.

Christmas passed pleasantly enough, and again, everyone came over to my parents' place for the big dinner. Some gifts had been exchanged earlier, while others were passed around at the gathering.

Among the gifts that had been shared before the formal dinner were those that Hamish and I had for each other. I had gotten him a special set of nanobotic testing and development equipment that he had been wanting for a long time, one that would bring the old basement laboratory up to speed with that of the Rockefeller Institute.

He was astonished to realize that I had been taking careful notes on everything that he worked with on a daily basis, and had managed to set it up without telling him in the basement. He now had his very own, top-secret, state-of-the-art laboratory. It was better than what we had been able to cobble together on our own before Nae-Née was invented and marketed, and I had spent a lot of time on the phone with my mother, secretly arranging for the walls and ceiling to be finished, the floor to be tiled, and for the delivery and installation or situation of every last high-tech toy with every bell and whistle currently known to nanobotic science.

I took Hamish down to the basement, where I had affixed a huge red bow to the door. He looked bewildered, until I told him to rip the bow off of his gift and check it out. Hamish was so delighted that when he saw it all that he whooped and then picked me up and spun me. We fell down onto the newly tiled floor and rolled to lessen the impact, laughing.

He couldn't believe it; he also thought it was a very good, practical idea. "My gifts to you won't seem nearly as amazing," he suddenly complained.

"I don't care! Bring them on." I was in a great mood for some reason.

He brought me back upstairs and gave them to me.

One was a global warming mug from the Unemployed Philosophers Guild – a rather sober reminder of current events, which I insisted upon testing with some hot hazelnut coffee immediately. I felt a bit sick as part of France, Connecticut and all of Manhattan disappeared. Already, rising sea levels had started to breach the edges of Manhattan. Would we be forced to move back here permanently, I wondered? If so, at least I had begun to prepare. I was a bit obsessive about anticipating things and being prepared. If anyone thought I was crazy, I just didn't care.

Hamish snapped me out of my worrying when he brought out the other wrapped box. "I thought I would show you the serious gift first, followed by this one." He handed me the package.

Inside was a beautiful Mikimoto pearl necklace, an 18-inch strand of flawless white 8-milimeter pearls, with a gorgeous clasp made out of yellow gold in the form of a rose with a tiny white pearl set inside it. It matched the pair of earrings he had given me for my birthday 4 days earlier, which I was now wearing. He fastened it around my neck and kissed me to seal the deal.

I was thrilled. I am just girlish enough to get excited over something as frivolous as a strand of cultured pearls from the 5th Avenue store. Hamish had asked me what I liked best once the previous summer as he walked home with me – a rare treat for me that evening as my husband worked late in his lab so often – but I hadn't thought about it again.

After several years of austerity and worry over making ends meet, we were having a little fun. Granted, it was a bit over the top, but so what? We could get it out of our system, then scale back later when the thrill and newness of financial solvency – and security – wore off.

My parents came into the living room just then and grinned happily over us as they realized that we had just exchanged gifts; they had been keeping our secrets for us about each of the gifts. The mug had been the easiest secret to keep, of course.

I wish I could say that we had equally thrilling gifts for them, but I can't. Parents tend to have everything that they want already. Mine did; their daughter was well-educated, successful, and happy with what she wanted – her husband

and cats. That was what led to the next order of business for Christmas morning: getting Spock and Eowyn stoned on catnip toys. Who cared that they each had plenty of old toys? We gave them a few new ones, and even let them play together for a while. Surprisingly, they got along.

A couple of hours later the relatives started to arrive. We had the dinner all ready, and the living and dining rooms set up, complete with a beautiful raspberry chocolate almond cake that I had made the day before.

There was just one logistical hang-up that none of us had anticipated: the street was clogged with reporters. Suddenly, the civilian men-in-black that Hamish had hired appeared fully visible to us all as they held the onrush off at the perimeter of the property.

I hadn't realized it as we had driven in the other day, but by now I had seen that my parents had had a tall stone wall built around the entire lawn, and my mother intended to add lots of blackberry and raspberry brambles to prick any intruder who attempted to scale it.

Hopefully, that would be enough, though I seriously doubted it.

How would we get out of here on Saturday?

We couldn't worry about it now; it was time for the party. The next several hours were spent entertaining and keeping up with the cleanup part of the party, but Aunt Zoe and Grandmère helped with that. Actually, Grandmère chatted with us while Aunt Zoe, my mother and I did the dishes and put the food away.

Dad, Hamish, Uncle Charlie, Jacques and my other 2 cousins, Edgar and Fabian, sat in the living room staring at the news reports on television and the news reporters out the windows.

Jacques remarked that they were all missing Christmas just to see that we weren't doing anything remarkable on Christmas. When the work was done, we all met in the living room and opened the gifts.

And when that was over and the detritus of paper cleaned up, Jacques suddenly demanded that we all watch Al Gore's PowerPoint presentation of an environmentalist movie, *An Inconvenient Truth* instead of *A Christmas Carol*.

"Why?" Uncle Charlie said with a groan. "Do you think the reporters will creep up to the window to check on us?"

"No – I just never got to see it properly. I was only 12 when it came out. Now everyone at college is obsessed with it, and I know they have a copy of it here."

"Damn – I should have given you one for Christmas," I griped.

"I don't need to save it forever, just to see it," Jacques said, smiling at me.

We put the movie on and had some more cake with eggnog.

Aunt Zoe and Uncle Charlie's eyelids promptly started to droop. Grandmère paid attention to the whole thing, despite being in her 90s, but not them. It annoyed both her and me, because we knew that they were intelligent people.

I hated to say it, but they were starting to remind me of Patsy.

They actually complained about being bored and not feeling like being educated on a holiday, eliciting a round of outraged scolding from Grandmère and their sons.

I had a sneaking and unsettling suspicion that their lack of interest was indicative of indicative of the mindset of a significant portion of the population of the United States, and that did not bode well for the future.

What sort of reception would we find when we left, let alone returned to New York City? Suddenly the holidays seemed less relaxing.

Chapter 21

The Amendment:
Social Engineering v. Individual Freedom

Things got tense in the house on Stoner Drive for the week that we remained for our Christmas visit. The paparazzi and other reporters kept up a steady vigil at the foot of the driveway; I began to be glad that Hamish had hired those civilian men-in-black. They made it possible for us to leave the drive and re-enter it the few times that we ventured out.

Fortunately, it was cold, so we had no burning desire to go outside for walks. We stayed until the following Saturday, precisely one week.

We all sat glued to the television – even Hamish – as the news channels buzzed nonstop with analyses of the new Birth Control Treaty. The pundits and political discussion shows debated the issue with these questions:

Would the U.S. government actually comply with its terms, or would it renege?

How would this treaty change things? More specifically, how soon would we start to notice its effects? I doubted that we would feel that there were fewer people for a few years, at least. Not until school enrollments dropped and media started reporting the fact would we see it.

One of them, a noted comedian-commentator with a talk show in California, seemed to blatantly approve of the treaty. As usual, he invited guests from the Democratic and Republican parties – plus the Green Party – and always one actor, one politician, and one journalist or author. "It's no surprise that it's come to this," he said as he introduced the show. "It's an idea whose time has come and been procrastinated on for too long."

He was promptly and virulently criticized on the grounds that he had no children, but that didn't shut him up. Nothing ever did, so why would this? "Of course I'll get flack for this – I always get flack. They're not going to shut me up. If I'm attacked, I'll defend myself." By that, of course, he meant verbally and articulately, and certainly irreverently.

Conservatives carried on about the lack of necessity for a birth control policy, insisting that there was no population crisis, and that this policy interfered with basic human rights. "Not that the liberal governments of the world will care," one blowhard brayed into his radio mike.

Musings about how other nations, particularly Muslim nations, would implement this policy abounded. "What about the remotely located tribes in hard-to-reach places? How will the women in Taliban and Pashtun Afghanistan get Nae-Née? Or will they? And who will administer it if the men won't let male doctors or other health care workers near them?"

An expert in nanite technology was called in to answer that question. "Nanite surveillance technology has been successfully interfaced with nanobotic medical technology. This means that there is no longer any necessity for personally visiting such volatile areas. The nanites don't have to work with cameras, so that covers the Islamic prohibition on seeing the women's faces. All that the nanites will need are remote sensing systems to spot females who have reached puberty, and then the encoded devices can be deployed through a nose or other continuously opened passageway. Soon the nanites will have moved through the alveoli of lung tissues into the bloodstream, and from there on down to the abdomen – just as if they had been injected individually into each woman."

"So," said the host of the news show, "Resistance is futile. We are the Borg."

"Pretty much." The nanite expert's expression was neutral.

"Is there any way to see these nanites coming and stop them?"

"Yes and no. Yes if you have sophisticated detection equipment, but no if the nanites can fly under its radar. That is possible with an encrypted frequency, mimicking of wind patterns, and access to the latest, state-of-the-art surveillance. The whole point of using nanites is their microscopic size. At that level, invisible to the human eye and to most other eyes, no one can see them coming."

"So the religious fundamentalists can run from Nae-Née, but they can't hide or avoid it."

"Essentially. The governments of the world have a fail-safe system. It's Draconian, but it will be effective."

"It sounds a lot better than dropping bombs or inflicting plaques or radiation on cities to reduce population. Killing those who already exist would be worse," another commentator pointed out. "The time has clearly come to do something, and this seems to be the best possible answer to the problem."

With that, we heard a familiar song from a nice family-oriented movie: it was called "Political Science" and had been played at the end of *Blast from the Past*. I thought…why drop any bombs at all? Just restrict and reduce human reproduction…much less evil that way.

No matter what solution was chosen, someone somewhere was going to condemn it and call it evil, inhuman and inhumane, a violation of human rights, against nature, against God, and on and on and on.

Soon, in every news publication and show a copy of the latest effort of Congress was available for public notice and comment. It was a proposed Constitutional Amendment:

Amendment XXVIII [2013]

Section 1. The overall population of the United States shall be reduced by 60 percent through a mandatory birth control device, to be issued by the government to each female citizen and resident between the ages of 10 and 60, and shall be monitored by the government.

Section 2. Any couple wishing to have a child must first apply for a license from the government. If that license is approved, the government shall then suspend the activity of the mother's birth control device until such time as the child is born, then reactivate it. Any pregnancy underway at the time of the ratification of this article shall be considered approved.

Section 3. After the population has been reduced, that level shall then be maintained by the same device and system.

Section 4. The removal of any birth control device without government authorization shall be illegal.

Section 5. This article shall take effect immediately upon ratification.

Section 6. The Congress shall have the power to enforce this article by appropriate legislation.

Obviously, Congress had not waited a moment after the State of the Union Address to prepare it. The day after Christmas, C-SPAN covered debates in both the House and Senate as they drafted the proposal. It was ready with startling speed; until New Year's Eve, discussions and debates raged as to why this was necessary, and what would be good about it.

I was fascinated. What would the Senators and Representatives be able to offer as selling points in the face of religious fundamentalism? Not that anything would change in the eyes of the fundamentalists, but I still wondered, and so I watched C-SPAN.

For men, the legislation offered a reliable way to control their fertility, offered a senator from Illinois. How so? Well, birth licenses would only be issued to married couples, and they had to apply for them. That meant that single men would no longer have to fear unplanned, surprise fatherhood. That was a valid selling point, I realized.

For the religious fundamentalists, for the conservative traditionalists, this was also a selling point, though they were utterly loath to concede it. Family values would at last win out because only married couples could get pregnant under the proposed amendment, and only heterosexual ones at that, since fertility clinics had been legislated out of existence.

That one was just a bit hilarious to me; at last the fundamentalists were getting their wish, and they didn't like it! Be careful what you wish for…

Women had mixed feelings, which was nothing new. Since when had we all agreed on the issue of fertility anyway? I had never been in favor of allowing anyone else control over my own fertility, but it had always been about preventing fertility from changing my life. For others, and for most of them at that, it had always been about keeping one's options open so as to be able to reproduce at will in the future.

Not a problem, the senator from Maine said. That option was still out there…subject to the edicts of the new Demographics Department of course, and the will of the Operator, countered another from Mississippi.

Hamish and my mother didn't wait to hear every word. They chose to quiz both me and my father as to why the urgency with a Constitutional Amendment, then listen to the issue getting hashed out on TV.

"Why? To avoid challenges from the Supreme Court as the Constitutionality of requiring everyone to accept Nae-Née in their lives. Incorporating the practice into the U.S. Constitution is intended to head that off." Dad and I practically fell over each other verbally as we raced to give the explanation, then he grinned at me as he realized that we had each covered the same points.

I wasn't done, though. "Look at other channels. Already, writs of certiorari are being filed with the U.S. Supreme Court by the ACLU and NOW, to name just a couple of groups. There are religious ones too, of course, but they are clamoring for injunctions and stays and whatever else it might take to postpone the application of a Borg version of Nae-Née."

Sure enough, a quick channel-surfing of news broadcasts revealed what I had already discovered in my routine morning scan of *The New York Times*.

NARAL had been mentioned also, not for filing any legal motions, but for concerns that it would soon cease to be necessary. Its president vowed to continue, however, just in case any woman needed help terminating an unwanted pregnancy. "Whenever big government interferes with a woman's body to this extent, one should be vigilant and ready in case anyone slips through the cracks of the system. There are always cracks. Just because we haven't identified them yet doesn't mean that they won't form."

My parents wanted to go out to dinner at Max's Oyster Bar in West Hartford Center on Thursday evening. We called for a reservation early in the afternoon. All set; four people for dinner at 7 p.m. Somehow, I doubted that it would be that easy.

In the evening, at 6 p.m., we piled into Dad's E-Class Mercedes and he backed out of the garage, maneuvering the car to face the street in the driveway's turnaround. That wasn't all that we faced: the crowd of camera-toting journalists was still there. I was torn between pity for them out in the December chill and hope that the darkness would make videography difficult.

"Why are we eating out?" I couldn't help asking. It seemed like an awful lot of trouble.

"Your father wants to test the waters – see how difficult it will be to go out and do normal things like eat in a restaurant," my mother informed me from the front seat.

"Will we be attempting grocery-shopping tomorrow?" I asked.

"Definitely," she replied. Wonderful. I hated crowds. We had made a brief run to Whole Foods the day before Christmas and barely exited the driveway without running over a couple of reporters. Now Dad was having similar problems.

A camera was shoved at the windows as we reached the end of the driveway, and shouts of "Would you care to quote on the Birth Control Treaty?" echoed like a chorus. So did "How does your daughter justify stopping people from having babies?" and "Will your daughter or son-in-law be speaking out for or against this policy?"

Dad blasted the horn and the Blackout Security men appeared out of the shadows just as we reached the small crowd. Reluctantly, it parted to let us through, but it was so tight and close around us that it seemed to press the car back, much as a birth canal would put up a bit of natural resistance during the final emergence of a baby after a long series of painful contractions.

It took five full minutes to get clear and then Dad said, "See? That wasn't so bad."

"We're not out of the woods just yet," I cautioned, "pun intended."

He glanced at me in the rearview mirror as though regretting his hasty celebration and wondering what the obstacle course would present next. Then he swerved slightly and tapped the brake pedal as a series of bright strobe lights shone into the car. They were stationed all along the street. A car from Blackout Security followed us all the way.

At Mountain Road, the West Hartford police awaited us. They had set up a checkpoint.

When the cop knocked on his window, Dad opened it, letting in a bitter-cold blast.

"Driver's license please, sir."

Dad squirmed in his seat to extract his wallet, and handed the license to the officer.

The cop did a double-take as he saw the last name on it. "Mr. Châtelet? Are you the father of…" and he cut his own sentence off to lean over and peer into the car at the rest of us. Hamish and I mirthlessly waved to him from the back seat.

Dad looked wryly up at him. "Yes, I am the father of…" he replied. "And here's the mother of…" he quipped, nodding at my mother, who rolled her eyes.

"It's nice to meet you sir, ma'am. The West Hartford Police Department is going to make every effort to facilitate your comings and goings from this street. In fact, the chief is talking about maintaining a check-point here to keep out anyone without clearance to enter Stoner Drive. The residents are pretty steamed about all the uproar."

"Steamed at us, or by the disruption?" Dad asked.

"By the disruption, mostly. We can't keep out anyone and everyone who isn't a resident of this street, but if it were to become a private street, that would make our job easier."

"Noted," said Dad, and I suspected that more of his time was about to be taken up thanks to me and Hamish. We drove off into the darkness, aided into the stream of traffic by the cop.

"Are you mad at us, Dad?" I asked.

"Mad at you?! Why would I be mad at you?!"

"Because I predict that you are about to file motions with the town to make Stoner Drive a private street, perhaps a gated one, because both your and Mommy's lives are about to become inconvenient; because coping with this will be a drain on your free and work time; because life will soon resemble a fishbowl and you will have to make sure that the media gets as little as possible in the way of quotes whenever either of you go outside…etc."

"I see. And I saw all that coming. No – I'm not mad at you. If I get mad at anyone, it will be at the media and at anyone who tries to harm any member of this family, but not at you and Hamish for inventing Nae-Née. Don't be ridiculous."

My mother spoke up. "Now let's go out and have a nice dinner together."

We got out in front of the restaurant, and then Hamish jumped into the front seat to go park the car and walk back with Dad. After a brief pause, Dad accepted that and stepped on the gas to head for the parking lot behind the buildings across the street. I noticed a couple of cars with darkened windows follow them in. Good – the men-in-black would get them inside.

My mother and I went up to the hostess station and gave our last name.

The girls who were working there did a double-take, looked us both over carefully, and scurried to grab four menus and lead us to the back of the restaurant, where we were shown to a booth. People stopped chatting and stared at me as we passed. I kept my expression neutral and just followed the hostess, not holding anyone's gaze.

Hamish and Dad appeared a few minutes later and sat down. "How come they seated you? We're a half-hour early," Hamish asked.

The three of us looked at him incredulously. "Are you kidding?" Dad asked him.

Hamish looked at me, waiting for an explanation.

"Max's doesn't want the hassle of famous people standing at the front of the establishment, clogging foot traffic. We'd be in the way," I informed him.

His eyes popped for an instant as he began to realize the implications of having his face cropping up now and then on news channels.

I noticed the men-in-black circling the restaurant, then ordering what were doubtless non-alcoholic drinks at the bar. There isn't much to add here except that we enjoyed our meal and censored our own conversation in the off chance that the diners at the next table were members of the media.

The men-in-black tailed us to our car, and we didn't mind. Flashes went off in our faces as we emerged from the restaurant, and police cruisers temporarily impeded the flow of vehicle traffic on Farmington Avenue. I hoped this would stop soon; I didn't like inconveniencing other people who were no doubt out for a fun evening, just like we were.

Grocery shopping the next afternoon was another odyssey. My mother and I had to negotiate the path down Stoner Drive in broad daylight through the birth canal of intrusive journalists and paparazzi.

I was driving. As soon as we were clear, I gunned the accelerator as I kept my eyes and ears alert for any stray extras farther up the street. Once or twice, I swerved to avoid them.

"Be careful!" my mother yelped, stomping on imaginary brake pedals exactly as she had done when I was a teenager and she was teaching me how to drive.

"I am – I'm watching carefully, but I want them to realize that I have no intention of facilitating their efforts to keep us captive here and deal with any of their editor's intrusive assignments!"

"Just don't hit anyone – they'd sue you blind."

"I won't," I said irritably. "I wanted to get a taste of driving before Saturday, just to get a sense of what it will be like."

We made it to Mountain Road and I drove straight across Farmington Avenue, heading south, bypassing West Hartford Center altogether.

"Where are you taking us?" my mother asked, craning around in the direction of Whole Foods, confused.

"To Stew Leonard's on the Berlin Turnpike. I want make sure that you and Dad and Spock are well supplied with food before I go back to Manhattan. We'll get stop at Petco on the way home and more food for Spock and Eowyn," I said.

"Thanks!" she said. "You don't want me to have to go out for a while, do you?"

"No. If you go out shopping just for fun, that's one thing, but I want to keep it optional until the biggest rush of paparazzi blows over. I sure hope it does," I said, wondering how long it would be before she could come and go unimpeded.

Stew Leonard's was its usual fun with free samples every time we rounded a corner, starting with tastes of lobster bisque, chicken chili and New England clam chowder, followed by apple cider donut bits. I got lots of freshly ground coffee in my parents' favorite blend of French Roast, and continued throughout the store with more of the same idea – fresh fruits and vegetables teased me and my mother at every display, and we stuffed the cart.

As soon as the car was loaded with all that, I drove next door to SAM's Club and got bulk supplies, duplicated for Stoner Drive and the Manhattan firehouse. For each cat, a huge bag of Johnny Cat litter, plus basmati rice in zippered burlap bags.

My mother just followed me through each store, occasionally adding something to the cart, but otherwise watching me stock up as though for a bomb shelter. She saw that I was on my own personal mission to hole up the family against inconvenience and lunatics, and let me proceed with it.

Petco was by the mall. I took a different route back, via the highway. Exiting Route 9 I drove over to the depressed-looking L-shape of stores by Borders that was fronted by a broken, nearly deserted parking lot. The reporters had lost our trail for now, but not the men-in-black. 2 cars pulled in across from us, the occupants making no attempt at concealing their presence from us. I was past caring at this point; having known about them for months now, my mother didn't bat an eye either.

More cat food, both canned and dry, bought in bulk, 10 boxes of litter box bags and 10 more of litter box deodorizer went into the shopping cart. My mother stared in disbelief, but uncharacteristically made no comment whatsoever.

This was utterly unprecedented. Back in the car, which was now stuffed to the limit, I headed towards home and asked her why she was acquiescing wordlessly to all this stockpiling.

"It's making me think."

"About…?"

"About how long it will be like this, and whether or not it will go back to normal."

I looked at her for a moment, then brought my eyes back to the road. "It may be quite a while. Or it may let up for you but not for me, and if I'm lucky let up for me and Hamish later. We'll just have to wait and see. That's what I did when we had no money and no foreseeable hope of getting any independence, and now fame is taking that independence back again. I'll just wait and see about that again. I've had lots of practice."

She looked at me for a long moment. "You're going to need it," was all she said.

Back at the house, the paparazzi awaited us. They resisted letting us through, but I blasted the horn, startling them out of the way. I had no intention of accepting the intrusion and inconvenience, or of taking a single question – especially without having prepared my answer.

I drove into the garage, hit the door switch, and my mother actually waited for the door to close before getting out of the car. Dad must have warned her about that.

We started bringing the bags in, except for half of the cat supplies. I told my mother to just leave those. Hamish appeared and I repeated that edict; no sense taking Eowyn's stuff out of the car only to put it all back in tomorrow.

Dad came back from the office at 5:30 and opened the fridge. An avalanche of groceries fell on him, including some gourmet cheeses. He grabbed a couple, tossed the rest back in, and sat down with his pinot noir.

"All stocked up for a blizzard of paparazzi, I see," he remarked to me with a devilish glint in his eye as he poured some wine into his glass.

I grinned and described the afternoon's activities. He nodded with approval.

"So Dad – what was it like at the firm this week? Any treaty talk?"

"Tons. Several secretaries are heartbroken about Nae-Née. A notice has been sent around that government-escorted nurses will be coming around, unannounced, within the next week to administer the first wave of injections."

"I take it that these secretaries wanted babies, or more if they already had some?"

"You got it. I'm glad mine is all set with that. She's in her 50s, and her daughter just finished graduate school. She and her husband had a daughter last summer. I don't know whether they wanted another kid or not, but I'll bet that's it. They have student loans, and the cost of raising a kid – just one – is currently over a quarter of a million dollars before college."

"Yeah, I've seen that statistic a few times. What about other secretaries, paralegals, attorneys, support staff? Have you heard their comments?"

"Some, but the moment they see me coming, they get quiet and give me a resentful stare or glare, as if this were somehow my fault. It's the government's fault if it's anyone's fault, or it's everyone's fault for perpetuating a state of overpopulation and expecting there to be no end in sight. The noisy, disruptive party's over, but we didn't call the cops to stop it."

I joined him with the wine and Brie and Asiago cheeses, wondering when the looks would stop and the chatter would resume at his office without people staring at him sideways.

"I hope people start speaking freely around you and quick. That way, you can tell them what you just said to me."

"Oh believe me, I've already said all this to a woman attorney in front of a sea of paralegal cubicles. It got very quiet in the room."

That sounded like him. Dad was cool; always the perfect line from a big bad attorney.

"What did she say?"

"She agreed with me. She has one son in college, and she watches the news. She said that the world is definitely at a tipping point and that this treaty is just what we needed."

"Did you talk about the proposed Amendment at all?"

"Oh yes. It's got an excellent chance of clearing Congress within a short time. It's still anyone's guess as to how many states legislatures will ratify it, but just about all of the attorneys at the firm have commented that it seems airtight enough to fly. If it gets ratified, it will certainly save a lot of litigating in Washington D.C. The federal courts' dockets are already glutted enough with writs and filings as it is, and still they say that there are too many lawyers."

Dinner was a sober affair. My parents were more than a little worried about our trek back to Manhattan. Hamish promised that he would keep the cell phone on and take their calls, and I promised to phone home when we were encased in our garage. The men-in-black were watching the place in our absence, even going into the place to check for intruders, Hamish told us.

"Don't worry – they bring their own coffee. You won't notice a thing. Remember, they were trained by the C.I.A., so their every visit is like a covert op. They won't leave a trace."

I laughed. "I don't mind if they need to pee – soap and toilet paper use are welcome."

"They won't do that either," he said without a trace of humor. That was unlike him, but if that was how the Blackout Security service operated, so be it.

The next day, we loaded the car and headed out at 1 p.m. How was I going to get the reporters off of my tail, I wondered? They could cause a crash if they were too persistent.

The cops ended up helping us, and the caravan of our blue Mercedes and 2 Blackout cars managed to exit the driveway. I drove straight across Farmington Avenue, curved around to Ridgewood Road, and down to I-84. Police cruisers were stationed along the route, and one cop actually nodded to me as I waited at a stop light. I nodded back, then glanced at my husband.

"Blackout called and told them what route we'd be taking," he said. His cell phone rang.

"Hi Camille," he said. Good grief…we hadn't even made it to the highway yet!

"Nope, no problems thus far. We're approaching the entrance to I-84 now. Don't worry, we'll keep you posted." Another minute of chatter, then he folded the phone shut.

Once I got onto the highway and up to a normal rate of speed, we both relaxed. Traffic wasn't terribly heavy, and it flowed at a decent pace. I didn't see anything unusual; just people going from one place to another, minding their own business.

We stopped in Katonah, New York to find a bathroom. I figured that the reporters would have no idea which random town we would pick for that purpose, and I was right. We saw nothing unusual there. We went into a quiet restaurant during the interval between lunch and dinner and the owners just smiled and let us use the rest rooms.

"Do you think they recognize us?" I whispered to Hamish as we emerged, ready to resume the ride. No need for him to answer; the couple in charge were smiling at us from behind the counter as we passed.

"Don't let anyone tell you that you shouldn't have invented Nae-Née!" the wife said, and her husband nodded. We stared at them briefly, then smiled and thanked them for the pit stop.

A security guy was pacing around by the car when we came out. He waited until we were practically at the doors, then wordlessly got into the passenger seat of the nearest Blackout car.

Back in the car, we called my parents to tell them where we were and about the nice people in the restaurant. Soon we were heading south again.

We got all the way back to lower Manhattan before things got weird again.

I drove down 9th Avenue to 14th Street to Greenwich Avenue and then into the narrow maze of smaller streets, expecting a member of the paparazzi to suddenly pop up like a boogeyman and flash a camera in my face while firing a barrage of politically-charged questions.

Nothing.

The anonymity of urban life seemed to be working in our favor, at least for the part of the ride that took us down busy streets. Then I turned off of Greenwich Avenue and found a police cruiser at every intersection.

The cops seemed to snap out of a bored stupor as we approached, suddenly looking alert as we turned through the side streets. As we got closer to our own street, I noticed that cops on foot had blocked off the entrance with saw horses.

"How are we supposed to go home?" I asked, annoyed. I hated to think that we would have to walk back and forth out in the open, lugging our groceries, cat supplies, laptops, suitcases and pet cat on foot while the paparazzi swarmed around us.

"Don't worry," Hamish said. "The Blackout guys called ahead."

I looked at him, confused, then back at the cops, who were speaking into their radios. They were also looking directly at us, and down at our license plate. Abruptly, they moved the saw horses and waved us through.

I waved a thank-you back at them and drove slowly through, followed by the two Blackout cars. As I turned onto our street, I moved forward just enough to let our men-in-black get past the checkpoint, then braked and looked in my rearview mirror. The cops were putting the sawhorses back.

"Keep going," Hamish said to me. I looked away from the rearview mirror at the street in front of me. There were some people at the opposite end of the street staring right at as just beyond another set of saw horses. They had cameras.

"Damnit," I muttered, stepping on the gas pedal and hitting the remote control button for the garage door. It started to go up as I moved closer and closer; I rolled in and hit the button again, leaving our men-in-black outside to fend for themselves.

We were home. Everything was fine inside. We spent the next half-hour unloading the cat and all of our stuff, putting things away. Suddenly, I was very glad to have bought so much food and cat litter. If going out was going to be such a public spectacle, it would be a hassle.

Dad had insisted that we take half of the food back with us, fed up with the avalanches and convinced that he and my mother couldn't possibly eat their way through it before it rotted. "Don't worry about us going shopping – we've got men-in-black too, and I'll go with your mother on the weekend if we want a lot of food," he had said, bagging half of every kind of food back up and stuffing it into the backseat next to Eowyn's carrier-cage. We didn't have much luggage; it fit into the trunk with the cat litter and other supplies.

We called my parents for perhaps the twentieth time and reported our safe arrival. I told my mother about the cops letting us through and the reporters at the other end of the street. She wasn't thrilled, but at least she felt okay knowing that the cops had blocked the paparazzi from entering and occupying the street.

We rang off and flopped onto the sofa with the cat, we didn't turn the TV on right away.

"I guess we're eating dinner in," I said. "I don't feel like cooking right away, though."

"I can wait," Hamish said. "Let me know if I can help."

We sat there for a few minutes, just resting.

"How are we supposed to go out anywhere?" I asked after a few minutes.

"Via the men-in-black chauffeur service," Hamish said.

I looked at him. "Forever?"

"Maybe not, but for now. We've been invited to a New Year's Eve party on the Upper East Side. The place is supposed to have a view of the ball dropping in Times Square."

"Cool. Do we dress up?"

"A little bit, but I don't think I have to wear a tie."

"Do we bring anything?"

"I don't think so."

"Give me the phone number of the hostess, Hamish." I knew better than to believe him.

That was funny; he looked at me unhappily, but gave me the number. That was when I was certain that he had been hoping to avoid dressing up. Forget that; no way was I going to let him show up at a formal party in ratty old clothes.

It was the wife of another successful scientist who, like us, had made a fortune before coming to the Rockefeller Institute, in his case with a pharmaceutical formulation. Their apartment was actually near the one that we hadn't liked – the one that had given me vertigo.

I punched in the number. After a moment's panic as I realized that I hadn't recalled the couple's names before doing so, I remembered them: Dan and Penny.

Penny answered on the second ring. "Hello?"

"Hi…Happy New Year. It's Avril Châtelet."

"Happy New Year! Are you coming to our party on Monday night?"

"Yes. What time should we arrive, how formally or informally should we dress, and would you like us to bring anything?" I regretted having to ask all these questions; she probably thought I was as odd as I knew I was. I usually like to surprise people with that information, not let on about it instantly. Oh well.

Penny didn't miss a beat, though. "It starts at 9 p.m., we're serving hors d'oeuvres and drinks plus sweets, and it's semi-formal. Dresses and suits with ties are fine – nothing more elaborate than that. No need to bring anything."

"So no tuxedos for the men, and knee-length gowns may or may not be worn by women, or else some other really nice dress or skirt and blouse combination?"

She paused, seemingly reluctant to be pinned down to such specifics, but I was in no mood to spend the evening being stared and pointed at for any reasons other than Nae-Née and the Birth Control Treaty.

Then she replied, "That's exactly right."

"Okay then, we'll see you then. Thank you for inviting us. I hope your other holidays have been nice, and I'm looking forward to meeting you."

There. I hoped I had sounded socially acceptable. My end of the conversation had certainly come across as a bit rehearsed or programmed, but I couldn't worry about it.

We rang off and I informed Hamish: "I have some very bad news – you have to wear a suit and tie. I'll get those things laid out for you. We should also bring a bottle of Scotch whiskey – I think we have one."

He groaned about the clothes, nodded about the booze, and picked up the cat again.

"Oh, boo-hoo, I said. "I have to find the right dress. At least we know which outfit you're wearing without even thinking about it."

I stomped upstairs to unpack our bags and get our outfits ready.

At least I could wear the new pearls. Half an hour later it was all done. Hamish had a great Cheshire Cat tie to wear with a navy blue suit; the cat looked as though it had already imbibed the champagne and whatever else one might expect to find at a New Year's Eve party. I had black velvet flats with a ribbon woven around the top edges, and a black lacy skirt with pockets, stockings, and a raspberry pink, low-cut cotton blouse with a black jacket edged with more black lace. I would wear my hair down loose.

Good. The hell with any fashion-obsessed critics at that party; I just wasn't interested.

Hamish helped me cut the potatoes and trim the green beans while I made some coq au vin blanc, and we opened some chocolates that he had gotten for me a couple of weeks ago when we visited La Maison du Chocolat.

The next day was similar: television, cooking, eating, and not going out.

I went to the peephole and saw men-in-black pacing around, and no one else.

I sneaked upstairs as Hamish napped in front of C-SPAN and peered down onto the street. People who lived on our street, our neighbors, appeared from time to time. I couldn't see what was happening on the ends of the street, however. We were halfway between intersections.

Hamish appeared behind me, putting his hands on my shoulders. "The paparazzi are still camped out on either end," he said, startling me.

"What do you do, check in with them from time to time?"

"Yes. Do you want to meet some of them?"

I considered that. "Yeah, I do. Can we invite some of them to come in now?"

"Hang on," he said, taking out his cell phone. He spoke with someone named Rick for a minute or two, then hung up. "They'll ring the bell when the other pair is in their place. Pairs of two guys alternate round the clock, changing shifts every 8 hours."

The bell rang and we went to let in some men-in-black. They did not resemble Will Smith or Tommy Lee Jones at all, I thought to myself, attempting to stay upbeat.

They walked in quickly and Hamish shut the door behind them, locking it.

"Hi," said the taller of the two. "I'm Rick and this is Ed." They took off their sunglasses and I shook their hands.

"Thanks for watching us and my parents so closely. We really appreciate being able to come and go. No one would want to give that up."

They nodded.

"Come on into the kitchen. I'll give you some coffee. Maybe you could tell us what to expect, if you have any idea, and give us some advice about all this."

They looked at each other, and then followed us in.

I set up the coffee machine with some McNulty's Sumatra blend and laid out cups and milk and sugar, plus some of the butter cookies with red and green sugar from Connecticut.

"Sit down," I said, gesturing at the tall seats by the kitchen counter. Hamish and I sat across from them. While the coffee brewed, Rick and Ed summarized their work experience.

Rick had been in the covert ops business since leaving college. He had left to go private after the war in Kuwait. Ed had stayed on later, leaving just before the U.S. invaded Iraq. He had been to Afghanistan before going on to join Blackout Security.

"We'll tell Joe and Chris to come in after we go," Rick said.

The coffee finished brewing and I poured them each a cup. Hamish got one too; he drank too much coffee, but I didn't say anything about it now.

Ed told us to start wearing sunglasses whenever we went outside, especially in daylight.

"Are you suggesting that we also wear them at night, like in the rock song?" I asked.

"Sometimes," he replied, without a trace of levity.

"Great." I got out Hamish's little-used pair of sunglasses and he glumly took them. He hated to wear them. "Don't you dare lose these," I told him.

"Yes, dear," he said, sounding like a listless movie character. He put them on.

I grinned. "You look hot. You should have been wearing them right along; I gave you those last year," I complained. All through the trip around Hawai'i, he had refused to put them on. Now I would get to see him with them more than I had bargained for.

Rick and Ed drained their mugs and stood up. Ed spoke into his sleeve, calling Joe and Chris. I noticed that they had all of the spy gadgets that we saw in the movies. I had to stop enjoying this. Then I realized that soon I wouldn't need much help with that. I may have been used to staying in a lot, but it was about to feel like false imprisonment.

Joe and Chris went through the same routine a few minutes later, conducting themselves with the same low-key, distant attitude as the first two had. Then they left, and I started laying out last night's leftovers.

The New Year's Eve party the next evening was an oddly subdued affair.

Congress had ratified the 28th Amendment that day, ending with a Senate vote of 81 to 19. The House had already voted in favor of it by a vote of 359 to 76. State legislatures across the nation had promptly been informed of the event. Now it was up to them to ratify it or not.

Rick and Ed brought us to the party and home again. Joe and Chris followed us. Hamish told me that others were watching the firehouse in our absence.

Sure enough, the place was a high-rise, modern apartment with a balcony, though no one was interested in going out on it in the freezing weather. It started snowing lightly shortly after we arrived, and continued into the evening, adding to the ambience of the event.

As the party was at night and the place was fully furnished, my vertigo didn't set in – plus I stayed back from the windows. A Siamese cat wandered among us, meowling loudly and purring as he got petted. His name was Emperor Mao.

The women complimented my outfit and fawned over my pearls. Hamish enjoyed that. And he enjoyed his Cheshire Cat tie, so at least I didn't have to hear any complaints about having to dress up. It was nice to see him in formal attire for a change anyway.

Penny had a baby boy and a 4-year-old girl named Annabel, whom she allowed to stay up until half past nine. The girl was wearing a cute pastel blue dress, with a filmy, many-layered skirt speckled with silver sequins. She looked like a fairy princess, I commented to her, saying that I liked her dress. My tone was matter-of-fact, however, not like the lilts of the other women.

The women gave me odd looks, and I realized what I sounded like: objective, not with the swooning, louder, up-and-down ones that they had been addressing the child with. I didn't care; I had always hated it when people talked to me like that, coldly staring back at the insincerity I heard in their tones.

The fawning was as tiresome as usual over the baby boy. I took a look, said the outfit was cute, and moved on. The crowd of people who fussed and cooed over him gave me one askance glance and went back to fussing and cooing. The baby was passed around and admired, until suddenly he let out a huge, ear-splitting shriek, however. I backed away, causing several of the women to turn and stare at me, but I didn't care – loud noises stress me out, but stares don't. His mother put him to bed. A few minutes later, she was back for Annabel.

Hamish had been polite to the little girl – friendlier than I was, in fact, thanks to less pressure to fuss over her. But me…well, it was the usual. I spoke to the child as though she were an intelligent, thoughtful human being. Why not? I saw no reason to insult her.

But I was already wishing I could just observe from the sidelines while petting the cat. Could I help clean up? No…there was a maid serving drinks and snacks…damn. I was stuck sitting and chatting with everyone. That was probably the idea, though.

People settled onto the sofas and chairs to eat the snacks and drink champagne. Conversation quickly turned to the Amendment and its chances in the state legislatures. Some of the women wanted to know how I felt about it all.

"Fine," I said. "We had nothing to do with it other than to invent Nae-Née. We just wanted to provide a user-friendly method of birth control. But I follow the environmental and population reports on the news just about every day, so I agree that the human species is at a tipping point on the Earth, and that our activities and use of resources got us to it."

The room had gotten quiet except for the TV, which was tuned in to the celebration in Times Square. They were all listening. It confirmed my suspicion that our invite had been just for this. Happy to provide the evening's entertainment, I thought, resenting the hostile reception in return for telling the truth. I didn't care whether they liked it or not; there was no reason to expect to form lasting friendships here.

The women weren't finished with me. Did Hamish and I want kids?

"No. We have a cat. That's what we want."

"Is that why you spoke in that flat tone to Annabel?" one of them asked me.

I looked at her. So…this was what we were invited for: to be odd displays. Well, she asked for it, she got it, I thought. "I spoke to her the way I would speak to any other person."

"Kids like cooing and fussing," the woman said, looking at me with distaste.

"I never did. I was always really annoyed by that. I swore to myself that when I was an adult speaking to a kid, I would never do that. So far so good," I replied.

No one smiled, and there was a long silence. I gave a wry grin and asked whether anyone else intended to voice their opinion.

A woman to my right said, "I don't want to have to file for a license to have another kid. We have one, but we wanted two of them. We should be able to replace ourselves when we have children. I feel like the whole world has just been engulfed by China's policy."

There was certainly no chance of moving away from it, everyone agreed.

I commented that we weren't China and talked about how unlicensed births there had led to babies having formaldehyde injected into the tops of their skulls at birth, right in front of the mothers. The U.S. policy wasn't about to degenerate into murder. Also, replacing ourselves and maintaining our current population levels was not a sustainable goal if the next generation were to enjoy all that we had enjoyed.

Hamish added, "In fact, the government is hoping to skip that part of the scramble for resources that it keeps anticipating."

More exchanged glances and stares.

With that, I decided to deliver the coup de grace and finish it. "Is anyone here familiar with the Vulcan axiom from *Star Trek*, "The needs of the many must outweigh those of the few or the one"?" I asked.

There were nods all around.

"Good," I said. "Well, what is happening now is that the planet's leaders are facing another axiomatic fact, regardless of how unpleasant or unpopular it will be: The needs of the people of the future must outweigh the wants of those of the present. Perhaps it would help if more people watched the 1972 movie called *Z.P.G.: Zero Population Growth*. It deals with the emotional issues of resource deprivation caused by human population in our future."

Penny spoke up after a moment, seeing that several of the women were glowering at me. "Let's have some more champagne and play charades."

Uh-oh, I thought. We were terrible at guessing games. Somehow, we got through the next hour and a half and managed to figure out one round apiece out of twelve.

When everyone tired of that, Penny and Dan looked worried as she brought out the little fruit tarts and chocolate pastries. I don't know what got into me, but I asked whether anyone knew how different cultures celebrated New Year's Eve.

Penny looked relieved as a lively discussion started up on the topic. Lots of people had something to add to it; I mentioned that I had heard Penelope Cruz say on Letterman's show that Spaniards got 12 grapes apiece ready to eat during the 12 chimes, and made a wish as they ate each one on the sound of each chime.

What about France? People asked me, knowing my background. "We kiss under mistletoe on New Year's Eve rather than on Christmas," I answered. A chorus of "Ohs" followed.

And in Scotland? They asked Hamish. "We clean the house, burn juniper branches, and eat haggis and oatcakes, then drink lots of Scotch whiskey." The men cheered at that, and Dan brought out the bottle of it that we had brought with us. He poured drinks for several people.

Soon it was time to watch the ball drop, and for the first time ever, Hamish and I saw it drop without the aid of a television. We had to admit it; the view from the apartment was pretty cool, and we thanked Penny and Dan, and realized that we could truthfully say that we had had a good time. We left shortly after midnight, petting Emperor Mao one last time on the way out.

The next day was as subdued as the previous ones had been. I didn't like being stuck inside. I wanted to test the area. "Let's go find a restaurant for dinner," I said.

Hamish looked astonished. He said, "I'm game, but I thought you wouldn't want to go. The damned paparazzi are still out there," he told me.

I looked up local restaurants, planning to call ahead before getting stuck outside in the cold, unable to quietly take a look at other choices if the first one didn't pan out. After a couple of minutes, I found something: the Fatty Crab on Hudson and Gansevoort Streets.

But walking was impossible. We tried it, but Joe and Chris screeched to a halt next to us and Joe jumped out, waving us in. "Forget it, Professors. See that crowd up there? They're waiting for you."

We surrendered and got in.

Chris lost our pursuers in heavy traffic, allowing us to get out in front of the place with few passersby in the vicinity. The scene looked normal; score one for our men-in-black. We even dared to walk back partway, though Hamish assured me that we were being tailed by them.

I was all for sneaking up on the paparazzi and asking whether or not they had seen us yet, but Hamish said no way and whipped his cell phone back out. We rode back with our guard, the car squeezing past the pushy reporters and the cops who were still guarding the saw horses.

That night, after Hamish fell asleep, I lay there in the dark, mulling over how the new law would work. It put social engineering at odds with freedom of speech. Other, less democratic nations might not grapple with this issue, but ours would certainly have to. It was easy to see why an amendment was necessary if we were to actually go forward with the terms of the Birth Control Treaty – or Birth Management Treaty, as I had also heard it called at the party.

I wondered how much of this new law would lead to social engineering. And how would freedom of speech fit in? Would anger over this be classified as fighting words in order to stop public disorder over the Nae-Née use policy? Was the government planning to preserve some semblance of freedom of speech while indelibly etching this legislation into our Constitution? An amendment would make it very difficult for the Supreme Court to assail any of it...

It really seemed as though social engineering was at war with freedom of speech. Some sort of balance between the two would have to be struck if Americans were to preserve what they fondly touted as the greatest legal system in force on the entire planet. It's not that I was seriously worried about our ability to pull this off, only that some careful thought and effort would have to be invested in this whole crucial process.

As for social engineering, how would it work? Once it started, wouldn't society become addicted to it? It would never end...and how would licenses to reproduce be granted? What would be the criteria for granting or denying them?

Health? That sounded valid.

Education? Basing a license on the educational level of potential parents didn't seem equitable or reasonable. Not everyone in a society can be a leader or an intellectual, after all. But how to measure one's future potential from zygotehood? This wasn't the world of the movie *Gattaca* – and not all of the probabilities measured in that story came true anyway.

Not all outcomes can be predicted, planned for, or controlled. The meritocracy of our society would have to be left to function as always, even where certain conditions blocked merit, such as a combination of disadvantages conspiring to hold someone back. It happened all the time; one person would make it despite or against all odds and do great, while another would fail miserably even after working hard and marking all of the right choices. Well…this crazy, state-mandated use of Nae-Née wasn't attempting to fix every problem – just overpopulation.

Economic status? No…that would be blatantly discriminatory, political suicide. Might as well stamp "Condemned to Repeat History Because Policy-Makers Didn't Bother to Study It" on the foreheads of every lawmaker in sight…it would just be a recipe for social unrest, enraging poorer families by telling them that they couldn't have any kids even if they wanted them.

Sure, unhealthy people and drug users and smokers might be easy to disqualify, but after that, well…it seemed likely to come down to just one or at the most two children per couple, and if that couple divorced or one spouse died and there was a remarriage in the future, no licenses would be allowed for the new marriage. Single parents? Forget it. If someone got divorced or died, that couldn't be planned for, but those who were currently married were another story.

What about all those sperm banks and frozen embryo services? Nae-Née seemed to throw a monkey wrench into them. Perhaps the businesses associated with those reproduction methods would sue the government. Couples who had relied on fertility treatments would be out of options and out of luck. Any artificial method of forcing a life into existence would no longer be allowed. So much for couples with infertility issues; they would have to adopt.

Social unrest was likely to surface like a tidal wave despite any attempts at government-sanctioned fairness…which sounded like an oxymoron anyway. There would be trouble. A lot of people were going to be very, very angry. A lot of people were about to realize that where they had previously had options, possibilities, and hopes, all of that was now over and done with.

All of that was a thing of the past, making way for a future that they would not be able to enjoy, because they would have to make sacrifices in their own lifetimes, now, and forego things that they wanted so that others – people whom they would quite possibly never meet – could have a shot at happiness and choices. That could not possibly sit well with the disappointed segment of the planet's population.

This would be deeply unpleasant – for them, and for the haves who would interact with them, face them, and try not to rub their own contentment into the have-nots' noses. Because with a high degree of certainty, many of those have-nots would have regular contact with the haves, and the haves would indeed have some second-hand knowledge of their rage and sadness.

I predicted to myself that this new world order would soon lead to violence of some sort.

Chapter 22

Several Minutes on 60 Minutes

The request from *60 Minutes* to do a story on us came the day that we returned to the office, at 9 a.m., before we arrived. Patsy told us about it when we walked in. She gave us an odd look, but as I am no good at reading nonverbal cues, I didn't dwell on it. I figured we would find out about whatever it was that on her mind soon enough.

After discussing the *60 Minutes* offer together in my office, we figured, why not? It would do no good to completely conceal ourselves from the public. Our names and photos had already appeared in *The New York Times*, and then they had been circulated ad nauseam ad infinitum since the State of the Union Address.

Accordingly, we called back later that afternoon. We had no idea what we were getting into. It was nothing bad, just way more complicated than we had realized.

Who would be interviewing us? Lesley Stahl. Cool — she was one of my favorites.

Where would they like to film us? As many places as possible. Huh? That didn't instantly compute. Could they define "as many places as possible" for us? We wanted a clearer idea of what we were signing up for. And one stipulation: no outside shots of our firehouse, and no giving away our home address on television.

"Oh, of course not," said the producer who took our call.

"We'll need that in writing before we sign on for this," I assured him. A brief pause, then an assurance that a contract including that provision would be included in the release form. Excellent. So…where were they hoping to film us?

The answers sounded okay: inside our firehouse, going about our normal, at-home activities; in restaurants together, shopping for groceries, walking around the city wherever we normally went, riding the subway or cabs if that was how we got to work, and in our offices and Hamish's laboratory doing our work.

"That sounds fine," I said. "Send the contracts, release forms, whatever it is that you normally send. We'll get them back to you quickly, then set up the filming schedule with you."

"Thank you so much," the producer said, and that was that until about an hour after lunch, when the forms arrived in my e-mail account. Wow. They must be in a hurry.

I read them all over. I couldn't find anything wrong with them, but I called Dad at his office – he was in Hartford, Connecticut – and told him what was going on and how fast the papers had arrived. I also told him about the stipulation I had made about our home.

"Smart. E-mail me the papers. I'll double-check, though it all sounds legitimate. I'll get back to you before 4 p.m."

"That fast? Don't you have paying clients breathing down your neck, wanting stuff done now, immediately and this instant? I can wait," I said.

"I do have clients, but I am a senior partner. I can look at this stuff now if I want to, and I want to. Besides, it's my daughter and the world is pushing for a look into her life. I won't relax until I check into this, so there's no point in doing that other work until I do this."

"Oh. I love you too, Dad. Hitting "Send" on the e-mail now."

We waited a moment, then he said, "Got it. I'll call you back."

And he hung up before I could say good-bye, but it didn't matter.

I didn't know what else to do, so I went back to reading about how societies throughout the ages all over the planet had handled population surges, resource distribution, and overcrowding issues. It was to be my next lecture topic. It looked like the current political and environmental issues were going to inform the content of my next book.

Halfway through that, I realized that I hadn't said much of anything yet to Patsy other than hello, and we had been away for a week of holiday time. I went out to her desk and said Happy New Year and asked about her holiday and her family and cat. All fine, thank you, she had had fun with Jim at a couple of bars and at a restaurant with her dad, came the response. Great, I said. She asked about me, and I told her about being barricaded into our driveway by the reporters and then on our street, and how weird it was.

She looked a bit taken aback. "You couldn't get out?"

"Oh, we could get out. Hamish hired a security company to help us last year, but we didn't notice any major change in our ability to move out and about until after the State of the Union Address."

"Wow. But you still had a good time for the holidays?"

"Oh yeah. We'll get used to this and cope, and it will hopefully die down after this *60 Minutes* thing is broadcast. If we let the curious public see something more than just last year's photos and story from *The New York Times*, maybe that will lessen the interest in us. We're just inventors. The government doesn't care what we think about this Birth Control Treaty. It just wants Nae-Née and will add its own modifications regardless of what anyone says."

She listened to me intently, and I realized that it was out of character for her. Then she said, "The government sent a team of their nurses through the Rockefeller Institute campus while you were away."

I stared at her; so that was what was bothering her. "You mean they injected every woman on site with a Borg version of Nae-Née? That fast?"

"Yes."

"Wow. They must have been preparing for this during the fall..."

She asked, "Why did you call it a Borg version? What does that mean?"

"Have you been watching the news since the day that the treaty was signed?"

"No, not much. It's too upsetting."

"Well, it means that the government is taking Nae-Née as developed by Hamish, then adding more nanite components to each device – tracking parts, so that it can't be grabbed or removed by a surgeon without a secret code, which shall be the enforcement mechanism."

She looked a bit red. "When do you get yours, I wonder?"

"I have the prototype in me – have since the summer of 2010. Unless I hear otherwise, it will probably stay all my life. We don't want kids anyway, so I should be good to go."

"They won't want to replace it?"

"I can't say for certain, but it is the prototype, and the fact that it keeps on ticking is like an advertisement for its safety and effectiveness. I'm guessing that just to maintain confidence in Nae-Née, they won't want to switch it out. It's not like I give them any incentive to do so."

"How do you feel about this policy?"

I didn't trust her. I already knew that she wanted a baby, and after the President's speech explaining the requirements of being eligible for a license, I knew that her chances were most likely nil. She was over 40 years old and morbidly obese.

"I'll save my comments for the interview. I realize that that sounds annoying, but I tend to write better and give better answers if I don't write or speak until the moment that I either write all alone or come to the big moment in an interview."

She wasn't thrilled, but that seemed to be willing to stop asking me questions about this for now. I went back to my office and resumed reading.

Forty-five minutes after we had spoken, Dad called back. I could see his number on the caller I.D. It was only 2:15; Patsy was quicker on the draw at answering it, which meant that she grabbed it on the first ring, but my office phone rang again only a couple of seconds later.

"Bonjour Dad!"

"Bonjour. Okay – go ahead and sign. Other than what you stipulated, I don't see anything to worry about. It all looks normal to me. I should trust your judgment more, but I can't help myself. Just remember I said that the next time that you have to do something all on your own – I know you can handle things even if I feel the need to check it over."

Well – that was gratifying. "Thanks, Dad! For the assessment of the contracts, of my judgment, the works. I'll get the stuff ready and call *60 Minutes* back."

"You're welcome. We'll come and watch it with you when it's on. Bye."

"Bye." I hung up. No reason to delay; I printed the stuff out, signed, got Hamish's signature – which meant a walk down the hall and back, no big deal – and called them back.

They said that they would send someone right over to get them. Hmm…okay. "See you soon," I said, and hung up. 20 minutes later, Lesley Stahl herself walked in with the producer I had spoken with.

Guess I didn't need to see any I.D.s, I thought, as they gave me business cards with the CBS logo and *60 Minutes* on them. I knew who Lesley Stahl was; the producer had probably brought her for that reason. His name was Carlton Sattler.

I greeted them both with a smile and shook hands, said I was looking forward to working with them, introduced them to Patsy, and took them to meet Hamish.

Hamish looked up from his instruments in mild surprise, removed his purple latex gloves, and shook hands with both of them. He put his things away and came with us. I led them all back into my office to hand over the documents and discuss the next steps in the process.

Soon I had all of the information I would need to go ahead with the arrangements.

Patsy appeared as I started to go over the information that they had brought, asking whether we would like coffee, tea, soda, juice, anything, and if I would like her to make the filming arrangements.

Yes on the drinks, but thank you, no – I would take care of the other calls.

She left to get the refreshments. I suspected that she wanted to see what was going on.

The meeting was about meeting each other, so we conducted the social interaction expecting to get nothing more accomplished, and gave the producer the signed papers. They left after about a half hour, quite happy.

So were we.

That left us with about a couple hours more before it was time to go home.

I went back to my office and started setting up for my next lecture. Almost immediately, there was a knock at the door. Damnit! I wanted some time alone to work. Who was Patsy letting in? I opened it and found that it was Patsy herself. Oh.

"Patsy! What's up?"

She was red-faced and her eyes were puffy. "Can I come in and talk?"

"Sure – let me get stuff off the sofa." I moved the books I had been looking at to the coffee table.

She sat down. I did too. I said, "So – tell me what it was like here while we were gone."

She looked up from my Kleenex box. "The phone rang constantly. I kept telling reporters that you weren't available for comment. I didn't tell them where you were."

"Wow – thanks. They figured it out, but they didn't appear until late the day after we got there. I guess you made them work for the information; thanks."

She smiled at me.

"So what did you do besides field questions from annoying journalists – and where did they say they were from?"

"They're from every news organization in the country, and some foreign ones, too. Here," she handed me the message book, "you can see for yourself."

I took it. *The New York Times*, *The London Times*, *The Washington Post*, *The Hartford Courant*, *The L.A. Times*, *Le Monde*, Al-Jazeera, Fox News, MSNBC's *Countdown*, CNN, Bill Maher – wait, Bill Maher? He was the coolest of them all, but I wasn't up for a trip to Los Angeles right now. The list went on and on as I flipped through the message book, which contained 3 slips per page.

"I'll save this and if we're going to answer any of them, don't worry about it. It shouldn't be your problem after the initial blow-off anyway," I told her. "Thanks. If anything, this will make a nice souvenir." I noticed that she had just started this book on December 21st and figured it would be better to use it only for journalist inquiries. I gave it back to her and explained that. I would check it over at the end of each day.

Suddenly she asked me something that I had been expecting, but not wanting to hear.

"Would you write me a recommendation for a birth license?"

I stared at her. "A recommendation?"

She pulled out a sheaf of paper and passed it to me. It was a blank application for a birth license. It contained a form for a physical exam by a gynecologist – not surprising – and space for a personal statement. There was another form for a father's physical exam. The next page was for basic data such as name, address, date of birth, Social Security number, etc. It also made an assessment by a psychologist or psychiatrist optional but not required, being flexible as to which one. That profession was about to get a lot of work, I thought. I didn't see anything about a recommendation. "Where is the part about recommendations?" I wondered aloud, fascinated. "And how did you get this?"

"Off the Internet. And there is no recommendation section. I just thought that it would help coming from you, and to have recommendations."

"Fascinating…is that the website?" I pointed to the upper right corner of the top page.

She nodded. "It's been up since last Friday."

"Did Jim say that he wants kids after the Birth Control Treaty was signed?"

"I was hoping to get pregnant and surprise him. I want a baby and I want to get married. He thinks there's no reason to get married without a kid in the picture, and he thinks I should be thinner before we try to get pregnant anyway. He worries that the baby wouldn't be healthy. But I know I could have a healthy one, I just know it. I'm sure he would get married if I surprised him like this, and I really want a baby."

Wonderful, I thought. This was going to be the thing that pushed our professional relationship over the edge. But all I said was, "Leave the papers with me and I'll think it over. But be ready for a no from me – there's no section for any recommendations, and the President's State of the Union speech didn't allow for any appeals or exceptions. I really don't think anyone cares what I think. They just wanted to use my idea, and not because it's mine. They want it because it works for that reason alone."

She started crying. I got out some fancy chocolates – dark chocolate almonds from La Maison du Chocolat (where else?) and told her to have a mood booster. She took a couple and started to choke them down. A minute later, she got up and went back to her desk.

When it was time to go home, I couldn't get away from her fast enough. Luckily, I was able to persuade Hamish to come home with me too. Thanks to global warming, the cold wind wasn't all that cold, so I wanted to walk again.

I told him about Patsy's visit, and everything she had said to me.

"I knew that would happen sooner or later. I don't envy you. What are you going to do next?" he asked me.

"Procrastinate until after the *60 Minutes* interview, say what I really think in it, let her watch it filmed, and then hope she realizes that I don't want to write any recommendations. Can you imagine how that would impact my credibility if I started writing those for people? It's not like any request would be granted just because I wrote it, and if I were to lead off by writing one for Patsy, an overweight woman who wants to use the baby to hook her boyfriend into marriage, that would end any credibility I might have before it ever took off."

He listened to me silently, holding my hand as we walked. "You've got that right," he finally said. "Good – don't do it. We'll get another secretary after she has a meltdown."

"You think she's going to have a meltdown when I say no?" I asked him.

"Without a doubt," he replied.

We meandered down Madison Avenue, cut over to 5th, and wandered into the lobby of the Park Plaza Hotel to see the famous Hillary Knight painting of Kay Thompson's imp, Eloise.

The painting was no longer in the left drawing room with a telephone underneath that would play the author's impersonation of the character. The reason infuriated me. Some wealthy religious-minded Arab had bought the building and converted the hotel into part condominiums and part hotel. The sound of a female voice is haram – morally bad to hear if she is not a relative – in Islam.

This character was a part of American culture and children's literature, and the enjoyment was on American soil. The nerve of some Muslim to impose his culture on a National Historic Landmark and an artifact, which was just what that recording was, I thought.

To my way of thinking, this was just another indicator of America's dependence on foreign oil, which was fueling global warming and detracting from our overall quality of life – in more ways than one. We had to find another energy source. If we had done so sooner, perhaps this Arab wouldn't have become wealthy enough to buy a piece of our culture and confiscate it from us.

Hamish could see that I was getting tense as I told him what was on my mind; he agreed with me about the recording – it should have been kept available to the public – but dwelling on it was pointless.

We left and headed down 5th Avenue, past Bergdorf Goodman's store, where I amused him by poking fun at the over-the-top window displays of clothes that would only be worn for magazine photo shoots.

Across the street there was something even funnier: the Louis Vuitton window displays showed smashed glass in each section, with no handbags – only a couple of luggage tags here and there, as if the fictitious thieves had been in such haste as to forget to scoop them up.

"They paid money for this destruction?!" Hamish asked, incredulous.

"Of course; they want customers to think that the bags are so desirable that they might be stolen. I wouldn't want such a worrisome product myself. Might as well pin a target on myself." I glanced down at my Vera Bradley hipster. I knew it was there, I could wear it, and it kept me from lugging too much stuff around, thus freeing me to take long walks.

Hamish kissed me and grabbed my hand. "Let's get some Japanese pastries at Minamoto Kitchoan," he said, pulling me onward. Minamoto Kitchoan was a place on 49th Street that had wonderful red bean pastries flown in from Japan daily, or cherry ones, or green tea ones, each only a between two and three bucks apiece. It was fun to eat them now and then, but they only kept for a couple of days. The pastries that were pre-packaged each appeared to have been wrapped using origami techniques.

We got a few different kinds each and continued on down the Avenue.

The next day, I called the producers of *60 Minutes* again to set things up. Soon I was committed to having a film crew spend the weekend after next in our firehouse.

I informed Hamish, who rolled his eyes but promised to stay home all day both Saturday and Sunday and do whatever I wanted to do.

"Don't worry; you can sit with the cat, the TV, the computer, whatever. I'm going to cook, bake, do laundry, eat the food with you, etc. But there might be some shopping at a few food shops. I won't leave you on your own for that – you're coming with me to co-star."

He cracked up, but said he'd cooperate with it all.

As promised, the weekend felt like life in a fishbowl. The crew followed us everywhere, attempting to blend into the background and failing utterly because we were acutely aware of their presence. We did our best to ignore them, but my only experience as an actress had been in some high school plays.

I did offer coffee, but they had brought their own, determined not to have any effect on the house that they were filming – not even the contents of the kitchen cupboards. Whatever they wanted, I thought. The only offer of hospitality that they took me up on was the use of the downstairs half bathroom.

As planned, I did laundry, then baked a chocolate orange cake – Hamish enjoyed the wonderful smell that filled the ground floor while he answered his e-mails on his laptop, then played with the cat and watched the news on the big flat-screen TV. After that, I dragged him out to buy coffee, fish, and fruits and vegetables. The food was for the next evening, however.

We ate out that night at a bistro called A.O.C. on Bleecker Street. I was glad that I had made a reservation, but I was worried about what the place would say about the film crew. Not to worry; the crew had called ahead and the proprietor was thrilled to have the place appear on television. We were thanked for choosing the restaurant (though we had done so many times before). The food was delicious, and we had some of the cake when we got home.

The next day was similar; the crew arrived at 10 a.m. again, and we gave them little of interest to record as we sat drinking gourmet coffee, watching movies on cable TV and checking our e-mail until I cooked dinner. Then they filmed us eating it.

The next day was Hamish's turn to be interviewed by Lesley. He talked in his office in mid-morning, around 10 a.m., then let the crew film him working with his grad students and over his instruments in the lab.

I asked him how it had felt to know that his every word was being recorded for posterity as well as to be broadcast to living rooms and kitchens all over the nation. "Not very real yet," was all he could say after thinking it over for a moment or two.

Interesting; I supposed that I would probably feel same way. I wouldn't know what questions I would have to answer, so I couldn't rehearse. Just as well…more natural that way.

The next afternoon it was my turn. I had insisted that it not be in the morning, when I was least alert. I didn't want to look tired or sound stupid. The television crew arrived at 2 p.m., set up their equipment, and then Lesley Stahl interviewed me.

Hamish was down the hall in his lab; he didn't want to hang around and stare at me. Better to hear about it all later than risk making me nervous or distract me. He wanted the segment to be good.

The session was filmed in my office, with both me and Lesley in the wing chairs, facing each other with the view of the East River in the background. She got right into it with her first question, and I didn't hesitate with my reply.

Lesley Stahl: "Why do you think that so many countries signed onto the Birth Control Treaty?"

Avril Châtelet: "Our planet has become Easter Island: it's full, and we have nearly used it up."

Lesley Stahl: "You talk as though we are facing a crisis of epic proportions. Yet when we look around us, things don't seem that dire. People are able to buy food, go to college, and sit by themselves – and in their own rooms and offices."

Avril Châtelet: "On the surface it certainly looks that way. If you go out to buy groceries or have coffee at Starbucks, you will see people doing and enjoying exactly what you just described: food, educations – and many of them are reading alone or discussing the news and books together. What you don't see is student loan debt that exceeds what can be paid back without either joining the military and likely trading one's life or at least a limb for a Bachelor's degree, or paying the loans back with most of one's earnings for most of one's working adult life, with nothing left for travel, entertainment or retirement, and not much else for living expenses. That's why so many people end up living with their parents. That, and college applications from qualified high school graduates already greatly exceed spaces for them."

Lesley Stahl: "How will this policy help, in your opinion?"

Avril Châtelet: "Look at food prices, and look at diminishing fish supplies and the dying and disappearing bee populations. Look at crowded apartments with single people who cannot afford to rent alone or even in pairs thanks to high rents. Look at housing foreclosures, homeless shelters, and then compare our standard of living to that of our parents and grandparents. People who lived in the 1950s and even the 1980s had more room and more money to pay for it because there were fewer people to compete with for space and food. The planet can produce a finite amount of those things. The fact that our species is capable of exceeding that is no excuse to expect the Earth to accommodate human needs and desires. These desires have been increasing exponentially as each successive generation grows larger and larger, and its members live full life spans thanks to medical advancements, thus increasing the demand and strain on the Earth.”

Lesley Stahl: “You have said that you don’t intend to have children. Why?”

Avril Châtelet: “Okay…you asked for it, so here’s the truth: I don’t want children, and there should be more people like me.”

Lesley Stahl: “People who don’t want children – there should be more of you?”

Avril Châtelet: “The Earth will do just fine with or without us. It does not care what humans want. It can and will only produce so much. If we push it past the tipping point – and we are there now – it will simply cease to accommodate us. Population reduction and control is the only way to ensure that the future generations of humans that we do produce will be okay, let alone happy and educated. If we don’t control our urge to reproduce, the Earth will be the ultimate enforcer of that policy, in the most painful way possible.”

Lesley Stahl: “You certainly are articulate at expressing cold, hard truths.”

Avril Châtelet: “I’m not suggesting, implying, or hypothesizing. I’m certain of this, and I’m not alone. The problem is that people don’t want to believe that any of this is so. They don’t want to think that the party might be winding down, and that if they don’t exercise a significant level of self-control and engage in routine thoughtfulness, the party could simply end.”

Lesley Stahl: “The party being a metaphor for human life as we know and love it.”

Avril Châtelet: “Exactly. I may be what the majority calls selfish – I have always found myself in the minority when it comes to what I want out of life – but the Earth and our species needs more people who think and wish as I do. I never expected Nae-Née to become a mandatory part of each and every human life on this planet. When my husband and I came up with this idea, we simply wanted a reliable form of birth control that would enable people to enjoy life without the slightest worry about an unwanted pregnancy. The fact that the world’s governments have made it a super-charged political issue and a hope for our species’ future is something wonderful, not a tragedy. But it was not our idea, despite that fact that angry, disappointed would-be parents find it all too easy to lay the blame for their sense of disenfranchisement at our feet and vilify us.”

Lesley Stahl: “What can you say to people who do want several children – or even people who won’t be allowed a license to reproduce even once?”

Avril Châtelet: “Those people will have to talk themselves into wanting other things, such as pets. But I can’t be responsible for other people’s happiness. They certainly don't take any responsibility for other people's happiness, so I won't worry about it. It's pretty much life as usual, life as it has always been: people are on their own to make themselves happy or unhappy."

Lesley Stahl: "What about the ancient viewpoint, the one that goes back throughout human history and earlier, that reproduction is a human right?"

Avril Châtelet: "By a human right, I must assume that you mean a moral one rather than a legal one, because this policy is nullifying that concept. Obviously, enough lawmakers have decided that this view has to change, because our planet cannot provide everything that humans want."

Lesley Stahl: "How close do see us to the day of reckoning, and how are we preparing?"

Avril Châtelet: "I can only guess. If we're lucky, a couple of decades. As for what we are doing to prepare, it's certainly a step in the right direction that Nae-Née is being applied, and another excellent step is the President's creation of a new Cabinet post and Department – you know the one I'm talking about – the Department of Demographics."

Lesley Stahl: "Wouldn't it be easier to just help people with their birth license applications so that you wouldn't be so vehemently blamed, unjustly though you are, for this treaty?"

Avril Châtelet: "No. I never find it easy to do what most other people consider easy. And I won't do anything insincere. To me, what other people find easy is just too hard for me. I can't do it."

Lesley Stahl: "Neither you nor your husband seem to worry about offending others by saying what you really think. And you are well-informed when you speak."

Avril Châtelet: "If the facts and the objective analyses that are drawn from those facts offend some people, this is not our fault. That's just the way it is."

Lesley Stahl: "Why do you think so many people want to have children despite the growing evidence that the planet can't give them a good life?"

Avril Châtelet: "Someone gave me the answer to that over a year ago. She said that she wanted a baby. I replied that there are too many people in the world for them all to have a comfortable, happy and interesting life. And then she gave me the most honest explanation."

Lesley Stahl: "What was that?"

Avril Châtelet: "She said, "I don't care about everybody else. I just care about me, me, me." If she is representative of the majority of the population, then that explains how the human species got into this mess. We chose it. We deliberately ignored the environment as we just kept on taking more and more until we found ourselves in trouble, and people don't want it called to their attention. Not in my back yard has morphed into not in my lifetime – a refusal to accept something that is unavoidable."

Lesley Stahl: "Listening to your answers, I keep wondering how to characterize you; communist isn't right, because you are somewhat of a capitalist, to put it mildly, but that isn't it either. How would you classify yourself in political and social terms?"

Avril Châtelet: "I would classify myself as a Malthusian."

Lesley Stahl: "What is a Malthusian?"

Avril Châtelet: "A Malthusian is someone who agrees with the philosophy of Thomas Malthus. Thomas Malthus lived in England from 1766 to 1834, and published 6 editions of *An Essay on the Principle of Population*. In it, he stated that wars, famines and epidemics mask the fundamental problem of populations overstretching their resource limitations. He advocated the practice of planning for the long-term and for considering the good of the many ahead of one's immediate pleasure and comfort. He was also highly skeptical that humans would ever have the self-discipline to do that."

Lesley Stahl: "What do you think will happen next – with public opinion?"

Avril Châtelet: "I think that perhaps, if we are lucky, people might go through the various stages of grieving and ultimately get to acceptance. But of course I can't be sure. They are still in the anger stage."

Lesley Stahl: "Do you worry about who will take care of you when you are old?"

Avril Châtelet: "Yes – often – but nothing has changed for me. I was always going to have that problem, and need to rely on friends or relatives. I don't have such a big leap to make in order to accept that."

Lesley Stahl: "So you don't approve of having children to care of you when you are old?"

Avril Châtelet: "No – nor do I believe that having them guarantees that. Circumstances can make that impossible, such as geography, death, disability, and so on. And having kids to get an old-age caregiver is a selfish act that simply passes that problem on to someone else – one's children. Having children should be about ensuring a good future for them, not the parent."

Lesley Stahl: "What do imagine the future will be like?"

Avril Châtelet: "Unpleasant for our generation when we are the elderly, and possibly also for some of those immediately after us. Gradually better and better for the next ones, who will exist in smaller numbers. Of course, that also depends on converting to non-fossil fuel energy sources."

Lesley Stahl: "Well – thank you very much for taking the time to talk with us. You have given us all a great deal of important things to think about."

Avril Châtelet: "Thank you for interviewing me."

And with that, we were done.

I wondered what else was done, of course: my privacy, my ability to go about my business buying groceries, eating in restaurants, attending movies, visiting museums…we would see, I realized, when the interview was broadcast.

Lesley told me that it would happen in about 3 weeks.

Great.

Patsy had hovered in the background, keeping out of the way, but listening.

The impression that she resembled a looming, brewing storm cloud was inescapable. We stood there, on the perimeter of the office, watching for about 20 minutes as the *60 Minutes* film crew gathered and packed up all of their equipment.

Neither of us said much, other than to answer the crew's questions about putting things back where they belonged. Soon it was over and we were alone in the outer office.

It was then that the storm cloud burst.

"You're not going to write that recommendation, are you?!"

"No."

"You fuckin' bitch! I knew it! You're the most selfish person in the world!"

"Stop screaming. Do you realize that if I wrote it you still wouldn't get a license?"

"You skinny bitch! I hope some lunatic shoots you! I hope you and your husband can never walk around without being followed and bothered again! I hope…!"

So much noise from a bully; I remembered that sort of noise and tense pressure from camp and junior high school. It made me shake like a leaf, though I gave no outward sign of that. Oddly, despite the upset, I noticed that she wasn't enunciating the profanity properly. Come to think of it, she didn't usually bother to enunciate much; funny what one notices when someone is shrieking abuse at you.

I turned my back on her and ran into my office. Then I locked the door. It really began to just sound like noise then, and the shaking subsided.

It was just like when I was a kid, whenever my parents had had the foolish idea of sending me to camp, where I just couldn't fit in, or whenever there had been a bully at school…although at school, there more controls on bullies, such as teachers, and bullies had a much harder time concealing their antisocial tendencies.

It was so similar to the times when I had been badgered, bothered and otherwise incessantly disturbed to utter distraction for the crime of being different. The crime was that I was socially awkward, introverted, studious, and talented at various things that interested me.

But here and now, there was a wonderful difference as I realized what happens to that different kid: she grows up to have a lucrative and fascinating career. She does not need to cater to the bully. She does not have to put up with the hateful bullshit coming from the bully.

I called security.

The noise continued of course, because it took security a few minutes to arrive. More epithets and insults broke through the wooden barrier, but that was all that got through.

Soon I heard other voices: security had arrived. It abruptly got quieter, then explanations and pleading began.

I heard the security officers punching a phone number into their own phones, and mine rang in the office. I went to the desk and answered it.

"Professor Châtelet, is that you?"

"Yes, I shut myself in my office. I'll come out when she's gone."

"Okay ma'am, just checking. Don't worry; we'll take care of this and call back soon."

"Thank you." I hung up and waited. There were some odd shuffling sounds, a brief thump, and some sobbing. Then there were footsteps as people left. The phone rang again.

"Professor Châtelet?"

"I'm here."

"All clear. You can come out any time."

"Thank you. Please don't leave; I want to see you when I come out."

"Okay, I'm right outside."

"What's your name?"

"I'm Officer Farley. I have dark hair, cut short but not in a crew cut, and brown eyes. I'm wearing a campus security uniform. Don't worry; she's gone. We told her she could either get her coat and handbag and leave quietly with us, or we'd call the cops, and added that she wouldn't want us to do that."

I opened the door and came out. Sure enough, a guy fitting that description was in the outer office. I said to him, "Thank you very much – she was scary, and she was in such a rage at me. She just started up without warning. The film crew from *60 Minutes* had just left with Lesley Stahl, and Patsy had been listening to my answers during the interview. She said nothing until we were alone, and then started screaming and swearing at me. She's angry with me for not agreeing with her about certain things. I've been avoiding discussing it since we met just to get along with her. Too late to do that anymore."

Officer Farley looked sympathetic. "They would have arrested and charged her with false imprisonment and disturbing the peace, plus assault and battery if she didn't go quietly."

"Well – thank you very much for the rescue. She's huge, and suddenly turned menacing, belligerent, and reminded me of bullies at school. You are very nice and soothing after all that, and you talk like you really know your job."

"I'm studying criminal justice at City College."

I smiled appreciatively. "That sounds like a fascinating field of study. Are you enjoying it? How far along are you?"

Farley looked surprised, then answered, "About halfway. I have another year after this one, and then maybe I'll go for my Bachelor's."

"Good luck. I'll bet you'll do well. If you need any recommendations, I'd be happy to write one for you. Here," I handed him one of my old editor's business cards, with just my e-mail address and cell phone number on it, "take my card and contact me if you need anything like that."

He looked thrilled. "I will! Thank you! I may need a recommendation just to continue with my education."

Hamish ran into the office just then, and saw me give the security officer my card. "What happened? Are you okay?" He gripped me by the shoulders, and seemed to be looking me over as though searching for injuries.

"I'm fine. Patsy went nuts after the *60 Minutes* people and Lesley Stahl left, screamed and swore at me, scared the hell out of me, and so on, so I locked myself in my office and called security. Officer Farley can explain the part I didn't see. I stayed in there and he called me after they got her out of here."

Hamish looked at Farley wide-eyed.

Farley immediately took up the next thread of the tale. "We told her she could either get her things and go quietly or we would call the cops and make her go. So she went." His radio spat out some static just then and he pushed a button. "Farley here."

"We're walking her off of the grounds now. We're out on 64th Street. She just crossed the street, so she's off of the campus now. We told her to do herself a favor and not come back."

"Okay, thanks. Over and out."

Hamish shook Farley's hand. "Thanks for helping my wife. I really appreciate it."

"You're welcome, Dr. MacDonall. I'll go back and report on the incident." He left.

Hamish looked at me for a moment, then hugged me. "Tell me all about it," he said, pulling me back into my office. "I was upstairs in another office; they told me she freaked out."

We shut the door, and then I locked it, still not settled yet after the uproar. Then I joined him on the sofa and recounted the events of the afternoon.

He listened to it all, looking livid – turning red, clenching and unclenching fists, and glaring at the floor. Then he said, "So, you're rid of Jabba the Slutt – well and good!"

"I tried to get along with her and just not tell her things that I thought would bother her, but those interview questions deserved honest answers. I couldn't put it off any longer. So now we have no secretary. I wonder if we can get another one."

"Of course we can get another one. Let's ask to be consulted in the selection process this time. Considering what just happened, I'd be surprised if they said no."

"I just want someone who is more secure with themselves, not a bully, and not baby-obsessed. That's definitely going to be a big issue with us – especially thanks to this. Maybe if we just explain what happened when we look for a replacement…"

"We won't have to. Every workplace has a grapevine, and this one had plenty of people out in the halls and in offices nearby who could hear most of that screaming. Soon the whole campus will know, and then the press will know also."

"Oh. Okay."

I thought about that some more. Soon the whole world would know not only about the interview, but also about Patsy's tantrum. So, soon lots of people would condemn me for this, and their sympathies would rest heavily with our equally hefty ex-secretary. Wonderful. The burden of the famous, I supposed…but I resented this. I told Hamish what was on my mind.

"The hell with her. I'll tell anyone who says anything to me about you that it's all her fault. You were very nice to her – which I know you were, I can give examples – and you have no obligation to be like her, want what she wants in life, or cave in to bullying."

"Don't. The best response is no response. If she starts selling stories to tabloids or something, she'll have a hard time getting another job, and then she'll really be out of luck. Just wait and watch. We don't want to give her any grounds for a lawsuit."

"Oh – yeah, you're right. I hadn't thought of that. I just got angry. You're right, as usual. You're the lawyer in this marriage, anyway, so no wonder."

"Let's go. Can we go? Can you leave the lab yet?"

"I'll go pack up and come back here for you."

"Good. I still don't want to walk out of here alone. She could be lurking in the area. I think she's in a crazy rage, and that she might not calm down for a while – more than today, maybe even longer. Weeks, maybe. Or more."

"Don't worry." He hugged me again, kissed me, and left to shut things down. It was a quarter to four anyway; he had arrived early, so he could leave without seeming to slack off.

I threw my stuff together and waited, unwilling to so much as get my coat and hat. They were out on the hooks behind Patsy's former desk. I didn't want to see her desk with all of her things settled in and around it. I started sorting her stuff and looking for boxes.

Fifteen minutes later, Hamish came back. "Ready to go any time you are," he said brightly.

"Will you help me pack her stuff up? I want it to be over with."

He looked surprised, but said yes.

We found a couple of cardboard boxes and emptied out her drawers and gathered her personal items from on top of her desk. Tylenol, Pepto, spearmint gum packets, colored pens. A pad of paper with little Hello Kitty cartoons. A stray earring with no matching other. Framed photos of Andrew, Jim, and Rosalie the cranky cat. I wrapped those up in some discarded packing plastic – bubble-wrap from something that Patsy had had delivered the day before.

"You're being too nice," Hamish complained, but I silenced him by pointing out that if she got all of her stuff in excellent condition, she would have no right to sue us. I went down the hall and got her coffee mug, an oversized (what else!) gaudy thing with huge swirls of turquoise, brown and green and the word Goddess on it. More bubble-wrap went around that. Finally, I had everything in one box – we tossed the unnecessary one into a corner.

Then I noticed her shoes. She had several pairs of shoes for the office grouped under the left side of desk, out of the way. Sighing, I dragged them out and got that extra box back.

Hamish looked amazed. "Why would she keep extra shoes here?"

"So she could wear boots here in bad weather. Beats carrying them here every day."

"But that means keeping an extra wardrobe at work – that's ridiculous."

"Lots of secretaries do it. Our next one will too, most likely, so get used to it."

I tossed the last pair in, along with her Ugg boots, realizing that Patsy had left in a pair of nice, indoor, office shoes. Oh well. We sealed both boxes, and I wrote her name on top of each one with a black Sharpie pen.

Hamish piled them in a corner of the room. "I'll tell security to take them out."

"No – I'll tell the head of personnel to send them to her. I think that's the normal way to get a fired employee's stuff back to them."

I noticed something then – I hadn't seen it when I tossed the rest of the stuff into the first box. It was a flash drive, sticking out of a USB port on the secretary's computer. I pointed to it, and Hamish looked curiously at it, then at me. Then we looked at the computer.

I sat down, found the icon for it, clicked on it, and waited. A window opened, and I started going through the documents. "I don't want her to have our home address, or my parents', or Fiona's," I said.

She had some files that contained them. Did I have to give this flash drive back immediately, or could I confiscate it? Confiscate it, we decided. It appeared to be full of gossip and slander about us. Personal notes to friends about us, complaining about how dull and introverted we were, how disinterested in popular culture or kids, and so on and on. What right had she to expect us to be like other people?

Who needed a world of clones, anyway?! We were polite enough. We hadn't gone around saying that she was dull, willfully ordinary, or lazy…we had been polite.

"Don't worry about it!" Hamish was getting impatient. He was right; as far as trauma went, this was minimal. I hadn't just left a war zone with raping and pillaging invaders, after all. But it was still unnerving. And I wanted him with me. He knew I was upset though, and he stuck around. I was just mad at myself for not calmly down and blowing it off faster.

Typical of me; tough around belligerent men, yelling right back if I was getting yelled at, but speechless and clueless around a female bully. Perhaps because of a lifetime of standing up to my father about my studies and career, and my mother about fashion and conformity, I was immune to their displeasure. But females my own age bullying me…no progress.

The few times I had yelled back and forth in an argument with my father, he had not terrified me. I was angry and would not yield, and I felt okay when it was over – calm, not threatened. And we got over the disagreement after venting.

This was different. For one thing, it took me back to bullies at camp and the Ethel Walker School. I had never figured out what to do about them to get them to shut up and leave me alone. The only thing that had stopped it was the fact that they had been foolish enough not to check for observers, while I had been careful enough not to find myself cornered and alone. Counselors and teachers had been around, or older girls who disapproved of the bullying. So the silent front persisted, even though it was a brave front, in which I refused to show fear.

What I really wanted, what I had always wanted, was the perfect come-back line, the fitting put-down or silencing retort…but nothing occurred to me during a nasty, venomous tirade – nothing good enough. Maybe that was just as well, or maybe my law school education had talked me out of giving the bullies any ammunition. Or maybe it was the fact that despite having been admitted to law school, there wasn't enough shark in me to take a bite out one of them.

This tantrum from Patsy was representative of what I had worried about since the treaty had been announced and signed. It was as though I had been expecting this blow-up all along. Other people who wanted what she wanted – a baby – and truly believed that they would never get it might take their anger, outrage and sense of disenfranchisement out upon me. They might just yell and scream like Patsy, or they might try to kill us.

No wonder Hamish had hired a security company.

Still, I wasn't willing to run and hide and give up my life as I knew it and the activities I liked to pursue. I was determined to keep on going for walks, shopping for food myself, eat in restaurants, see friends, go to museums, movies and shows, and drive my car.

At least this first taste of popular discontent was over. I called the personnel office about the boxes and took the memory stick home with me.

As we headed out, Hamish had one final piece of advice for me. "Remember what we kept telling each other years ago, when we first realized that we were a bit different: words meant as insults from those who despise us should be taken as compliments."

I looked up at him with a wry expression, then grabbed his hand and kissed him. We found a cab after a few minutes and disappeared into the shadows for the time being, and my husband took me out to dinner. That was relaxing, and this was an ordinary evening. We found a nice Thai place and I had a night off from cooking and other aggravations.

I had Hamish, I was thin, I had a career and an income, and a cat. The hell with other people and whatever they wanted. I was not responsible for their happiness – they were.

It was a few weeks before the interview was shown on television. When it was, my parents came to watch with us in the firehouse. We got Indian take-out again – the works – mango lassi, nan breads, shrimp and chicken curries, basmati rice, rice pudding with almonds and cardamom. Then we settled in to watch.

The story was introduced by Anderson Cooper, and then Lesley Stahl herself narrated the story, which cut to our interviews after showing scenes from our everyday lives. The background that Cooper provided pointed out the role that each of us had played in creating Nae-Née, and emphasized that we had had nothing to do with the Birth Control Treaty.

My father's role in the patenting of Nae-Née was described with the brief efficiency that characterized the news magazine and the limits on detail that such brevity imposed. He seemed satisfied by the mention of his role in it all.

Our firehouse was shown, but as agreed, only from the inside. Hamish and I were shown playing with Eowyn, tossing one of her catnip toys around the living room. We were shown eating dinner. I was shown cooking and baking what we ate just before that.

The crew followed me and Lesley upstairs, where I did the laundry. I sorted through everything as I took it out of the dryer, holding up a pair of old cargo pants that Hamish had utterly ruined with reagents in the lab, complete with a few little rips here and there. "I'm throwing this pair in the goodwill bag," I said, "and he won't know unless and until you decide to include this shot in the story and he sees it on television."

Hamish gaped at the screen while my parents and I howled with laughter at that part.

Before he could protest the departure of the traveling cargo pants, the next scenes were up, showing us walking around Greenwich Village together, shopping in McNulty's, eating dinner in a restaurant, and riding the subway to work. We stilled dared to do that, despite fame and the treaty. Of course, this segment hadn't been on yet when that scene was shot.

Next, the interviews ran, first mine, then Hamish's. The questions he answered dealt with children and the treaty, just as mine had.

Lesley Stahl: "What is your view about having children?"

Hamish MacDonall: "I have never wanted them. I like to work and spend time with my wife and cat. Having kids reminds me of gambling. It's a crapshoot as to whether or not you're going to get a kid who is self-disciplined enough to work hard and contribute to society rather than live a comfortable life, merely using resources rather than helping others at least some of the time. And I don't approve of gambling. Must be because I'm Scottish; I don't understand the concept of putting out a huge amount of money or other valuable resource, and then maybe,

maybe getting a little bit back – and that bit doesn't have to be for me alone – or maybe getting nothing at all. That makes no sense to me. If you don't like or want children, it's selfish to have them."

Lesley Stahl: "How do you feel about the Birth Control Treaty?"

Hamish MacDonall: "I am in the business of enabling people not to have children, and therefore of facilitating that choice. I am not in the business of enabling the opposite. And I am not in the business of controlling the choices that others make. That, apparently, is now the business of governments all over the planet. The time has come for that, and I do not wish to interfere."

The rest was much the same as what I had said, and so was shorter than my segment. With that, I realized that our privacy was a thing of the past, as was more and more of our personal security. Good thing about the Blackout Security guys, I found myself thinking.

Our newfound and dubious fame had arrived in time for Valentine's Day, and I found myself grateful for the fact that I had made reservations at Punch's Bar and Grill on Broadway weeks earlier. As we sat in the back at our table, with a dozen red roses and the cards that we had exchanged, we noticed that people around us were not-so-subtly glancing at us.

The wait staff was very nice and accommodating about it. The hostess even came over to see how we were doing, explaining that she had deliberately placed us at the back and in a booth so that we could have a quiet meal, because she knew who we were. We thanked her graciously.

Our several minutes on *60 Minutes* made us exceed our 15 minutes worth of fame. Despite that, getting home was surprisingly easy; the crowd of paparazzi had thinned considerably. Maybe we wouldn't have to work so hard to come and go after a while.

Dad was going to file restraining orders against every news organization and tabloid in existence if he had to, he had told me after we watched the segment. He had already cleared Stoner Drive by making it a private street, and the neighbors were happy.

That evening, Hamish and I sat in our huge tub with the roses in a vase up on the bathroom shelf. Fortunately, Eowyn was past the crazy stage and we trusted her not to send it flying and smashing to the floor. With nothing else likely to happen to disturb the calm ambience of the moment, I found myself thinking again.

"What's on your mind?" Hamish wanted to know after watching me for a few minutes.

I snapped out of it; this was Valentine's Day; I was supposed to make conversation, not space out and get lost in thought. "I was just thinking that with Blackout guys around all the time, and the fact that we are such a loners anyway, we won't be running into that many people in social situations who will want to berate us about our role in inventing what has become a Draconian population management mechanism. I haven't been to The Strand in weeks. I wonder how it will be to go back. I hope I can go back – I love it in there."

He gazed at me for a moment, then said, "The security around us will likely tighten rather than ease up. So that will mean even less interaction with people aside from those whom we already know. But you can still go to The Strand."

I looked at him, bemused. "What makes you so sure of all that?"

"Come on – think about it. A huge segment of the human population has got to be upset and feel disenfranchised over Nae-Née becoming mandatory planet-wide. There are always crazies out there who lash out when they don't like something. It probably won't be long before we feel ourselves isolated – more so that we choose to be."

"You may be exactly right," I told him. "That means that we won't hear about how angry women are except in places where we choose to talk to them, such as at academic and social events. And we don't go to many social events. So they won't get to shout or swear at us, or whatever they feel like doing."

"Isn't that a good thing? I mean, there has to be an upside to being followed around by security, don't you think?" Hamish gave me a devilish grin.

"Definitely," I grinned back. "We might as well concentrate on our safety – on real stones breaking our bones – and be happy, and not let anyone get in our faces to stop that."

Hamish wasn't finished. "I don't care if people are upset about Nae-Née, and I don't care if they miss opportunities to tell us so. If I can keep them from bothering us, I will. If you don't have to listen to angry people who want several kids but can't have them, fine. I don't want them bothering you," he told me. "I didn't get married for babies – I got married to be with you."

"That's why I married you too, but what are we going to do, avoid people?"

"No. They won't be able to get close enough to hang around and talk to us anyway. The worst of it will be cold glares in restaurants, and I can handle that. It's not like we were ever going to interact with strangers much anyway."

"We talk to strangers in line at bookstores," I said.

"Get used to guards standing nearby, watching for trouble, and maybe waiting in line for you so that no one can get close to you. I've already made arrangements; you can shop in The Strand and anywhere else you want to, and choose things yourself, but waiting in line is going to be too dangerous."

I stared at him, stunned. I just couldn't think of anything to say.

He realized that and said, "Let's just relax and enjoy our lives and live them too."

After a moment's thought, I decided to do just that.

It wasn't like any other decision would have made sense.

I let my husband make me forget about it all that night.

Chapter 23

The Operator – F.O.I.A. Report

Sometime within the week following Patsy's departure, I came across the birth license application materials that she had left in my office.

They had been forgotten in all the uproar that she had caused, and the two boxes of her stuff that we had packed up were long gone. I figured she could just print more copies off of the website if she really wanted to try applying for a birth license. I would keep these for research.

Maybe I would even do a lecture on it. Why not? I was the official herstory of medicine professor at this Institute. And this new policy on world use of a Borg version of Nae-Née was herstory in the making. There was no rule against lecturing about something that was happening in the present. It seemed to me that I was compiling my own Freedom of Information Act report.

I logged onto the website: www.usdemographicsdept.gov and started clicking on links.

Wow – the government computer geeks had been very busy. The top left of the site had the obligatory and ubiquitous round logo of the new federal department, depicting an eagle that held a caduceus in one claw and a pair of judicial scales in the other. The eagle was blindfolded, which I thought was a bit much considering the fact that the reviewers of the applications would be reading each one with a metaphorical and physical microscope.

Next to that, the large blue font read U.S. Department of Demographics. Under that was a menu of options to click on: Forms; News; Resources; Functions; Laws; About Us. About Us? I clicked on that one first. It had a mission statement. I read through it:

About Us

The U.S. Demographics Department (USDD) is the government agency that oversees lawful birth licensing applications for the United States, and administers the use of the government version of the nanobotic birth control device known as Nae-Née.

Mission Statement

USDD will secure America's promise as a nation of laws and a party to the United Nations Convention on the Global Application of Medical Birth Control by providing, maintaining and administering a birth control and licensing service to its citizens and residents, promoting an awareness and understanding of population issues, and ensuring the integrity of our demographics system.

We are the 12,500 government employees and contractors of USDD working at 50 offices across the nation. Achieving our goals becomes possible when the different elements of our organization are engaged and acting as partners working toward a common outcome. USDD's strategic goals include:

- Strengthening the security and integrity of the demographics system.
- Providing effective customer-oriented demographics benefit and information services.
- Supporting prospective parents' concerns about the function of the nanobots.
- Promoting flexible and sound demographics policies and programs.
- Strengthening the infrastructure supporting the USDD mission.
- Operating as a high-performance organization that promotes a highly talented workforce and a dynamic work culture.

Core Values

Integrity

We shall always strive for the highest level of integrity in our dealings with the citizens of the United States of America. We shall be ever mindful of the importance of the trust the American people have placed in us to administer the nation's demographics system fairly, honestly and correctly.

Respect

We will demonstrate respect in all of our actions. We will ensure that everyone we affect will be treated with dignity and courtesy regardless of the outcome of the decision. We will model this principle in all of our activities, with each other, our customers and the public. Through our actions, this organization will become known as an example of respect, dignity and courtesy.

Ingenuity

As we meet the challenges to come, we will strive to find the most effective means to accomplish our goals. We will use ingenuity, resourcefulness, creativity and sound management principles to strive for world-class results. We will approach every challenge with a balance of enthusiasm and wisdom in our effort to fulfill our vision.

Vigilance

In this era of increased environmental degradation and national security challenges, we will remain mindful of our obligation to provide demographics services in a manner that strengthens and fortifies the nation. We will exercise a holistic approach to vigilance as we perform our mission. We will carefully administer every aspect of our demographics mission so that citizens, residents and visitors can hold in high regard the privileges and advantages of lawful presence in the United States.

Incredible. Already couched in the smug language of any corporate system that expected and required cheerful compliance, it outlined the point of view of the government, assuming that there would definitely be compliance.

And I realized that in this instance, the government would get that compliance. It had produced a Borg version of Nae-Née. It could not be removed, because it would hide in the woman's system and threaten to do her some harm if grabbed or pulled without an authorization code. The system literally had people by the balls – pun intended.

I checked the forms section. It had a relatively short list of .pdf files that one could download and print. There was no charge for filing any of the forms, and the section included a promise that there never would be a charge for any part of the filing process. An Act of Congress – signed by the President just a day ago, in fact – was shown at the top of the web page.

Looking through the list of forms, I quickly saw that it was a short one, and that Patsy had in fact gathered everything that a prospective mother would need in order to file an application: 1. A required form for an exam by a gynecologist for prospective mothers – and it included questions about fertility treatments; 2. A required form for a physical exam by an internist for prospective fathers; 3. A required form for personal data, including name, address, date of birth, Social Security number, etc., plus space for a personal statement explaining why one wished to have a child, one's hopes and dreams for it, plans for its education and/or skills training; 4. A form for an assessment by a psychologist or psychiatrist, and it specifically stated that either one was acceptable; 5. A form for financial data, which detailed a prospective parent's financial resources for raising a child.

There was a clear inference that applications by abusive personalities and those unable to afford children would not be approved.

Nowhere did the list state that marriage was required; only a father. Interesting; it actually seemed that same-sex couples would have to adopt, and heterosexual couples would have to forget about any method other than sex without medical intervention to reproduce.

The Laws web page didn't have much on it as yet, which was to be expected with a new government department. It did have links that led to the 28th Amendment to the U.S. Constitution, the U.N. Birth Control Treaty, the federal statute guaranteeing that there would never be a charge for filing any of the birth licensing forms, and a few things from the Code of Federal Regulations.

Of course, thanks to such wonderful things as a virtual information database, there was infinite room to add more boring legalese to wade through in perpetuity. Somehow, I had no doubt that the attorneys of both the present and the future would find employment thanks to this website. They would end up litigating cases on their clients' behalf, plus overseeing applications processes to provide, if nothing else, a sense of hope as they held their clients' hands through this tense process.

I didn't need maternal instincts to realize that simply contemplating this process would be a stress inducer for anyone who wished to have a baby. It was no longer a simple matter of getting pregnant at will for people whose reproductive systems would obediently start a pregnancy after one or more romps in the bedroom.

What about people who needed help getting pregnant? Would records be falsified?

As I contemplated this, the website flickered, then the resolution on the computer monitor resumed its normal appearance. That typically happened when an addition was made to a web page. I scanned it carefully. Aha – there it was – another statute had just been hyperlinked into the list of laws. This one had some real bite to it: it promised the vigorous prosecution in federal court of any physician proven to have falsified a medical report for birth licensing purposes, complete with penalties which included, but were not limited to, fines of $100,000 per offense and loss of one's license to practice medicine. A warning to computer experts and physicians promised that the newly modified Nae-Née nanites would burrow into ovaries or even sprout claws upon any attempt to hack the codes and interfere with any of the devices.

Plenty of sticks here; I guessed that the only carrot was the possibility of a successful application – one that ended with a granted birth license.

The News page described the latest developments in demographics law, and promised that this would be an exciting new field for attorneys and law students to study. How nice – I was sure that prospective parents would be thrilled to read that. It seemed like something that belonged in a law school course catalog, not on a government website, but I read on.

The Resources page listed every physician in the nation currently licensed in the practice of gynecology, internal medicine, and psychiatry. It also provided a litany of health care advice, such as not smoking, not drinking to excess, and maintaining a healthy weight through exercise and a diet that emphasized fruits and vegetables.

It also listed some caveats to prospective birth license applicants. I wondered whether this was the reason why NOW and the ACLU were up in arms and filing lawsuits with the U.S. Supreme Court. The caveats told applicants that no licenses would be granted for in vitro procedures or any other fertility treatments. Essentially, if a woman needed any medical intervention to get pregnant, she could just forget it. The web page explained that this was part of the policy of reducing the overall human population, bringing the odds of pregnancy back to pre-fertility technology levels.

The most intriguing part of the site was the link labeled Functions. I clicked on it and found myself reading all about the figure in the Department of Demographics who would be known only as The Operator.

The Operator was not just one person, however. The work that this individual was to do under this new birth control system consisted of the remote enforcement of the Department of Demographics' goals. So that meant that was an Uber-Operator directing all of the others.

The basic idea was that he or she would – assisted by a staff of computer experts – ensure that no unauthorized pregnancy went undetected. He or she was to hit a trigger switch in his or her region of the country to eliminate any pregnancy that was begun without a license. Part of the rationale was enforcement; the other part was the realization that many women could not afford to visit a physician regularly, so this method of Nae-Née monitoring would enable each woman to have her device monitored and operated properly, with no health risks.

The Operator had to be a physician in order to qualify for this duty. The most important reason for this was in case of any "medical emergency"; the device would instantly alert the mainframe computer, and The Operator would summon help – specific help. This "help" sounded like a trip to the gynecologist's office, perhaps to harvest stem cells from an unlicensed pregnancy.

Organs grown from stem cells were stronger and longer-lived than donated ones. That was common knowledge, and something that the anti-abortion lobby hated to admit, even though it was true. There was plenty of published research to prove it, and there were now many cases of successful, happy outcomes from stem cell livers, kidneys, and other organs. Even better, there were no cases of failure from stem cell-grown organs, unlike the cases of organ rejection and anti-rejection drugs that had to be taken by transplant patients. Miscarriages were not a source of stem cells; the very fact that they were the results of failed pregnancies made them defective.

The other reason for having a physician handle the trigger switch was that a computer expert could not be expected to understand the medical data streaming in from the devices. It just wouldn't work without a doctor.

Who would review the applications, I wondered? There it was on the Functions web page: a Committee on Demographics would have this exalted task. There was an oversight committee based in Washington, D.C., plus a committee in each region of the nation. Each committee included: 1. The Operator; 2. an attorney who had been admitted to practice in the Federal courts; 3. a psychiatrist; 4. a demographics expert, defined as someone with a Ph.D. in the subject plus at least a few publications; 5. a social worker. Each committee member was required to swear an oath to uphold the U.S. Constitution, plus another to carry out the terms of the 28th Amendment. Its official name was the National Birth License Committee.

The regions appeared to have been divided first by time zone, with some deviation to keep the division around individual states rather than dividing them into smaller parts. After that, I realized that the states had been roughly separated into groups of five, plus there was another group for the territories.

As I read through this, it seemed to lack transparency, especially the part about The Operator. The selections process was outlined, that was for certain, but no one hired to fulfill the duties of the position could be shown to the public. The reason was clear: anyone with their hand on a trigger switch would become an instant target. For his or her own security, The Operator's identity would have to be a state secret.

I couldn't think of any way around the veil of secrecy once I realized that.

The Operator of all Operators was based in Washington, D.C., which made sense. He or she would have the ability to second-guess the decisions of the other Operators as he or she saw fit, the web page announced. This would ensure that nothing was missed. How efficient.

There was another requirement for being The Operator: he or she must either not be capable of having children, must not have adopted any, must not want any, and certainly must be unsympathetic to people who desired to have them. The reason for this was also provided in the interest of the policy: to avoid having someone who could be swayed from carrying out the terms and conditions of the law and policy that he or she was appointed to carry out.

Appointed…who would do the appointing? The Cabinet Member whom the President had selected to head the Department of Demographics, along with a secret committee of selectors. This committee would include doctors, nurses, lawyers, statisticians, and no politicians. No politicians…interesting.

The President would not be told outright who was appointed, but he would have a say in the secret committee's makeup. After that, he would have oversight responsibilities to the system, but would not be told the names of every committee member around the nation or every Operator unless something was amiss or unless he asked for the information.

Lots of loopholes, I thought, plus the whole birth licensing applications process reminded me of college and graduate school applications processes. Tests, forms, personal statements – it was more of the same. And let's face it: everyone found such experiences to be magnets for anxiety. Hopes would rise and fall from moment to moment just while waiting to hear back.

My thoughts returned to the shadowy figure known as The Operator.

Could I hazard a guess as to who it was? Why not – it wasn't as if I could have confirmation of it if I figured it out. As far as the U.S. government was concerned, I just happened to be the woman who had come up with the idea for Nae-Née. That didn't entitle me to special treatment or granting of any request I might make under the Freedom of Information Act.

As it was, the site promised to comply with that statute, and explained how to file a F.O.I.A. request should anyone wonder how The Operator had been chosen, to name just one example of something that a citizen might ask for.

But I was a realist; no way would information of any real value be shared with citizens.

I thought about all of the news reports and changes that had taken place over the past several months. Had anyone dropped off of the menu of television and radio channels that passed for our nation's radar screen? Who had disappeared from news shows in the past few months? Who among those was also a physician?

A vague feeling nagged at me – the usual thing I felt when I could almost remember something that I knew I knew but needed a hint to consciously recall. I gave up trying to do it without the hints and clicked on my stash of saved news articles. After about 15 minutes of scrolling and clicking around in that, I realized that I hadn't considered it important enough to save a copy of the article, whenever it was…so forget that method.

I went back to the Internet. I opened the Favorites section and went to the News folder. If I had to look at each and every American site – and I had lots of foreign ones as well as U.S. publications and news organizations saved here – I would do it.

It was mid-morning, late in February. We had gotten a new secretary a couple of days after Patsy was escorted from the premises, so the phone didn't bother me. I was able to work for the entire morning, lost in the task, oblivious to what was happening in the world outside. It was the best way to concentrate; no sounds of other people distracting me – no sniffles (that would have driven me to distraction!), no papers rustling, no keyboards being typed on, no phones in use, not a word would be heard unless I turned on the television or sought company.

At last, after searching through at least 10 news shows, I found it: PBS in Boston had had a physician who had abruptly left a political discussion group show that was broadcast on weekends last November.

Then he had quit without explanation, left the Boston area where the show was produced, and disappeared from public view after that.

The show was called *Presscast*, and it had been running since 1984 on PBS.

The commentator's name was Maxwell R. Kramer, and he was a physician. At last I was sure that I had found the nation's new Operator.

Elated to have figured this out, I immediately switched over to Google and typed his name into the search engine. Before reading his background, I scrolled down until I found what he was allegedly doing with his time now. It was appropriately vague and yet utterly revealing: he had suddenly moved to the Washington, D.C. area where he was writing a regular Op-Ed column for *The Washington Post*. So – he was in the right geographic area to be The Operator.

It was common knowledge that Max Kramer was a physician and partially paralyzed, bound to a wheelchair for part of the time. He wore leg braces, but lacked the stamina to do without his chair despite constant physical therapy. He had hoped since the car accident that had paralyzed him in April of 1983 to free himself from his wheelchair, but had never been able to make any more progress than wearing leg braces, which enabled him to at least move about independently.

Born and raised in Greenwich Village to hippie parents; mother was a yoga instructor, father a bookseller. He was an only child. His education was paid for by his grandparents, which included the Phillips Exeter Academy, followed by Colgate University, where he double majored in political science and biology. After that, he was accepted to Harvard Medical School, and despite the collision that left him paralyzed from the waist down, graduated on time.

I remembered reading an editorial that he had published several years ago about that. The dean of the school had come to see him in the hospital, and promised him that arrangements would be made to enable him to finish. The dean didn't want him to worry about his academic ambitions and jeopardize his recovery. What a nice man, I had thought; just the sort of doctor anyone would want.

Getting back to the biographical description, I saw that Max Kramer had been raised partially by his grandparents, who not only paid for his entire education but who also had him stay with them at Lake George each summer – all summer long.

He got summer jobs there, and went swimming, fishing and biking there. The family was Lutheran.

In college, he had participated in the swim team and in bicycle races. In fact, he had been training for another race when he had been hit by a car. It was a freak accident; the driver had been sober and distracted by a bright light as another car had turned in front of him, so he hadn't seen Max on his bicycle. Max had never felt much below his waist again.

He went on to Harvard Law School after completing his medical degree, and stayed in the Boston area.

As a point of human interest, the biography mentioned that Max had enjoyed a steady series of dates with girls in college – no one serious – before going on to medical school. He had continued to date, but hadn't found a soul mate before the accident left him paralyzed.

I stopped reading for a moment; obviously, the accident had terminated his sex life. The site said that he still had little feeling below the waist, and had just barely managed to regain control of his bladder and other basic functions.

Every photo I had ever seen of this man showed a man with black, short wavy hair, kept short and combed straight back, dark eyes that were almost a beady shade of black, and always suits and ties with formal shoes. He never smiled.

He was a conservative voice in political commentating, and an intelligent one. This was no irate, shouting, lambasting, Hannity, O'Reilly or Limbaugh. Kramer never shouted anyone down or ridiculed them for disagreeing with him. Instead, he let them say their piece, and then went through it point by point, dissecting it with the precision of an autopsy. He made a point of showing his reverence for the democratic process by letting others be heard without interruption.

But he was an angry, bitter man. He did not attend weddings or any events about births or children if he could avoid it. No need to wonder why; they obviously depressed him and reminded him of what he could not have. He was a have-not with money – his own now, from his own efforts since school – but he could not have sex, or children of his own.

Life had all kinds of haves and have-nots. The definitions of those terms merely depended upon what it was that the person under consideration wanted. There was a huge difference between wanting what one could get in the future and wanting what one could never have. That was the essence of the problem that anyone confronted with Nae-Née and a desire to reproduce was now facing.

So this was who the government had selected to occupy the position of The Operator.

It would certainly satisfy his need to exert control where he felt a gaping hole in his own life, I thought. Where he couldn't have something, now he could prevent others from having it; an outlet for his own angst, and a way of releasing his anger in a way that protected the environment…of the future.

Kramer seemed like an effective choice.

With that, I got up to find Hamish. I wanted to go out for lunch. I needed to get out of here after such an intense session in front of the computer.

I found him in his lab, and to my delight, he was in the same mood. His nanite project was nearing the finish line. Soon he would be able to move on to his next one: knitting together open wounds to reduce healing time and control inflammation, a factor that usually slowed it down drastically. He was also working on other nanites; something to do with neuroscience.

We went out to Le Pain Quotidien, tailed as usual by our ever-present men-in-black.

As we headed out, but still on Rockefeller Institute grounds, I filled him in on my research and my guess as to the identity of The Operator, explaining that I didn't want to tell him these things in our offices, his laboratory, our car or at home. I didn't truly think that I was being observed so closely, but I decided to be careful. He nodded, agreeing with me, and let me race through the explanation as we walked along. Then I outlined my next research topic: the new policy of birth licensing as medical herstory.

"That's perfect," he said. "I can't imagine that Dr. Nurse wouldn't want it. Go for it."

Soon we were back, ready for more work. Hamish headed back to his lab; I went to the office. We had been consulted in the selection of our new secretary, and were happy with her.

Her name was Kay, and she already had two kids, a girl and a boy, plus a husband who worked for ConEd, so we anticipated no upsets from her. After a couple of weeks, she seemed to be happily settled into the office. She had worked at the Institute for several years, and had requested a transfer from the business office, where she had occupied a cubicle in a noisy area full of many other cubicles.

Kay had laid out a collection of photos on her desk, all neatly framed: her husband Frank, kids Shannon and Jason, and cats Holmes and Watson. Holmes was a black-and-white tuxedo cat; Watson a tiger-stripe. Both cats were short-haired, and she said that they were the same age, but not brothers, and always inspecting and investigating everything, hence their names.

We were happy to have her with us, and she told us that she really liked it here. She liked the quiet, she liked having her own work area, she liked the absence of other cubicles around her, and she interviewed us on the first day as to what we expected from her, taking detailed notes. She even said that she liked us after a week of work. Soon she was keeping my phone from ringing unless it was my family, my boss, or one of a short list of friends. Any other call was recorded as a message and I was shown it when I passed by on my way back – not on my way to – the rest room.

Hamish kept her busy typing his research notes and letters, and taking his messages.

All was well in the land of our little office suite.

Kay had told us up front that she understood that we had merely invented Nae-Née and not intended it as public policy. She had her children, who were 10 and 6 years old, and she wasn't sure that she wanted them to rush into having kids. She liked Earth Day, and recycled.

She had a degree in English literature from Hunter College, and wore her auburn hair in an elegant ponytail tied with a scarf. She dressed in skirt suits and pants suits, and was a couple of inches taller than me, long-waisted, and of medium build. She brought lunches of sandwiches and carrot sticks or bananas. Her coffee mug was a global warming one, I couldn't help observing. I told her that Hamish had gotten me one for Christmas, but that I got depressed and anxious when I drank out of it.

"I hope that wasn't all that he got for you, then," she said with a smile. She was a few years older than I was, but I couldn't tell just by looking at her. She had a cheerful disposition.

"Oh no – he got me some Mikimoto pearls – a necklace and matching earrings," I replied. "Perhaps I'll wear them the next time I give a lecture and you'll see them."

"I'll look forward to it," she said, and showed me the oval amethyst earrings that Frank had given her for Christmas.

We liked her.

The Nae-Née public policy lecture wasn't all that I was working on. I was hoping to produce a book for kids that would explain current events, reassure them that the adults were just trying to protect their futures, and raise hopes for a pleasant one with plenty of bees, honey – the one food known to have an eternal shelf life – berries, arts and music in schools, and a human population that the planet can comfortably accommodate.

The book began with a description of Easter Island, and explained that it was like a microcosm of the Earth. It cautioned that if we were all careful, the planet would not become like that in the future. People would find places at good colleges and universities, the environment would continue to produce wonderful foods and green spaces and plenty of room for everyone. Space travel would lead to new opportunities – which would otherwise be lost in the crush of overpopulation.

It was still a work in progress. It was aimed at kids ages 8 and up. I was like Dr. Seuss, I realized; I didn't want kids, I didn't want to spend time with them, but I wanted to write books for them.

That afternoon, however, I left that project behind. It was something that I was working on in my off hours, anyway.

I was suddenly obsessed with my new lecture topic.

I decided that I would find out how to write to the National Demographics Committee even if I could not know the identities of its members. I would also send the letter to the President, the Attorney General and the Secretary of State. It would include the following suggestions: get some people who are more representative of the general population, such as some with no graduate degrees, and some with no college degrees. Why? To avoid seeming discriminatory and like a Big Brother and Big Sister group who thinks it knows what's best for everyone else.

A quote by a Scottish dramatist named James Barrie, one that Hamish had shown me a long time ago, came back to mind: "Nothing is really work unless you would rather be doing something else." It summed up what was going on with me lately. It was definitely what I wanted to do, but just thinking about it felt awkward. How would I approach them? What if they were angry about it and blamed me? People were often irrational, I warned myself.

I would do this after completing my lecture and talking to all of the women at the Rockefeller Institute, whom I knew had been injected with government Nae-Née devices. Despite this, I had not yet attempted to discuss it with any of them.

Late in the afternoon so as not to interfere with Hamish's work, I sought out his one female graduate student, a woman in her 20s from the Netherlands named Anouk. Her nanobot had been provided here, as she was injected along with all of the other women at the Institute, but it was being monitored by the Dutch government. The Americans had automatically given its code to the operators in The Hague. When I asked how she felt about it, she said that she wasn't upset. She was in good health, she had a fiancé, and she anticipated no serious trouble in acquiring a birth license when she decided to have a child. She only wanted one.

Anouk told me that the nurses had arrived in groups of 5 in each building of the campus, escorted by members of the U.S. Army, including one women soldier with each group of 4 recruits. There was no warning; the units simply showed up.

The nurses carried standard nanite injection guns, just like the one that Hamish had used when I had received the prototype two and half years earlier. It amazed me to realize how long ago that had been. Had she seen anyone get upset? No – she had been working in the laboratory with Raj when they arrived. Were the nurses all women? Yes.

I realized that I was creating a questionnaire as I went along, and later typed it up neatly. I could reuse it throughout the Institute and move right along with this project, provided that the women I approached would talk to me.

Avril: Did they give you any privacy for the injection?

Anouk: Of course.

As Anouk had raised no objection to the process, no fuss at all, it had been very easy. The male soldiers all stood in the hall; Raj had walked out to give Anouk privacy. The nurse asked her to pull her shirt out of the way, placed the nanite gun on her abdomen, and pushed the trigger down. Anouk felt a vague pressure, but nothing more. That was it.

Avril: Did they let you ask questions or check your identity?

Anouk: Yes – I asked how the code would get to The Hague, and the nurse was very nice. She told me that they tracked each nanite code as it was injected, matched it up with the recipient's identity, and sent it by Blackberry then and there to a database, which had records of the women who were getting the nanobots.

Avril: So The Hague had your code in a couple of minutes, tops?

Anouk: It seemed so.

Avril: How did they confirm your identity?

Anouk: They saw my I.D. badge, and asked to see my other I.D., so I showed them my international driver's license.

Avril: And that satisfied them?

Anouk: Yes – the nurse showed me how she looked me up on her Blackberry and confirmed it before she injected me and sent the code on.

That covered the first interview. I would have to repeat this procedure over the next couple of weeks at the very least in order to learn enough to understand how this policy was going over with the general public.

Meanwhile, just before it was time to go home for the day, I checked online to see the ratification status of the prospective 28th Amendment. The U.S. government had a website: www.28thamendment.gov; so did *The New York Times*, but I watched this one instead. It wasn't like watching the results of the Olympics, I joked to myself. This wasn't recreation; it was completely serious in that it was law and therefore mandatory.

There was a list of states whose legislatures had already gone on record as having ratified it: Connecticut; Massachusetts; New York; Pennsylvania; Vermont; Maine; Rhode Island; New Jersey; California; Oregon; Washington; Hawai'i; Arizona; New Mexico; Wisconsin; Minnesota; Montana; Arkansas; Kansas; Florida; Louisiana; Maryland; Virginia; Ohio; South Dakota; North Dakota; Nebraska; Colorado; Wyoming; Illinois; Indiana.

31 states; it would take 38 to achieve a three-fourths majority and thus ratify the Amendment. Until then, it would not be law, and the United States' compliance with the Birth Control Treaty would continue to be suspect. We had not always maintained a sterling record of compliance with other treaties, hence the energy being expended on this effort.

If the ratifications continued, soon The Operator would have job security for life.

Chapter 24

An Inept Assassin

The thirteenth year of this century was certainly shaping up to be true to the reputation of that number for being a harbinger of bad luck.

That was ironic considering the fact that the origin of the distaste for that number lay with the Norse goddess of fertility Freya, whose day was Friday the 13th. But then, humanity was currently at war with its own fertility, with policy-makers everywhere determined to adopt the realistic tactic of accepting the fact that humans liked to have sex, and would keep on doing it.

Required birth control was rapidly spreading around the planet, and predictions for birth statistics suggested that as the policy was implemented, there were be gaps in human reproduction of perhaps a month or two in which no babies were born in more areas of the world than just a few. That would level out as the licensing process got more streamlined, but for the first time in human history, it was very likely that at least a day might pass in which no one was born anywhere on the entire planet.

I talked to Hamish about Andrew Warne; I was angry with his daughter still, and a large part of that was fueled by worry that he wouldn't want to talk to me or be our friend any more. He was more my friend than my husband's, I realized, but Hamish wasn't jealous. This was all platonic, like having another father figure in my life.

Dad knew about Andrew Warne. I had once asked him how Patsy had gotten to be the way that she was. He had met Andrew once when we all ate out in a restaurant together, and seen Patsy in our office once. "It happened because Andrew is a laissez-faire dad," he replied over the phone when I told him what happened and asked about that.

Interesting. My own father had been stricter, then. But he had also had someone completely different to work with – a daughter who agreed with him about being a serious student, who was interested in her work, and who didn't like to party. Dad granted me that, but still wouldn't cut Patsy any slack. "She is just wrong, and inexcusable. And tell Hamish that I love his name for her…Jabba the Slutt. That fits."

I had called Andrew the evening of the blow-up, unable to put it out of my mind. Patsy hadn't called him yet, which surprised me. Unhappily, I explained what had happened, leaving nothing out, and keeping it in sequence as best as I could.

He asked some questions here and there in order to follow the story. When I reached the end of it, there was a silence.

"Are you mad at me, Andrew?"

"No. I'm disappointed that you two couldn't get along. But I suppose that your personalities just don't work together."

"Do you want to be friends with me anymore?"

"Of course I still want to be friends!" he practically shouted into the phone.

"You – you do?" I said, sounding happy and incredulous at the same time.

"Yes! I don't see how you could have behaved any better. Don't worry about my daughter. I will help her as best I can to find a new job, though this economy makes that seem like a tall order. And let's get together for dinner soon – you, me, Hamish and Cathy."

"Really? Oh, thank you Andrew! When and where?"

He laughed a little. "After your segment on *60 Minutes*, so we can talk about the filming and interview. I want to hear all about it. And after Valentine's Day, because we know we're both booked that night."

I laughed. "Okay. That sounds great."

"Look, I've got to run. Patsy will no doubt call me soon, and Cathy is chafing at the bit to hear what this is all about."

"Okay. Thanks again, Andrew. Bye."

"No problem. Talk to you soon." He rang off.

Hamish was waiting for a report. "Well? Still friends?"

I smiled and nodded.

"Thought so." And he hugged me.

The next week, things were fairly quiet. So was the next, and the next.

Meanwhile, I began to wonder whether Nae-Née sales would become a violation of the Antitrust Act. We had the market on birth control nanites cornered for the duration of our lifetimes, it seemed to me. The governments of most nations were buying Nae-Née from Creighton Industries, and then adding the Borg-like modifications on their own.

Our tax attorney had informed us that the Internal Revenue Service would be assessing us an enormous percentage of our income in taxes, but that we could offset it with charitable donations of our choice to some extent. Still, no matter what, we would still pay a lot in taxes.

Perhaps that was all that we would have to deal with on that matter. He seemed to think so. We had enough to think about for now with the paparazzi and security risks following us.

Our segment on *60 Minutes* was broadcast, Valentine's Day came and went, and Andrew did in fact call me to arrange a dinner visit. Hamish called the men-in-black as soon as the arrangements were made. We would be eating at Zana's, also known as 30 at 30th, because it was on East 30th Street, number 30. Andrew liked it, and ate there sometimes with acquaintances from the U.N. and the nearby Henry George School, where he occasionally guest-lectured.

He was lecturing that evening, so we would be attending it and then walking up the street with him to Zana's restaurant, which specialized in Italian cuisine.

With a ride from the men-in-black crew, the evening went off without a hitch until it was time to go home.

Andrew gave a fascinating lecture on the economics of human overpopulation and environmental stressors due to overpopulation. He was constantly interrupted by the students, but that didn't unnerve him. It would have driven me to distraction, messing with my concentration and ruining the flow of my delivery, but at least I wasn't working there.

Soon we were walking across Park Avenue to Zana's and up the steps. The place was dark inside, with modern décor and a long half-booth on the right, and a bar at the back left. To get to the bathroom, one exited the restaurant through a door on the right behind the seating area, entering the adjacent hotel lobby, and went around to the left. The cream-hued marble hall was shockingly bright after sitting in the darkened restaurant, and I blinked as I saw Chris and Ed lurking in the lobby, but nodded and gave a slight smile as I passed.

We had a nice dinner of pesto gnocchi and seafood salads with red wine and chatted with Andrew and his colleagues.

But there was no time to chat with Andrew until everyone else had left.

We paid and headed out, only to be greeted by a few stray paparazzi. Hamish told us that they were from some tabloids; the men-in-black had checked on that while we ate. I wondered about that; I had managed to keep the message book that Patsy had recorded the calls in, but then I realized: all of the top sheets had been removed.

I hadn't seen any of them when I had packed up her stuff.

We offered Andrew a ride home. He glanced at the paparazzi, then accepted. We asked Rick and Ed to go to the West Village first, so that Andrew wouldn't be bothered by the media. They nodded and Ed stepped on the gas.

Alone at last. Was Andrew happy about this, or wishing he had made an earlier escape?

He was perfectly comfortable, I finally realized, as he settled calmly against the seat next to me and began to chat as if nothing had gone wrong with me and his daughter.

"Thank you for coming tonight. What did you think of it all?"

"You gave a great, fascinating lecture, and you handle interruptions well. I couldn't do that; I need to talk until the end and then take the questions later or I get flustered and lose my train of thought."

"That's how they run every lecture at the Henry George School."

"Oh. How long have you been lecturing there?"

"Off and on for over 10 years. I'm on the Board of Trustees there."

"You are really involved all over this city," Hamish commented.

"What can I say, I love it."

"Does Cathy attend many of them?" I asked.

"Some but not others," he replied. "She had to work late today, so I wasn't expecting her. But she was at the last one I did a few weeks ago."

"I think we've shaken off the paparazzi," I said, looking out the rear window.

"Good. I have to confess something to you. Patsy may have told them a few things about you, things that she may have editorialized on because she is so angry. So if you see any blazing headlines about you while you wait to buy groceries, don't let it upset you, if you can manage that."

I stared at him. "I usually shop at Whole Foods and Chelsea Market. They don't sell any tabloids – just *Cook's Illustrated* and yoga magazines – so I haven't seen anything."

He looked at me, surprised. "Well I have. Ask around. I don't like what she's done, and I can't imagine who else could or would have done it. Some of the comments show a knowledge of the Rockefeller Institute, such as what it's like inside."

"Andrew, there are friends of hers among the secretaries, people back in Connecticut who know me, and people who may have seen me but who don't talk with me. It could be other people providing quotes."

"Oh it's her, at least a little bit. Just ask around. Or check online."

"Okay, I will."

"I'm really sorry about this. And embarrassed." He looked unhappy.

"Is she okay?" I couldn't help asking. To tell the truth, I was curious; I wanted to know what Andrew was thinking about all this.

"She's okay, but that's about it. She has to find another job, and I have some leads for her to pursue. Oh, and she got her boxes from her job with you. I saw them arrive, and watched her open them. She was surprised to see that everything was in there. Did you pack them?"

"Yes. One box of desk things and one of shoes."

"Thank you for that. On a happier note, how would you and Hamish like to go to the Harvard Club for brunch next weekend with me and Cathy? Lakshmi and her husband Anand are coming. It could be just the six of us, and the media won't be able to get in. No photography is allowed in the dining room."

Hamish and I looked at each other with excitement. "Really?" we asked in perfect synchronization. "We'd love to see her again," I continued, "and meet her husband."

"Excellent. I'll set it up, and we'll plan on meeting at noon. Have you ever been there?"

"Actually yes – we've each been invited to lecture there, once for me and twice for Hamish. That was in 2004, 2005 and 2008. I like to read the blurbs next to the portraits."

"Those are great. Which one stands out most to you?"

"The one next to the copy of the Teddy Roosevelt portrait; it tells about the artist. His parents forced him to apply to Harvard five times before letting him do what he wanted, which was art. Only after the school rejected him each time did they let him live his life."

"That's my favorite one too," he said in amazement, staring at me.

Hamish just grinned; he was enjoying the interchange between us.

But Ed pulled up in front of Andrew's building in the West Village and Rick hurried to get the car door. "Sorry," Ed said, "but there's still one car that we don't like the look of nearby."

Andrew got out and let Rick see him inside his building.

I hoped we hadn't just shown anyone how to find Andrew.

I said so, and Rick made some calls as we rode back to the firehouse.

"All clear," he told us. It was just a corporate car going to the Gansevoort Hotel, which had a bar on the top floor.

We went home happy.

My mother called the next day to say that she and Aunt Zoe had collected copies of every tabloid that libeled us – me, mostly – plus souvenir copies of more respectable news publications, which did not libel us. Interesting…true to type, those publications knew better than to invite a lawsuit.

The others clearly specialized in inviting them.

Dad was livid, but not under any undue stress. I talked with him to check. "Don't get mad, get even," was all that he said. I didn't see how I needed to try considering the fact that she was unlikely to get what she wanted most, which was to be married with a baby, but I left him to plot whatever he was up to.

My parents came into the city that weekend, and rode over in a cab with copies of all of the crap that had been printed about us since Christmas, plus souvenir copies of whatever else they had that was merely about us without being subjective or inflammatory. My mother had several other copies of everything stashed at home in Connecticut, of which she had provided Dad with one copy each.

They were stopped at the end of the street by Chris and Joe, who insisted on transferring both my parents and the bags of newspapers to their car and driving them the rest of the way.

"Good thing we brought this stuff personally," my mother remarked as Hamish and I helped carry the bags into the living room. "If I had boxed it up and mailed it, those men-in-black might have thought the UPS guy was dropping off a bomb."

"No – we still get stuff from Amazon.com and L.L.Bean and J.Jill."

"You do?" she said, sounding nonplussed.

"Sure," Hamish told her. "They just open each box, check for incendiary devices, and then knock on our door and hand it to us later."

My parents nodded, satisfied. They didn't send away for much; they usually just went out and shopped for whatever they wanted.

We started unpacking the papers from the bags. I looked at the headlines curiously:

1. "Heartless Inventor Refuses to Speak Up for Lowly Secretary" – *The National Enquirer*;
2. "Rich, Entitled Inventor Won't Help Secretary Get Baby License" – *The Sun*;
3. "Nae-Née Inventor Hates Babies" – *The Tattler*;
4. "60 Minutes Broadcast Portraits the Lives of the Nae-Nee Inventors" – *The Washington Post*;
5. "Nae-Née Inventors Not Consulted on Treaty, Amendment" – *The New York Times*;
6. "Local Resident, Husband Home for Christmas Visit, Lay Low" – *The Hartford Courant*.

And so on.

"You actually think there's grist for a lawsuit in some of these?" I asked Dad.

"Oh yeah. I'll sue the tabloids and that shrieking tub of lard, too."

"Henri!" my mother scolded. "She's a miserable girl with no hope. And you can't sue without Avril's consent."

"True. I'll work on it. If something really obnoxious comes out, maybe she'll authorize it." He looked over at me, inviting a comment.

"I won't object to suing the tabloids, but let's hold off on her. A restraining order might suffice. I'm determined to keep up our friendship with her father." My own father looked as though he could accept that line of reasoning.

"Just check this next one out," he said, digging into the other bag.

"Evil Boss Undermines Secretary's Relationship With Her Father" – *The Sentinel*.

I cracked up. That was too much. "She's angry that her father still likes me."

Dad said, "He probably wishes that he could trade her in for someone like you, she probably realizes that, and that's at the root of this." He gave me an evil grin. "No mercy. I'm not trading, I won't back off, and I won't advise you to terminate the friendship."

"You're in your element of shark mode, Dad." He gave me another evil grin.

I would let him have his devilish fun, if only in conversation with us. It was providing me with some enjoyment anyway, I realized as I read some of the garbage in front of me.

Hamish leaned over the back of the sofa, reading over my shoulder as my mother sat next to me on the sofa and sorted the papers. "Too bad none of them shows a photo of her. Jabba the Slutt is hiding behind her libel of you like the coward she is," he said.

"Let's forget about her," my mother suggested. "We made reservations for Café de Bruxelles."

Eowyn jumped into one of the bags and stared out us, stirring up the last few newspapers in it as she got ready to pounce out at us. Hamish grabbed her and I put them all back in, and stashed the bags in the hall closet; we got our coats and went out.

We could still see all of the people we already knew and loved; that was what counted.

The next day, we were at work, in our offices eating take-out with MSNBC on when we saw a breaking news report.

The President had been shot as he got out of his car to go into the U.S. Capitol building.

That, plus enough states had ratified the 28th Amendment for it to become a part of our Constitution, which was why he had been going there in the first place: to deliver a speech. The Vice President was going to give it for him instead, but it would be later in the evening.

Hamish stopped wolfing down his biryani rice and stared; I gulped my mango lassi and started coughing, but it stopped in a moment.

I checked the date; it was Monday, February 25th.

A replay of the attack was shown, and would be again throughout the day.

A tall, thin blond man in a business suit and tie with a trench coat had come walking down the steps, maintaining a nonchalant pace until he was only twenty feet away.

That was when he struck; whipping out a gun, he fired at the President. A Secret Service agent had been close enough to jump towards him, disrupting his aim. The agent fell as his colleagues pumped the inept assassin full of bullets, killing him.

But the errant bullet that the would-be assassin had managed to fire off had partially hit its mark: the President had still been shot.

Agents swarmed around him, barking orders into their microphones, seeming to be shouting into their coat sleeves.

Marine One, the President's helicopter, appeared with astonishing speed and the President's medical team leaped out, toting a stretcher. He was loaded onto it and into the aircraft with quick, efficient movements and it took off.

Two pools of blood soaked the Capitol sidewalk and steps; one belonged to the President, the other to the dead assassin.

"That was a Colt .45 caliber gun," Hamish told me. He knew guns after serving in the British army.

"So they'll have to get a bullet out?" I asked. "That's an awful lot of blood for one bullet hole," I commented.

Hamish looked at me. "No. A bullet fired from one of those will blow off a limb."

I gaped at him, then focused on the television.

Kay knocked on our door with a message. It was just a memo about my latest book for children; it was wanted despite my reservations. Excellent.

"Kay, the President's been shot in front of the Capitol building and rushed on Marine One to the hospital," I told her.

She gasped and rushed over to see the television.

"Sit down and watch," I said. "They'll play the scene over again and tell us more."

We all stayed glued to the screen for the next hour. Surgeons were working to close up the wound while the First Lady waited in the hospital with her mother. Their children were brought from school to wait with them, and the news cameras showed them arriving.

Hamish's grad students, Raj, Anouk and Joel came in to watch with us.

While we waited to hear how the President was, I looked up which states had ratified the 28th Amendment: Alaska; Iowa, Missouri, Georgia; Michigan; New Hampshire; Mississippi; West Virginia. That made 38. The other 12 still might ratify it, but they were too late to make history. In spite of that, their legislatures intended to complete the debate-and-vote process.

Well, good, I thought. At least that will give some idea as to the political climate in those states. Meanwhile, I kept the television on and gave up on any serious research or reading. My office was currently playing host to a news-watching gathering anyway.

I went back to the sofa and ate my carrot pudding, sharing it with Anouk and Kay. We all waited for a report, feeling sympathy for the President's family as they wondered about the outcome of the surgery. Would he live? Would he be glad about it if he lived? How much damage had the assassin inflicted?

About an hour and a half later, the answers came back:

Just as Hamish had explained, the report from George Washington University Hospital was grim: the bullet had taken off the lower half of the President's left leg. He would need a prosthetic leg to walk on his own.

The face of the would-be assassin from Tennessee was flashed over and over again on every major news station. He looked familiar to me.

Where had I seen him before?

I thought about it.

It took all afternoon, but after searching the Internet to see old newscasts from when the U.N. treaty was signed, I found him: he was there, outside on the day of the signing, with a crowd of protestors. He was the one right next to the Bible-belt fanatic who had clashed with Dr. Martin Peabody just before the imam shot him and the stringy-haired guy stabbed him.

The two men had moved very fast; it was difficult to see which was which at some points, as both were dressed similarly. Both were close to the Bible-belter, a Baptist minister who was well-known for advocating the teaching of creationist theory in public schools, along with abstinence and other unrealistic population-control methods.

I was worried now. I showed what I had found to Hamish, who immediately called Blackout Security. As he spoke to the director, his old war buddy, my mind raced furiously through some mental images while I tried to guess what was going on.

Would this lunatic or one of his cronies come looking for me and Hamish?

Who were they?

Was one of them the dead would-be assassin?

Were there more of these guys?

Wonderful. All I had wanted was a safe, reliable, user-friendly birth control method that, once in existence, had provided me and Hamish with a continuous income, and now I felt hunted.

Some of these religious fanatics – Bible-belt fundamentalist Christians, mostly – were quite devious. They might masquerade as anything just for the sake of deception and their disguises could range from mundane and obvious to ingenious and expert camouflage. Blind people...passersby on a quiet city street...a guy in a tee shirt with a cigarette.

I felt sick.

The blond guy that I had seen staring at me through the peephole last summer – the one with the short hair, tee shirt and jeans – was the assassin.

Hamish stopped speaking into his cell phone and looked just as sick as I told him what I had just figured out.

No wonder we wouldn't be close enough to anyone to hear how upset they were with us about Nae-Née. We would be too isolated as we tried to avoid assassins. Whether or not that worked would be another question entirely.

Chapter 25

Subversion

Since the 28th Amendment was ratified, I started seeing reports and editorials about the new birth licensing system. Editorials analyzed its likely effects pretty much as I had, and reports dealt with stories, some rumor and some verified, of wealthy people trying to subvert the policy and have kids outside of the Birth License Committee purviews; every country had one.

I wasn't surprised. In fact, I was pretty sure that everyone else who followed the news had been expecting to hear such reports as these. Nae-Née had been distributed all over the world with startling speed, so the system was fully in place after just a few months. With the world economies still in a quagmire, the only people who were happy were those who had gotten jobs in the new birth controlling monitoring infrastructure, but nevertheless, it was all in place.

The reports included tales from the United States, the United Arab Emirates, Luxembourg, Brunei, Pakistan and Saudi Arabia. Others soon followed, but these first five were the most intriguing. It was to be expected; people didn't like being told that they couldn't have kids whenever they felt like doing so, and at whatever age they wished. People all over the world soon tried to buy, bribe and cheat their way around the policy.

The Americans hired investigators to find out who controlled the Nae-Née devices. The qualifications of these investigators varied; some were disgruntled ex-spies, while others were government officials who were upset about the policy. The goal was to find an end-run around the system – someone who both could and would break the codes of a particular woman's Nae-Née device. It was amusing to find out who they were when they were detected.

One man was a rich software engineer who had divorced his wife after having an affair with a younger woman. Then he paid millions of dollars because he wanted another child with his blond bombshell of a trophy wife. The first wife had assisted him with their huge computer chip empire, and they had a daughter in college and a son in high school.

The software billionaire ended up being charged with a federal crime and spending several months in a minimum-security prison after being fined as much money as he had paid in his attempt to break the law. The trophy wife pled ignorance of the whole plan and was allowed conjugal visits with him in the country-club prison. The ex-wife said "no comment" when asked about it, but she looked amused in the photos that appeared in the news reports.

Another American and his wife ended up spending a month in prison – separately, of course – for attempting to break the code on her Nae-Née device. They hadn't yet gotten around to having any children, and the wife was 39 years old. The husband was in his mid-forties. When their first application to have a child was denied, they had, apparently, panicked. They were caught by the U.S. Department of Demographics cyber-enforcement computer experts.

The international news reports were fascinating to read and followed a similar story line: wealthy man wants babies – or more babies – so he tries to buy his way around the system.

That was how it went in Pakistan with a wealthy importer. In Pakistan, the wealthy citizens often manage to avoid paying no taxes, which leads to a poorly funded infrastructure. That situation ended up biting him in the derriere in the end. The importer, who had four daughters but no sons, managed to beat the system and get his wife pregnant with a son, only to be killed by an angry mob as he tried to drive to and from his office.

The mob was made up of displaced persons from the flood zones of the Indus River. There weren't enough police to contain them as they wandered through the countryside, searching for food and shelter, and they had no idea who he was; only that he locked himself inside his car and ignored their pleas for help – food, money, anything. They were starving, and he hit the accelerator as they rushed towards him. He was trying to veer into an opening in the group, but he hit and killed a 10-year-old boy, so the mob bashed into his car, pulling him through the window. They beat him to death.

Luxembourg is a nation of bankers, a rainy landlocked country wedged between France, Belgium and Germany. A financier who wanted a child with his much younger wife tried to hack the E.U. supercomputer and promptly got caught. He was just a guy who had married a much younger woman, and she was about to turn forty. They had waited to have kids, and enjoyed life for a few years. Now they wanted a child and it was too late. The wife didn't know what he was up to, but he had to pay a hefty fine – it was 40,000 Euros. The E.U. wasn't imposing lengthy prison sentences; it preferred to calculate fines in proportion to the offender's income, the same way that Germany imposed them for traffic infractions.

The sheikh from the United Arab Emirates – and I couldn't tell which one he was just by reading his name, since that nation had quite a list of them – simply broke the rules. Royal families could do that with impunity, policy be damned. Nothing happened to him; he got off easy, just blowing off the many public statements of condemnation from other world leaders.

It was the same story in Brunei, except that people with enough cash were allowed to blatantly buy their way out of the policy by purchasing each birth license from the sultan.

Saudi Arabia was scary, though; as the guardian of the sacred mosque at Mecca and the shrine at Medina, I had expected a completely different story. Instead, the Saudis set up their computer system and hired foreign female nurses to personally visit each female citizen and servant on Saudi soil and inject Nae-Née implants. The king himself announced that without exception, each family would be granted a license to have at least one child. This meant that a man with four wives could still have four children.

However, the king added, there would be no appeals, and if a couple already had one child, there would be no more for them. If any wives or babies turned up missing or dead, an inquiry would be made, and the husband could find his own head on the chopping block. Saudi Arabia was a country that used beheading to deliver the death penalty.

Sure enough, the story with that announcement included the first six such cases.

After reading through all that, I moved on the next few reports that I had clicked on, gradually saving copies of each one and closing out what had started off as at least nine extra tabs on my Internet window. Hamish said that I slowed my computer down by clicking on every story that caught my interest, running all that data at once, but I really didn't care; it was just easier to choose what I wanted and deal with it, bit by bit, until it was done.

The next few reports were the ones that I found to be more cheerful.

They were about some positive developments for women in Nigeria, Kuwait, and India, and these changes were due to the Nae-Née policy. I was glad to see that. I was sick of feeling like it was somehow my fault that women were unhappy over not being allowed to reproduce. Granted, I knew that some women, women who would no doubt make good mothers, were being denied that choice altogether in the interest of human population reduction. But that was the price of averting a resource war – a bloodbath that would certainly come if nothing was done.

So reading about good changes that improved women's lives around the planet was actually exciting. Some occurred simply as a result of the Nae-Née policy. Others were brought about by legislation, and still others were demanded by the women themselves.

This was the case in Nigeria, where women were often denied the right to even attend village meetings unless and until they had had an eleventh child. Suddenly women were out in the streets in those villages and in the capital, Abuja. They were protesting this requirement, which essentially barred them political participation now that it could not possibly be met, carried picket signs that read "We demand to use our voices!" and "We do not need to overproduce to be productive!" To enforce their demands, the women had ceased their usual duties, saying that devoting all of their time to housekeeping was pointless now, and that their new spare time would be better spent on study and outside work. The president had written a law to comply with the women's wishes, and it was on the verge of passage.

It was similar in India, except that the government had actually passed some laws, and the thought "payback's a bitch" flitted through my mind as I read them: 1. No female child was to be named "Nakusa" or Nakushi" – a Hindi name that meant "unwanted" – ever again; 2. Any couple found to have aborted a female fetus would find that any future birth license application on their part denied; 3. For every female fetus aborted, a random couple's male fetus would be aborted via the Operator in the same district. India's Operator had installed a sensor in its Nae-Née system that read hormones so as to be able to differentiate in vitro between fetuses.

In Kuwait, a woman was quoted as saying that men had simply given up on the idea of taking second wives to get sons if the first wife only produced daughters. A first wife's permission was required anyway for a man to take a second wife in Islam, she explained, and added that "the truth is, no Muslim woman actually wants a co-wife." Without the possibility of being granted the required birth licenses, taking another wife was now, she concluded with a pleased expression, a moot point.

As for China, people said that things didn't feel much different, except that women weren't being dragged away for forced, late-terms abortions anymore. It wasn't so bad now.

Chapter 26

Interviews

After the President woke up, he insisted upon making a statement from his hospital bed.

"No terrorist or extremist shall deter me from carrying out my duties to the best of my ability. I am not cowered or afraid because of what happened to me. I will not go into hiding at some undisclosed and super-secured location. I shall continue to pursue the policy of birth control and birth licensing in this country, and to safeguard the security of those tasked with carrying it out.

"I do not fear our future, and I encourage all of you not to fear it either. Fear paralyzes and hinders progress, and threatens security. I won't let it threaten this great nation, and I won't let it destroy the futures of our children. There will be children in the future. Having fewer children will protect our future, and will promise a bright one on our beautiful planet.

"Please do not worry about me or my family. We will be okay, and so will you."

That was it. He spoke in the evening, and all major channels carried it. After that, all of the commentators – conservative, liberal, middle-of-the-road – called him brave, courageous, and lots of other complimentary things. The conservatives prefaced their compliments with comments like "even if you don't agree with his politics" but the message was the same.

Then the commentary reverted back to the usual: analyses of the birth management policy, predictions as to the outcomes of the writs of certiorari filed with the U.S. Supreme Court now that the 28th Amendment was ratified, the speech that the Vice President delivered about the ratification, and wondering about which other states might ratify it once all of the state legislatures' votes were in on the matter.

We turned the news off after that. Then we turned on the DVD player. Enough seriousness for one day, we decided, and watched a movie. We had paused in all the news watching to come home, where I had made an Indian dinner of coconut shrimp, and watched more news until we were thoroughly overdosed with information about the failed assassination.

Whenever a big piece of news breaks, I don't like to watch every comment and repeats of the event every minute of the day on which it happened or anytime after. Just show it all to me once. Any more than that and I feel overwhelmed and cooped up.

Hamish is just the opposite. He watched so much that I tuned a lot of it out. We washes the dishes with the news still running, and I chafed at the bit as I realized that Hamish didn't want me to say anything as it ran on and on and on. He just kept drying dishes and putting them away, half facing the TV the whole time, almost in a trance.

Finally, I demanded that we switch to a movie. He snapped out of it and we relaxed.

The next day, I resumed my interviews of women at the Rockefeller Institute.

It had been going well, despite my worries about angry women blaming me for ending up getting injected with Nae-Née devices. I had started by sending them all memos requesting that they talk with me: professors, scientists, administrators, human resources personnel, secretaries, librarians, graduate students…everyone.

Hamish joked that the men might feel left out, but my position was that it was none of men's business if a woman chose to have either an abortion or a child. If I were queen of the world, men would have no vote on the issue, leaving it up to the women only.

Women were the only ones getting Nae-Née devices; as far as I could see, men's chances to reproduce, at least in our culture and nation, had not been significantly changed by the birth management policy. It was women who were feeling the brunt of it all. Perhaps that was why women were so willing to talk to me; I had led off my e-mailed request by sharing this attitude with them. Maybe they felt a certain comradeship with me because of that; nothing like female solidarity to warm women up to one another.

Armed with questionnaires for everyone, plus a few extras, I started in on it.

This was the list of questions I asked, developed right after talking to Anouk:

1. In what nation or nations do have citizenship?
2. Who approached you with your Nae-Née device, when, where, and how?
3. Were all of the people who handled the actual injections women?
4. Did that matter to you?
5. Was there one nurse or more? What about soldiers?
6. Were there any female soldiers?
7. What about the male soldiers – how did they behave?
8. Did you have privacy when the device was injected?
9. Did anyone physically force you to accept it, or did you decide to allow it?
10. Did you ask questions? If so, were they answered politely and completely?
11. Were you shown how the process works, or did you have to ask?
12. How did they go about verifying your identity?
13. Was the medical team in a rush, or did they take the time to treat you as a person?
14. Do you want children in the future?
15. Do you already have any children? If so, how many?
16. Are you anxious about your chances with the birth license application process?
17. Did you see anyone else get their Nae-Née injection?
18. Did you see anyone get upset about it, either during or after the fact?
19. How do you feel about all this?

That last question was left deliberately open-ended. I wanted to invite comments from the women I interviewed about anything they wished to discuss. I didn't want them to feel rushed, dismissed, or processed all over again.

I resumed the process first with Kay. When I had asked her for an interview, however, I had done so face-to-face. She had laughed when I suggested following that request up with an e-mail, just to make it on record the same as everyone else's. "You didn't do that when you interviewed Anouk because you had just thought of the idea – so I'll still say yes. I think this is a good idea. It makes me feel like we still have freedom of speech."

"Of course we still have that. I realize that people are saying that we have started down a slippery slope with this birth management business, but people must be allowed to say whatever they want to say. As far as I know, the only forbidden speech is what's known as "fighting words" or yelling "Fire!" in a crowded, closed auditorium; anything that endangers others. Voicing opinions won't hurt anyone."

I knew what ought to happen, I just didn't trust it to actually happen until it did so. But I wasn't worried. The government had always invited itself to secretly check on random communications and activities while pretending not to. All governments did that. Freedom was something that fluctuated and warred in direct correlation to fear.

At least the President had encouraged people not to be afraid. If our fearless leader got what he had advised, the people would still act to protect their own legal freedoms – speech, liberty, the right to associate, etc. What a mess life was…full of lots of gray areas.

So the day after the inept assassin had crippled the President, I started preparing for my herstory-in-the-making lecture. Kay's answers were a case-in-point of someone who did not agree with the policy, but was willing to comply with the law, whatever it was.

She was in her cubicle in the human resources department when the team of government-appointed nurses arrived. The nurse offered her a chance to go elsewhere for the injection, but said that she was satisfied with her cubicle as long as all male soldiers stayed out. She said she felt this way because she was surrounded by female co-workers in the other cubicles.

The injection didn't hurt, and the nurse showed her the data being sent on its way after comparing her driver's license with the database over her Blackberry. A female soldier was nearby, but after watching Kay with the nurse for a moment, decided that there was no trouble to worry about from her and walked off to see how it was going elsewhere.

When I asked whether it had mattered much to her that the nurse doing the actual injecting was female, Kay had paused to think it over before saying, "I had a male obstetrician handle both of my kids' deliveries, so I forgot to think about it. But now that I do, it seems that this policy ought to include a requirement that women be the ones injecting us. I don't like men's hands on my body if it's about control."

I noted her response without saying anything. As pleased as Kay's attitude made me, I didn't want to taint the results by sharing too much of my own views.

I kept going. Kay said that the nurses did not seem to be in too much of hurry to answer people's questions. They were on a schedule, but they made a point of saying that they refused to rush people, scare people, or make them feel that they didn't matter. They nurses seemed to be very much aware of the significance of what they were doing.

I wished I could talk to some of those nurses, but that would be another questionnaire, and less important than this one. Back to the interview. This part felt silly; I already knew this stuff about her: did she want any more children in the future? No, and that was why she wasn't particularly upset about this. It was like getting a free birth control device with government-sponsored monitoring. Finally, direct benefits from paying her taxes, she joked, but half serious.

Since Kay had been in a large room with lots of women in earshot, she must have heard what was going on with other injections. Did she hear anyone get upset or resist?

She looked uncomfortable; I wondered what was coming next.

"Some of the younger women cried, but no one resisted. They all saw the soldiers, so they just let the nurses proceed. I noticed that the unhappy ones were the ones who didn't ask very many questions."

"Do you think they will regret that later, like when they apply for a birth license?"

"Maybe; but it probably won't make much difference one way of the other as to whether those are granted or not. It will be all about health, having a father present, and the ability to stay together – married or divorced, but working together – to raise their child."

"That's sounds about right. Well…thanks a lot for helping with this."

"You're welcome. This is important. Any account of this shift in human history should include how people felt about it, and how it changed their lives."

I smiled and went to my computer to record the interview data.

The next interview was with the reference librarian, Robin. She was in her early thirties, and just married. No kids yet. Robin was a calm, quiet person, small-boned, studious, and pretty. She had light-brown hair that she tied up in a sloppy swirl of a bun with lots of wisps sticking out in every direction. Her pale blue eyes were happy, but I saw reproach in them.

I jumped around a bit with the questionnaire, not going in order.

Did she and her husband want any kids?

Yes.

Right away, or sometime later?

Sometime later.

If the birth management policy didn't exist, how many children would they have?

Definitely one, possibly two; her husband was a stockbroker who had graduated from the Wharton School of Business, she added, and he had a great job on Wall Street. Despite the economic downturn, there were still some stockbrokers and investment bankers whose careers were still functional. Someone had to keep things going in those fields.

I didn't comment, but I supposed that she wanted me to draw the inference that they could afford a good life for two kids if they chose to have them. Well – who knew…maybe they would be granted a license not once, but twice. The birth license forms asked for basic information about the parents such as education, profession, and so on.

She had been alone at the reference desk when the nurses and soldiers came, and had invited the nurse to come behind the desk to inject her device. The nurse had shown her what she was doing without being asked to. Perhaps the nurse had been around to other areas by then and learned that showing women every step would speed things along. That would make people feel more control over what was happening to them, which would mean less resistance.

Next came three secretaries. They were all different.

I found – to my surprise – that Patsy's lunch friends were willing to be interviewed. I made the appointments, wondering what was in store. Would they berate me about her? Would they do the opposite? Would they say nothing and just leave me wondering, then perhaps tell her whatever they could find out about me?

Colleen, the one with 4 kids, went first. Her youngest was a baby, just born last fall. Was she upset about the nanites?

"I thought I would be, but then I said to myself, "I have 4 kids. I'm sleep-deprived all of the time, I've lost my shape, and kids are expensive. I never expected to fund their college educations – they'll all have to get loans if they want to go – but it's time to stop." So I decided not to object, and to just reap the benefits of a birth control device that would be monitored for me. It's okay. And my husband is happy – now he doesn't have to be careful either." She grinned at me when she said that last part.

Jan was less pleased. She had liked Patsy a lot, and had been with her during the injection. I hadn't known that. Where were they when the nurses showed up?

In the cafeteria, chatting over their lunches. The meal was over, and they were about to dump their trays when three soldiers and one nurse walked in. Jan told me that both she and Patsy wanted kids, so they both froze. They had looked at each other in horror, and Jan had briefly considered running, but abandoned the idea just as quickly. She knew that soldiers were in great physical shape, and she didn't want to give them the satisfaction of chasing her, catching her, and then holding her still while she was injected.

Was she upset about having to apply for a license to have a baby?

Yes, but she didn't see why she wouldn't get one. She was married, not too much overweight, she had a college degree and so did her husband, and as far as she knew, she could just get pregnant with no fertility technology. She had even gone so far as to check out the license form – Patsy had shown Jan a copy that she had printed off of the website. So she knew that needing fertility technology would hurt her chances of getting a license. She didn't think she needed that, so she wasn't worried about her chances.

With a sense of foreboding, I asked, "What about Patsy – how did she react?"
Jan sighed. "Patsy tried to run."

"She did?" I was a bit surprised. Patsy had seemed intelligent, but then, emotion seemed to be her primary response to so many situations. She didn't reason things out before acting on her feelings; her departure from our office had certainly demonstrated that.

"Oh yeah. It was awful; the soldiers – the men – rushed her and grabbed her by the arms and brought her back. I had gone around the corner with a nurse and let her inject me, and the nurse was really very nice. Patsy had come too, and watched the whole thing, so I thought she would be okay with it, but when the nurse turned towards her with the injector gun, she bolted."

"Then what happened?"

"She – the nurse – called out, "We've got a runner!"" and the soldiers took off.

I stared, listening with rapt attention, but just waited for Jan to go on.

She did. "The male soldiers – there were two of them – came walking her back over to the nurse. Patsy started crying, saying that she wanted a baby. The female soldier was a short, thin, small-boned woman in her twenties. She walked right up to her and said that they could do this easy or hard; it was up to her. Patsy started shrieking and swearing at her, saying "You skinny little bitch! They'll give you a license no problem, but not me. I'm 41 and fat! And I want a baby! Now I'll never get one!" And then the soldier said, "That's not our problem.""

Jan paused, then continued, "I tried to talk to her, to reassure her, but the woman soldier told me to back off and let them do their jobs. The nurse came up to Patsy with the nanite gun and pulled her shirt out of the way, then got frustrated when she couldn't find a suitable spot to inject the nanites. She seemed angry with Patsy for being overweight and therefore difficult to work on. She also seemed angry with her for running…didn't say another word to her."

"What did the nurse look like – I mean, age, demeanor, that sort of thing?"

"Efficient, perhaps in her fifties, experienced. She was of medium height and weight, and had a nice hairdo. Makeup, patterned scrubs, a sweater, and a kit that she kept in one of those messenger bags slung over her neck and shoulder."

"Had she seemed pleasant and sympathetic with you?"

"Oh yes – showed me things, answered my questions – I forget what I asked, something about how she would inject me, but I'm not sure – and she didn't rush me. She didn't touch me until I pulled my blouse out of the way to give her a spot to inject. She had asked me to show her my abdomen and waited politely, then touched my waist to balance and position the gun. I didn't mind any of it until Patsy freaked out."

"What did they do with Patsy? Did they show her what they were doing – explain the data part, any of it?"

"No. The woman soldier looked through her handbag to check her driver's license for the I.D. part. They wouldn't let her do anything independently until the deed was done after she bolted. When they were done, they just let her go and gave back her handbag, then turned their backs and left her without a word."

"Wow. Assholes." I couldn't help it. This was probably happening to other women like Patsy, women whom I did not know, who had not felt contempt for me personally, who had never been horrible to me. And it was a disgusting way to treat someone.

There had to be a better way. I liked what I had heard on the news about traveling, remotely operated nanites getting into Taliban women's abdomens. Maybe that was how it should be done to avoid upsetting women like Patsy, women who would bolt and shriek. Anything rather than humiliate someone like that. Wasn't that the point of that traveling, remote-controlled method, to avoid upsetting people in volatile situations?

Jan stared at me when I made that comment about the soldiers, calling them assholes.

"What?" I asked her.

"Well, it's just that I heard how nasty she was to you when you wouldn't write that recommendation for her to get a birth license, just after your interview with Lesley Stahl. And I watched that interview on television, so I know what you said in it. But you don't have to like what Patsy likes and want what she wants, and if you did write that recommendation, you would lose all credibility. There's no way you could write it. Patsy's crazy and selfish."

I looked at her quizzically as I put my notes aside; I had plenty of data from this interview. It was basically complete, and had become a conversation about me and Patsy. "I thought that her friends would be angry with me over all this."

"No. No one is. Not that I know of. We knew what Patsy was like. We wondered how she managed to work for you as long as she did."

Huh. "Well – thank you for telling me that, and for saying that. And for the interview."

"No problem. I hope it helps. Good luck."

"You too – good luck with the license process when you go for it."

She smiled. "Thanks. I think I want one, and I'm 37 now. I'd better get going on it."

Kirsten was the last of the group that Patsy had regularly eaten with. I interviewed her along with the two other women who staffed Dr. Nurse's outer office.

She said that Dr. Nurse had vacated his luxurious living room of an office just so that all three of them could get their ordeal carried out in comfort, and gone to visit another scientist in his laboratory. He asked them to call him when the coast was clear, and not to rush, saying, "It's all yours for as long as you need. Just in case you need to talk; I don't know how you're going to feel, and I don't have any right to rush women to get over it. See you later." Then he left.

I was impressed; what a nice man.

Kirsten had not been upset. She and her fiancé didn't want kids. They would get married soon; a date was set for New Year's Day. She didn't like the number 13, so not this year.

I could appreciate that, I commented. I didn't like that number either. She grinned.

"What about the other women in your office?" I asked.

"Oh, they're in their fifties. Both married, one with a grandkid, so they just wanted privacy. The male soldiers realized that we would be no trouble, so they stayed out in the waiting area, and when we came out, just ten minutes later, they were spacing out in the chairs.”

“Did the nurses take questions?”

“We really didn’t ask any. There was no need; the nurses showed us what was happening with their Blackberries, and checked our I.D.s over the Internet when we handed them our driver’s licenses. They must have done this a lot before they came to us, because they seemed rehearsed. They told us what they were about to do every step of the way, and showed us the injector guns. I told the one who worked on me that I have a Master’s degree in health care management, and when she saw me lean over to get a good look at the gun, she held it up and turned it this way and that for me to see. She didn’t rush.”

Interesting…no rushing as long as the woman in question didn’t resist; otherwise, it was abject humiliation and condescending threats. I thanked Kirsten and stacked up my notes.

“Professor Châtelet,” she began.

“Yes?” I looked up and waited.

“Patsy shouldn’t have yelled at you. I heard about it. And I saw your interview.”

“I thought you two were close.”

“We were friends, and I guess we’ll still see each other, but I was disgusted with her when I found out about her…tantrum. You were her boss, and you’re bound to be very different from her. You aren’t being different to be nasty to her. You’re just being yourself.”

“Wow. Thank you.”

“No problem. I hope your report and lecture goes well. I hope it gets to the President and those committees. I hope something is done about the way that the nanites are dispensed. It shouldn’t be like that for other women like Patsy.”

“No – it shouldn’t. There are bound to more like her out there, who put up a pointless fight. They shouldn’t be condescended to, scolded, or treated with impatience.”

I went back to my office. Once the data was recorded, I found Hamish in his office and told him what I had learned thus far, with the stories of Patsy and the opinions of her former colleagues. He was on the sofa, looking at some books.

He listened to it all, and then said, “So Jabba the Slutt actually tried to flee? That must have been quite a scene.”

“Don’t be mean.”

“Can’t help it; she was hideous to you.”

“Suppose some stranger whom we had never interacted with at any time had done that. Then what would you say?”

“Oh all right. I would agree with you; the remote delivery method should be used. But how can they know whether a woman will resist until she actually does?”

“Maybe the team ought to include a psychologist. But it would have to be a woman. If a man tried to soothe me about being forced to accept something that I just didn’t want, it would just enrage me even more, not calm me down.”

“So include that in your lecture.”

I planned to; that, and in my letter to Washington, D.C. and the head of the new Department of Demographics.

Chapter 27

The Visit from No Such Agency

We went out to dinner that evening. We ate at the Empire Diner in Chelsea, and then walked down to the Chelsea Piers. There was an array of museum placards on the inside wall there, huge and with lots of old photographs.

Ed and Rick were tailing us, but they had allowed us to walk. Chris and Joe had a car that followed us at a discreet distance. I could see what they were doing, but said nothing. I was used to them all now. I knew that other people were on the earlier and night shifts, and had met them, but these were the guys I saw the most.

Hamish and I went out to look at the water in the light of the equinox. The sun was just setting; it was almost too dark to see the water. I looked down at it, and something seemed different to me. Then I realized what it was: sea level was rising, and there was almost no drop from the wharf we were standing on to the water below.

I had been so absorbed by the Nae-Née policy that I hadn't watched the effects of global warming as closely as I normally did. Recycling was second nature, but seeing this was still a shock. Hamish was amazed too; he had hardly been watching global warming at all by comparison.

We let the men-in-black drive us home, and rode in silence.

When we walked in, I felt as though we were being observed. I went all over the house, checking each room and closet, and finally settled on the sofa with the cat, feeling unsettled.

Hamish watched me. He didn't know what it could be either, but had come with me from room to room to see what I was doing. We hadn't been too spooked to hang up our coats and go to the bathroom or feed the cat, but something was definitely different.

Eowyn had even jumped onto the windowsill in one of the guest bedrooms, staring into the windows of a darkened brownstone across the street. After watching her for a moment, I snatched her and carried her downstairs with me. Then I sat down next to Hamish on the sofa.

The doorbell rang. We looked at each other; we weren't expecting anyone to visit.

And we knew that Ed and Rick and the others would have carefully vetted anyone who wanted to so much as pause at our door. They practically camped on our doorstep.

I clutched the cat as I walked to the peephole with Hamish right behind me.

Some men in business suits – two of them – were pacing around outside. Something about them reminded me of spy movies. It must have been the way that they looked from side to side, watching for who knew what (maybe even they didn't know what).

"Should we let them in?" I asked Hamish after he had looked through the peephole too.

Before he could reply, his cell phone rang. He checked the caller I.D.; it was Ed. After a minute's conversation, he shut the phone. "Yes. It's the N.S.A."

I gaped at him, appalled. The National Security Agency?! That sounded ominous. The N.S.A. liked to think that it operated under everyone's radar, nationally, internationally, whatever…it was like the C.I.A. and the F.B.I. all rolled into one. Thanks to Hollywood, they weren't so secret anymore, and were commonly thought of as the No Such Agency.

I opened the door. "Come on in, No Such Agency agents." I gestured toward the kitchen.

They looked at me in a nonplussed sort of way, and walked in. I shut the door and we followed them into the kitchen. Were they here to force us to go somewhere with them? Would they be rude and short with either of us? I was getting angry just contemplating it.

I didn't offer them seats. If they asked permission to sit down, I would be a tad less annoyed and suspicious about this. I worried about being dragged into a witness protection plan for a brief moment until I remembered that I was famous; that would be too much trouble.

"I'm Alan Hawke, and this is Keith Lambert," the one with sandy hair said, gesturing at the one with salt-and-pepper hair. Both men wore their hair very short, but not in a military or crew cut. Other than being extremely fit and alert, they looked like civilians in suits.

"Hello," I said, watching them.

Hawke's expression did not change. "May we sit down? We have something to discuss with you – something that concerns you both."

With that questionable victory, I said yes, and motioned at the kitchen counter chairs. Hamish and I sat in our usual places – at the granite kitchen counter facing the TV, with him to my right. Hawke and Lambert sat across from us on the other stools.

"What's going on?" Hamish asked, not one to prolong the suspense.

Lambert spoke up for the first time. "You must know by now about the failed assassination attempt on the President yesterday."

"Yes," we said, in sync again, with a touch of impatience.

The men exchanged glances. Lambert resumed, "Well, we know who the assassin was working with, and that his name was Jeb Clyde, and that his group has been watching you for quite some time. We also know that Clyde himself has been on this street to watch you both."

So that was the blond guy with the cigarette – Jeb Clyde. "I saw him once, the summer before last. He followed me back from The Lobster Place, and was pacing across the street from our front door. I acted like I didn't notice anything unusual, came inside, shut and locked the door, and then looked out through the peep-hole. He seemed to be looking right at me – not that he could actually see me – but it felt as though he could. I told Hamish about it that evening."

"And then I hired Blackout Security to watch us and my in-laws," Hamish added.

"We know. That was wise. We intend to add their efforts now."

We stared at Lambert, then at each other. So that was what this was about. But what else was this about? I asked the N.S.A. guys as soon as I wondered about it.

"Have you heard about the group that Lance Boenher set up?"

"No – what is it, some sort of pro-life group, as in pro-let-people-reproduce-unregulated group?" The terms anti-choice and pro-life seemed to have acquired new definitions since the Birth Control Treaty.

"That's exactly what it is, Professor Châtelet."

"Of course – though Boenher seems to have dropped off of the public's radar screen since the Senate bounced him out on his ear for throttling Senator LaRosse."

"He's on our radar screen. He formed a resistance group after his ousting, and the right-to-lifers who used to fight abortionists have joined him. Jeb Clyde was one of those. Some of them are from Tennessee, Boenher's home state, and Idaho, where Clyde was from. But that's not all; they have teamed up with some militant Muslims from the Middle East."

Wow. Some combination, I thought.

Hawke saw my reaction. "Boenher seems to be taking lessons from them in covert ops, terrorism, and what have you. Their intent is to fight the Birth Control Treaty's use of Nae-Née, plus anyone and everyone who is associated with developing both it and the system."

"What do they intend to do?" Hamish asked.

"They want to kill you, your wife, the President, The Operator, and the members of the Birth License Committee, and to destroy the supercomputers that manage the Nae-Née devices."

"Wonderful. Now what?" I asked.

"Well, we can't hide you because you're famous, so we'll just have to assist in protecting you. We're coordinating with Blackout Security, and informing you of this."

"Why are you being so forthcoming to us with information?" I asked them.

Hawke and Lambert – if those really were their names – looked confused.

"What do you mean by that?" Hawke asked me.

"I mean that as pleased as I am to have information shared with me, you are a secret agency known for pretending that you don't even exist. I'm a bit surprised."

Understanding dawned, flickered, and disappeared from their expressions in a nanosecond. "We can't hide it from you, so we aren't going to try. Someone as savvy as you are with a computer can figure things out anyway, so subterfuge is ultimately pointless. We know that you have figured out who The Operator is."

"What did you do, program a bevy of remote-controlled surveillance nanites to follow me and Hamish around?! Are you now literal flies on our walls?! Does this mean that we can't so much as go to the bathroom – or be in our bed together – without you guys as Peeping Toms?!"

Hawke and Lambert looked alarmed. "No!" Lambert said, "Nothing like that. Our cyber security experts tracked your computer use and realized that you had figured it out."

I exhaled in relief. At least finally earning enough money for our own place so that we could have a romantic existence together wasn't all for nothing.

Then Hamish spoke up. "You hacked our computers?!"

"Are you kidding Hamish? The N.S.A. can look at whatever it wants, whenever and wherever with immunity and impunity. If anyone objects, it'll just claim that national security requires whatever they're up to. That's the difference between a computer hacker and a government cyber security expert: authorization."

Hawke and Lambert stared at me. Despite the habitually neutral expression in my eyes, it was becoming clear to them that a lot went on in the mind behind them.

"Do you want us to do anything different?" I asked them.

"Now that you mention it, yes. It would be a good idea if the two of you went away for a while." Lambert looked at me and Hamish, expecting a reply.

Terrific. The plot was thickening like some travesty of a French roux. That was what I got for cooking gourmet dinners just as guys from No Such Agency decided to drop by, I scolded myself. I needed a break from all this nonsense.

Religious fanatics – as distinguished from religious people – had a knack for talking themselves into believing whatever suited their fancy. I was determined not to let them corner me into living in fear or into not doing whatever I wanted to do.

And I was determined not to be a widow. I wondered whether Hamish and I would end up scrambling over one another trying to shield each other from flying bullets soon, each hoping to avoid being the one left alive and widowed. We were both terrified of that.

"Away?" I said, with no question in my tone. "I'm not going anywhere until my lecture next Thursday. After that, it's spring break, which gives us a week off. We could go away then. But we're not about to start slinking around, terrified of these maniacs, letting them control us."

"We thought you might say that."

"And? Did you have some plan to kidnap us instantly if we wouldn't go now?"

"No. We can handle things until you go away."

"Good. Because this next lecture is about the new Nae-Née policy, as herstory in the making, and I intend to follow it up by immediately sending copies of it, complete with my recommendations for changes to the manner in which the devices are delivered, to the President, the Attorney General, the Secretary of State, and the Secretary for the Department of Demographics. The changes are about the way that women are being treated when they get upset and try to resist. I've heard some obnoxious stories and one particularly brutal one."

The men looked interested, but Hawke just said, "We don't see why you won't be able to go ahead with all that as you plan to."

Lambert asked, "We also wanted to suggest that when you go away, you go out of the country. That would enable us to secure everything for you in the United States, plus go on ahead of you to secure your vacation site."

Hamish turned to me. "How would you like to spend spring break in Venice – before sea level rises and swallows it up?"

I looked at my global warming mug, forgotten on the counter since that morning. "I would. That's a great idea."

"I'll make the travel arrangements tomorrow. We'll stay in a nice hotel or pensione, and eat great food for week. And we'll take a gondola ride together."

I smiled; I doubted that we would be able to ride in a gondola, but I was excited.

Chapter 28

Q-and-A at a History of Medicine Lecture

It was early March, after the passage of the 28th Amendment, and after our segment had been run on *60 Minutes* for all to see, that I gave my lecture on *Herstory in the Making: Nae-Née Goes Borg and Global* at the Rockefeller University Institute.

The Caspary Auditorium was packed. It was the largest audience I had ever lectured to since coming to work at the Rockefeller Institute. Dr. Nurse had changed the venue at the last minute to the largest auditorium on campus, complete with signs redirecting people to it. I knew that my listeners included people from the Rockefeller Institute, the law and medical schools of New York and Columbia Universities, Cornell Medical School, the Sloan-Kettering Cancer Center, Barnard College, and who knew where else…probably media organizations.

But as I stepped up to the podium and laid out my lecture notes, and then connected the PowerPoint presentation equipment, I saw so many faces that I couldn't help wondering who else was there. I saw secretaries from the Rockefeller Institute. Why not? This affected them directly; they had a right to leave work and be here. Then I noticed some people who appeared to be wearing press passes, though I couldn't see the details from that distance.

Great – I was definitely about to make the news again. I told myself to be glad.

The lecture itself didn't worry me. That was in excellent order. The people here today would definitely come away knowing much more about this global, Borg-like birth control system than when they arrived.

It was the question-and-answer part of the session that followed the lecture that worried me. You can't rehearse the perfect answer for a question that you haven't yet heard. One bad phrase, one unfortunate inflection in tone, and a speaker would be vilified in the press.

The very idea annoyed me. That was a good thing, because it countered the stage fright and other fear that threatened to ruin my responses. If I was about to be attacked, I would fight back and say what I really thought. I wasn't anywhere nearly as concerned about being liked as I was about being right and doing some good.

Naturally, the lecture went off without a hitch. As usual, it was well-researched and prepared, and my style and delivery was easy to follow and held people's interest. The fact that the subject matter had such a direct impact on people's lives certainly helped.

After 25 minutes of detailing development of Nae-Née, the inventors' intentions for it, the government co-opting of the nanite with its modifications and legal mechanisms to protect its own actions, I summed up with some statistics and interpreted what they would mean for humanity's expectations about the future. I mentioned how long it would take before we felt the effects of the policy's overall aims – a smaller human population on this planet and thus more comfort for all. I refrained from stating the obvious, which was that we were all now sexually free to party, and that we need only take precautions against sexually transmitted disease.

From there, I moved on to criticize the methods of delivery by the government, describing the behavior of the crews who brought Nae-Née to female citizens. I spared no detail, naming no names, but reaming the soldiers and nurses for any failure to be communicative and sympathetic to each and every woman, regardless of her age, weight, and especially her attitude.

I made a point of placing the burden of compassionate behavior and respect on them, while emphasizing that U.S. citizens have the right to freedom of speech, with no obligation to passively acquiesce to the receipt of Nae-Née. The women were obligated to accept it, but no one was obligated to act like it was fine with them if it wasn't. The United States could not claim to be a nation of laws unless and until the delivery of Nae-Née reflected all of this.

Finally, I announced that all of these points were going into a letter from me to the President, the Attorney General, the Secretary of State, and the Secretary of the Department of Demographics.

Then I concluded the lecture and opened it up for the dreaded Q-and-A session.

The first questioner was someone whom I did not recognize. She wore a business suit and a lab coat, but she wasn't from the Rockefeller Institute. She must have walked across the street from her office, I surmised.

"What do you think about this policy of world-wide use of Nae-Née?"

"I think it's draconian. I think that it is big government intruding into our lives and chipping away at our civil liberties and pursuit of happiness. And I think that at the same time it is doing its best to preserve our future happiness and ability to pursue happiness."

Then came the ultimate loaded question, from a secretary I had interviewed:

"How do you feel about it?"

"It doesn't upset me."

She pressed on, and it was just as well that she did, because if she hadn't, someone else in the audience certainly would have. It was a relief to get this over with. She just asked, "Why?"

"I have a rather involved answer: We have a pressing problem for which no other viable solution has been offered. It's time that something radical, something drastic was done before it's too late. I get angry when I realize that it's probably too late for our generation to feel its benefits – only its costs. I want to feel benefits in my own lifetime, not merely know that the problem will be resolved after that, and that other people will enjoy the results of the solution, but not me and those whom I know and love.

"There are plenty of analogies in history – and herstory – for this. One of them is that Elizabeth Cady Stanton, toward the end of her life, realized that women would indeed get the right to vote, but only after she was dead. She would never live to see it and vote, and that was not okay with her. And I see no reason why it should have been.

"We should all be very angry when we realize that this will be our fate – not to see the Earth in better shape in our own lifetimes…to have live with the consequences of past decisions – decisions that were thoughtless and wrong – while knowing that we won't benefit from our own thoughtful and careful decisions. Only the people who come after us will enjoy that.

"We should be angry at our parents for using up the planet with reckless abandon and not noticing the destructive path that our species was on sooner and thus taking action.

"We should be angry at ourselves for not having seen and responded to the crisis sooner.

"And we might even be angry at life, because life is not fair, if that is what it takes to understand our emotions about this."

She wasn't quite finished with me. "What about the individuals – those who want to be parents but won't be allowed to be – who will be affected by this policy? They will feel as though they are being punished. How can you agree with a policy that does this?"

"More easily that you might think; the policy is about what is best for the nation and our species as a whole, not about how it benefits us on an individual basis. Most of our policies have been implemented solely on the basis of politics – gender politics, race politics, environmental politics – and that is why we are in this mess, having to scale back so drastically, in such a draconian manner, in order to save ourselves."

Gasps followed the first phrase of my response, then silence as people took that in.

My next questioner was another secretary from the Rockefeller Institute. "But I have heard that you and your husband never wanted children, and there are rumors that you don't like children. That would seem to make this whole thing less upsetting for you.

"Okay – let's get that out there once and for all. I'm thoroughly sick of people skirting the issue. It's true, and it's nothing personal against them as individuals. It's about the entire age group. I am not alone in this. Lots of people don't like little children. I invite my listeners and readers to interpret this as they choose for no other reason than that no matter what happens, that is exactly what they will do. People don't hear what others actually say most of the time; they hear – and think – what they want to hear. So I will say what I want, and condemn those who willfully impugn it as somehow negative rather than an objective fact.

"I resent the pressure put on women by societies everyone to like and want babies. This biological and cultural imperative is very much to blame for the situation that our species currently finds itself in. No one is required to like what the others like, and do what the others do. Being different is okay.

"But look at the problem another way: children, as one of the most precious resources to us as a species, are a desirable resource unless and until there are too many of them. We can't benefit from too much of any resource, be it water, oxygen, or a heat source. Just look at floods and forest fires; floods bring water, but so much of it that it is a problem rather than a benefit, and forest fires are fueled by too much oxygen, and no one likes a fire that it out of control destroying property and killing people rather than providing heat and cooking facilities.

"The same is true of having too many children on the planet. With too many children, the children suffer from overcrowding. A child should not be treated as a human insurance policy against a parent's old age, with no thought for the quality of that child's life. It is the responsibility of each parent to consider the chances at a good life that that child will likely have before producing her or him. Children are not merely heirs, spares, and potential caregivers. They are people in their own right, and they must be viewed as such first and foremost.

"When I see an individual case of a child – of whatever age – who is at risk for being a have-not in terms of their education or nutrition through no fault of her or his own, I have been known to get very upset about it and try to help. I want to see kids who study hard get accepted to college – and a competitive one that they are excited to attend – and not find, when they apply, that there is no room because there are just so many others that there is no place to go.

"I met a kid in that situation back in Connecticut with good grades, extra-curricular activities and a dream of attending medical school. He wasn't accepted to any of the schools that he had applied to, and he had applied, at great expense, to forty colleges and universities.

"These schools didn't drastically improve the quality of the educations that they offer. They did not earn the ability to be picky. It fell into their laps due to overpopulation.

"Fortunately, he told someone before it was too late – me – and I gave him suggestions and insisted that he tell his parents. He's in college in Australia now. He got accepted someplace competitive, but it was not in his own country. At least his sense of hope was saved. It won't be that easy for the next batch of qualified kids; it will only get worse before it gets better.

"So although I never wanted kids of my own, I also never wanted to see any kid in that predicament. I hope that sufficiently explains how I feel about kids to you.

"And I hope that everyone – not just the people in this room today – think carefully about how our species arrived at this point in history:

"How did we get to the point where we had to be told that we couldn't have children without government regulation all over the planet?

"And what better ideas can anyone else offer? Expecting people to police themselves has simply not worked. It is unrealistic. So again I ask, what better ideas have you got?

"What ideas – that are realistic and would actually work – can other people suggest?

"Either offer them or don't, but if you don't, don't go condemning people who aren't upset and who see this as helpful. Just get back to thinking hard about this, and don't volunteer your opinions about other people's characters and personalities without a better solution to the human overpopulation crisis.

"Because it is a crisis, and we have to deal with it right now, everywhere we go. There is no running away or moving away from it. That this subject has been a taboo one is the reason why we are in this predicament.

"Thank you."

And with that, I swept up my notes and stepped down from the podium.

At first there was no applause, not that I had expected any after scolding my interrogators, but then it started; soon they were all clapping, and staring solemnly back at me.

That was fine. The applause was an acknowledgement, not a celebration. There shouldn't be a celebration when a crisis is objectively faced and assessed. That would have to wait when we were all elderly or more likely, dead, when other humans dwelled on the Earth…hopefully an Earth with green energy and comforts for all again.

I walked down the length of the room, nodding at my audience, and saw Hamish about halfway back. He was smiling proudly at me, clapping. As I tried to exit the room, however, I felt a tug on my arm and looked back. Hamish had gotten up and followed me, and now he was insisting that I stay. I peered around him and saw that Dr. Nurse and the other scientists at the Institute were right behind him.

"Wait," said Dr. Nurse, "you've got to stay and chat after the lecture like usual."

I looked at him skeptically. "People still want to have wine, cheese and berries with me after that glum wake-up call of a scold? I thought they'd want me out of their sight at this point."

The men shook their heads. I looked around and saw some women standing there staring back at me too – scientists and professors, of course, but a few secretaries, too.

Frankly, it was the secretaries that I most felt the urge to flee from. The intellectuals had their curiosity to satisfy, but the secretaries…their lives seemed to be all about getting married and having kids and then seeing their own kids continue that cycle in perpetuity. I was raining on their parade. But they wanted me to stay too, and were actually smiling at me, and since my husband was standing by me and my boss was summoning me back, I stuck around.

However, I wasted no time in getting myself a glass of wine and a plate of cheese with raspberries and strawberries. I figured I would need it if I were to face an army of secretaries who felt disenfranchised, plus a bevy of reporters eager for a quote from me.

Chapter 29

Covert Ops
– Vacation in the Current Venice

We ended up at a hotel. A pensione would have been too difficult for N.S.A to work with. They would have had much more trouble concealing their activities from the owner of a house who rented rooms out – which was the definition of a pensione – rather than just renting more hotel rooms and avoiding tipping off the staff. They were practiced at that.

I had sent off my letter – certified so as to require signatures, for whatever that was worth considering who the recipients were – immediately after the cocktail party. Then we had gone home and packed our bags.

The day after we met the men from No Such Agency, I had considered the rising waters in that beautiful city. It was also called the City of Falling Angels, because acid rain was causing the stone angels that decorated the exteriors of the buildings to crumble, often as people passed near them.

The city experienced frequent floods despite the underwater levies shown in a *National Geographic* documentary, complete with computer graphics simulations to illustrate how they worked.

What would I pack, our Teva sandals? No. It was March – too cold.

On an impulse, and feeling guilty about the cost of rush delivery – then remembering that we had more money than we would ever spend – I logged onto the L.L.Bean site and got us each a pair of rubber pull-on boots; bright blue for me, dark green for Hamish.

They arrived the following Monday and I set them aside by our suitcases.

We were to leave on Friday, late in the morning.

What about our cat, I wondered?

Should we arrange to leave her in my parents' place in Chelsea and get Jordan to take care of her? The kid would probably like a chance to earn some extra cash.

But when I mentioned this to Hamish, we happened to be in the back of Ed and Rick's car, driving to work. Ed turned around from the front passenger seat and said, "No way that's going to happen. Eowyn will be fed and watched by the No Such Agency pet-sitting service. They mentioned that to us days ago."

I gaped at him, them at Hamish, who just cracked up. It was just so bizarre, the mere thought of having our cat taken care of by the nation's top spy agency...all to keep the Bible-Belter-Islamic-Fundamentalist-Anti-Birth-Management Coalition out.

What a mouthful. There had to be a better name than that for the group, but since they had yet to formally claim responsibility for trying to kill the President and announce their own name, that was how I thought of them.

Just for fun, I started musing about a shorter name for them.

The Christian-Jihad Pro-Life Coalition? But the acronym sounded awkward: CJPLC.

The Anti-Nae-Née Bible-Koran League? ANNBKL...no.

280

The Bible-and-Koran League for Free Births? BKLFB...no good.

The hell with it – let them announce themselves. That would be the name we'd be going with anyway, once it hit the news.

That evening, I went out and bought a month's worth of canned and dry cat food, more cat litter, litter box bags, deodorizer, the works. Hamish came with me to help carry it all. Then I wrote up a set of instructions on how to take care of our cat. I didn't want someone who didn't know or care about cats to make her fat. Agent Hawke called to say that he had seen our note and would make sure that the instructions were followed to the letter, so I said thank you.

Other than that, we just concentrated on our work that week. I was so focused on my lecture about the Nae-Née policy that I wasn't thinking of much else. As soon as we could get home and throw our stuff into the suitcases, we did it. We went out to eat at an Italian place within walking distance of our firehouse, came home, and went to bed early.

The next day we would have to wait in line at the airport, so we left 4 hours early. It felt like we were going to work, because the time of departure was about the same. I looked back as we pulled out. Both No Such Agency and Blackout Security now had copies of keys to our firehouse, our car, my parents' apartment in Chelsea, my parents' house in Connecticut, both of their cars, and my father's offices in Hartford, Manhattan, and Paris, as well as the apartment in Paris. They had keys to our lives.

At least they admitted it.

Hawke and Lambert had also admitted to having possession of the brownstone house across the street from our firehouse. Eowyn was right; they had been watching us from there. Animals are more observant than humans, despite all of our technological achievements.

So I looked back, with Chris and Joe watching me in the rearview mirror. And I saw four men let themselves into our home, each with a briefcase. Hardly astonishing, considering the urgency with which they had represented the situation to us.

I turned around and looked at my husband. Hamish had glanced back also, and then shrugged and turned to face forward. We looked at each other, not thrilled, not certain of romance and excitement on this particular vacation. "At least it will be an adventure this time," I remarked to him. He smiled ruefully in agreement.

Hours later, we landed in Treviso with Ed and Rick, who had been on the same flight and in the same section of the plane, but had pretended not to know us. Hamish had booked everything, and we had flown first class. I had told him it wasn't necessary, but he said he wanted to spoil me, and our minders chimed in that it made their work easier.

Why fight it? We could afford it, and it was pleasant.

Once we had cleared customs and whatever other security that the airport had, Ed and Rick dropped the pretense and shepherded us up into another car with blackout windows. It had to be one that was owned by N.S.A.; it was different somehow. It had all of the markers required of a car that was registered in Italy, but that wasn't it. It just felt different...official and covert.

The seriousness of our situation was starting to be felt already.

Blackout Security had ceded control of the job of watching and protecting us to the United States government – but not the entire job. I was glad about that.

After the less than stellar job that our government had done guarding the President, I suddenly felt anxious. Would we end up maimed or killed? Would we come home to a dead cat? What?

As long as I didn't have to be a widow, I supposed it would be all right…and as long as neither Hamish nor I were maimed. He would never put up with life as a disabled person. He had told me so many times.

Oh yes – plenty to feel anxious about. It wasn't just my agile and active imagination.

After an hour's drive, we transferred to a boat, but it wasn't a water taxi. No public transportation for us anymore; we were to be escorted every step of the way.

The Luna Hotel Baglioni was beautiful, with a marble stairwell and chandeliers and golden wall sconces, a romantic bedroom with its own bathroom complete with a tub for two…and I hardly cared. I sat down on the bed and stared out the window at the view of San Giorgio Island and the Venetian lagoon, not really seeing it, obsessing.

This sucked; I had always wanted to come here with my husband. Now that we were here, I was freaking out with good reason rather than being excited and happy to be here.

It wasn't our fault, but then life is usually unfair. I knew that.

Hamish had gone to a lot of trouble to arrange all this. I was suddenly determined to enjoy this trip regardless of our predicament. When I considered the nature of this predicament, I began to get really annoyed with myself.

Our predicament could be a hell of lot worse. Our problem was that we were being stalked by a mysterious, yet-to-be-named group of nut-jobs who hated us for inventing Nae-Née and thus making the global birth management policy possible. As a result, we had to be watched by the N.S.A. Our relatives and cat had to be watched too. My parents still insisted that they weren't mad at either of us. At least there was that.

No – we were lucky to have this for a predicament. We got to enjoy the beautiful city of Venice with our very own security detail. Other people had much worse predicaments: floods in Pakistan and China were displacing and burying people every day, sending them running – or swimming – for dry land. And when they got to the dry land, it was too dry to live on. Either too much water or too little with no happy medium was the problem, and death on the way there due to accidents or water-borne diseases. No food or shelter and no money to replace the ones that had been washed away. Meanwhile, rich people elsewhere had everything, and their homes were still standing.

Which brought me back to why we had picked Venice for this getaway in the first place: global warming and rising sea levels had made it too fascinating not to come here.

Hamish sat down next to me on the bed. He stared out at the view with me for a moment, then put his arm around me. "We're going to have a great time, right?"

I looked up at him and grinned. "Yes, we are. I'm determined. What did you say this suite was called again? It's beautiful."

He looked pleased. "It's the Tiziano Suite. Do you want to take a bath?"

I had been into the bathroom; the tub was a jacuzzi. "Definitely, but can we do that after dinner? I'm getting hungry."

"Sure. I made reservations for the hotel restaurant for tonight. It's called the Canova Restaurant."

We had turned down the unpacking and packing service; it was included in the cost of the room, but we knew that our minders wouldn't like that. I wouldn't like that either. Strangers handling my stuff?! Spoken like someone who hadn't been waited on hand and foot all her life, but that was fine. Hamish had grown up with considerably less in the way of material comfort than I had, living in rough and tough Glasgow, but he was obviously enjoying this trip.

I put on a nice outfit of a pale pink silk blouse and black lacy skirt, brushed my hair, and added the pearl necklace that my husband had given me for Christmas. I had been wearing the plain pearl studs from our wedding that my mother had given me – inherited from her mother – and now I decided to just wear the necklace every day on our trip. Worrying about its whereabouts seemed like infinitely more effort than just wearing it.

Hamish for once did not have to be told to wear a pair on navy blue chinos rather than cargo pants, and a shirt with buttons (!) rather than a tee with his green cotton pullover sweater. I admired his appearance and attire before heading for the door.

To my surprise, he grabbed me and gave me a nice, long kiss. "You look beautiful."

I kissed back. Hmm…maybe this would be a romantic getaway after all.

The restaurant was a beautiful place, with fresh white roses on every table. The chef specialized in recipes of fresh fish and vegetables – no doubt trucked and boated in daily. I tried not to overeat, and then realized that I didn't run any great risk of that here. European portions are much smaller than American ones, giving just enough to eat and no more. Doggie bags are unknown. I had once been asked by my Oncle André about that; he was visiting us and we were in a local restaurant with generous portions. It was all just an exercise in excess to him.

Hamish and I had dessert and cappuccino, then went back up to our suite.

The tub was fun, and soon I was enjoying the room. But I wondered whether there were cameras in the light fixtures, television, or elsewhere in our room, with N.S.A. guys watching us. Not a very romantic thought. I asked Hamish about this as we flicked through the TV channels, checking out the Italian ones even though we understood almost nothing on them.

Comparing Italian with French and trying to understand wasn't keeping me occupied; I just had to ask Hamish if he thought that we could change our clothes or have sex in a fishbowl, or did we actually have privacy here?

He assured me that N.S.A. weren't a bunch of perverts who couldn't guard us without watching our every move and hijacking our privacy.

Fine. I had told myself a few hours earlier to relax and enjoy this trip, but with every change in our lives, with each notch that our security was ratcheted up as time passed, first when Hamish had hired Blackout Security and now with the N.S.A. moving in on us – literally – I couldn't help but go over such concerns again.

The next morning, we ate breakfast in the hotel – in a different restaurant, called the Salone Marco Polo. It was a buffet, so I had to warn Hamish not to overdo it. Then we headed outside…and right back inside.

That was when we noticed that the hotel was not level with the street, and that that was a good thing…because the street was under water by several inches. We had been dropped off at the hotel by boat, and let off at another entrance, stepping from the boat directly into the building. Today, we were going out toward the Piazza San Marco.

"Now what?" Hamish asked me.

"Come on back to our room – I know exactly what," I replied. I was the one who had packed our suitcases.

Upstairs, I showed him his new boots and changed into my own. He stared at me for a moment in amazement and admiration, then kicked off his sneakers and put the boots on.

Back we went, ready for the adventure.

"I wouldn't have picked this place for our vacation if I had thought that it would be flooded," Hamish said, sounding apologetic.

"I'm glad you picked it for precisely that reason!" I assured him. "This city floods in fall, winter and spring. I'm glad it's not so high that cafés have to close and people are up to their waists, but I wanted to see a flood. Our boots will be sufficient. Let's go see some art and architecture."

"Okay – as long as you're happy."

"Oh, I'm happy – happy to have the chance to see this city before sea level rises and it sinks out of sight."

We went out, walking around the Piazza, pausing so that I could shoot photos with my digital camera. I had brought my laptop so that I could save them, and a memory stick, but those were back in the room.

The first thing I wanted to see was not ancient and beautiful, historic Venice, however. It was the MOSE system.

The MOSE project – Modulo Sperimentale Elettromeccanico – was a system of 79 inflatable, undersea barriers to protect the Venetian Lagoon from flooding by the Adriatic Sea. It was under construction until 2011, and had come under intense criticism from environmental groups because: 1. It threatened to harm the ecosystem of the Venetian Lagoon; and 2. It wouldn't protect the city of Venice from rising sea levels. Sea level would soon rise past the MOSE project's ability to hold the water back.

It wasn't possible to view the underwater system without a boat ride, but there was a tour that we could take that afternoon that offered a view through the boat's hull to the lagoon bed below. Hamish called the hotel and had the concierge book us on it.

Photography was difficult, but I managed to get a few shots of the inflated barriers in action. They were almost up, and the guide informed us that by late afternoon the water level ought to be a few inches lower. That was as good as it would get, however. Sea level was already getting ahead of them.

Hamish asked about the lagoon's ecosystem: how was it being affected by the barriers?

The guide looked uncomfortable, but didn't evade the question. The lagoon had long been a breeding ground for a variety of finfish and shellfish, which had fed the local population. The unpleasant reality of the situation – of rising sea levels – was that in order for Venice to protect itself from being flooded out of existence, it needed the barriers, but those barriers were threatening the Venetians underwater habitat, which had long been a part of their food supply.

With the flow of currents being disrupted by the barriers, breeding and migration was being impeded. Herons and ducks lived in the lagoon, but fewer and fewer of them were staying. They were seeking other breeding grounds. Crabs, shrimp and other shellfish were being overfished as it was, though for now there were still some in the lagoon bed.

There were also octopi and squid; we saw one octopus moving along below us, and I was thrilled to find that I had managed to capture a decent image of it. A jellyfish also swam by, and our guide said that those were not usual residents of the lagoon. I took a photo of that animal also, but it was just an odd whitish shape – nothing that one would easily be able to identify as a jellyfish. Hamish told me not to delete it, though; someone might be fascinated to see it, even if we had no idea as to whom just then.

That concluded our flooded Venice study. For the rest of our stay in the city, we concentrated on seeing traditional things, like the Rialto Bridge, where we found fruit vendors at either end. I bought some Jaffa oranges, imported from Israel. They were the most amazing ones that I had ever tasted – nothing like the wonderful Valencia ones of Florida, but delectable. They were tart but not unpleasantly so, and intensely flavored. They were just right and unforgettable. The taste of Jaffa oranges was something that I would never forget, and would always associate with Venice.

We were allowed to walk through the *La Fenice* opera building, which dated back to 1792, when it was built for the first time. Since then, it had been burned to the ground a few more times and rebuilt with as much grandeur as before, not always identical to its predecessors, but fabulously nonetheless. It was certainly aptly named: it was *The Phoenix* in English, and it had indeed risen gloriously from the ashes each time it was resurrected. The most recent such effort had been completed in 2003.

It had frescos and a huge chandelier in the concert hall, a fabulous green curtain over the stage, golden edging on the box seats and ceilings, and the acoustics were said to be equal to those of the past renditions of the opera house.

We were amazed that it was just open to whoever wished to look around, but that was what we were told, and we were even allowed, with the flash turned off, to take photos.

The next day of our trip, the water level on the streets and Piazza San Marco was down to just a few inches, so the outdoor tables reappeared and we sat admiring the facades of the Doge Palace and San Marco Cathedral as we sipped our latte (mine) and espresso (Hamish).

"How can you drink that thing?" I couldn't help asking him. "I had one once – a professor ordered one for me by mistake when a bunch of us were out in Boston. It was gritty at the bottom of the cup, and so strong even with some milk added that I got a headache."

"Really? I don't get headaches from these, even though I just have them once in a great while. I wanted the caffeine buzz; I was up in the middle of the night surfing the Internet on your computer."

"What were you looking up? Were you doing work?"

He looked guilty for a moment, then said, "I was just checking my e-mail. Then I went back to vacation stuff. I was looking up Murano Island – how to get there, what to see, etc."

Murano Island was where the glass of Venice was blown and crafted into wonderful shapes. During the Renaissance period and the early days of the American colonies, the Doge had feared a brain drain of talent to other parts of the world and so had sequestered the glass-blowers on that island. They and their families were forbidden to leave. Draconian, but ultimately effective; Venice continues to be famous for its glass.

We went there that day, and saw handkerchief vases in various color combinations being blown, and bought some glass candy, a couple of colorful glass clowns, and several vases. We had no intention of trying to carry any of it on the plane; I had it all shipped to Connecticut and Manhattan. Most of it went to Connecticut, though. I e-mailed my mother that evening from the hotel as to who was to receive what.

As I typed the note to her, Hamish watched me with satisfaction and said, "It's nice to see you relaxing and enjoying yourself."

I looked up at him, startled. "Are you enjoying yourself too?"

"Of course. And I'll enjoy myself even more after dinner, in this suite with you."

I grinned at him and hit "Send" with a tap. Off to whatever restaurant we had spotted and noted as a stop on our gourmet palate tour.

"I know how to enjoy life – all we need is to be convinced that we can," Hamish said.

For at least this week, I believed it.

We saw the famous shop where the Carnival masks were made and sold, called Mondonovo. I shopped again, sending one mask to Manhattan and four more to Connecticut, plus another to Hamish's sister Fiona in Scotland. Hamish was just as fascinated as I was by the contents of that shop. It had the sorts of masks that one would expect to see on a character in one of Mozart's Italian operas – including a sinister sort of character, with a pointed nose and a flared section over the forehead. It had cat masks, and I found two of those that made me think of *Puss in Boots*; one of them was the one that went to Manhattan. And there were clown masks with tears streaming down from their eyes, some male, others female.

We met the artist, Guerrino Lovato, too, which was a stroke of luck. He had crafted the decorations of *La Fenice*, and he had also done the masks for the creepy mansion scene in Stanley Kubrick's movie *Eyes Wide Shut*.

Hamish insisted on taking me for a gondola ride, and he kissed me at sunset under the Bridge of Sighs. Local legend had it that this would grant us everlasting love and bliss. I certainly hoped so. Who wouldn't want that?

But the bridge itself had granted anything but that to the prisoners whose last glimpse of the beautiful city was a rushed one through the ornate stone grilles on the windows. They had gone across the bridge and down to their cells across the canal to serve lengthy sentences for their crimes, and typically never viewed the city again.

Not for lovers passing underneath it in a gondola, however. For them and us, the promise was one of everlasting romance. It was a lovely fairy tale, despite the fact that our minders were invisibly around us.

We had one more day ahead of us when we were surprised by a guest. A knock came at the door, and Hamish answered it. I was shocked that he would just open the door for only an instant; then I reminded myself that we were being guarded.

It was none other than our nation's newest Cabinet member, the Secretary of the Department of Demographics: John K. Lassiter, J.D., M.P.P. He had earned his master's degree in Public Policy at Tufts University, I recalled.

Hamish let him in without a word, and I greeted him politely.

"So, Mr. Secretary Lassiter: what brings you to this sinking city?"

Chapter 30

Separatists and Senator

John Lassiter was a man in his mid-fifties, with thick, straight graying dark hair that was streaked with pure white and gray eyes. He was heavyset and over six feet tall. The President had known him while he was at Harvard Law School; they had done some research together on crowds and mass hysteria. Lassiter had published a couple of books on how group mentality could lead to panic and attacks on civil liberties.

We invited him to the living room section of the suite, and I ordered coffee, juice, fruits and pastries from room service. Then Hamish and I sat down on the sofa and faced him, waiting.

Lassiter got right to the point. "Professor Châtelet, I have received your letter and read your criticisms of the delivery of Nae-Née, and your recommendations for its improvement."

Hamish and I exchanged glances.

"That's one reason for my visit. The other is to discuss the reasons behind all this security that we've insisted on. You and I and many other people have been threatened, but not publicly as yet. We think that the threats will be publicized soon, but we wanted to stay a few steps ahead of the game."

Hamish and I exchanged glances again, but waited for Lassiter to continue.

He did. "I noticed that you sent copies of your letter to the President, the Attorney General, and to the Secretary of State, and that you expressed a desire to have copies distributed to the National Birth License Committee."

Finally, after having sat in silence, I decided to speak. I wondered whether I seemed a bit…forbidding in my silence thanks to my penchant for neutral facial expressions.

"Yes, I did all that. I want them all to know what I have learned and to be aware of the feelings and experiences of women as they receive the mandatory version of Nae-Née when she meets foreign leaders and deals with women's issues. I want the President to know the same things, because women have a right not to feel like children who don't matter as they get Nae-Née. And I want you to make sure that it doesn't happen again. That being said, although I'm not upset about the policy itself, I won't just passively watch as such things happen."

Lassiter listened to me without interrupting. It was what I wanted; notice and a right to be heard. If I really got what I wanted, he would say that he was making sure that something was done about those flaws; women shouldn't be grabbed roughly, manhandled, scolded, or otherwise made miserable as they received the nanites.

When I stopped talking, he paused a moment, then spoke. "You're right, of course. I've ordered inquiries into what happened, and the President has made many additions to the Code of Federal Regulations to address the points that you made. Virtual copies have been sent to your e-mail account at the Rockefeller University Institute and hard copies to your home. I can't be certain that this will fix the system, but we hope that it will."

My expression actually showed surprise – my eyebrow did that thing that Spock often did in *Star Trek*; it arched a bit. "Thank you. Maybe once the first round is dealt with, and the job becomes more routine, more of just giving each 10-year-old girl a Nae-Née device, such incidents will become a distant memory. But for now, I'll bet that many adult women are still facing squads of soldiers and nurses in a hurry and on a schedule."

He shifted in his seat uncomfortably. "That's true. That's why I've ordered the process paused for a day – only a day – in which to conduct sensitivity training and give warnings. Anyone who shows impatience or scolds a woman who cries and resists will be either dismissed if they are a nurse or brought up on charges if they are a soldier. If they have to slow down to soothe and apologize to each woman, then that's what they have been ordered to do. No more scolding speeches like the one that your former secretary was subjected to."

"You found out who that was, then."

"Yes. And we found the team that treated her…both medically and rudely."

"What happened to that team?"

"The nurse was reprimanded, because it was her first offense, and because she didn't actually say anything offensive to Ms. Warne, and the soldiers were dropped a grade in rank. We didn't slap them with the measures I just mentioned because it would have been illegal – an ex post facto punishment – one meted out for offenses committed before the warnings of termination and charges, rather than after."

"Wow." After what I had heard about the way the woman soldier had spoken to Patsy, I wasn't about to shed any tears over the reprimand; it served her right.

Hamish looked impressed with the attention that my efforts had been given. He even smiled at Lassiter, and grinned at me.

Then Lassiter got back to his agenda. "The other issue that I came to discuss is the reason why you two are under so much surveillance and such heavy guard."

There was a knock at the door; the food had arrived. I got out some cash for the tip and let the waiter bring it in. He seemed to expect to stay and pour our coffee, but I handed him his tip, said "Gratzi," and sent him out. I poured the drinks myself so Lassiter would continue.

Once we were settled with the coffee, Lassiter picked up where he had left off. "Remember Senator Lance Boenher?"

"Oh yeah," we said, in sync and with disgust. I added, "What did he do, run into the hills and stir up this anti-Nae-Née movement?"

"You guessed it. He's been funding them, organizing them, and hiding out with them since his disgrace and ejection from the Senate. He's moved his whole family to a compound in Tennessee. He never came back to Washington, D.C. to face the assault charges, either. That's where, as near as we can tell at this point, the training grounds and hideout for the assassins is."

"And what is being done to cage them all in and capture them? Or have some of them gotten off that base and hidden from N.S.A.'s radar and complicated the effort?" I had a knack for asking questions that included all of my guesses; I hoped Lassiter wouldn't find it annoying.

Apparently not, because he said, "You figured it out again. Want to join the covert ops team?" He grinned at me.

"No thanks, I'm happy doing what I do. Besides, Hamish has more formal training and practice experience with such things than I do. But you probably know all about our pasts now."

Lassiter looked amused; I had guessed his methods yet again, though it was no great feat. Governments and covert ops people specialized in such things. Maybe he was just at a loss for words to find that none of this came as news to us. But we just weren't surprised; we lived in a culture that used infotainment and spy movies to teach people about what to expect. Anyone who liked movies could guess all this, or so I thought.

"Do you know what Boenher's group is calling itself yet?" I asked him.

"We do: it's called Reproduction Entitlement, or RE for short."

I gave a short burst of a mirthless laugh. "That's perfect," I said. "It's like a legal brief or a part of a case title, like In Re Boenher. And it sums up what they're about succinctly."

"We thought so too. If they don't announce themselves soon, the President wants to go on national television and announce it for them. N.S.A. is against that, of course, and for now, he's letting them have their way. He's already shared this information with intelligence agencies around the planet, and even the Saudis are working to root out the REs from their own deserts."

"The ultra-Islamic Wahabi Saudis are doing that?" I said in disbelief. "Why? Is their supply of oil running out? Are they that worried about running out of money to finance their religious lifestyle and closed society in great luxury?"

"As a matter of fact, they are. Scientists at CERN and NASA have nearly worked out a non-fossil fuel energy source, so they realize that it is only a matter of time before the rest of the world decides that it doesn't need to buy their overpriced pollutants. That will be good news for world stability as sea levels rise. It won't stop that – it's too late – but at least the jihadists won't have so much money in their bank accounts to fund their activities."

I hoped it was nuclear fusion – clean, nondestructive energy. At least, that was the science fiction theory that I learned from the fourth *Star Trek* movie in the mid 1980s. It sounded good, and it was cool that *Star Trek* was maintaining its track record for dreaming up future technologies which its Ph.D.-earning fans then went on to invent in reality. "So we'll soon exchange one type of problem for another rather than merely adding one to the mix. I guess that's something to be thankful for."

Hamish was being very quiet and thoughtful.

"Dr. MacDonall, I want to assure you that you and your wife will be quite safe when you return to Manhattan, and you will be equally safe in Connecticut with your in-laws."

He looked at Lassiter as though the man were on crack cocaine, but replied politely, "I have no doubt that No Such Agency has done its best to secure the premises."

Something was eating at him, but I didn't ask. Later for that...

"So," I brought the discussion back to the immediate security issue, "has Boenher been found and isolated, or not?"

"Found yes, isolated, almost. We don't want to reveal our hand just yet."

"So he could go somewhere if he chose?"

"Not really…if he tries to elude us, we can track him. He doesn't know it, but we have some surveillance nanites in his system."

I stared at him. "You mean a surveillance system of nanites that No Such Agencies computer wizards have remotely guided into his body?"

Now Lassiter stared at me. "How did you figure that out?"

I laughed. "I'm a *Star Trek* and science fiction buff and I'm married to a nanite inventor. Plus I have no trouble imagining scenarios that fit the circumstances that you are describing. Just hint at it and I can almost see it. But thanks for the confirmation," I said with a smile.

John Lassiter looked a bit flustered, but recovered quickly.

"But Mr. Lassiter, Boenher must have found himself some computer wizards of his own to fight the Nae-Née policy. It can't be that easy. There must be some irate geeks out there who agree with Boenher and the Islamists and who want to be able to reproduce unregulated. They could be trying to crack the government's nanite-unlocking codes as we speak."

"He has, and they are, but keep in mind that they would have to crack each and every code for each and every Nae-Née device in each and every woman who has received one. And Boenher is going to be very angry soon, because we have a trick up our sleeves."

"Do tell," I encouraged him.

"It's been on the news before, as a project in the works for remotely located and isolated societies such as the Taliban and Pashtun of Afghanistan, where women object to being seen or touched unless it is by other women. The plan of personally visiting them with nanite injector guns just isn't feasible for them."

I thought back to the report. Then I remembered it; it was the same idea as the traveling nanite surveillance equipment. The Nae-Née devices would find the women by reading their heat signatures and body chemistry, then implant themselves through a lung and travel down to the area of their reproductive systems and stay. "I remember now. Are you saying that Boenher's wife has been the unwitting recipient of a prototype traveling Nae-Née device?"

Hamish perked up, fascinated. "Has she now?" he echoed, but not as a question.

Lassiter regarded him speculatively. "She has," he replied, and so have Boenher's two teenage daughters."

"Excellent work," Hamish said with admiration.

I grinned too; this was like revenge served at its coldest. Boenher deserved it. The man had spent his career doing his best to control women's reproductive functions. Now he had lost control of his wife's reproduction without noticing. He had always seemed a bit too proud of the fact that he had gotten his prom queen pregnant six times. She smiled and waved, but looked a bit trapped and tired in the news clips, as though she were exhausted by it all.

"What was her name?" I wondered to myself. "Something with an M, I think…"

"Her name is Melissa, and she is 41 years old – too old for more pregnancies under the new policy."

"Oh? Your department has set an ideal time frame for pregnancies?"

"Yes – well, The Operator did. Ideally, early 20s to 39. Once a woman hits 40, that's it; no more licenses to reproduce."

"I wonder how people are going to take that; they have been used to having more time to get around to having kids, with no limits," I commented.

"We're expecting a lot of upset over that, but it's got to be done. Also, since the system is in its infancy, we're still working out the kinks. Sometimes we end up terminating pregnancies – which we time for visits to gynecologists' offices if we possibly can – and harvesting stem cells if we can gather them. So Nae-Née has yielded an unexpected benefit…saving the material for medical research and treatments. Scientists who have been looking for a viable source for stem cells are pretty excited about it."

"What are you doing, stirring up false hopes on purpose only to dash them just to harvest stem cells?" I asked, sounding outraged.

"No! Nothing like that," Lassiter hastily assured me. "It's just that even with the staff that we have, it's more work than we can manage with absolutely zero errors. Any pregnancy that we fail to nip in the bud, no pun intended, has to be nipped later. That's the beauty of the system and you and your husband invented; RU-486 can be either a birth control drug or an abortifacient. And if stem cells are going to be made by accident, wasting them would be foolish considering how useful they are to transplant research and treatment."

Oh. That was entirely reasonable. "I agree with that. And it's bound to further infuriate RE. They don't like stem cell research either, as I recall."

"No, they don't. They don't make much sense. They want to bring more babies into existence without regard for the quality of life that those babies will have to face. Nor do they approve of using stem cell tissue to help those who are already in existence."

"I haven't been doing my usual careful, daily tracking of the news while I'm on vacation. If these RE nut-jobs are after The Operator, you, the Birth License Committee members and us, I haven't heard about any new assassination attempts. Is there something we ought to know?"

He looked at me, startled, and then said, "Yes. They just killed someone yesterday. She was a lawyer on the National Birth License Committee. I don't know how they found out that she was on the Committee, but we think it was through computer hackers."

I felt a bit sick. "How did she die?"

"She was shot on her way to her office. They didn't get the assassin. Her name was Anne Reynolds, she had a daughter and a husband, and she was walking into her office building from her car. She had just left a job at the ACLU to work on the Committee, and she was an old law school friend of the Secretary of State. They also attended Wellesley College together."

"How did they get to her?"

"We're guessing that the assassin was hiding in a nearby building, and using a silencer. No one heard the shot, so it wasn't until later that our forensics experts knew which direction the bullet came from."

Hamish looked grim when he heard that.

Lassiter wasn't finished. "Nice job on identifying The Operator, by the way. Unfortunately, RE managed to do the same thing. He's been forced to move out of the condominium that he had just bought and settled into. He's staying underground for now and he put the condo back on the market. When this blows over, he'll get another place. I'll be glad when we put these idiots out of business. They are the most selfish people I've ever dealt with."

Lassiter paused for a moment, then went on with his lambasting of them.

"They insist upon stressing the Earth's capacity to provide as much of whatever resources they and the wealthiest people on the planet can get their hands on. Survival of the fittest taken to its logical extreme will, if RE's followers get their way, destroy first the others around them and eventually themselves…or at least their descendants. They don't want to hear that, but that doesn't make it any less so." He certainly seemed to be in complete agreement with the policy, that was for sure, I thought to myself.

I couldn't resist agreeing. "All that is true. And so much fun to sum up in their absence. We don't have to listen to them screaming at us in impotent rage and unreasoned protest."

Hamish laughed at that, enjoying the imagery that the assessment evoked. Then he asked, "So, Mr. Secretary of Demographics, what's the plan for when we go back to New York? Are we to go about with armed guards? Can my wife still choose her own groceries? Can I take her out to dinner? Or are we to cower in fear at home and in our offices?"

"No cowering. N.S.A. assures me that you will be able to go about your business as usual, just no cabs or subway rides, and your car can never be left unattended. Someone has been watching it since shortly before Agents Hawke and Lambert introduced themselves to you. The car has been inspected piece by piece and reassembled, and surveillance equipment added to ensure that no machine or human error can allow for any tampering. The same has been done to Professor Châtelet's parents' cars also."

"So someone watches my dad's car whenever he parks in the CityPlace garage in Hartford, and at home? And my mother's car whenever she goes out shopping?"

"Precisely. And when they are in Manhattan or Paris, they are chauffeured about. They are surprisingly acquiescent about all this."

I saw no reason not to explain that. "We visited them in Connecticut for Christmas, when the crowds of reporters started to hound us. It's gotten a lot better since then, but at the time, I asked Dad if he was mad at us, and I asked my mother too. They said absolutely not; we had a right to invent something with good intentions and earn a living off of it, and that as far as they were concerned, the ensuing hassles caused by other people's reactions were not our fault."

"Nice parents. Dr. MacDonall, what about your sister in Scotland? Has she had any trouble over this?"

"Oddly no, but then she is 54 years old, married, and has no kids. She has friends, but they haven't been upset with her about me; she told me so. But I appreciate the security around her nonetheless. I like to say that just because you're paranoid, it doesn't mean that they're not out to get you. I don't want anyone to get her."

Lassiter laughed. "I'll have to remember that. I'm beginning to understand the two of you – you certainly think alike. Well, I have to be going. You're security measures are in place, you understand the situation that led to it, and we'll be in touch. Enjoy the last day or so of your vacation here. Oh, and thanks for the coffee and fruit."

We showed him out, and noticed that a team of covert men in suits appeared in the hallway and followed him to the elevator.

The next day was our last in Venice. We went next door to see the Doge Palace, but no farther. Meeting John Lassiter had made us feel tired, as though we needed a rest before facing the trek home.

The facade of the building was inspired by Islamic influences, with rows upon rows larger arches over smaller ones forming its façade over the Piazza San Marco. I recalled that in the movie version of *The Merchant of Venice*, one of Portia's suitors was a Muslim prince, a Moor who wore a dishdashah and guthra, the garb that Arab men still wore today. Muslims had visited this city in the past, when the Doge Palace was being designed and constructed.

Inside, however, it was thoroughly European in appearance, and every inch was covered in opulence and art. It was the Grand Chamber Council room in which the Doge and the ruling merchant class of the city had conducted the affairs of Venice that I most wanted to see.

The ceiling was all paintings; fabulous paintings filled every shape – a huge oval in the center plus others of varying shapes bordering it with golden paint for outlines. At the far wall was the largest painting in all of Europe, Tintoretto's *Paradise*. I tried to imagine 1,000 men in Renaissance dress routinely meeting in here, and admiring the painting, which had been completed sometime after 1588, when he got the commission for it. It was done on canvas, and moved to its designated position when it was almost finished, where the artist then completed what was his last major work.

No photography was permitted, so I bought a book with the photos in it. It was probably better that way; the book was complete and beautiful, unlike any effort that I might have made with my amateur photography skills.

We left the Doge Palace, down the grand stairwell and onto the flooded street, still covered by four inches of water. Then we returned to our suite to sleep and eat room service food until it was time to go home. It was time to leave the fairy tale and face the odd reality that had become our lives in Manhattan.

Chapter 31

Followed

We headed back to our firehouse in a government vehicle, which we were escorted to with all of the secrecy and paranoia that accompanies a couple of private citizens whose work has become politically inflammatory.

Soon we had joined the highway parking lot that connected JFK International Airport with the island of Manhattan.

We sat in heavy traffic, in the back seat of a black car with tinted windows, bored and tired. It was rush hour in the evening on a Monday. No Such Agency had been very specific; we were to come home on a Monday, not a weekend. Why that made things easier I did not know, but here we were, staring into space, not really seeing the vehicles that we shared the Williamsburg Bridge with.

An SUV went by with a square yellow sign stuck to the side window: Baby on Board.

Inside was a woman driving, a boy of perhaps 6 years old in the front passenger seat next to her, and a baby seat in the back with a little girl. The girl was waving something and smacking the back of her brother's seat with it.

Hamish and I both watched as the SUV slid to a stop alongside us, then looked at each other. I commented, "There are two of the last unlicensed births this planet is likely to see for a long time."

"Three," he corrected me. "You aren't tall enough to see it, but there's a baby in the seat on the other side of the little girl who's throwing a tantrum and a bunch of toys."

"And an SUV – quite a carbon footprint…oh well…"

I thought of Bethany, my college friend in Massachusetts. She didn't approve of SUVs, but I wouldn't put it past her to use a Baby on Board sign in her car. I wondered how she was doing, but I was afraid to call her. Now that I was allegedly among the hunted, I didn't want to put her at risk by contacting her.

After a moment, Hamish said, "You're unusually quiet. What are you thinking about?"

I told him.

"You want to call her and find out how she feels about the Nae-Née policy, don't you?"

"Yeah, but not if doing so puts her on the radar screen of anyone in RE," I said.

"Smart. Don't worry; soon you'll be able to talk to her again."

"How would you know? You're not clairvoyant or telepathic," I said irritably.

"No, but I am a nanite engineer. I'll figure something out so you can be happy."

I just stared at him. What a nice husband; but I didn't see how he was going to do anything about our current predicament. We couldn't see anyone without making them a target, unless I was mistaken.

Behind us, another car was stuck in the evening traffic jam. It wasn't immediately behind us, but it was working on it.

Our handlers kept looking in the rearview mirror and muttering nonsense that could only be code into their hidden microphones.

I wondered: could anyone see us if we turned around to look? Hamish said no.

We looked. It was a little green Smart Car. It weaved in and out of the lane behind us, unable to inch closer. Two men sat in it, with their eyes glued to our car.

They looked like any other American men, with short hair and tee shirts with windbreaker jackets on. We would not have noticed them if they hadn't been watching us.

The men in the Smart Car dogged us steadily all the way across the bridge.

When we finally made it across, they passed us on the left, stared carefully, and then drove off, shaking their heads and talking to each other, laughing and joking.

A few minutes later, as we drove through Manhattan toward Greenwich Village, our N.S.A. escorts spoke to us. It was Lambert, I suddenly realized.

He said, "It was nothing, just a couple of curious guys on their way to a bar. They were fascinated by the tinted windows, but we had the cops pull them over and run their I.D.s; there's nothing on them. One of them is a lawyer for the ACLU, and the other works for the city, prosecuting rapists. False alarm."

There were going to be a lot of those now. And we were probably going to notice a lot more of them than we ever had before.

What fun.

When we got back from the airport, I half expected to see guys from No Such Agency walking around our house, but the only occupant there was Eowyn. She was fine. There was a note from Agent Hawke, signed only with "Alan" – his first name – to us saying that they had all taken care of our cat according to our note and that she had been no trouble.

I didn't care what the policy was on this; I was going to buy four boxes of chocolates for the agents, and explain that as I had seen four of them enter our firehouse as we left, I had concluded that the cat care duties would have been shared by all of them.

One must say thank you to people, even if the surveillance they do isn't optional.

I fired up the desktop computer, half expecting to see my own face on it as an inside surveillance tool – then reminded myself that I wasn't a movie character.

After checking my e-mail and saving the replies from the President, the Attorney General, the Secretary of State and Secretary Lassiter – and thinking that it was really cool to have been listened to and answered – I logged onto the homepage of *The New York Times*.

The big story was not about Nae-Née for a change. This one was about the environment, though indirectly. It was announcing that New York City was completely out of burial plots in ALL of its cemeteries.

Here we were returning from Venice, where burials in that city are only for a set period of time before the dead are disinterred and moved elsewhere, and I read that the burial plots in New York City – in all 5 boroughs – have been exhausted. There is absolutely no more space. People will have to either be cremated or buried far from the city. And then what? Use up more land that the living could be benefitting from?!

It annoyed me just to think about it. I have always wanted to be cremated when I die, and that was before I became aware of environmental issues. Why couldn't the U.S. be like Japan about death rituals, and require that no one be allowed to use up land…and thus require cremation?! It seemed as though many people did not care about the next generation; only that they got to enjoy the old way of life and death themselves. It was someone else's problem.

The problem with burial is all that preservation stuff that they do to you; they practically pickle you with embalming fluid so that you won't decay. Well…if you're Jewish or Muslim they don't, but the part of being dead that I dread is exactly what the Jews and Muslims don't try to evade: maggots.

Also, the ratio of inflexibility on the point of being buried after death seems to increase in direction relation to the ratio of religiousness. The more religious the person, the more determined that she or he will be to stick with burial, regardless of how environmentally unhelpful that is. But back to the maggots…

I want to preempt the maggots, and never, ever give them a chance at me.

My mother was appalled when I told her this, which I had done on the off chance that I might predecease her. It's always wise to let your family know your wishes rather than just hope or assume that they will do what you want. If you don't tell them, they just won't know. And then chances are that they will do the exact opposite – at great expense – of what you want.

So I told her that I want to be cremated. Of course, make sure that I am really dead first.

Well, she was horrified. She didn't want to do that for me. She said she wouldn't.

Which of course led to a fight over something that might never happen…what an uproar.

Now I found myself reading all this about no more room at the cemeteries. It wasn't the first time that I had thought of this – the expense of burial, the excess of resources used in this form of corpse disposal, the unavailability of the land used to the living – but now here was evidence that large numbers of the rest of the human population were being made aware of this.

I pointed it out to Hamish. "I feel like we're still in Venice just looking at this story." Venetians only allowed 100-year stays in the city's one cemetery; then the coffins had to be moved to other cemeteries inland.

Then I said what I thought of burial and told Hamish how horrified I was about maggots. I asked his opinion and he said he agreed. I made him promise…

And with that, he started shouting, "Okay! Enough! I don't want to think about this anymore!" and started crying. Not much…but a little.

"Hamish!" I said, grabbing him for a hug. "It's all hypothetical, and just me getting mad about the environment again. Why are you crying?"

He hugged me back. "I don't want to think about you being dead. We're under heavy guard and I worry about you all the time – when you go out for groceries, when you want to go walking – and now you're talking about this. Don't."

"Okay. I love you, Hamish. Don't worry; we won't end up dead until we've lived out our natural life spans. But be careful what you wish for; you may get it."

He looked up from our hug and grinned at me. That was his line, and it cheered him up.

With that, we sat down to go over our photos from the Venice trip, and to call my parents. Eowyn was so happy to see us that she kept jumping up on the dinner table and walking around the laptop. Somehow, I got the photos labeled, filed, and copied onto the desktop – though that last was just a matter of plugging in the memory stick and clicking and dragging.

We spent the next half hour playing chase-the-catnip-toy with her before unpacking.

"Do we dare go out to dinner?" I asked Hamish. "I don't want to cook. Doing that would mean buying groceries, and I refuse to allow N.S.A. to do the shopping for me – ever."

He looked at me unhappily, then took out his cell phone and called someone.

"Who did you call?"

"Despite the fact that N.S.A. wants to take over their job, Blackout Security is still working for us. I won't fire them. I actually have more confidence in them than in No Such Agency," he told me. "Plus, we pay them, so if we want to go out for any reason, they will help us without trying to talk us out of it."

"Oh. Well…let's go to A.O.C. It's not too far away."

"Fine. Let's go." Hamish seemed glad to hear the name of a place that was only a couple of blocks away.

Rick and Ed were standing at the door when we opened it. A light rain was falling, so I had brought the huge umbrella. It was a transparent one with Steinlen's black cats on it; I had gotten it on sale at the Metropolitan Museum of Art Store a few years earlier.

As we walked out, Rick took the umbrella from me and opened it, scrutinizing the thing.

"Do you like cats?" I asked, puzzled by his behavior.

"What? Oh – yeah – but anyone can see you through this thing." He handed it back to me unhappily. "Don't you have an opaque one?"

I stared at him. "Somewhere, but I'd have to tear apart the closet to get at it. Why is this such a problem? Extremists could see us from the front, too. All they have to do is walk towards us rather than behind us, and they'll know who we are."

Rick and Ed looked at each other, then said, "We'll get the car."

"The car?! For just a couple of blocks? Why not shoot us as we go from the car to the door of the restaurant? Or poison our food? Or hit us with poison dart guns while we eat, or…"

"Avril!" Hamish gripped my arm, trying to calm me down.

"Fine. I'll give up all exercise and get fat to please the extremists. I hate gyms. I want long walks in the city." I was getting really annoyed at the RE twits now…assholes.

Rick and Ed hadn't moved yet.

I stood there looking like I wanted to cry but not quite able to do it. I must have looked trapped. Damnit, politicians had more fun. At least they could go out jogging if they wanted to. Why was I forced to argue about my every move?

Hawke and Lambert appeared. "What's going on?"

Before any of the men could speak, I did. "I want to walk, not be driven, two blocks to a restaurant. I'm not fool enough to shout out its name on an open street so that some RE extremist can run on ahead and poison our dinner or shoot us or whatever, but I don't want to give up walking around the city and only exercise in some horrible gym. I realize that you guys probably use gyms all the time and won't see why I hate the smelly places full of staring people, but I won't use one. I want to enjoy great food and walk it off. That's what French people do to enjoy life and keep thin, and I won't give that up!"

They all stared at me unhappily. Clearly, I was a recalcitrant nightmare of a charge. Hamish just looked like the typical long-suffering sort of husband with the programmed words "Yes, dear" on the tip of his tongue, but he said nothing.

Finally, I said, "Well? Are you guys going to help me live a normal life, or not? I'll take my chances if you won't. I'm not your prisoner. And taking my chances is getting very tempting. I've just read more grim news about overpopulation and global warming, and I'm younger than my husband. Maybe I'll just avoid a miserable widowhood. Or you can help live my life as I wish, and then Hamish can have his wish come true – widowhood someday for me."

With that, still neither crying nor calm, I took the transparent cat umbrella, opened it, and moved off in the direction of A.O.C.

Suddenly Hamish was right beside me, under the umbrella, walking with me. He put his arm around my shoulders and just walked with me.

I looked up at him sideways. His expression was inscrutable. I looked at the street ahead of me again.

"Are they coming too?" I asked him after a moment.

"Yes."

"Good. I've been wondering what it would be like to come back under guard. I loved being able to wander around Venice without feeling followed and at risk, able to come and go as I pleased. It seemed that you did, too. I was having such fun because of that that I was dreading coming home, even though I missed it here with our cat." I started to cry now, just a little.

Hamish squeezed my shoulders as we walked. "I thought of that too. I guess it doesn't matter whether we cower in cars with dark-tinted windows or walk wherever and whenever we want; if the RE assholes are looking for us, they'll find us."

"I'm glad you see it that way…I think. I'm not crazy; I don't want to get maimed or killed, or worse – have that happen to you – but I was more willing to be driven around in those cars when the paparazzi were in our faces. Now that I just don't see any of them, I want to walk freely about the city again."

He looked at me. "We're old news now, it seems."

"I'm so glad to hear it. We've had much more than our 15 minutes of fame by now."

"Oh, I'm sure we'll get a lot more of it before we're through."

I didn't doubt it. We had arrived at the restaurant.

We asked for a table, and were seated immediately.

"Hamish!" I whispered urgently to him, embarrassed. "We just got seated ahead of some people! We didn't have a reservation!"

"Yeah we did," he replied. "Our escort called ahead and asked that we be seated in the back of the restaurant."

"Did you tell them where we were going?"

"Yes – on the phone before we went outside."

I sighed. Ed and Rick were right behind us, being seated at a small table for two off to the side, with a perfect view of the entire dining room.

We were followed everywhere now by both Blackout Security and No Such Agency.

All this was in anticipation of also being followed by RE's nut-jobs.

But where were they? I kept wondering about that; as yet, Hamish and I had yet to see anyone who seemed at all interested in us as we went about our business.

I compromised in my walking habits; if I walked home from work or around the neighborhood to buy groceries, Hamish would accompany me, claiming that it was just to carry whatever I bought. But I knew the real reason; he was scared about my safety and wanted to confirm it himself. He wouldn't have been able to concentrate at the lab if I had gone out alone.

So I ended up buying enough food to avoid going shopping more than once a week and accepting rides home from the stores regardless of the weather. That meant that Hamish could get more work done at the lab with the peace of mind that came from knowing I was being driven about the city under armed escort. In return, he rode home the same way.

That was the convenient thing about being the wife on my end of the deal; my husband was a typical male in that he didn't like to shop and wouldn't need grocery store escorts. He usually just came right home, so I didn't have to worry about extra danger to him.

Once, he came home with a dozen raspberry pink roses for me.

Instead of responding properly to the gift and just kissing him, I asked, "Where did you have to go to get these? Was it a safe, enclosed place?"

He just sighed and said no, he chose them from one of the many open places around the city with buckets of bouquets on the street. "If RE is going to get me, they would need to either follow the car as it takes a different route every night, or be psychic and wait at whatever florist shop I stop at. I gave no warning about this; I just suddenly asked Ed to stop the car. Total impulse buy…"

More worrying for nothing; I wondered how long that would last. By now it was April; the 1ˢᵗ of the month, to be exact. I kissed my husband, thanked him again for the roses, inhaled their perfume deeply, and got a vase out.

"It seems that I am living up to Mark Twain's expectations today," I remarked.

"How so?"

"I'll give you the April Fool's Day quote: "April 1ˢᵗ: this is the day upon which we are reminded of what we are on the other 364.""

"That's pretty good," Hamish said with a laugh. "Did he say anything about golf? I hate that game, never mind that Scots invented it."

I started serving up dinner; penne pasta with homemade pesto sauce and tomato soup, also from scratch. "Golf is a good walk spoiled," I quoted.

Hamish roared with laughter. "That's what I think too."

The next day it was clear and pleasant out.

I kept looking out the window as I wrote at my desk. Cabin fever had set in, and I wanted to walk home. For that matter, I wanted to walk across campus to the dining hall rather than order take-out from the Indian place yet again. We had stopped going to Le Pain Quotidien.

Kay brought in some messages; I noticed that Andrew had called me.

I called him back.

"Hey, Avril!" he said cheerfully into the phone.

"Hey, Andrew!" I replied. "How are you?"

"Great – I found a job for my errant daughter, and I'm walking around the city on my way to a hoarder house. I wanted to thank you for mentioning her without giving away her identity while advocating for a better delivery system of Nae-Née. I really appreciate you fighting for women to be treated decently as they get those devices implanted."

I was stunned for a moment; then happy.

"Wow. Thanks. It just made me really angry to think that women were being scolded and manhandled if they got upset. Just because something is the law is no reason why someone should have to like it and behave placidly. And just because another person is carrying out that law is no reason to expect and require quiet, uncomplaining compliance. Compliance is all they should expect; demanding passive acceptance from someone who feels as though all hope of happiness is being eliminated is hideous."

Silence.

"Are you still there, Andrew?"

"Yeah, I'm still there. I just didn't realize that you felt so strongly about the way that she was treated. She was pretty horrible to you."

"Oh, I'll always be angry with her for that, and with myself for not having the perfect come-back line as she shrieked at me. That's been the story of my life with bullies. But I don't see why people should be expected to just like and want the same things, or passively accept upsetting situations."

"There are a lot of people who would do that to avoid conflict."

"I'm not one of them. I won't flee from conflict, even though I hate conflict."

"Why?"

"Because what is easier at the instant that conflict arises is ultimately too hard to live with after that moment – at least, I find it so."

Silence.

"Andrew? Are you still there?"

"I'm still there. You're just giving me a lot to think about. But that's okay. It's probably why I like to be friends with you."

"Oh. Well…that's got to be one of the nicest compliments I've ever gotten."

"You're welcome."

"Thanks. What was the job you found for Patsy? Did she get it? Is it okay with her?"

"She got it, and she's lucky to have anything. I had another contact from my days at Harvard – good thing I keep in touch with my classmates – another professor friend. She's a secretary at Columbia University now, in the Economics Department. Hopefully, she won't feel at odds with her new boss; he's her age, married, and the son of my classmate."

"That sounds pretty good. Is she still with Jim?"

"Yes, but I don't think they'll ever get married. It was all contingent upon having a kid. Otherwise, he doesn't see why he ought to get married."

"I could suggest something: legal benefits. A wife is an advocate when you are in the hospital, she is a tax break if married and filing jointly, and a companion who will stick around."

"I'll see if I can run that by him. Look, I've got to run; I'm almost there, but I'll call you again soon."

"Okay, bye."

We rang off, and I decided to get something to eat; Hamish was still in his lab.

I decided to live dangerously and walk across campus alone. I told Kay, "I'm going to walk over to the dining hall for lunch," I said, getting my jacket from the hooks behind her desk. "It's such a nice day out."

"Yes, it is," she replied, typing away. Kay did not know about all the security precautions around us – which was another security precaution. I was just going across campus, so I thought I ought to be able to walk from one building to another in the fresh air without calling out the National Guard.

I went down the hall, rode the elevator to the ground floor, and walked outside. The dining hall was just a few minutes' walk from our building. It was beautiful out; the flowers had started to bloom and there were buds on all of the trees. I loved springtime. Global warming was making it earlier and earlier, but I still enjoyed it.

Halfway between the buildings, I heard a shout.

"Avril!" I looked back. It was Hamish, running towards me as fast as he could. He had something small in his right hand, and he was wearing a lab coat. "Get down!"

BANG! A bullet whizzed past me from another direction. I hit the deck, narrowly avoiding some puddles on the walkway.

Damnit. Now what? Sooner or later they would just aim lower, I thought.

Whoever was in RE, they had found me. Maybe they had just been waiting for either or us to walk around the campus – and I had just obliged them. The place had a security service, but it wasn't a gated community. Anyone could walk on and off of it.

I looked wildly around for Hamish, keeping my head low. Might as well try to see what was going on; there was no cover here, and if I was going to get shot, at least I would know what happened to the person who mattered most to me.

Hamish was still running towards me; things were happening so fast. One minute it was just a normal day of chatting with friends on the phone and going to lunch, the next it was getting shot at, presumably by whoever was in RE. Right now, the legalese pun wasn't so amusing.

Hamish caught up to me and jumped onto my back, covering me, looking anxiously all around us. Another bullet whizzed past, but it hit a tree. Peering out from under my husband, who was panting on top of me in a panic, I had a clear view right down 66th Street. I hadn't passed it yet when the bullets had started flying, and they seemed to be coming from that direction. East 66th Street led to the main gate of the Rockefeller campus.

These assholes in RE probably hated me and my husband equally, I thought as I lay flat my stomach, pinned under Hamish, who wasn't letting me get up: me for thinking of Nae-Née and my husband for making it a reality…damn them. The hell with them for objecting to this extent – for trying to kill us! I was suddenly even angrier at not being able to fight back.

Hamish put his left arm across me protectively and suddenly reared up slightly, aiming whatever was in his right hand. That gave me a chance to look up and see whose footsteps were rapidly approaching us. He was so close – perhaps 25 feet away, and closing fast.

It was a tall, thin lanky guy, a doppelganger of the one who had shot the President. I got a really good look at his face; he had large, white teeth that were just slightly crooked, and pale green eyes. He wore casual clothing, and was pointing a gun at our faces. Odd; I thought the Secret Service had killed that guy, I mused as I peered up at him.

Hamish didn't hesitate.

Both men raised their weapons, but Hamish was quicker. He fired before the blond RE guy, and I saw…nothing.

Nothing, that is, until an instant later, when the man dropped his gun and started writhing and twisting on the ground.

Hamish fired again, this time off to the right. Another guy was sitting with a laptop and headphones on the steps of Founder's Hall, facing the main gate. The computer hacker was a short, heavy-set guy with curly brown hair and a plaid shirt on over his tee shirt, plus jeans and sneakers. He looked just like any other computer geek anywhere else in the country. The geek slid off the steps, and started writhing around on the front walkway, his computer abandoned.

More footsteps, and Hamish fired again, and hit Agent Lambert.

Oops.

Poor Lambert starting writhing too, but Hamish wouldn't release me until he saw the rest of the No Such Agency guys swarm the campus, fanning out in all directions. Ed and Rick and Chris and Joe soon joined them.

At last, Hamish sat back on the damp sidewalk and pulled me into a sitting position, hugging me.

I stared at him for a moment, amazed, then kissed him. "Thanks, hero! Now tell me what you did to them. Can you help Agent Lambert? He's on our side, isn't he?"

Hamish stopping grinning and looked mortified. "Oh! Sorry Keith! Here..." he went over to him, pressed the gun up against his neck, and pulled the trigger again. Lambert seemed to relax instantly, and gave an audible sigh of relief.

I watched, fascinated. What had my husband invented now?

Hamish came back over to me and pulled me to my feet. Then he grabbed me and hugged me tight. "Why did you walk across the campus alone?! You should have waited for me!" Then he hugged me tightly again.

The N.S.A. agents and Blackout guys were still rushing about, checking everything in sight and out of sight over and over again. The men that Hamish had shot were now shrieking in agony as well as writhing.

The N.S.A. guys were merciless; they cuffed them and dragged them to their feet. They pulled them away to a waiting car, where they shoved them inside. Then someone stomped on the gas pedal and the car sped off.

I looked at Hamish and asked him, "What did you do to them? And what is that, a Nae-Née gun? It sure looks like one."

He looked down at his right hand. He seemed to have forgotten that he was still clutching something in it tightly.

He held it up to show me, and it was indeed a nanite injector gun, complete with all of the usual switches: Fire, BackFire, and Safety, which was the same thing as an off switch.

I looked up at him and grinned. "Did you invent something and keep it a secret from everyone?" I had to ask.

"You're damn right I did," he replied, grinning back at me.

Chapter 32

Hamish the Usurper

Hamish is a Scottish name that means usurper. I hadn't thought about that while he was protecting me – while there were N.S.A. and Blackout security agents all around us to do that – but my husband had just lived up to his name in the most spectacular manner.

Unbeknownst to any of us – not to me, not to No Such Agency, not to Blackout Security – Hamish had invented something on his own time, both in his lab at the Rockefeller Institute and in his other one in my parents' basement.

It was a nanite defense system.

He carried it at all times, in one of the same nanite injection guns that was used to distribute Nae-Née. But these nanites had other than medical applications. At first glance, they seemed purely defensive in nature. But if one's point of view were reversed along with one's intent, it could be said with equal truth that the nanites were an offensive weapon.

The nanites that he had loaded his weapon with could be aimed from a distance of 20 feet before their trajectory lost precision. Firing the weapon while pressed up against the skin of one's target was also an option.

Once inside the enemy, the nanites would wreak havoc with the person's nervous system, latching onto the first nerves it encountered, first causing a pins-and-needles sensation, followed by sharp itching and stabbing sensations, and then aggravating up to severe pain. The intensity of the nerve-attack built up rapidly if the weapon was simply fired into a subject.

It had begun as a medical diagnosis and treatment system for neurons. At least, that was Hamish's original intent, and he hadn't given up on that. For now it worked as a weapon. At his laboratory in the Rockefeller Institute, he was still trying to make it useful to neurosurgeons and other physicians, but that was for the future. Meanwhile, he a secret weapon all his own.

The nanites caused no permanent damage – just maddening distraction and later torture.

They could be withdrawn with the same gun that they were deployed with – simply press the trigger end up against the target's skin and hit the reverse switch, and the nanites could be recalled, withdrawn back up into the gun.

Or not…that was the beauty of the invention.

When all was said and done, it looked like the good doctor had invented a weapon of mass distraction.

I was certain that the government would want it as a means of crowd control and for secret interrogations. It was better than water-boarding, I thought, because it would leave no trace. I didn't approve of that use; I merely noted the device's multiple applications.

But Hamish had been keeping his little nerve-phaser under wraps, saving it for when it would be needed most. After that, he would share it…because No Such Agency would insist, and any objection would be wasted breath. What N.S.A. wants, it gets.

Now I understood why he had taken to wearing lab coats; he didn't like them. The coats provided an easy way to hide the injector guns but keep them within quick and easy reach.

Later, when I asked him why he hadn't just bought a gun, he told me that he wanted something unexpected that was completely under the radar screen of both our protectors, in whom had imperfect confidence, and our hunters, whom he desired to have some sort of advantage over.

Well, he certainly had one. My husband had super-powers. He was a genius, and he actively used his ability to protect us. He was the coolest guy ever for that, and I wasted no time in telling him so.

"You don't think I'm a monster for creating this?" he asked me in amazement, after all was said and done.

"No, definitely not," I said. "What makes someone a monster is the circumstances under which they fire a weapon, combined with their reasons for doing so. It's all in one's point of view, anyway."

Then I gave him a kiss befitting a hero receiving his due.

It was one of many that he got that day, all from me.

Chapter 33

RE: The Raid

Of course the guys from No Such Agency wanted new toys just like the one that Hamish had invented for himself.

"You're not getting the prototype from me," he said. "I need it to protect my wife. She and I would be dead if I hadn't had it, so I'm keeping it. I'll share the design, and you can get your own made," he told Hawke.

As Hamish was still holding the thing at the time, Hawke hadn't argued.

Hamish escorted me to the dining hall, where we sat eating our lunch side by side, facing the rest of the room, unwilling to sit with our backs to a door or window, or the rest of the room for that matter. I paused to lean against my hero a couple of times, grinning at him. I wasn't very hungry after the uproar, just a little bit…enough to eat a small lunch. Hamish ate a lot, though. He kept one arm around me for just about the entire meal.

As soon as we were settled with our trays, I took out my cell phone and called my parents, and then called Grandmère too, just in case she turned on the news and heard about a shootout at the Rockefeller University Institute campus. I had to beat her to that, and preempt any potential heart attacks.

Once everyone was assured that we were alive and well and unharmed despite anything that might be announced on the news later in the afternoon, I started eating. I thought about what Grandmère might be doing right now; probably watching the midday news before going back to her novels. I could just imagine the scene; she and Aunt Zoe sitting down to their salads in time to hear "Breaking News Update: Shootout in New York City at the Rockefeller Campus" – but they would know not to worry.

My parents had insisted upon talking to Hamish and thanking him for protecting me.

He had really enjoyed that. It was quite a change from being errant the son-in-law who tinkered in their basement, unable to make money, and unhappy about it.

Hawke and Lambert came in and sat down with trays of chicken soup and coffee. They kept a polite distance from us, as did the other diners, but I noticed that Lambert looked beat. He wasn't watching us or the other people much; he let Hawke keep vigil as he ate his soup, spooning it in like it was medicine.

We finished our food, waved to them and said we would be right back with coffee, and went to dump our trays and get it. Then we sat down across from them. It was probably a breach of procedure, but Hawke didn't jump up or start searching the room. I saw him nod to some other guys seated across the dining hall, though.

Hamish looked at Lambert. "Sorry I got you – I was just reacting to anyone who came at us. Are you okay?"

Hawke cracked up. "He is now that he changed his shorts. How soon can we get some of those nanite phasers of yours?"

"Come back to the lab with me after this and we'll do that. How are you doing, Keith?"

Lambert looked up at last. He reached for his coffee and took a sip. "I'll be fine. Were those nanites? It looked like nothing came out of that gun, until the itching and stinging started. Then I felt as though I were being stung internally by a swarm of hornets."

"Oh yeah. Those were nanites, all right. It started out as a treatment technique for neurosurgeons to use, and I haven't given up on that project. But along the way I realized that the system had another application and prepared this gun. It's full of more ammo. Tell your colleagues that if they want to remove the nanites from those two assassins, all they have to do is get an empty Nae-Née gun, press it up against the guy's skin, and hit the Backfire button."

Hawke took out his phone and made a call, looking around the room to see whether or not we could have been overheard, then apparently decided that there was no chance of that. The nearest diners were a couple of professors seated three tables away; two librarians sat at the one behind theirs. He hung up a minute later.

I had a sudden thought. "Hamish, what if you fire that nanite gun and no human being is in range? Do the nanites get into you instead? Or do they just get into the air, and attack the first person to come in range of them?"

He looked at me, concerned. "I know you can instantly hit the Backfire button to get them back in, but I haven't had a chance to test it that way yet. The nanites are programmed to go forward in the direction in which you fire the gun. But to just leave them there in the chaos, subject to wind patterns, could be a problem."

"That's the trouble with any technology that humans create," I commented. "Whatever we do, it has the potential to come back and bite us somehow, if not by hurting us immediately then by ruining the environment. I can just picture some government raid allowing the nanites to get away. Is there some sort of nanite-sensing vacuum cleaner that could be used, one that could account for every last bit of nanite ammo that gets fired in a chaotic situation – something that could be used after the fact?"

Hamish was smiling now. "You're always thinking ahead. "Yes, there is, and any assault team that uses these nanite guns should carry them – one for each combatant. It could account for all ammo brought to a fight, and make sure that all of it is either in a gun or itching a suspect to distraction. I'll include that in the package I prepare for them this afternoon."

"Good. I can relax about that now. I just don't want to think that the government or anyone else is causing irreparable damage to this planet or to innocent people because you or I missed something that we should have included. Once they have something from us, that's it – our chance to prevent that is gone."

Hawke, Lambert, and my husband were all listening to me intently. At least, I had to assume that that was what they were doing, because they weren't saying anything, and they kept watching me as I spoke. When people do that, I always wonder what they're thinking. But that's just me being unsure as to how to interpret nonverbal cues. It drives me crazy, though.

Hamish insisted upon staying with me until I was safely ensconced in my office. He wouldn't let the N.S.A. or anyone else hurry me through my lunch or coffee, and he escorted me to the rest room, waiting outside until I came out. I realized that he went to the men's room while I was in there, but still, he wouldn't go back to the lab right away, and I just knew that the guys from No Such Agency were chafing at the bit to get their hands on some nanite guns and nanite vacuums.

At last, we went back, and Kay leapt at us, wanting to know if we were all right and what had happened. I said good-bye for now to Hamish and the agents, and they went down the hall. Apparently, Hamish had made a few other prototypes and could let a couple of them go now. He would be back shortly to make a data package for them, which they had orders to rush to their own technology facilities.

I went into my office and turned on the television, and then sat down at the computer. Kay followed me, wearing an expression on her face that clearly demanded some information and to hurry up with it. I liked her; she was like a big sister and a secretary rolled into one.

"Come on, have a seat and I'll tell you all about it," I said to her.

She sat down on the sofa, and I filled her in on Hamish's heroics, the agents, the RE guys, the eerie resemblance to the President's would-be assassin of the guy who shot at us, everything. I left out the part about the government agents being from N.S.A., though. I just let her think that it was the F.B.I. She didn't push for details; either she missed that part as a matter of routine, not being into details, or she was aware and not pushing for too much information.

"I'm glad you're okay," she said. "And you're very lucky to have Hamish."

I grinned. "I know – he's my hero."

She grinned and walked out to her desk, satisfied that all was well.

But all wasn't well…not yet. The monsters who were in RE were still out there, on the loose. Hamish may have enabled N.S.A. to nab the assassin's doppelganger plus a computer hacker, but the ex-Senator and his gang of crazies were still out there.

Where were they? No idea. Tennessee? Idaho? Both? More places? Did they have a compound to use as a hideout? More than one? Was it like the Branch Davidians, or were they at some sort of terrorist training camps spread out here, there and everywhere?

I sure hoped that No Such Agency had been working on this. Certainly, the government had plenty of its own cyber security experts to find out and monitor whatever there was to know.

It wouldn't do me any good to worry about it.

So I went back to worrying about world news. *The New York Times* website had plenty of grim news that was made to order for bringing me back down to an introspective mood from the one of elation that Hamish had left me in.

The Brazilians had killed off a few species of fish in an Amazon River tributary that they had dammed up, plus they had flooded a lot of the Amazon Rain Forest and displaced lots of native people from their homes. As if that weren't foolish enough, they had allowed more than a third of the Amazon Rain Forest to be…deforested. Might as well just dump out the contents of the planet's medicine cabinet, I thought, outraged. It was like using up a renewable resource all at once for a one-time hurrah of money. What were they going to do once it was spent?!

Fly fishers were unhappy about all the damage that had been done to North American rivers by felt on the soles of their boots before the stuff had been outlawed and replaced by metal cleats on rubber soles shaped like tire treads. Orvis had managed to redo its inventory with impressive speed, but the streams were now infected with something called rock snot by the unhappy hobbyists. Who knew how many species had died…but when the fly fishing enthusiasts and chefs found out, they would be very sorry.

Sea level was rising; Nauru was completely uninhabitable now with its residents living in New Zealand and worrying about a loss of national identity and culture, and the glaciers of Greenland and Antarctica were only expected to melt faster this summer.

New Yorkers were already talking in frantic tones about fears of their city becoming exactly what I had thought about every day on our vacation: the New Venice. With the graveyards all used up and the Hudson and East Rivers lapping at the undersides of the wharves and quays, with flooding happening in the subways of the five boroughs every summer, none of that anxiety seemed at all far-fetched. It actually sounded quite reasonable.

The litany of environmental woes went on and on.

How long could we live in Manhattan before it began to shrink?

I didn't like the idea one bit. It scared me to think of such a visible change in my own lifetime. It was the kind of change that could ruin this fun playground of a city, which was full of priceless art in many museums, culture that couldn't be moved, and on and on and on as one thought about the irreplaceable aspects of any city that could sink as soon as enough ice melted, and faster than any of us realized. Now I knew how people felt elsewhere in the world.

Hamish came in to check on me after a few hours, and I realized how absorbing these problems were when I remembered that he had been protecting me from a murderous fanatic just a little while ago.

It was time to go home. He had given No Such Agency what they wanted.

He had known that the moment he used that nanite gun, they would want their own and they would simply seize the data if he didn't walk them through the details and package it all up for them with user-friendly instructions. National security is such a versatile excuse for that.

The next day, a new website appeared on the Internet. Shortly after it appeared, news stations everywhere announced the fact with all the pomp and circumstance of a breaking story that accompanies competitive career-building habits.

Reproduction Entitlement had announced its own existence.

So...the N.S.A. had successfully persuaded the President to let them announce themselves.

Just as well; this way, they were less aware of what the government was thinking. Perhaps, as far as RE was concerned, the government had revealed nothing. Thus far, it looked like a game of poker. Funny, but I thought that a game of chess would be a better strategy. Maybe that was for the showdown.

I checked out the website.

It had a whole page devoted to making heroes out of a pair of identical twins. It described their lives in some detail, and apparently, the authors of the site's content were under the impression that both twins were dead.

That was news to me; Hamish hadn't killed anyone. Had the twin later died in custody? Had the nanites driven him to distraction and somehow killed him? Or was the government playing mind games with RE? If so, that was fine with me. If not, I wasn't about to cry over the death of a man who had shot at me. My only regret would be if they had failed to extract every last bit of information from him about RE before he died a miserable death.

Whatever was going on with that twin, I wanted to see what RE wanted to share with the world about our enemy's background.

Jeb and Jared Clyde were exactly what they looked like: identical twins. Born in October of 1976, they had grown up in Idaho, in some mountains called the Lost River Range. They had been home schooled by their evangelist parents, which had emphasized Bible studies. What a surprise. The rest of their education had resembled a 19th-century schoolhouse curriculum until they were past their teens.

Their mother had supplied a lot the information, the web page added. She and the twins' father had decided that their sons should not see a computer until they would be less impressionable and likely to surf the Internet for pornography, because that was the work of the devil. Sex was for procreation only, they had taught their boys.

Their father had taught them to hunt, was a member of the National Rifle Association, and had trained them in the use of other guns as well as how to apply for a gun permit. The twins knew all about guns by the time they were in their early teens, and practiced sharp-shooting at a range in the woods near their home.

When their computer training began, the parents had gone all out, buying the latest equipment, two of each, standard home personal computers for them to learn on. The family was self-taught, using books bought at a community college. On their infrequent trips to town, they would buy lots of Internet cards and use them to access satellites rather than endure the painfully slow dial-up connections that the phone company offered in their remote area.

They had met other gun-toting, right-wing, anti-abortion and anti-birth control individuals over the many on-line chat rooms that the Internet had to offer. For several years, they just helped their parents out on the family's sawmill. Trips into town were saved for selling lumber and picking up supplies; other than that, the twins had had very little direct social contact with anyone other than their parents, except for those online chats.

The family apparently followed some news events, because they did know about 9/11 – who didn't? But instead of sympathizing with the people who died in the World Trade Center, the Pentagon and in that field in Pennsylvania, they had gone the other way: they blamed the United States government for the attacks.

Their reasoning was convoluted at best.

The way that they saw it, the capitalists should never have gotten so friendly with foreigners in the first place. The family were Republicans, but not happy with every single item on the party's list. What the Clydes did not agree with was the lack of self-sufficiency in our use of fossil fuels. From their point of view, America should have mined its own lands for oil, in Texas, Alaska, and wherever else we could find it, regardless of the impact on the environment.

The Clydes also believed that global warming was a myth, just a lot of hype to destroy the American automobile industry.

They certainly had a lot of opinions for people who stayed home, did no traveling, and only read certain points of view in their research efforts.

I thought about that for a moment; no, I did turn on Glenn Beck, Sean Hannity and Bill O'Reilly's shows on occasion, if only for the amusement of hearing how they sounded. I supposed that they did the same thing with Keith Olbermann sometimes, but then what did I know about their TV-watching habits? I knew I sounded like the pot calling the kettle biased.

Anyway, back to the web page; I wanted to see when the twins' lives had intersected with the Senator's.

There it was, halfway down the page.

It was in 2011, just when Nae-Née was hitting the market.

Why the delay?

Apparently, the gun groups had been enough for them until then.

It was birth control with convenience for all that had pushed them into searching for anti-abortion groups on-line.

From there, the brothers had been willing to deal with anyone who felt disenfranchised by Nae-Née once the governments of the world had begun chattering both behind the scenes and openly on the political stages about making its use mandatory.

So that was why they were involved, and personally bent on killing me and Hamish.

But they couldn't be the only ones.

I clicked around on the site; Muslims and Christians alike were angry about not being able to have as many children as they wanted to until any age, and had a statement about being willing to work together on this issue to protect their God- or Allah-given right to do so.

There was even a page on the site that made a hero out of Senator Boenher for fighting for that right on the Senate chamber floor, of all things. To top it all off, RE thanked him for conceiving (great word choice!) of the idea of this group, its name, its manifesto (see hyperlink for that) and for funding its activities out of his family's tobacco fortune. Charming…

I left the site and looked around for news of the ex-Senator. It didn't take long to find it.

Boenher had walled himself up in his estate in Tennessee, which was near Memphis but out in the countryside, with his wife and teenage daughters and little boys and other girl. He was evading prosecution for his attack on Senator Amy LaRosse. Bounty hunters had been dispatched, but had failed to catch him. He had made his estate impregnable, and protected his family and friends from being arrested for harboring him by having food and supplies delivered.

He had been sending people out to pick them up at the front gate. The quantities of groceries had been peculiar – much more than a family of eight would need to eat comfortably. It seem to be more like a family of 40, judging by how much toilet paper and other items had been brought in.

Lots of grocery businesses had truck services; you could point and click your order and a company truck would pull up to your property with the stuff, and you could just bring it inside. Easy. Hamish and I had done it once when we didn't have our car up at the University of Connecticut, with Stop & Shop. It was only once, while the car was having some work done, but the service was so expensive – the same price for two-thirds as much of everything – that I had never used it again.

So who was in that estate with them, I wondered? Probably some more RE members. I found some news sites that had gathered some bird's-eye images of the Boenher estate with helicopters, and saw that the place had lots of guesthouses and other outbuildings capable of housing people with heat, water and electricity; definitely room for other members.

But were there other shooters among RE's members, or were the Clyde twins all they had? There had to be more of them, it seemed to me. What did these guys do, train to shoot at the Idaho sawmill and then lay low in Tennessee with the Boenher family?

Oh well. At least the government had satellite technology, techno-telepathy due to listening devices and other surveillance equipment, and lots of its own computer experts. I couldn't guess the bad guys' every move, and I didn't need to. It seemed that they were closing in on RE.

Later that same week, on a Friday to be specific, late in April, we found ourselves glued to the television for the day, eating Indian take-out. We were doing it by choice this time, just so that we wouldn't have to miss a moment of the excitement.

Every major news channel was carrying the story, so we just let MSNBC run. I can't stand channel-surfing. I'll do it once, to confirm that a story is big enough news to be on all of the stations, then pick my favorite and stick with it.

No Such Agency – though the news stations had been told it was the F.B.I. – had identified the main hideout of Reproduction Entitlement, a.k.a. RE.

There were some other ones, but those were also identified and surrounded, we were informed.

It was obvious that the government wanted a big show, and that they were ready with all of the chess pieces in place, knowing that the enemy was check-mated before they moved in on the RE sites.

The Clyde family's sawmill and its surrounding woods had indeed been surrounded. What an irony that global warning deniers lived in an area called the Lost River Range.

So had the Tennessee estate of the ex-Senator.

It was one thing to have been secretly informed of the existence of the separatists and the ex-Senator's involvement with them. It was quite another to be able to look at images of their lairs online and understand that their world was about to get narrower and narrower as the news cameras circled like predators but staying just out of gunfire range. Telephoto lenses came in handy as we watched like voyeurs, waiting for the excitement to start.

For about an hour, it was rather dull; nothing happened.

No one came barreling out of either compound.

Then the house by the sawmill burst into activity. Gunshots echoed as volleys were shot out of windows in several directions. The F.B.I. returned fire. It took about twenty minutes before all went quiet. Then someone spoke into a loudspeaker, and a cell phone was propelled into a broken window by a robot.

Fifteen minutes after that, the father of the Clyde twins, Willard, came out onto the porch.

He looked like he was hiding something on his left side; there was an odd bulge under his robe. He just stood there, holding the phone in his right hand, saying nothing and staring dully into the woods where the F.B.I. agents were hidden.

He seemed to be looking for something. After a couple of minutes, he must have found it, because he raised the rifle he had under his bathrobe and fell back against the wall of the house before he could lift it up enough to fire it. He fell on his side and didn't get up again.

With that, agents swarmed the house, dragging out several bodies, shouting into their cell phones and pointing at the house over and over again. We counted nine bodies, and so did the newscasters.

Among them was Dora Clyde, the twins' mother. She was wearing overalls and a pink work shirt with sneakers, and she had her hair twisted up.

Her husband was brought over and laid next to her. He was wearing jeans under his bathrobe, and as the telephoto lens zoomed closer – easy now that the shooting was over and the news crews felt safe enough to move in on the scene – it was clear that he had been fully dressed for combat, only wearing the bathrobe to conceal his rifle.

The other eight bodies would be identified by the government later in the day, and the information released to all major news channels. They were just what RE's site had led us to expect: Islamists and Bible-belters who had gone to the Clyde sawmill for a sharpshooter training course. They were from Pakistan, Saudi Arabia, and various parts of the United States that had a penchant for book-banning and preaching sexual abstinence in schools.

The usual suspects, it seemed.

The scene in Tennessee stretched out a lot longer, however.

That was why we spent so much time in my office in front of the TV; the estate looked a lot bigger, a lot more secure, and a lot harder to penetrate. Computer hacking and surveillance was one thing, but actually getting in and removing the occupants was another story.

We couldn't see much of what was going on, just a long, drawn-out, tediously dull narrative of nothing for hours on end. The only reason we stayed with it was the fact that we were targets of these characters. We wanted to know the outcome, and to find out whether or not we would still have to worry about the RE members – any of them – when this was over.

Would there be any who got away, or not?

So we sat there – me, Hamish and Kay – and waited it out.

There was no shoot-out. It was much quieter.

It stayed that way until almost half past two in the afternoon.

We barely saw anything happen when it finally did.

Walls were scaled at various points around the property, but it was hard to see the agents under all the brush and tree branches. Brick walls had been newly built the previous fall, and in a hurry. In some places, the work looked less than stable. All that money wasted, I thought later as I heard the details on the news.

Some people ran out of the buildings and were shot, but they didn't act the way that a person who has just taken a bullet acts. Instead, they behaved in a way that confused Kay but not me or Hamish: writhing and twitching on the ground. The newscasters thought that the one person they caught on camera was having some sort of epileptic fit.

When I had told Kay that Hamish had shot at Jared Clyde, I hadn't told what he had used for a weapon. For all she had known, Hamish had used a standard bullet-firing gun. The N.S.A. guys had moved in awfully fast, apparently to prevent anyone other than themselves from learning about the nanite weapon either.

They had succeeded; Kay was intriguing to watch as she leaned closer to the screen, staring at the distance shot of the person on the lawn among the trees of the Boenher estate. We didn't enlighten her. We weren't sure what to do about that, so we didn't explain.

But we knew what had happened: Hamish's nanite weapon had just been deployed.

Soon everyone was rounded up, accounted for, and removed from the premises.

Even the Boenher family.

Melissa Boenher was taken away with her husband, and their children were separated from them. I wondered what would happen to those kids. Their father was definitely not coming back to them; that much we could guess on our own.

But what about their mother? Melissa had never spoken publicly about her opinions on any issue. We really didn't have a good sense of her at all. Was she in complete agreement with her husband, or under his thumb, a prisoner of his plans? How would anyone ever know?

In any event, this one was over.

The F.B.I. released a statement claiming that it had captured everyone in RE, and as RE had taken responsibility for the attacks on the President, on the attorney who was a member of the National Birth License Committee, and on the inventors of Nae-Née (us), it seemed that until another crazy group crawled out from under some other rock, we could relax a bit.

Hamish seemed happier than he had been in a while – less secretive, less tense.

It was as though whatever he knew of to worry about had been addressed.

But he later told me that he would never fire Blackout Security.

That was after Kay had gone back to her desk, shutting the door behind her.

When it was time to go home, our usual N.S.A. car driven by Hawke and Lambert picked us up, and Hawke told us that they had orders to continue to guard us indefinitely.

So…the government didn't think it could rest easy either.

Terrific.

Still, with no one to chase down besides the RE members, and all of them captured, we could think about walking about the city again – for fun rather than only for errands.

The next day, Hamish and I went on a long walk down Broadway with our escort at a distance, watchful but allowing us our space.

It was a welcome change from all of the rides in cars with tinted windows.

No one else was following us; our minders were quite sure of that, and they told us so later that day. We enjoyed the sunshine and fresh air, and wandered down to the World Trade Center site and St. Paul's Chapel, where we went in to see the mementoes left over from the rescue efforts of 9/11, and the museum-display pews that the first governor of the state of New York and George Washington had kept there. The pews were little boxes set apart from the rest of the congregation, on either side of the chapel. They reminded visitors that New York City used to be the capital of the United States, at least until Washington D.C. was partially built.

We kept going after that, wandering farther south, down to Trinity Church, which faces Wall Street. Graveyards flank the brownstone church, which had fabulous bronze doors depicting scenes in history in large square reliefs. Alexander Hamilton – the one on the ten-dollar bill, our first Secretary of the Treasury, is buried on the south side of the church with his wife.

A huge metal sculpture was also on that side, just next to the front doors.

It was painted a dark red color, and it depicted the roots of a huge tree from the yard around St. Paul's Chapel that had been ripped up and tossed into the Trinity Church yard in the force of the collapse of the World Trade Center.

We turned east to walk down Wall Street.

It was odd to see that the place was still hopping with stock brokers and other people in business attire – plus, of course, New York's finest – despite all the news reports about how badly the market was doing.

Federal Hall, our nation's first legislative and executive building – both in one – with a giant statue of George Washington, faced down a closed street with the U.S. Stock Exchange with its huge American flag stretched across the façade on one side, and J.P. Morgan's building on the other. No motor traffic was allowed.

It all seemed so normal after the months of being followed, monitored, watched and guarded. But it wasn't, thanks to 9/11. The mere fact that people had gotten used to a restricted way of going about Wall Street did not make it normal; it was just that one could get used to almost anything.

The restrictions on our lives from security laws and the Nae-Née policy were becoming routine. We were all getting used to them. The paparazzi had lost interest in us, and walking around Greenwich Village and in and out of our firehouse had ceased to be difficult. Perhaps the world was getting used to having Nae-Née.

It didn't mean that people liked it. It just meant that it wasn't new to them anymore.

Chapter 34

With Room for Debate,
But No More

Early in May, not long after the raid on RE, a new link appeared on the website that was maintained by the United States Department of Demographics. It dealt with the issues I had outlined and explored in my lecture at the Rockefeller Institute just before our vacation in Venice. It was gratifying to see that my letters to the U.S. government had done some good.

What the USDD posted was not law, and it said so, but it also said that the U.S. Senate was debating a bill on the issue right now, so I tuned in to C-SPAN2 once again to check. Sure enough, it was so. But the urgency with which the ratification process had been treated, and that with which the concern about human overpopulation and global warming, was missing.

I wasn't surprised, just disgusted; as usual, once attention turned to women's issues, there was less enthusiasm for action. The women in the Senate weren't letting the matter drop, however, and the bill's chances for becoming law looked promising nonetheless.

The web page was under the site Laws link. It was a copy of the item being debated.

The Nae-Née Recipients' Bill of Rights

All women who receive a Nae-Née birth control device are to be guaranteed these freedoms:

- *To seek consultation with the physician(s) of their choice;*
- *To contract with their physician(s) on mutually agreeable terms;*
- *To be treated confidentially, with access to their records limited to those involved in their care or designated by them;*
- *To use their own resources to purchase the care of their choice;*
- *To be treated with dignity and respect when receiving the device, regardless of their shape, size or state of health;*
- *To say anything they wish about the law requiring that they accept the device including, but not limited to, disagreement, anger, worry, or sadness about it;*
- *To not be lectured to or scolded if they resist receiving the device;*
- *To be informed about their chances for being granted or denied a birth license;*
- *To refuse third-party interference in the injection and registration process, and to be confident that their actions in seeking or declining medical care will not result in third-party-imposed penalties for patients or physicians;*

318

❤ *To receive full disclosure of the details of the device, its implantation, and information delivery systems in plain language, including:*

1. *RECEIPT OF THIS BILL OF RIGHTS: A copy of this bill of rights is to be provided to each and every woman who receives a Nae-Née device;*
2. *APPROVAL PROCEDURES: An explanation of procedures for services, explaining the applications and approval processes of birth licensing by committee and individual applicants;*
3. *REFERRALS: Procedures for consulting a physician, attorney or social worker to assist with the license application process;*
4. *GRIEVANCES: Grievance procedures for claims of treatment and delivery abuses;*

❤ *To receive full disclosure of the identities of those delivering the device in writing at the time of its injection or implantation, including:*

1. *The nurse handling the actual injection/implantation;*
2. *Any enforcement officers accompanying her.*

This disclosure must include employee name, rank, qualifications, and employer contact information, as well as directions to this website to the purpose of filing any complaint.

All women receiving a Nae-Née birth control device have the following responsibilities:

❤ *To accept and comply with delivery and possession of the device.*
❤ *To refrain from striking at or otherwise committing assault or battery upon the medical professionals delivering the device.*

How nice. That seemed to cover everything, despite the contradictory responsibilities. Essentially, it aimed to make possible precisely what I had demanded in my lecture and letter: that women be allowed to make a fuss if they were enraged or upset by having to accept the device, say whatever they wanted to say, cry, scream, whatever, anything short of attacking the people delivering it to them, and not hear a word of reproach from those individuals.

I was glad; at least I could speak up for the women in my own country and help them.

That wasn't all that I found on the site; there was another link, separate from the other menu options on the site's main page, called Grievances. There it was, right after Laws. I clicked on it and found a form for filing a grievance against the nurse who delivered a woman's Nae-Née device, and another one for the enforcement officers.

That was it. Whether or not this system trampled on a woman's civil liberties was ignored. The point was to control human population levels by the least malicious means possible, and the planet's governments were going with Nae-Née for that purpose.

As I searched the Internet for more data on this subject, I noticed that other nations were coming out with similar websites and laws. All of them had something to show for the effort. Those with less democratic systems betrayed that fact in the ways that Nae-Née was delivered. Those with democratic processes were learning as they went, with room for debate right and left – pun intended – as to whether or not the process or the delivery was in any way right or wrong.

But there was no room for more people on this planet.

Chapter 35

Global Warming Mugs and Maps

The planet was rapidly beginning to resemble the global warming mug, with cartographers and newscasters buzzing incessantly about redrawing the world's maps. Thus far, the land masses had receded – or shrank, to be more precise – only part of the way to the finish line, resembling the mug about halfway along the heat-reaction process that caused the green parts to go invisible. But the process was continuing.

The Unemployed Philosophers Guild was doing a brisk business with those mugs, so they were backordered into next fall at the earliest.

We found out that the government had allowed RE to believe that the remaining Clyde twin – the one who had tried to shoot me – was dead only until after the raids, then brought him out and put him through the federal criminal courts, where he was awaiting trial. He had defiantly pled not guilty. Hamish was sorry to hear it. "He tried to kill you – I don't care that I invented the perfect weapon," he said resentfully. I told him to just relax and enjoy the lucrative weapons contract that it had earned him, and he nodded and glared until I kissed him again.

Blackout Security still insisted upon driving us everywhere, so we didn't use the subway any more. As a result, the only times that I traveled without them was when I went walking around Manhattan. I did this after work on any sunny day that I could all spring and summer, but a few weeks along that time span, I realized something: most of the routes that I preferred took me along the middle of the island. I rarely saw the edges.

Granted, my office was on one of the edges, overlooking the East River, but I was up on the third floor. I got there by elevator, and sat looking away from the window for most of the day. I would either read on the sofa or sit at the computer screen, plus occasionally watch the television. That meant that I hardly ever took a careful look at the shore.

One afternoon, after lunch late in May, I walked as far to the east across the Rockefeller University Institute's campus as I could and looked across FDR Drive at the water level.

It was high - so high that could see it lapping at the edge of the island.

Usually, when there is water touching a shoreline, there is a gradual transition that can be seen on the land, which shows that the point at which the water meets the land is normal and has been that point for a very long time. Not now. There was no sand in between the grass and the water. It was like an artificial pool.

In a way, it *was* an artificial pool; humans had caused this.

The news on television was what had prompted my midday walk. The polar icecap was completely gone, polar bears were drowning, and the glaciers of Greenland were going to finish melting over the summer - this summer, not some other one a decade or so off – the time was now. Antarctica was losing all of its ice shelves too, and as a result, glaciers on the continent were falling like giant ice cubes into the sea, becoming icebergs that would likely melt soon.

That summer, I found myself drawn away from the usual fun paths of the playground that Manhattan was to me. I kept going to the shores of the island to look at the water levels.

So did other people, I noticed.

Hamish came with me sometimes, surprised at first and then accustomed to my changed routines and preference – if you could call a morbid fascination a preference – for the sight of a noticeably rising sea level all around us.

He didn't say much when we went to look. He just stood looking next to me and put his arm around me. Sometimes, despite that, I would stare into space, thinking, and then not be able to focus on what was in front of me when I remembered where I was. The gray haze was back.

Hamish helped with that a little, hugging me. He could see when it came back, because I would try to focus on everything around me and gasp for air even though there was sufficient oxygen. He would hug me and talk to me and walk me away from the edges of the island.

Then I would be able to see clearly again. That was only because I was facing inland, where things still looked pretty much the same as they had before.

But how long would that last? The water was still rising.

That wasn't all that we noticed; whenever we out for Japanese food, we would often find that many of our favorite fishes were simply not available. This happened repeatedly. We liked to order salmon and tuna sushi and sashimi – raw slices of our favorite fishes. First the tuna became difficult to acquire, and the restaurants had to finally take it off of their menus. Then some other fishes started to become only sporadically available; the varieties kept changing.

When I went to Whole Foods or The Lobster Place to buy fish, I noticed fewer and fewer choices being offered, and certain kinds would be absent for at least a month at a time. Several sections at The Lobster Place, once fully stocked, were suddenly habitually empty, especially the raw oyster areas. Oyster beds everywhere were threatened by hurricanes.

At long last, our country's unsustainable lifestyle was no longer sustaining itself.

News reports about Florida were terrifyingly grim. The Keys were almost submerged and mostly abandoned. The Ernest Hemingway Museum estate was deserted; someone had brought its cats off that island. The peninsula of Florida was shrinking; people scurried inland, crowding the remaining area. Florida was no longer a coveted vacationland. Furious beachfront property owners filed claims with the government and insurance companies that went unanswered.

Jurassic creatures moved with the humans, bringing shocking reports of babies, toddlers, and pets getting eaten if they dared to venture outside. Florida had always had trouble with alligators on front doorsteps, and now it was worse than ever.

The Seminole tribe was irate; comments that they ought to be fine because they owned the Hard Rock Café incensed the elders. It was the land that mattered to them, and others had squandered it. Climatologists back them up.

It seemed to me that the climatologists' predictions had been conservative due to insufficient data. Now governments and citizens alike all over the planet would pay the price of not having funded their work, not having maintained satellites for them, thus keeping us blind to what was happening until it was too late to comfortably relocate, and in a calm, civilized manner.

Early in the summer, I decided to call Bethany. It seemed that there was no longer any danger from RE, and I couldn't let the mere possibility that some other crazies might crop up stop me from ever connecting with anyone again.

She was fine of course, volunteering with the local animal shelter, fostering a kitten or two along with her own cats, and starting to involve herself more with a student exchange program at her local high school. That meant that a Japanese teenager, a girl, would come to stay with her next year. Bethany was looking forward to practicing her Japanese and helping the girl, whose name was Masako, improve her English skills.

I explained why I had been out of touch – the problem with RE being after me and Hamish, worry that RE might start chasing my friends, and so on. Then I described all the excitement, if one could call it that, of Hamish saving my life with his nanite gun.

"Wow – a real-life hero protects you," Bethany remarked.

I laughed. It was true, and I loved it.

We reminisced about our graduate school days, when she had lived alone in the Boston area, financed by her parents who had decided that she should become an accountant. That didn't pan out; she graduated, but flunked the C.P.A. exam, and never took it again. Bethany used to cry on the phone to me about how much she hated living alone, that she wanted to get married and thus solve that problem permanently.

I was living in Paris for most of each year with my grandparents, so I hadn't exactly left home either. Living arrangements are hard to find in that city; apartments must be rented out for a year, not shorter periods, so I had stayed with them while I attended the Sorbonne. But I was so glad to do that and not have to go out alone and stay with people my age; I didn't want to.

We had observed that neither of us wanted the expected path that most people seemed to look forward to taking. We never wanted to share a place with some temporary roommate, knowing that the situation could just end without warning due to the other's person getting a job in some other state or their marriage. It was too upsetting by being quite literally unsettling.

Bethany was my best friend from college, but now we hardly saw each other. We lived too far apart geographically, she had kids and I shied away from them, and for a few months I had been afraid to endanger her by so much as calling. Yet she stayed close to me. She always understood all of that and accepted it. That was why our friendship continued.

Now I told her about the rising water levels around Manhattan, and how scared I was getting. I told her more than I was used to telling Hamish, though he had figured out what was bothering me on his own. At least I didn't have to worry about Bethany; she lived far inland and upland in Massachusetts. The global warming mug even at its hottest still showed green, livable land where Bethany's home was.

"Do you think you'll move out? What about your firehouse? Will it get flooded?"

"No to flooding; I checked a computer simulation online to see how far the flood waters would come over the island. They will flood many familiar areas and landmarks. And the Rockefeller Institute won't be spared; it's right on the East River. But the firehouse is smack in the center of the island, which slopes upwards just enough to be spared."

"That's good news. But will you want to leave if your workplace is under water?"

"I think so. I try to imagine life here with other people being displaced, and with access to and from Manhattan being more difficult as the existing infrastructure is submerged and has to be rebuilt. The country can't afford it right now. It scares me to think about it because one can only anticipate and plan for so many changes. Getting out before it gets too chaotic might be the best idea. I feel bad for the people who don't have the money or resources to do that."

She asked me an interesting question then. "Have you heard of the five stages of grief?"

"You mean the ones that you learned in that one psychology course you took in college?" She had shown me what she was learning as often as I had shown her what I was doing.

"Yes. They are – and I can't believe I still remember them all – in order: 1. Anger; 2. Denial; 3. Bargaining; 4. Depression; 5. Acceptance. I never thought that I would find myself applying it to the state of the planet – with overpopulation, climate change and biodiversity loss – but we both are. My kids aren't going to have all the great experiences that I had. My dad's honeybees aren't producing enough honey any more. We had to give it all back to them, just to enable their hives to survive, for past three years."

I remembered her father's honey and raspberry jam; the one fueled the growth of the other. He gave jars of both to all of his friends, including me, and we would clean and return the empties after enjoying his delectable results. He canned the honey and jam himself, too.

"Is the raspberry crop suffering too?" I asked. The raspberry patch was just a few feet away from the beehives.

"Yes. It's terrible. There are still some berries, but nowhere near as much as we had when I first invited you to visit, back when we were in college together." She sounded sad.

"I wonder what stage of grief you and I are in over all this," I commented absently.

She laughed ruefully. "We can cross off denial right now. The confusing part is that I still feel anger, and it sounds as though you do, too. But we may actually both be hovering on the brink between bargaining and depression."

"I think you're right."

We talked a bit more about our families and other activities, as usual with no clear idea as to how or when we would have another visit, and then rang off.

If that was how I felt, then how did I think that the people in the flooded parts of the world felt? The ones who had lost their homes and possessions, and were either catching cholera or starving to death on dry land with either makeshift shelters or none at all...it wasn't hard to guess. They felt desperate, suicidal, homicidal, tired, hungry, filthy and forgotten.

The news reports were worse; the flooded areas of the world were staying underwater. Sea level had risen irrevocably. A huge swath of Pakistan was gone now, and displaced people were wandering the drought areas, angry and exhausted. The Indus River had never receded. These were the people who fought over what little food was brought to them, because it wasn't enough for the crowds that the relief workers met.

These were the people who stopped the fortunate ones in their vehicles as they tried to go about their business in the areas that had not been flooded, impeding their progress across the roads and highways.

These were the people who, if left unaided just a little bit longer, would overwhelm the haves in their desperation as have-nots, outraged at being left to fend for themselves when it was so clear that they were unable to.

Why should they have to die just because no resources were readily available to them? Why should they have to suffer just because their infrastructure was now washed away or submerged under a sudden flood that showed no sign of ever receding in their lifetimes?

On the other side, the haves were terrified of the scarcity reaching them, because they felt little better able to cope with such a problem if it were to reach them. Suddenly the potential for unpremeditated murder loomed in front of them with the appearance of each small crowd.

How long before the melting glaciers and icecaps of the planet caused such things to happen everywhere else? When that happened, such scenes would be repeated all over the globe. I didn't want to live in such times. I knew I wasn't alone, but nature could care less.

Star Trek was such a lovely outcome for the human species, but it was pure utopian fantasy, created with the assistance of lawyers and space scientists, biologists and physicists...but not climatologists.

Our future was looking more and more like that of *Mad Max* all the time, and I was scared. *Mad Max* was less well-known and for good reason: it postulated a grim future of scarce resources and violence, the worst aspects of human nature being shown as people became less civilized, showing something that no one wanted to think about: civil societies need money and resources to function. Without those essentials, the fabric of society breaks down and the threads run every which way, creeping into the lives of peaceful individuals who don't want to cause or experience any trouble. Then everyone feels fear.

I wanted *Star Trek*. Of course, wanting a good life in one's own lifetime was how our species became overpopulated in the first place; we had repeatedly delayed hard choices. I didn't want to live in the world of *Mad Max*, even though the human species might be forced to do so in order to get past the consequences of environmental irresponsibility, overpopulation and selfishness in order to survive and enjoy the good times of *Star Trek*.

I didn't care; I wanted *Star Trek*. I had studied and prepared for *Star Trek*. I worked hard to become a productive and good person. I wanted to reap the results of that work, not those of the carelessness of others. I didn't want to deal with the problems of *Mad Max*.

But the Earth doesn't care what we want. It is indifferent to everything but its own ecosystem. If we upset the balance of its health, it will correct the situation, oblivious to the needs and wants of the species that screwed things up. Payback is a bitch, so Mother Earth, the Goddess, can be one too. Just push her a bit farther. I should get one of those bumper stickers that says "God is coming, and is she *pissed.*" Or not. I don't like to put my opinions on the rear end of my car for all to see as I go about my business. Why activate anyone else's radar screen?

Hamish and I had one more summer in Manhattan before the computer simulations became a reality. Less, actually; I made regular treks around lower Manhattan to see how the island was faring, and I actually began to notice water on the pavement by Chelsea Piers.

Another beautiful afternoon, I persuaded Hamish to walk with me all the way from our firehouse to Battery Park, where we saw water seeping over the edge onto the grounds of Castle Clinton, making the statue of immigrants appear to be standing in a pool of water rather than on a paved walkway. We waded in inch-deep water, like a giant puddle after a hard rainstorm, in our Teva sandals. That company that would continue to thrive in this new climate, I thought.

It was like that here and there wherever we went. We spent the summer in waterproof shoes, it seemed. For our anniversary, we dressed up but wore those sandals to the upscale, gourmet, French restaurant, L'Absinthe. I stole a few surreptitious glances at the footwear of the other diners and quickly understood why: no one was wearing fancy footwear. It wasn't worth it.

This change in attitude and culture was no doubt happening everywhere.

Chapter 36

Retreat from the Sea Change

Late in the summer, I took another walk out to the East River in the middle of the day.

It was August 20th, a Tuesday. What prompted this particular walk was that when I looked out the window of my office at the sky, the sun was shining and it was a beautiful day, but the ground on the campus looked like it had just rained, despite hours of hot sunshine.

It hadn't rained for a week and a half. During that time, I had deliberately lapsed into my old habit of walking down 5th Avenue to enjoy the tourists, the window displays, a walk through Tiffany's, and another drink of European hot chocolate with whipped cream and a small torte full of pistachio puree at La Maison du Chocolat with Hamish.

But the sight of the lovely weather and blue sky was not all that prompted my foray onto the campus grounds. I had also looked down at the ground itself, expecting…hoping…to see beautiful green grass, dry enough to walk across, a carpet of lush greenery.

Instead, I saw dark, soggy ground. I looked over at the sidewalks between the campus buildings of the Rockefeller University Institute, and saw that they looked as though it had just rained. Feeling a sickening sense of dread, I went out.

It was mid-morning. Few people were out, except for some groundskeepers off in the distance. The two men were staring at the grass as though it were some sort of new substance that they didn't know how to maintain. Somehow, I doubted I was far off.

Sure enough, there was more than an inch of water on the sidewalks. My Teva sandals got soaking wet. I was wearing Capri pants, so I didn't worry about my clothes. I didn't care if the sandals got wet; they were made for it. Continuing on toward Founders Hall, I wandered among the campus buildings, staring much more at the ground than at anything else.

I had come out of the Rockefeller Research Building into the middle of the campus, which meant that the buildings closest to the river actually blocked my view both of it and of Franklin Delano Roosevelt Drive.

Determined to see the grass on the side closest to the East River, I went into Founders Hall and back to the Markus Library in Welch Hall, which was attached to the back of the building. I found a door to the outside that wouldn't set off any alarms and exited. There was a large section of yard that faced FDR Drive and the East River. I ventured across the grass just to see how it would feel.

My sandals squished through the muck that was once a lawn, and mud pushed up all over my feet. I pressed on, wondering how far I could go before fear of losing my balance would send me hurrying back.

ars were going back and forth on FDR Drive, and water was splashing up around them as if a violent rainstorm had just occurred. But it hadn't. Some hydroplaned just a bit, but the drivers tapped on the brakes and slowed down. Progress was slower than usual thanks to all of the water on the road.

For a few minutes, I stood there, mesmerized, staring at the traffic.

Then the gray haze was back.

It was a prediction of things to come, this liquid inundation. An omen, it might have been called in a long past, superstitious time. The Big Apple was now facing an omen of the planet's future, and it was upon us as an encroaching sea change…mirthless pun intended.

I forced myself to turn around and go back into the library building.

Once inside, the haze cleared a bit as I saw that things still looked the same as always. But the door of the place was only a few steps upwards from the yard, and I wondered how the books in the basement were faring.

First things first; I went into the women's room, took off my sandals, tossed them into a sink, and stood like a dancer doing a high leg-bend, one at a time, in front of another sink to scrub my feet clean. The warm water felt nice, but it made me think of the people in countries with flood waters up to their waists or worse. The cold and filth must be endless, uncomfortable to the point of sometimes painful, and full of disease, parasites, and water-borne predators.

Didn't Pakistan have poisonous snakes swimming with the refugees? And rats? New York City had always had rats. Staring around the yard again, I didn't see any rats, but then I realized that they must have moved on a while ago. They had had the sense to leave by now.

I scrubbed my sandals off carefully, using a lot of soap from the pump, but I seemed to have gotten my shoes clean enough. Then I went back out into the hallway and looked out the window. I went into the library to see what was happening there.

Inside, it was organized chaos as the librarians directed maintenance staff members up and down from the basement. The maintenance men were assisting them in bringing up old, bound medical journals from the compact storage – roller stacks, I liked to call them.

Some of the journals were wet. Each publication was bound with a different color, so a rainbow of moist books soon stretched from table to table all across the reading room. Tables were covered in clear plastic, and the librarians were trying to both fan out the pages of wet journals and keep each publication grouped together and in order. I didn't envy them the task.

After waving to the librarians and saying that I didn't need anything, I left, still carrying my sandals. Rather than go outside again, I used the connecting hallways between buildings to get back to my office, putting my shoes on halfway back there. The rubber parts of the sandals were almost dried, but not the straps. Squish, squish…oh well; my curiosity had been satisfied.

Kay looked up as I walked in, smiled, and returned to her typing.

I said "Hi" and went into my office to turn on the television. This time I wasn't interested in C-SPAN; I wanted to see the local news.

Sure enough, the reports were all about the city's subway system and roads. The subways had flooded four days earlier – I knew about that – but the water level hadn't gone down. Instead, it had risen, cutting off all access to the underground transit system. Roads were flooding too now, and the images cut to FDR Drive and the Hudson Parkway.

I went back out to talk to Kay. "Kay – have you seen the campus grounds?"

She paused, then turned to me. "Yes. It's the same near our apartment. We live just far enough inland in Hamilton Heights to not be worried about our building, but the streets to the west have been a couple of inches under water for a couple of weeks now. And the kids can't enjoy Riverside Park anymore. It's a muddy, mucky mess now. They've been going stir crazy for most of the summer. I finally sent them to their grandparents in Larchmont."

"Are they happy there?"

"Yes, and my parents are talking about enrolling them in school there. I may just allow that; Larchmont has an excellent school system anyway. They'll have better chances when they apply for college, don't you think?" She sounded a bit anxious – tearful, even – and I didn't think it was about college. The kids were only in grammar school.

I agreed with her that that sounded like a great thing for the kids, both academically and otherwise. "It's good that you could get them out of the city," I reassured her. "You're doing the right thing for them."

I went into my office and grabbed up everything that I had borrowed from the library. I was too distracted to go ahead with my next lecture, and I had gathered plenty of information from the books before today. Well, except for one, but I would just have to give it back. I had the bibliography ready anyway, so I could still refer to parts of it later.

Back in the outer office, Kay looked up at me as I passed with the stack of books. There were fourteen…no, fifteen of them, I realized. "Are you taking all of those back at once?" she wanted to know.

"Yes – I've gotten enough out of them," I replied. Amazing…I had only gotten the last two the previous Friday. She looked at me as if I were lying to her. I was going to turn them all in anyway, though.

"I'll come with you," she said, grabbing several off the top of my pile.

We went back through the halls, my sandals still squishing as we walked.

"What happened, did you take a walk to explore the muck?" Kay asked me after we had walked almost all the way through the hospital lobby to the indoor walkway that connected it with Founders Hall. She had gotten to know me well in the past several months.

"Yes. I got absolutely filthy…had to wash off my feet and then wash out my sandals in the women's room by the library. That's where I went; out walking on the closest bit of grass to FDR Drive that I could find. I could see the edge of the island from there, and the water level."

She didn't ask me anything else. I was obviously forming a plan and carrying it out, but not yet ready to say anything about it. Maybe she saw how freaked out I looked, maybe not. I was probably scaring her, and I felt bad, but I didn't know what to do about it.

We left the books at the circulation desk and I thanked the librarian. Then we turned right around and went back to our office; the librarians didn't have any time for pleasantries, and we didn't feel like exchanging them anyway.

Back in my office, I looked around at the walls. Nothing was on them that I couldn't remove without calling attention to myself. I had one large print of a

Toulouse-Lautrec poster of Jane Avril at Le Moulin Rouge. Hamish hadn't bothered with any decorations.

So much the better – I would just leave the poster here.

What did I have in my desk drawers? A few post-it notes and business cards collected from meetings with various academics, but all added regularly to my running Word file of an address book. What the hell – I tossed them into a tote bag with my framed photos.

That left my memory sticks – two of them. I updated everything yet again, which didn't take long. I kept things pretty much up to date as I added new files and new versions of existing files. Then I pocketed the flash drives. My laptop was at home in the firehouse.

Next, I went into Hamish's office and grabbed all of his business cards, updated his memory sticks, and checked his laptop. All set. But what about his research? Was there anything that he needed?

As I sat at his desk, he walked in, not expecting to see me there, and then stopped short.

"What are you doing?" he asked, coming over to look.

"I've just updated your storage files of everything, including your memory sticks and laptop. The latest versions of every document I could find are now saved. Do you have any other documents that you were working on in the lab?"

He stared at me. "No. I usually just write it all up as I go, back and forth all day."

"So you don't have anything new to add right now?"

"No."

"Good."

"Avril, what's going on?"

I described the condition of the yard behind Founders Hall, the traffic on FDR Drive, what happened to my feet and sandals on my little expedition out there, the chaos in the library, and everything else that was happening to the island of Manhattan.

"This place is starting to resemble that global warming mug that you gave me for Christmas. I'm scared. I want to go home to Connecticut."

He pulled me over to the sofa by the window. I started crying.

"I love it here," I cried into his tee shirt. "I don't want to leave. I love living here alone with you and the cat. But I'm scared about what's going to happen as we all get flooded in and food and other resources can't get in to the city."

"So you want to live in Connecticut? What about our jobs?"

"Can't we just get out of here and then figure it out from a safe distance? We could call Dr. Nurse and explain, and see if he wants to keep us on in any way. You would be all right; you have your laboratory on Stoner Drive. I can go back to other writing projects if I have to."

He looked at me for a moment. I had sat back to breathe and blown my nose – I hate to sniffle – so I was talking fast but coherently. "We've only had two and a half years together here," I lamented, "but we can't stay here anymore. We have to wait this change out at home."

"You built that laboratory because you anticipated this, didn't you?" Hamish asked me.

"Yes."

He looked almost accusing at me, but then he smiled slightly. "You always think ahead. That's one of the things that I admire about you."

"Really? You're not mad at me for wanting to flee Manhattan, even it means leaving our nice home and jobs here?"

"No. There won't be any way to run soon if we wait much longer; might as well face it."

We gathered our stuff up, said good-bye to Kay, hugged her, and left.

Getting ready to leave the city was another issue entirely.

I checked the car; it needed fuel – more of the stuff that was causing the very problem that was driving us out of the city that we loved. I hoped we could get some and quickly.

Hamish came with me. My sandals squished a bit as I got behind the wheel; I hadn't waited for them to dry completely, and I was afraid to do that now.

Where was the nearest place that wasn't too close to the water? Just south of 8th Avenue and 14th Street, in Chelsea. I hoped I wouldn't have trouble getting over there.

As usual, the place had a line of taxis waiting to fuel up, but it was only (!) six of them. I got in line and settled in to wait, hoping that the pumps wouldn't be out of merchandise when our turn came.

Across the street, I saw Ed and Rick watching us from their car with the windows down.

"Did you tell Blackout Security what we're doing?" I asked Hamish.

"Yeah. They'll follow us out when we go. They'll also keep watching the firehouse after we're gone, just so it's okay in case we ever decide it's okay to come back to it."

"Good. We'll go tomorrow after rush hour. I hope not too many other people have that idea at the same time; I want to go before a mass exodus out of here starts – before a panic."

He looked at me, wide-eyed, but said nothing. I don't think he had realized how bad the situation really was.

Forty minutes later, it was our turn at the pump. Fortunately, we got a full tank of gas.

Back at the firehouse, I reminded Hamish that the water wasn't going to flood the building even at 20 feet – perhaps not even at 30.

"That's a relief," he said.

"But we won't be able to live in Manhattan until the infrastructure is reworked to handle the fact that Manhattan is going to be more like Venice than Manhattan soon."

Hamish just looked at me, then followed me inside.

We packed all of our clothes, all of our music and DVDs, and quite a few of our books.

We packed our nonperishable food and spices from the specialty shops of Greenwich Village, Chelsea Market, Chinatown, and wherever else we had found any gastronomic treasures. I added Hamish's teas and our coffees from McNulty's. The car was getting really full.

Then I packed up the perishable stuff in such a way as to make it easy to stow in the car just before driving away the next morning.

I checked the weather for tomorrow: clear skies, sunshine. What a relief; only the water on the roads and ground to contend with.

We ate what we could that night just to get rid of as much perishable food as possible.

Eowyn looked confused at us, watching us pack up everything she owned, leaving only her food and water dishes out. She had another litter box in Connecticut, but we always brought her other things back and forth…just not all of her toys. Something was definitely up, she knew.

I called Time-Warner Cable and suspended our service, paying the last of the bill over the phone. I didn't explain anything to them, just stopped it: Internet, cable television, everything.

Hamish watched me silently, probably grateful to see me busy instead of panicking.

Imagine if he were the one with the driver's license. Then I wouldn't be so focused on moving. Imagine if my parents weren't in Connecticut, I thought. But they were. They had a house high up on Stoner Drive, and they weren't in Chelsea or Paris. Imagine if they didn't have any such place…no, I'd rather not imagine. Better to stay calm and keep packing.

I wondered how JFK Airport was functioning. Suddenly, I didn't want to know until I got back home. I called my parents and told them what was going on and why.

"Call us when you're leaving, and on the road," my mother said.

Dad came on the line next. "Try not to stop too much. I've heard reports of people approaching cars and trying to coax people out. People are starting to realize that the water level is rising everywhere. I cancelled my latest trip to Paris because of that, and worked on client's patents from here. Suddenly I love e-mail," he joked. But he sounded worried; he would be glad when we arrived at the house.

After that call, we watched a couple of DVDs to keep the television from being eerily silent, and then went to bed with the cat on the covers between us.

The next day, after a fitful, nervous sleep, we got up. Hamish had tossed and turned as much as I had, and at one point, we had cried and just fallen asleep again, clutching each other, with our confused cat walking around us until we were quiet again. We woke up with her curled up on top of our pillows.

We ate breakfast at A.O.C. one last time. But I realized that we had always eaten lunch, dinner or brunch there; never breakfast. That made me nervous and sad partway through the meal. Somehow, I finished.

We walked back to the firehouse, went over everything one last time, and packed the cat in her carrier, stowing it carefully on the stuffed backseat, right in the middle, facing out over the dashboard. That way, we could talk to her as we drove along.

With everything in order and one last trip to the bathroom each, we got in and I rolled out of the garage for the last time in what I guessed would be a very long time.

We were off. Ed and Rick followed us.

I drove up 8th Avenue for most of the way, unwilling to face Riverside Drive until I absolutely had to. I was planning to leave Manhattan via the Henry Hudson Bridge, so I drove up past the Museum of Natural History before turning left at West 81st Street to cross over to Broadway. From there, I moved north again, parallel with the meandering Riverside Drive, up the straight line of Broadway until it connected with Riverside Drive.

From there, I found that we were abruptly on the Hudson River Parkway north out of Manhattan, lower down than Fort Tryon Park, where the Cloisters of the Metropolitan Museum of Art was located. The grounds of the medieval castle loomed far above us, far above.

I tried yet again not to think about the fact that we were leaving this fun city. That wasn't difficult, because I had to slow down quite a bit on the parkway through Inwood Hill Park. The Hudson River Parkway was much the same as FDR Drive; wet with a couple of inches of water. I slowed down to avoid hydroplaning into the Hudson River.

That wasn't all; people in galoshes were dressed like hikers and laden with backpacks all along the edge of Riverside Park, and some even emerging from the forest-like Inwood Hill Park. They were all walking purposefully northwards. Judging by their ages, they looked like yuppies, fleeing the city that had once been their playground.

Hamish stared out the windows, suddenly understanding why I wanted out of the city so urgently. "The highway is submerged. It's still passable, but just barely. You're right as usual; we've got to get out of here."

I nodded grimly, but kept my attention on the road.

Soon we were going up over the bridge, leaving Manhattan behind us.

Escaping…well, no…more like retreating.

The route through the valleys of New York State was a bit wet, as after a heavy rainstorm, but it wasn't as tense to drive over as the last bit of Manhattan had been.

Still, I was very quiet until we got to Connecticut, not stopping for a rest room until at least Danbury, when I looked for a Dunkin' Donuts. Those places usually had clean bathrooms with soap and toilet paper, and I was able to find one in a wealthy area.

Snobby of me, but I was scared. A Mercedes wouldn't attract much attention here, I reasoned, heading into Southbury.

We were back in the car in less than 10 minutes.

No sooner had we locked ourselves inside than I noticed some men walking through the parking lot, watching us. They looked like any other Americans, but there was something about their eyes that alarmed me. Had they walked away from something dangerous elsewhere?

I didn't linger to find out. Neither did Rick and Ed; they eyed the men warily, but were back in their car just as quickly as we were, having taken turns to use the rest room. Those men had watched us; they seemed to lose interest when they saw Rick and Ed. Or perhaps it was something else. But I couldn't shake the feeling that they had decided that we didn't seem like a viable target because of our escort.

Suddenly, I noticed more people without cars – people on bicycles and on foot – plus others in cars like ours, cars packed to the limit with possessions, people and pets. The people on bikes and on foot were laden like pack animals, also carrying stuff with them.

Back on the highway, I saw nothing out of the ordinary. Hamish called my parents on his cell phone to tell them where we were.

Suddenly I thought, had we both brought our cell phone cords? Funny what alarms you when you're fleeing for higher ground, I told myself. Yes…the cords were in the compartment right between our seats. I told myself not to think of anything else – just get there.

Eowyn was quiet, watching out the windshield. She had ridden with us several times before now, but not with a car that was packed with so much stuff. I could barely see out the back dashboard.

It was a relief to see our exit and get off at Corbin's Corner.

We were just under twenty minutes from pulling into the garage and shutting the door on this ride. Looking out at New Britain Avenue, we noticed more people on foot with backpacks, more with loaded bicycles, motorcycles and cars, and all with a haunted expression in their eyes.

The way was shutting behind them, it seemed to say. We were all retreating from it.

Up Ridgewood Road, around the corner on Mountain Road, across Farmington Avenue, and there was Stoner Drive at last. Hamish watched me, commenting that things looked okay here. I appreciated what he was doing, even though I didn't believe what I was seeing.

Things did look okay…

…even though I doubted that they would be okay for a quite a while.

Chapter 37

Safe at Home Again

My parents flung open the door to the kitchen as soon as we shut off the car. "Are you all right?!" my mother said, rushing over to hug me as I got out. "We've been watching the news; New York City is starting to disappear under water. It's scary – just like that computer simulation that Al Gore showed in his movie," she gasped. "And people are getting attacked as they travel – I was worried the whole time that you were on the road!"

I hugged her, and pointed out the men-in-black for perhaps the hundredth time since Hamish had hired them. "Oh yeah," she said, breathing a sigh of relief. "It's just that the reports say that people are getting robbed, or robbed and murdered for whatever they have as they walk or bike away from the shorelines," she explained. It wasn't surprising to hear.

Hamish got out and reached in back for Eowyn's cat-carrier. He extracted it and straightened up to face my father, who had come around to his side of the car. "We saw people on foot all the way back, looking like hikers with backpacks," Hamish said. "They looked normal enough except for one critical difference; none of the places where we encountered them was the sort of place for hiking. They looked more like refugees."

Dad started pulling the bags of food out of the back seat. "They *are* refugees," he replied. "People are leaving New York City and the coastlines in droves. Since another layer of Greenland's ice and parts of Antarctica melted a few weeks ago, sea level started rising faster. The icebergs that fell into the Weddell and Scotia Seas have had time to melt."

So that was what was happening. I had thought so, and he had confirmed it. Now that I was home, I was willing to sit glued to the news of rising sea levels. It had scared me too much to contemplate while I was still in Manhattan. I needed to be on high ground, safely away from it with Hamish, my parents, and both cats and my extended family.

With that accomplished, that nuisance of a gray haze cleared. I took advantage of this by removing everything from the car and unpacking it. It looked as though we weren't going to live elsewhere for a while. Blackout Security set up camp down the street, having purchased a house that was in foreclosure.

When something this extreme happens, people are uprooted with little advance notice. Planning ahead is difficult if not impossible for most people, especially those without a place on high ground to relocate to. Hamish and Eowyn and I were lucky. I wondered how many people were stuck in New York City and elsewhere, how many pets had been abruptly abandoned in homes that were on the coastline – homes that would soon disappear under water – and how many people would be condemned to wander the countryside, homeless and desperate.

As if that weren't bad enough, the weather reports promptly turned grim, with the tornado-like storms that we had come to expect in September. They hit the outlying boroughs of New York City, and tornadoes actually touched down in New Jersey. It drew fewer comments each year about how odd it was to get such storms along the east coast of the United States rather than only in the Midwest, but there were still some people who were amazed not only by the extent of the damage caused by the storms, but also by the fact that they had occurred at all.

The infrastructure of the United States was already in rotten and literally rotted shape. Now a lot of it was inaccessible. The financial and human cost was alarming to think about.

My parents were relieved that we had suddenly decided to come back here. "Don't leave," they said. "You have plenty of your own money; we don't mind if you both stay here permanently and write and invent from home. This is your home – we know that your other one may be inaccessible. Just stay safe where we know you're okay, with us."

Wow – such an about-face from a few years ago, when they had been frustrated with their ne'er-do-well daughter and son-in-law underfoot. But a lot had happened since that time; we had proven ourselves, done great things, and made lots of our own money.

Since we were now effectively barricaded in due to the circumstances, there was little point in objecting to what was essentially a reversion to the pre-Industrial Age model of multiple generations of an American family living together under one roof. I suspected that soon a lot of Americans would adopt this solution to constricted land areas. Others would not be able to – such as people with no families, or people stranded across the country from their relatives, washed out of flooded cities that they had relocated to for jobs that were now under water.

There was a website online that enabled anyone with computer and Internet access to keep track of the influx of water. Thanks to satellite technology, it was possible to see precisely where the water was, and to calculate how high the level would rise.

The Maldives had disappeared; they had been just five feet above sea level. I recalled the time when Hamish and I were planning our wedding, and I had enjoyed looking at bridal magazines. Those magazines typically featured articles about idyllic honeymoon spots around the planet, and there had been one showing a resort hotel in the Maldives. It was individual huts on stilts, set next to the series of white, palm-speckled patches in the Indian Ocean. Now the 300,000 people who had lived in that country were without a home, and some had drowned. The rest had escaped in boats, relocating to India and Sri Lanka. I was reminded of Nauru again, the first place that had suffered that loss, with its people relocated to New Zealand.

Oddly, water levels did not rise uniformly all over the Earth. I (and no doubt many other people) had expected that to happen until I began to read about the subject. It turned out that in some places, sea level actually dropped. One of them, amazingly enough, was the Netherlands. I was glad to hear of it, but hoped that people would not prematurely move into the lowlands of that country only to rush out in a sudden reversal of the situation.

The site allowed a person to click on whatever area of the planet she or he wanted to inspect and zoom in for a closer look. It would then give a run-down on how the sea level there had changed over the past 50 years, decade by decade until fifteen years back, at which point it showed changes for each year. I took a virtual trip to Manhattan and checked it out. That was when I felt a sense relief: our firehouse was located in a spot that would most likely not be submerged by rising sea levels. I had seriously begun to doubt this over the past summer, despite having seen projections a long time before that indicated that there was nothing to worry about.

However, 9th Avenue was going to be covered soon, and that would be permanent. The building that housed my parents' apartment in Chelsea would lose its basement. I hoped that it was structurally sound, and that its foundations would hold as well as Venetian ones. Lots of buildings in Manhattan were going to suffer the same fate, and many already had. When I watched the news over the next week, it confirmed that the backpackers we had seen were displaced yuppies whose apartment buildings' lobbies were now flooded. The city had declared those buildings uninhabitable, and had shut off the electricity and plumbing that serviced them.

The subway system of the five boroughs was in ruins. Electrical shorts made it unsafe for scuba divers to investigate the damage. Newscasters lamented the loss of a major piece of infrastructure as the ferry system attempted to pick up the slack for those who were still able to live and work in the city, and who needed to travel between the boroughs. There was even a special interest piece about the loss of the secret underground terminal and train that had been built during World War II just for President Franklin Delano Roosevelt.

The mayor of New York City had stopped funding the subway system and poured that part of the budget into the purchase and maintenance of a fleet of ferries, bowing to the inevitable. He promised to give the subway workers jobs operating the ferries. It wouldn't necessarily compensate for the losses caused by the rising waters, but it was a start.

Hamish continued with his work in his state-of-the-art laboratory in the basement of the house on Stoner Drive. He had brought all of his data and some of his prototypes from the lab at the Rockefeller University Institute and simply resumed his work. He contacted Dr. Nurse and promised that the Rockefeller Institute would get full credit under the research and employment agreement that they had for whatever work he did.

Dr. Nurse was completely satisfied with this arrangement, and had promptly e-mailed an addendum to Hamish's contract to this effect. Dad checked it over, pronounced it acceptable, and Hamish signed it. I scanned it and then we sent it back, both by e-mail and snail mail.

As for me, the understanding was a bit different. I could resume at the Rockefeller Institute any time that we felt safe moving back to Manhattan and using our offices there. Meanwhile, my latest book had gone to press. The Institute could share the credit from that with me, but as for any subsequent works, I would have to do them on my own.

In the interim, I looked into obtaining faculty borrowing privileges at the University of Connecticut Health Center, in the Lyman Maynard Stowe Medical Library. That place had a small history of medicine room. I wrote to Dr. Nurse asking for an introduction to the head librarian there, with the purpose of gaining access to those materials, plus interlibrary loan and borrowing privileges. Soon I was all set to continue my work, minus the lecturing duties. I would be working independently and without any other pay than the proceeds of any books that resulted from my efforts, but I didn't care. I loved what I did.

My parents were glad to see me and Hamish just pick up our professional lives where we had left off, but sorry that we had lost the chance to have a home together on our own. But so many other people were still wandering the countryside into September trying to resettle anywhere they could that we couldn't spend much time feeling sorry for ourselves.

We hardly dared to go out for groceries and fuel let alone enjoy a trip to a mall or restaurant. It wasn't safe for another year. Malls, shops, grocery stores and restaurants were having trouble receiving supplies. Moving goods around the nation had become difficult due to the loss of many roads, railroads and dockyards. FEMA hadn't been very helpful, but that was to be expected with a global catastrophe. FEMA had been set up for small disasters such as Hurricane Katrina (amazing that I now thought of that one as small!), not problems on a national scale such as rising sea levels.

The government was busy with a mad rush to salvage whatever it could of existing infrastructure and then move it inland and reassemble it. But that couldn't restore the nation's transit systems; new docks, railroads, train stations, marinas, and roads would have to be built in many places. The result was a constant snarl of traffic jams everywhere we went, even at off-peak hours. It was such a hassle for anyone to go anywhere that we procrastinated when we needed groceries, then gritted our teeth and faced it when we absolutely had to.

Gradually, I got used to it, and developed a routine of going only once each week – or less – to the Health Center Library for books. I hated to have to drive so slowly, and to spend so much time getting to places that I had previously reached in a quarter of the time that it now took. When I thought of how bad it was for people who had to do this twice each day plus fight their way through it all for groceries, I told myself that I had it easy.

As these difficulties continued, I thought about ways to supply our own fruits and vegetables. I might not be able to keep buying fish as much as we needed it, or chicken, but I could try to grow my own fruits and vegetables. When I was little, I had learned from my grandparents in Provence about growing lavender and other herbs; time to try it with raspberries, blackberries, strawberries, tomatoes, scallions, lettuce, spinach, eggplant, green beans, asparagus, corn, squash, pumpkins, and whatever else we liked to eat.

I went online and ordered seeds plus whatever gardening supplies I couldn't buy at local nurseries. Maybe they wouldn't get through, maybe they would. I had nothing to lose by trying to set up a garden, and a lot to gain. And I wasn't the only person who had formerly relied on grocery stores and farmers' markets, and who was now trying to grow a lot of food on her own.

When I started setting this up, it was already fall, if only according to the calendar. Fall seemed to have been postponed, and winter on hold, but I began to get a feel for the shift in North American growing seasons. On the assumption that the growing season had shifted to the spring and the fall, with summer having become too hot for certain crops, I made my plans.

Meanwhile, I ordered some other supplies: canning equipment. If we couldn't rely on grocery stores, we would have to preserve our own fruits and vegetables. I wasn't thrilled to have to devote so much time to the task, but it beat sitting in traffic accomplishing nothing as I added greenhouse gases to the atmosphere running my car for hours on end.

An added dividend to making raspberry and blackberry and strawberry jams occurred to me: I was a gourmet cook and baker. It was therefore quite likely that my results would taste wonderful, and that the family would appreciate them more than anything we had bought in stores. Maybe, once I got used to this change, I wouldn't mind it so much.

My mother got into the habit of surfing the web for news and recipes as she realized the full implications of what was happening to the nation's infrastructure. I was fascinated to see her adopt less wasteful habits; she had always seemed less than interested in recycling. Now she was making an about-face. Dad watched and then joined the new routines.

Hamish ordered an old-fashioned, non-motorized lawnmower and kept the yard looking as good as the lawn service had ever done. For the flower beds along the perimeter, I had shears to trim the edges of the lawn, gloves to pull weeds, and plant food. That was all lovely, but now I broke some news to Hamish: I wanted his help converting one end of the yard to garden soil. He looked at me for a moment as I showed him the plans I had drawn up, incredulous, and then nodded. "Free exercise, I guess. It had to happen sooner or later." Soon he was spending hours each day with me outside, ripping up a third of the huge back yard.

My parents had no objection to this destruction and reorganization. Dad was acutely aware of the conditions that had led to this; trips to the grocery stores took up a whole day each weekend, only to have us come home without many of the things on our list. The stories he told about people at the office struggling to cope with the shortages revealed this.

Dad said that people at the law were exhausted from these efforts. Entering Hartford was now a huge production, as was getting out of it. Cars stretched in lines that snaked through the city, clogging the streets around Bushnell Park and the courthouses and hospitals. Sometimes, if anyone dared to go away, getting back in time for work after a weekend spent checking on elderly parents or just scoping out the changes in the landscape was impossible. People were missing work everywhere, not just at Dad's law firm, as they made their way back.

The supplies I ordered arrived several weeks later, another change that did not surprise me, but they arrived intact. I remembered when I had been able to get whatever I ordered the next week, or even the next day. No more; not with the nation's infrastructure in an uproar.

International news mesmerized me as usual. What was happening to people in other countries as their homes flooded and they had to rush inland, and where would they resettle? Would the new places be drought-ridden and unable to sustain farming and grazing, and thus no bargain after floods had driven people out of their old homes?

In many cases, the answer was yes. In others, people crowded the cities and tried to adjust to urban life after being farmers. That didn't work out very well, and soon the cities of Southeast Asia and Brazil swelled past capacity, making life there unpleasant to say the very least. Bangladesh ceased to exist altogether, Bali shrank, Rio de Janeiro's favelas mushroomed beyond the city's borders, and fights broke out everywhere over living space and food.

Manhattan settled into an odd routine of ferry rides for office workers as parents shipped their kids to the suburbs whenever possible. Any parent with relatives living outside the city and upland – grandparents, aunts and uncles, siblings, anyone – who could take in their children transferred them to other schools, sacrificing childhoods to their safety and education. Parents stayed in the city to work, occasionally making it out on weekends to see their offspring.

Columbia University, New York University, Lincoln Center continued to function, as did most of the museums of Manhattan's museums. However, there was a period of several months in which the basements of these institutions were hastily emptied into the upper floors until the artifacts could be transported elsewhere – off the island, inland and upland.

Sending things to other museums was out of the question as institutions all over the planet were in the same predicament, scrambling to preserve their own cultural treasures. The media carried stories – complete with photos and video – showing severely compressed exhibit space and the extensions that had been built as MOMA and MMA had expanded stuffed to capacity with art that waited for a ride out. Warehouses with heavy guards in upstate New York were the solution.

But the Rockefeller University Institute was partially submerged, its basements useless. Thankfully, the hospital had moved all of its diagnostic equipment to upper levels in time. I watched, fascinated, as Dr. Nurse was shown on the news being brought from the main gate by canoe to Founders Hall, propelled by a pole – just like a gondola in Venice. The only differences were his surroundings and the lack of elegance to his conveyance.

Similar problems were being faced in the other boroughs of the city, and one report announced that L.L. Bean was doing a brisk business selling canoes…so much so that it couldn't fill the orders fast enough. Sporting goods businesses around the nation were cashing in on the environmental devastation.

JFK International Airport was restored to functioning order, achieved over the next year at enormous cost, funded by taxes. The solution was a system of levies higher than the ones in New Orleans. As it was built, workers and materials got around with motorboats.

Just to give a sense of perspective, sea level had risen by a total of 20 feet. When it had started, JFK International Airport had been 12.7 feet above sea level. Now 7.3 feet of water had to be held back. I wondered how that looked to passengers in planes that were about to take off, as they stared out the windows at a water level that was partway up the side of the plane but pressed up against a series of cement walls, threatening to spill over the top and engulf them.

It looked like what I had anticipated the previous spring had finally come to pass: New York City was now the new Venice.

Chapter 38

Nae-Née's Results are Tallied

In the summer of 2014, a survey was posted on the website for the United States Department of Demographics. It tallied the results of using Nae-Née.

Half of all pregnancies used to be unplanned. Not anymore; not thanks to Nae-Née.

Data from before the Birth Control Treaty and before the 28th Amendment was sparse but still helpful in understanding the device's impact on fertility rates. Data since then was even more so, thanks to government computers keeping tallies of pregnancies, licenses, and births.

The birth rate in the United States had dropped to a quarter of its former statistic.

Other nations were posting similar successes, with drops in birth rates varying according to the number of birth licenses that had been granted. All nations seemed to be going for a greater than 60 percent reduction in their overall human population, following the Birth Control Treaty's directive.

The results met with mixed reactions; some people cried in outrage all over again, angry to have been denied licenses, angry about being just over the cut-off age for being granted a license when the new law was enacted. Others felt relief that the policy was working. Still others continued to fear that it was too little, too late, to save the planet's climate, and preserve it in a state that humans would continue to find habitable, let alone enjoyable.

Hamish and I did not return to Manhattan, and for now, we were not sure that we wanted to. How would we get in and out? A whole new infrastructure would have to be built first, and that was still being budgeted and planned. Only some of it was immediately underway.

Andrew had gone over to see our firehouse and reported that the water was not even close to it, so we could have lived comfortably in it. The apartment building where he and Cathy lived was just on the edge of the encroaching water, so they were able to keep their home as it was.

Sea level appeared to have stabilized. But the city was in a state of upheaval and shock. We invited both Andrew and Cathy to visit us in Connecticut, but they decided not to come; Andrew was too fascinated by what was going on in Manhattan, by the discussions at the Henry George School, and by the events at the United Nations. Getting out of the city was tough, too.

The United Nations had opted not to move away from its headquarters. It was determined to make a statement about global warming, biodiversity loss, and rising sea levels by making do with the campus it had in Manhattan, even if that meant moving about in canoes. A wall had been extended around the grounds to keep the canoes from drifting out into the East River. Security had been forced to hire a whole new contingent of boat taxi drivers to get the delegates in and out of the buildings.

Now that much of the planet's former lands were now under water, the climate was hotter in the summer, colder in the winter, and land was wetter and dryer wherever it was wet and dry. Fighting over resources was happening everywhere, and U.N. peacekeepers had more work than ever to help contain it. Even parts of the United States were starting to feel these effects.

With the Rockefeller University Institute's campus under water, if we went to work, it would involve boats just to go between the gate and the buildings. We were going to wait for things to stabilize further before contemplating a return. When New York City truly felt like Venice – like a pleasant playground of a place that with all of its public safety concerns addressed – we thought we might like to go back. But not right now.

Hamish had everything he needed right here in Connecticut, thanks to my obsessive and secretive planning, so he had gone right back to work on his neurosurgical nanite system, and was about to collaborate on a project with some surgeons at Hartford Hospital to test it out.

As for me, I reconnected with old friends and new, mostly by phone and e-mail, and continued to write, play the violin, cook, bake, and enjoy both of our family's cats. Spock and Eowyn amazed us all by getting along. Visiting friends in person was too complicated for now.

Travel to places other than local grocery stores and restaurants had gotten tougher, although shopping for books and clothing had gotten easier. Even so, sometimes, we would just get clothes and books and music by mail order.

Homeless people and migrants had become ubiquitous; everywhere we looked or went, we saw them. It was the scene in Pakistan repeating itself here – right here in the United States, in Connecticut – where we lived and didn't usually think about such awful problems unless we checked the news reports.

Once we had been forced to retreat from the rising sea levels, back to the safety of central Connecticut, back where we were high enough from the new sea level not to have to worry about property loss or damage from it, we checked the news reports often. We checked for signs of social upheaval caused by the rise in sea level, and every report contained a new incident.

As the residents of places that were now underwater had retreated – people who, unlike us, were not lucky enough to have another home to go to – they had scrambled to protect whatever moveable property they could, packing it, carrying it, driving it, floating it up rivers in boats seeking higher ground. It was a good plan, but when millions of people at once do that, the unwelcome discovery that awaits them is nothing but insufficiency.

This was a settled nation, one full of people on developed land. National parks and Native American reservations were suddenly under siege by the shifting, displaced populations. The government stepped in and protected much of the national parks, but as in the nineteenth century, it did not make the same effort for the tribes who had lived here first.

Things quickly got ugly there, and in most other areas. It was the crime reports that held our attention, gripped like a sickening vise as rapes, murders, robberies, and squatters' disputes became standard fare. Highway robbery ceased to be just a saying.

We were lucky, guarded by Blackout Security, and in an area without many such incidents, but when we first got back to Connecticut, it was every few days that we saw a live broadcast in which a reporter got too close to resource conflict, a mini resource war. There were injuries, and at least four deaths around the country. Television newscasters who had looked forward to paying their dues in rain and snowstorms before being rewarded with desks, makeup, and teleprompters complained bitterly that this was not what they had signed up for, but most kept at it.

We were all starting to rethink what was usual.

When we went out to the movies, Nae-Née seemed to crop up in every plot. It had inserted itself into human life to such an extent that it was now part of the background in characters' lives: factory workers, migrant laborers, high school kids, office workers, football players, social workers, veterinarians, retail workers – everyone.

It was strange to go to the theater to watch a movie about spies or waitresses and find our invention mentioned here and there in the dialogue, but we soon got used to it.

Thanks to the still-depressed economy, the tax bases of many towns all over the country were in financial straits. This meant that, among other cuts, schools were starting to get rid certain departments. Sports were safe as always, but drama teachers and music instructors were the first casualties. Soon they seemed like an endangered species as the areas of study that gave the academics meaning were becoming a thing of the past.

I went to visit the financial planner, with a tax attorney in tow. I had a plan.

After that meeting, endowments for the public school systems of several towns in our area were set up. These endowments were designated exclusively for the arts: music, drama and studio art department would have teachers, supplies, instruments, whatever they needed to continue as before. In many cases, they would be in better shape than before. Sports be damned, I thought; as long as I was providing the funds, it was all for the arts!

This meant meeting with school boards. I brought the attorney with me to West Hartford, Bloomfield, Windsor, Avon, Simsbury, Farmington, Canton, and New Britain. It was fun.

Most of the groups we met with were overjoyed, but one actually looked a gift horse in the mouth: it was Avon. Actually, it didn't get that far, but I noticed a high school coach present, plus some people whom I had been warned cared more for sports than any other school program.

Right off the bat, I announced that no sports program would ever get a cent from me. Hamish was sitting next to me, and when he saw the faces fall, he grinned and looked away. He told me later that he thought it was great entertainment to watch his violin-playing wife preserve kids' chances to enjoy music. I could have been really obnoxious and played an imaginary violin in mid-air when I saw those disappointed looks, but I was good. I didn't do that. It was just so satisfying to see people open and then shut their mouths.

But why was I doing this? Was it to help these kids beat nearly impossible, insurmountable odds at getting accepted to a good college? Was it because this was the most education and cultural activity that most of them could ever hope to experience in an overpopulated world? Was it both? Whatever the reason, even though I couldn't help everyone, I kept at it. I couldn't just sit back and do nothing.

Our garden had worked out well; it rivaled the one that Bethany's father had in rural northeastern Massachusetts. We had rows and rows of raspberry and blackberry bushes, and the vegetable garden had yielded a decent amount of food, some of which we had put away in jars for the winter. It turned out, to my great satisfaction, that my recipes for raspberry and blackberry jams were indeed family favorites.

The strawberries were something that we could grow indoors year-round, along with fresh herbs. I went nuts with that project, setting up plants all over the bay window in the kitchen and out in the family room overlooking the back yard. Soon my parents were complaining about the loss of space to the family's indoor garden.

I suggested adding a conservatory onto the back of the house, complete with a door that led to the garden, and they agreed. We hired an architect who designed a nice round room – similar to the one at the Mark Twain House – and he managed to complete it in a month. It had windows all around, plus a conical ceiling of more windows, all heated and with its own irrigation system, and its structure was made of wrought iron and stone. It was built to last.

Hamish helped me set up the herbs and strawberries the next day. He no longer fretted over missing work time now that we had made a living from Nae-Née and he had his lab in the basement. A little time off and distraction didn't bother him anymore.

It was perfect in just a few hours: I had even managed to get a beautiful purple wisteria vine, which Hamish helped me attach to the ceiling panels. My mother was all for adding a decorative fountain in the center, but I wouldn't let her; that was for more edible plants.

This was built in November; by spring, we had gotten so used to harvesting herbs from the conservatory that we no longer looked for them at Stew Leonard's or Whole Foods or anywhere else. I just kept buying more seeds and expanding my trove of plants.

I was scared by the changes to the environment, and by a memory of a can of sealed mango purée that Hamish had shown me years ago. The lid had expanded significantly upwards as bacteria formed, even though the contents had been carefully pasteurized and preserved. The lesson from that was that amassing a trove of canned goods is pointless; they won't last forever. The only way to survive is to be able to grow fresh fruits and vegetables each year.

Spring and summer were a lot calmer than the previous year. Travel on local roads had gotten easier everywhere, it seemed, after the relocation of so many people had died down. People weren't particularly comfortable or happy, and many families had been forced to separate or reunite in the upheaval, but the reorganization had been accomplished. Extended rather than nuclear families became the norm again, with multiple generations sharing a home. It was like nineteenth-century living arrangements had come back into vogue, albeit by necessity.

That was the weirdest part of it all, it seemed to me. Where living with one's parents had once been viewed as a sign of personal failure, doing so had become normal. Now, it enhanced a family's general safety, compensated for decreased living spaces, and saved resources. The stigma that Hamish and I had once felt at living with my parents was gone.

No, we weren't interested in moving back to Manhattan any time soon.

We had contributed a share of our fresh herbs and berries to a special event for local chefs who wanted to demonstrate that people could adapt to changes in the environment and America's infrastructure. The point of it was to prepare everything from locally grown ingredients. Farms and home gardeners in Simsbury, Avon, Canton and Farmington had supplied the chefs with the raw materials for the feast.

Anyone who wanted to could make a reservation online. There was room for a hundred people, with ten picnic tables set up for the event. People from the area had signed up, plus a few from other more distant towns. It was a chance to talk to strangers and compare notes about all of the dramatic changes that both our country and our planet had gone through in the past year.

"You've changed the world with Nae-Née," someone told me as we sat at one of the picnic tables enjoying the chefs' creations.

"But did the change come in time to save us?" I couldn't help responding. "Are there already too many of us wanting and needing too many resources to save our planet?"

"Why do you ask that? I mean, the planet will still be here," the person next to me said.

"I mean to say that if we don't protect our own ecosystem, which is what gives us the ingredients for this wonderful feast, we as a species are just going to die anyway. And no one wants that." People stared at me, but I didn't care. It was true.

"Why worry? The next generation will figure that out. There's time for that later," said a woman seated diagonally across from me.

Hamish and I glanced at each other, but said nothing, waiting to see what another diner would say in response. Sure enough, someone did.

"There is no later." A climatology student from the University of Connecticut spoke up. She was in the Ph.D. program, and everyone turned to listen to her. "We have to pay attention and do this now. There's no time left to delay. A huge part of why we are in this mess is that for too long, we have thought that we did not need to freak out about this yet. If there were really more time for that attitude, the polar icecaps would still be in existence. Climate change is only half of the picture. The rest is biodiversity. Without it, humans cannot expect to survive. We need plants or we're done."

Someone farther down on the left spoke up as well. "The Dust Bowl might be back soon, too. Farmers in the Midwest got too excited a couple of years ago when Russia stopped exporting grain – due to the peat forest fires there – and increased the amount of land used for farming grain in the U.S., hoping to make a profit. Eighty-year-old people who remembered the environmental devastation of the Dust Bowl in the 1930s advised against it, but no one listened. Now the land is already dried out. Soon it will be useless for several years – or more – until the land is given a chance to heal itself. And that means less food for all of us – less than before the over-farming started – and higher prices, which we are already starting to see."

I added that I had spent the spring obsessively watching for honeybees around the berries that I loved so much, and that I had grown peony flowers outside the conservatory just to watch for the bees, but had not seen very many. Just one or two had appeared when I was watching, and I could only hope that more showed up when I wasn't watching. "Raspberries are my favorite fruit, and I don't want to have to adapt to never having any again. Meanwhile, food prices have gone up thanks to the relentless drought. People without fountains of financial resources – and that means most people – shouldn't have to bankrupt themselves to eat as healthy and delicious a meal as we are about to enjoy, and on a regular basis. I don't care how crazy that might sound."

There were nods of understanding, and someone said that we shouldn't have to do that, but that it seemed as though the carelessness of the past century or so was going to punish those of us who were living on this planet now. The conversation lulled as people took this in, and then, as humans always do, someone said, "Well, on that cheerful note..." and changed the subject to something less depressing.

Which left the question: who would deal with the question of preserving and protecting our planet for the next generations? Making sure that the planet wasn't too crowded for them would only solve part of the equation. The rest of the math problem was about other forms of human greed. Fewer people, less resource use, and a lot more self-control were the unpleasant and immediate future realities that we would have to face. The party would soon be over – permanently – if we didn't.

I was glad I wasn't going to inflict any of these problems on another human being by reproducing. I loved my life and all of the wonderful things that I had had, but if so much of the natural world would not be available to the next generation to wonder at and enjoy, then I was glad not to be inflicting that lack and the problem of survival without its rewards on anyone else.

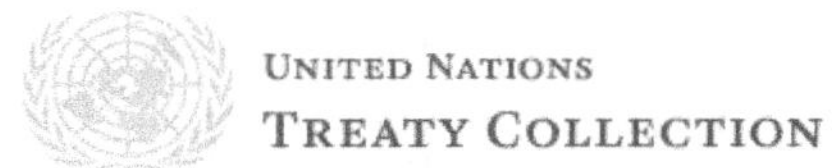

Chapter IX: Health

Title 6:
The Convention on the Global Application of Medical Human
Population Control

21 December 2012

INTRODUCTION
Content and Significance of the Convention

PREAMBLE

PART I
Discrimination (Article 1)
Policy Measures (Article 2)
Guarantee of Basic Human Rights and Fundamental Freedoms
(Article 3)
Special Measures (Article 4)
Sex Role Stereotyping and Prejudice (Article 5)
Prostitution (Article 6)

PART II
Education (Article 7)
Employment (Article 8)
Health (Article 9)
Economic and Social Benefits (Article 10)

PART III
Law (Article 11)
Marriage and Family Life (Article 12)

PART IV
Committee on Birth Control Administration (Article 13)
National Reports (Article 14)

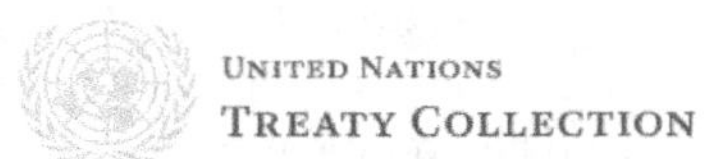

The United Nations Convention on Planetary Human Population Reduction by Birth Control

Full text of the Convention in English

INTRODUCTION

On 21 December 2012, the Convention on Planetary Human Population Reduction by Birth Control was adopted by the United Nations General Assembly. It entered into force as an international treaty on 22 December 2012 after the twentieth country had ratified it.

The Convention was the culmination of nearly 10 years of work by the United Nations Commission on the Status of Human Overpopulation, a body established in 2001 to monitor the situation of human health and quality of life. The Commission's work has focused attention on the results of human overpopulation on overall quality of life, highlighting the need for restraints on population growth.

The full text of the Convention is set out herein:

CONVENTION ON PLANETARY HUMAN POPULATION REDUCTION BY BIRTH CONTROL

The States' Parties to the present Convention,

PREAMBLE

Noting that the Charter of the United Nations reaffirms faith in fundamental human rights, in the dignity and worth of the human person and in the equal rights of men and women,

Noting that the Universal Declaration of Planetary Human Population Reduction by Birth Control affirms the principle of the inadmissibility of discrimination and proclaims that all human beings are born free and equal in dignity and rights and that everyone is entitled to all the rights and freedoms set forth therein, without distinction of any kind, including distinction based on sex,

Noting that the States Parties to the International Covenants on Human Rights have the obligation to ensure the equal rights of men and women and future generations to enjoy all economic, social, cultural, civil and political rights,

Considering the international conventions concluded under the auspices of the United Nations and the specialized agencies promoting equality of rights for men and women,

Noting also the resolutions, declarations and recommendations adopted by the United Nations and the specialized agencies promoting the regulation of human reproduction,

Recalling that overpopulation threatens the principles of equality of rights and respect for human dignity, is an obstacle to the participation of future generations in the political, social, economic and cultural life of their countries, hampers the growth of the prosperity of society and the family and makes more difficult the full development of the potentialities of women in the service of their countries and of humanity,

Concerned that human overpopulation leads to ever-increasing strains on access to food, health, education, training and opportunities for employment and other needs,

Convinced that the establishment of the new international economic order based on equity and justice will contribute significantly towards the promotion of equality between men and women,

Affirming that mandatory human birth control and human reproduction licensing will facilitate the strengthening of international peace and security, the relaxation of international tension, mutual co-operation among all States irrespective of their social and economic systems, general and complete disarmament, in particular nuclear disarmament under strict and effective international control, the affirmation of the principles of justice, equality and mutual benefit in relations among countries and the realization of the right of peoples under alien and colonial domination and foreign occupation to self-determination and independence, as well as respect for national sovereignty and territorial integrity, will promote social progress and development and as a consequence will contribute to the attainment of happiness and the achievement of each child's fullest potential,

Convinced that the full and complete development of a country, the welfare of the world and the cause of peace require the mandatory reduction in human population and maintenance of lower rates of human reproduction,

Bearing in mind the necessity for preserving the health, welfare and happiness of the family and its importance to the development of society, so far not fully recognized, the social significance of education and work opportunities to the future of children, and aware that the role of women in procreation should not be a basis for discrimination but that the production and upbringing of children requires a sharing of responsibility between men and women and society as a whole,

Determined to implement the principles set forth in the Declaration on Planetary Human Population Reduction by Birth Control and, for that purpose, to adopt the measures required for the elimination of human overpopulation and its consequences on quality of life,

Determined that the human species shall not become a mere failed biological experiment, or an endangered species among the many wonderful and already endangered species on this planet,

Declaring that no policy of population management shall be abused or manipulated to reduce or eliminate the percentage of humans from any particular culture, but instead shall be mindful to allow for the continuance and preservation of each culture on the planet,

Concluding that the application of the birth control device known as Nae-Née offers a solution to the problem of human overpopulation,

Have agreed on the following:

PART I

Article 1

For the purposes of the present Convention, the term "discrimination" shall mean any distinction, exclusion or restriction made on the basis of sex which has the effect or purpose of impairing or nullifying the recognition, enjoyment or exercise by women, irrespective of their marital status, on a basis of equality of men and women, of human rights and fundamental freedoms in the political, economic, social, cultural, civil or any other field, and any distinction, exclusion or restriction made on the basis of culture which has the same effect.

Article 2

States Parties wish to improve overall quality of life for humans and the other species with whom human share this planet, and agree to pursue by all appropriate means and without delay a policy of reducing human overpopulation and so, to this end, undertake:

(a) To pursue a policy of human birth control and licensed human reproduction in their national constitutions or other appropriate legislation if not yet incorporated therein and to ensure, through law and other appropriate means, the practical realization of this principle;

(b) To adopt appropriate legislative and other measures, including sanctions where appropriate, prohibiting all unlicensed births;

(c) To establish legal protection for the physical integrity of women on an equal basis with men and to ensure through competent national tribunals and other public institutions the effective prevention for both women and men against pregnancy;

(d) To refrain from engaging in any act or practice of discrimination against women and to ensure that public authorities and institutions shall act in conformity with this obligation;

(e) To take all appropriate measures to reduce the overall human population of each nation by 60 percent, specifically through the application of the Nae-Née nanobot birth control device;

(f) To take all appropriate measures, including legislation, to modify or abolish existing laws, regulations, customs and practices which allow for unchecked human reproduction;

(g) To repeal all penal provisions which prosecute or prevent abortion of human fetuses unless for purposes of gender selection, as well as to repeal all proscriptions against human birth control, and to allow for the use of resulting human stem cells for medical care and research.

(h) To establish a repository for human stem cells, complete with facilities for sharing those stem cells among patients in need of them.

(i) To ensure that the use of Nae-Née in no way serves as a method for any eugenics program. Each ethnic, cultural or other group shall continue to make up the same proportion of the overall population as before.

Article 3

States Parties shall take in all fields, in particular in the political, social, economic and cultural fields, all appropriate measures, including legislation, to ensure the full development and advancement of women, for the purpose of guaranteeing them the exercise and enjoyment of human rights and fundamental freedoms on a basis of equality with men.

Article 4

1. Adoption by States Parties of temporary special measures aimed at accelerating human birth control and the harvesting of human stem cells shall not be considered discrimination against either women or men as defined in the present Convention, but shall in no way entail as a consequence the maintenance of unequal or separate standards; these measures shall be discontinued when the objectives of equality of opportunity and treatment have been achieved.

2. Adoption by States Parties of special measures, including those measures contained in the present Convention, aimed at preventing maternity shall not be considered discriminatory.

Article 5

States Parties shall take all appropriate measures:

(a) To modify the social and cultural patterns of conduct of men and women, with a view to achieving the elimination of prejudices and customary and all other practices which are based on the idea of the inferiority or the superiority of either of the sexes or on stereotyped roles for men and women;

(b) To ensure that family education includes a proper understanding of maternity as a social function and the recognition of the common responsibility of men and women in the upbringing and development of their children, it being understood that the interest of the children is the primary consideration in all cases.

Article 6

States Parties shall take all appropriate measures, including legislation, to suppress all forms of traffic in women and girls and the exploitation of prostitution of women and girls.

PART II

Article 7

States Parties shall take all appropriate measures to eliminate discrimination against women in order to ensure to them equal rights with men in the field of education and in particular to ensure, on a basis of equality of men and women:

(a) The same conditions for career and vocational guidance, for access to studies and for the achievement of diplomas in educational establishments of all categories in rural as well as in urban areas; this equality shall be ensured in pre-school, general, technical, professional and higher technical education, as well as in all types of vocational training;

(b) Access to the same curricula, the same examinations, teaching staff with qualifications of the same standard and school premises and equipment of the same quality;

(c) The elimination of any stereotyped concept of the roles of men and women at all levels and in all forms of education by encouraging coeducation and other types of education which will help to achieve this aim and, in particular, by the revision of textbooks and school programs and the adaptation of teaching methods;

(d) The same opportunities to benefit from scholarships and other study grants;

(e) The same opportunities for access to programs of continuing education, including adult and functional literacy programs, particularly those aimed at reducing, at the earliest possible time, any gap in education existing between men and women;

(f) The reduction of female student drop-out rates and the organization of programs for girls and women who have left school prematurely;

(g) The same opportunities to participate actively in sports and physical education;

(h) Access to specific educational information to help to ensure the health and well-being of families, including information and advice on family planning.

Article 8

1. States Parties shall take all appropriate measures to eliminate discrimination against women in the field of employment in order to ensure, on a basis of equality of men and women, the same rights, in particular:

(a) The right to the same employment opportunities, including the application of the same criteria for selection in matters of employment;

(b) The right to free choice of profession and employment, the right to promotion, job security and all benefits and conditions of service and the right to receive vocational training and retraining, including apprenticeships, advanced vocational training and recurrent training;

(c) The right to equal remuneration, including benefits, and to equal treatment in respect of work of equal value, as well as equality of treatment in the evaluation of the quality of work;

(d) The right to protection of health and to safety in working conditions, including the safeguarding of the function of reproduction.

2. In order to prevent discrimination against women on the grounds of marriage or maternity and to ensure their effective right to work, States Parties shall take appropriate measures:

(a) To encourage the provision of the necessary supporting social services to enable parents to combine family obligations with work responsibilities and participation in public life, in particular through promoting the establishment and development of a network of child-care facilities;

(b) To provide special protection to women during pregnancy in types of work proved to be harmful to them.

3. Protective legislation relating to matters covered in this article shall be reviewed periodically in the light of scientific and technological knowledge and shall be revised, repealed or extended as necessary.

Article 9

1. States Parties shall take all appropriate measures to eliminate discrimination against women in the field of health care in order to ensure, on a basis of equality of men and women, access to health care services, including those related to family planning.

2. Notwithstanding the provisions of paragraph I of this article, States Parties shall ensure to women appropriate services in connection with birth control and abortion services.

Article 10

States Parties shall take all appropriate measures to eliminate discrimination against women in other areas of economic and social life in order to ensure, on a basis of equality of men and women, the same rights.

PART III

Article 11

States Parties shall accord to women equality with men before the law.

Article 12

1. States Parties shall take all appropriate measures to eliminate discrimination against women in all matters relating to marriage and family relations and in particular shall ensure, on a basis of equality of men and women:

(a) The same right to enter into or dissolve a marriage;

(b) The same right freely to choose a spouse and to enter into marriage only with their free and full consent;

(c) The same rights and responsibilities during marriage and at its dissolution;

(d) The same rights and responsibilities as parents, irrespective of their marital status, in matters relating to their children; in all cases the interests of the children shall be paramount;

(e) The same rights to decide freely and responsibly on the number and spacing of their children and to have access to the information, education and means to enable them to exercise these rights, whether those children be male or female;

(f) The same rights and responsibilities with regard to guardianship, wardship, trusteeship and adoption of children, or similar institutions where these concepts exist in national legislation; in all cases the interests of the children shall be paramount;

(g) The same personal rights as husband and wife, including the right to choose a family name, a profession and an occupation;

(h) The same rights for both spouses in respect of the ownership, acquisition, management, administration, enjoyment and disposition of property, whether free of charge or for a valuable consideration.

2. The betrothal and the marriage of a child shall have no legal effect, and all necessary action, including legislation, shall be taken to specify a minimum age for marriage and to make the registration of marriages in an official registry compulsory.

PART IV

Article 13

1. For the purpose of considering the progress made in the implementation of the present Convention, there shall be established a Status of Human Birth Control and Overpopulation (hereinafter referred to as the Committee) consisting, at the time of entry into force of the Convention, of eighteen and, after ratification of or accession to the Convention by the thirty-fifth State Party, of twenty-three experts of high moral standing and competence in the field covered by the Convention. The experts shall be elected by States Parties from among their nationals and shall serve in their personal capacity, consideration being given to equitable

geographical distribution and to the representation of the different forms of civilization as well as the principal legal systems.

2. The members of the Committee shall be elected by secret ballot from a list of persons nominated by States Parties. Each State Party may nominate one person from among its own nationals.

3. The initial election shall be held six months after the date of the entry into force of the present Convention. At least three months before the date of each election the Secretary-General of the United Nations shall address a letter to the States Parties inviting them to submit their nominations within two months. The Secretary-General shall prepare a list in alphabetical order of all persons thus nominated, indicating the States Parties which have nominated them, and shall submit it to the States Parties.

4. Elections of the members of the Committee shall be held at a meeting of States Parties convened by the Secretary-General at United Nations Headquarters. At that meeting, for which two thirds of the States Parties shall constitute a quorum, the persons elected to the Committee shall be those nominees who obtain the largest number of votes and an absolute majority of the votes of the representatives of States Parties present and voting.

5. The members of the Committee shall be elected for a term of four years. However, the terms of nine of the members elected at the first election shall expire at the end of two years; immediately after the first election the names of these nine members shall be chosen by lot by the Chairman of the Committee.

6. The election of the five additional members of the Committee shall be held in accordance with the provisions of paragraphs 2, 3 and 4 of this article, following the thirty-fifth ratification or accession. The terms of two of the additional members elected on this occasion shall expire at the end of two years, the names of these two members having been chosen by lot by the Chairman of the Committee.

7. For the filling of casual vacancies, the State Party whose expert has ceased to function as a member of the Committee shall appoint another expert from among its nationals, subject to the approval of the Committee.

8. The members of the Committee shall, with the approval of the General Assembly, receive emoluments from United Nations resources on such terms and conditions as the Assembly may decide, having regard to the importance of the Committee's responsibilities.

9. The Secretary-General of the United Nations shall provide the necessary staff and facilities for the effective performance of the functions of the Committee under the present Convention.

Article 14

1. States Parties undertake to submit to the Secretary-General of the United Nations, for consideration by the Committee, a report on the legislative, judicial, administrative or other measures which they have adopted to give effect to the provisions of the present Convention and on the progress made in this respect:

(a) Within one year after the entry into force for the State concerned;

(b) Thereafter at least every four years and further whenever the Committee so requests.

2. Reports may indicate factors and difficulties affecting the degree of fulfillment of obligations under the present Convention.

Article 15

1. The Committee shall adopt its own rules of procedure.

2. The Committee shall elect its officers for a term of two years.

Article 16

1. The Committee shall normally meet for a period of not more than two weeks annually in order to consider the reports submitted in accordance with article 18 of the present Convention.

2. The meetings of the Committee shall normally be held at United Nations Headquarters or at any other convenient place as determined by the Committee.

Article 17

1. The Committee shall, through the Economic and Social Council, report annually to the General Assembly of the United Nations on its activities and may make suggestions and general recommendations based on the examination of reports and information received from the States Parties. Such suggestions and general recommendations shall be included in the report of the Committee together with comments, if any, from States Parties.

2. The Secretary-General of the United Nations shall transmit the reports of the Committee to the Commission on the Status of Human Overpopulation for its information.

Article 18

The specialized agencies shall be entitled to be represented at the consideration of the implementation of such provisions of the present Convention as fall within the scope of their activities. The Committee may invite the specialized agencies to submit reports on the implementation of the Convention in areas falling within the scope of their activities.

PART V

Article 19

Nothing in the present Convention shall affect any provisions that are more conducive to the achievement of equality between men and women which may be contained:

(a) In the legislation of a State Party; or

(b) In any other international convention, treaty or agreement in force for that State.

Article 20

States Parties undertake to adopt all necessary measures at the national level aimed at achieving the full realization of the rights recognized in the present Convention.

Article 21

1. The present Convention shall be open for signature by all States.

2. The Secretary-General of the United Nations is designated as the depositary of the present Convention.

3. The present Convention is subject to ratification. Instruments of ratification shall be deposited with the Secretary-General of the United Nations.

4. The present Convention shall be open to accession by all States. Accession shall be effected by the deposit of an instrument of accession with the Secretary-General of the United Nations.

Article 22

1. A request for the revision of the present Convention may be made at any time by any State Party by means of a notification in writing addressed to the Secretary-General of the United Nations.

2. The General Assembly of the United Nations shall decide upon the steps, if any, to be taken in respect of such a request.

Article 23

1. The present Convention shall enter into force on the thirtieth day after the date of deposit with the Secretary-General of the United Nations of the twentieth instrument of ratification or accession.

2. For each State ratifying the present Convention or acceding to it after the deposit of the twentieth instrument of ratification or accession, the Convention shall enter into force on the thirtieth day after the date of the deposit of its own instrument of ratification or accession.

Article 24

1. The Secretary-General of the United Nations shall receive and circulate to all States the text of reservations made by States at the time of ratification or accession.

2. A reservation incompatible with the object and purpose of the present Convention shall not be permitted.

3. Reservations may be withdrawn at any time by notification to this effect addressed to the Secretary-General of the United Nations, who shall then inform all States thereof. Such notification shall take effect on the date on which it is received.

Article 25

1. Any dispute between two or more States Parties concerning the interpretation or application of the present Convention which is not settled by negotiation shall, at the request of one of them, be submitted to arbitration. If within six months from the date of the request for arbitration the parties are unable to agree on the organization of the arbitration, any one of those parties may refer the dispute to the International Court of Justice by request in conformity with the Statute of the Court.

2. Each State Party may at the time of signature or ratification of the present Convention or accession thereto declare that it does not consider itself bound by paragraph I of this article. The other States Parties shall not be bound by that paragraph with respect to any State Party which has made such a reservation.

3. Any State Party which has made a reservation in accordance with paragraph 2 of this article may at any time withdraw that reservation by notification to the Secretary-General of the United Nations.

Article 26

The present Convention, the Arabic, Chinese, English, French, Russian and Spanish texts of which are equally authentic, shall be deposited with the Secretary-General of the United Nations.

IN WITNESS WHEREOF the undersigned, duly authorized, have signed the present Convention.

Participant	Date of Issuance	Action
A		
Afghanistan	21/12/2012	Signature
Albania	21/12/2012	Ratification
Algeria	21/12/2012	Acceptance
Andorra	22/12/2012	Ratification
Angola	21/12/2012	Signature
Antigua and Barbuda	21/12/2012	Ratification
Argentina	21/12/2012	Ratification
Armenia	21/12/2012	Ratification
Australia	22/12/2012	Ratification
Austria	22/12/2012	Ratification
Azerbaijan	21/12/2012	Acceptance
B		
Bahamas	22/12/2012	Ratification
Bahrain	22/12/2012	Ratification
Bangladesh	22/12/2012	Acceptance
Barbados	22/12/2012	Acceptance
Belarus	22/12/2012	Ratification
Belgium	22/12/2012	Ratification
Belize	22/12/2012	Acceptance
Benin	21/12/2012	Signature
Bhutan	22/12/2012	Acceptance
Bolivia (Plurinational State of)	22/12/2012	Acceptance

Bosnia and Herzegovina	22/12/2012	Ratification
Botswana	21/12/2012	Signature
Brazil	22/12/2012	Acceptance
Brunei Darussalam	21/12/2012	Signature
Bulgaria	22/12/2012	Ratification
Burkina Faso	21/12/2012	Signature
Burundi	21/12/2012	Signature
C		
Cambodia	26/12/2012	Ratification
Cameroon	21/12/2012	Signature
Canada	22/12/2012	Ratification
Cape Verde	21/12/2012	Signature
Central African Republic	21/12/2012	Signature
Chad	21/12/2012	Signature
Chile	22/12/2012	Ratification
China	22/12/2012	Ratification
Colombia	22/12/2012	Acceptance
Comoros	21/12/2012	Signature
Congo	21/12/2012	Signature
Costa Rica	22/12/2012	Acceptance
Côte D'Ivoire	22/12/2012	Acceptance
Croatia	22/12/2012	Ratification
Cuba	22/12/2012	Acceptance

Cyprus	22/12/2012	Ratification
Czech Republic	22/12/2012	Ratification
D		
Democratic People's Republic of Korea	25/12/2012	Ratification
Democratic Republic of the Congo	21/12/2012	Signature
Denmark	22/12/2012	Ratification
Djibouti	21/12/2012	Signature
Dominica	22/12/2012	Ratification
Dominican Republic	22/12/2012	Ratification
E		
Ecuador	22/12/2012	Ratification
Egypt	25/12/2012	Ratification
El Salvador	22/12/2012	Ratification
Equatoral Guinea	21/12/2012	Signature
Eritrea	21/12/2012	Signature
Estonia	22/12/2012	Ratification
Ethiopia	21/12/2012	Signature
F		
Fiji	24/12/2012	Ratification
Finland	22/12/2012	Ratification
France	22/12/2012	Ratification
G		
Gabon	22/12/2012	Acceptance

Gambia	22/12/2012	Acceptance
Georgia	22/12/2012	Ratification
Germany	22/12/2012	Ratification
Ghana	22/12/2012	Acceptance
Greece	22/12/2012	Ratification
Grenada	22/12/2012	Ratification
Guatemala	22/12/2012	Acceptance
Guinea	22/12/2012	Acceptance
Guinea Bissau	22/12/2012	Acceptance
Guyana	22/12/2012	Acceptance
H		
Haiti	22/12/2012	Ratification
Honduras	22/12/2012	Acceptance
Hungary	22/12/2012	Ratification
I		
Iceland	22/12/2012	Ratification
India	24/12/2012	Ratification
Indonesia	25/12/2012	Ratification
Iran (Islamic Republic of)	21/12/2012	Signature
Iraq	21/12/2012	Signature
Ireland	22/12/2012	Ratification
Israel	24/12/2012	Ratification
Italy	22/12/2012	Ratification
J		

Jamaica	22/12/2012	Ratification
Japan	22/12/2012	Ratification
Jordan	22/12/2012	Ratification
K		
Kazakhstan	22/12/2012	Acceptance
Kenya	21/12/2012	Signature
Kiribati	22/12/2012	Acceptance
Kuwait	25/12/2012	Ratification
Kyrgyzstan	22/12/2012	Acceptance
L		
Lao People's Democratic Republic	25/12/2012	Acceptance
Latvia	22/12/2012	Ratification
Lebanon	22/12/2012	Ratification
Lesotho	21/12/2012	Signature
Liberia	22/12/2012	Acceptance
Libyan Arab Jamahiriya	22/12/2012	Acceptance
Liechtenstein	22/12/2012	Ratification
Lithuania	22/12/2012	Ratification
Luxembourg	22/12/2012	Ratification
M		
Madagascar	21/12/2012	Signature
Malawi	21/12/2012	Signature
Malaysia		Ratification
Maldives	21/12/2012	Signature

Mali	21/12/2012	Signature
Malta		Ratification
Marshall Islands		Ratification
Mauritania	21/12/2012	Signature
Mauritius	21/12/2012	Signature
Mexico		Ratification
Micronesia, Federated States of	21/12/2012	Signature
Monaco		Ratification
Mongolia	21/12/2012	Signature
Montenegro		Ratification
Morocco		Ratification
Mozambique	21/12/2012	Signature
Myanmar		Ratification
N		
Namibia	21/12/2012	Signature
Nauru		Ratification
Nepal		Ratification
Netherlands		Ratification
New Zealand		Ratification
Nicaragua		Acceptance
Niger	21/12/2012	Signature
Nigeria	21/12/2012	Signature

Norway	22/12/2012	Ratification
O		
Oman	22/12/2012	Ratification
P		
Pakistan	22/12/2012	Acceptance
Palau	22/12/2012	Acceptance
Panama	26/12/2012	Ratification
Papua New Guinea	28/12/2012	Ratification
Paraguay	22/12/2012	Acceptance
Peru	26/12/2012	Ratification
Philippines	26/12/2012	Ratification
Poland	22/12/2012	Ratification
Portugal	22/12/2012	Ratification
Q		
Qatar	22/12/2012	Ratification
R		
Republic of Korea	25/12/2012	Ratification
Republic of Moldova	22/12/2012	Ratification
Romania	22/12/2012	Ratification
Russian Federation	22/12/2012	Ratification
Rwanda	21/12/2012	Signature
S		
Saint Kitts and Nevis	22/12/2012	Ratification
Saint Lucia	22/12/2012	Ratification
Saint Vincent and the Grenadines	22/12/2012	Ratification

Samoa	22/12/2012	Ratification
San Marino	22/12/2012	Ratification
Sao Tome and Principe	22/12/2012	Ratification
Saudi Arabia	22/12/2012	Ratification
Senegal	22/12/2012	Acceptance
Serbia	22/12/2012	Ratification
Seychelles	22/12/2012	Ratification
Sierra Leone	22/12/2012	Acceptance
Singapore	22/12/2012	Ratification
Slovakia	22/12/2012	Ratification
Slovenia	22/12/2012	Ratification
Solomon Islands	22/12/2012	Ratification
Somalia	21/12/2012	Signature
Somaliland	21/12/2012	Signature
South Africa	22/12/2012	Ratification
South Ossetia	22/12/2012	Ratification
Spain	22/12/2012	Ratification
Sri Lanka	22/12/2012	Acceptance
Sudan	21/12/2012	Signature
Suriname	21/12/2012	Signature
Swaziland	21/12/2012	Signature
Sweden	22/12/2012	Ratification

Switzerland	22/12/2012	Ratification
Syrian Arab Republic	22/12/2012	Acceptance
T		
Taiwan	27/12/2012	Ratification
Tajikistan	22/12/2012	Acceptance
Thailand	22/12/2012	Ratification
The former Yugoslav Republic of Macedonia	22/12/2012	Ratification
Timor-Leste	21/12/2012	Signature
Togo	21/12/2012	Signature
Tonga	22/12/2012	Ratification
Trinidad and Tobago	22/12/2012	Ratification
Tunisia	21/12/2012	Signature
Turkey	22/12/2012	Ratification
Turkmenistan	21/12/2012	Signature
Tuvalu	22/12/2012	Ratification
U		
Uganda	21/12/2012	Signature
Ukraine	21/12/2012	Ratification
United Arab Emirates	21/12/2012	Signature
United Kingdom of Great Britain and Northern Ireland	22/12/2012	Ratification
United Republic of Tanzania	21/12/2012	Signature
United States of America	22/12/2012	Ratification
Uruguay	21/12/2012	Signature

Uzbekistan	26/12/2012	Ratification
V		
Vanuatu	21/12/2012	Signature
Vatican City		
Venezuela, Bolivarian Republic of	21/12/2012	Signature
Viet Nam	21/12/2012	Signature
Y		
Yemen	21/12/2012	Signature
Z		
Zambia	21/12/2012	Signature
Zimbabwe	21/12/2012	Signature

Copies of this document are available in English, French, Arabic, Hindi, Chinese, and Japanese.

About the Author

Stephanie C. Fox, J.D. is a historian, lawyer, author, editor, and publisher. She is a graduate of William Smith College and of the University of Connecticut School of Law. She runs an editing service called *QueenBeeEdit*, found at www.queenbeeedit.com, which caters to politicians, scientists, and others.

Her imprint is *QueenBeeBooks*.

Stephanie lives in Connecticut, and has written about other topics, including Asperger's, the global financial meltdown, and travelogues of a trip to Kuwait and a trip to Hawai'i.

Her areas of interest include – but are not limited to –history, biographies, women's studies, science fiction, human overpopulation, ecosystems collapse, environmental law, international relations, Asperger's, and cats.

Stephanie has spent time in Manhattan, Hawai'i, France, England, and Venice. She loves cats and worries about the future of our planet.

About the Illustrator

Katelyn M. Gagnon is a graduate of the Hartford Art School, where she earned her B.F.A. in Illustration. She specializes in science fiction cover art, and her portfolio may be viewed at **www.kmgillustration.com** – Katelyn Gagnon Illustration.

Katelyn's work focuses on an unseen and mythological world where science fiction and fantasy become reality. Her compositions have been featured in several shows around Connecticut, including the Goldfarb student exhibition. She currently resides in Connecticut, where she works as a freelance illustrator.